Emily®
the Strange

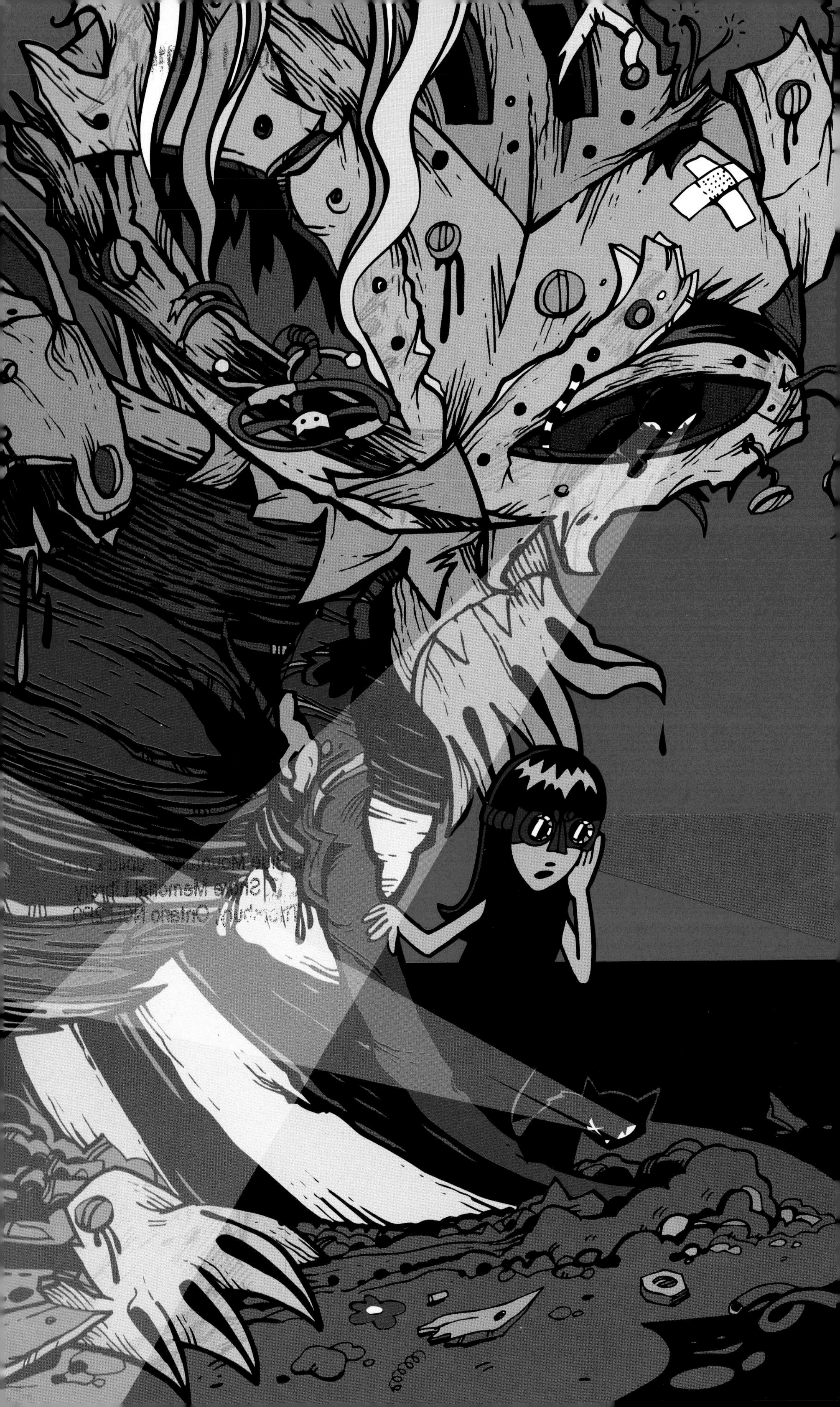

Emily®
the Strange

Written by **Rob Reger**

Art and colors by **Buzz Parker**

Letters by **Nate Piekos**
for BLAMBOT!

The **13**th Hour

Cover art by **Buzz Parker**

DARK HORSE BOOKS®

This book is dedicated to Lupa

Editor Shawna Gore

Publisher Mike Richardson

Published by Dark Horse Books
A division of Dark Horse Comics, Inc.

Dark Horse Comics
10956 SE Main Street
Milwaukie, OR 97222

DarkHorse.com
EmilyStrange.com

3 5 7 9 10 8 6 4 2

First Edition: June 2011
ISBN: 978-1-59582-700-5
Printed by Midas Printing International, Ltd.,
Huizhou, China.

MIKE RICHARDSON President and Publisher — NEIL HANKERSON Executive Vice President — TOM WEDDLE Chief Financial Officer — RANDY STRADLEY Vice President of Publishing — MICHAEL MARTENS Vice President of Business Development — ANITA NELSON Vice President of Business Affairs — MICHA HERSHMAN Vice President of Marketing — DAVID SCROGGY Vice President of Product Development — DALE LAFOUNTAIN Vice President of Information Technology — DARLENE VOGEL Director of Purchasing — KEN LIZZI General Counsel — DAVEY ESTRADA Editorial Director — SCOTT ALLIE Senior Managing Editor — CHRIS WARNER Senior Books Editor — DIANA SCHUTZ Executive Editor — CARY GRAZZINI Director of Design and Production — LIA RIBACCHI Art Director — CARA NIECE Director of Scheduling

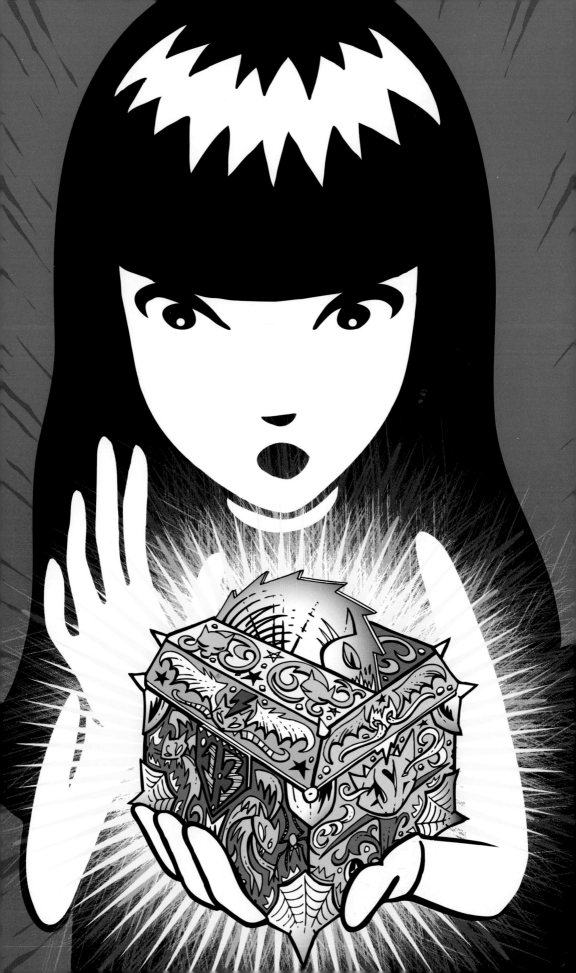

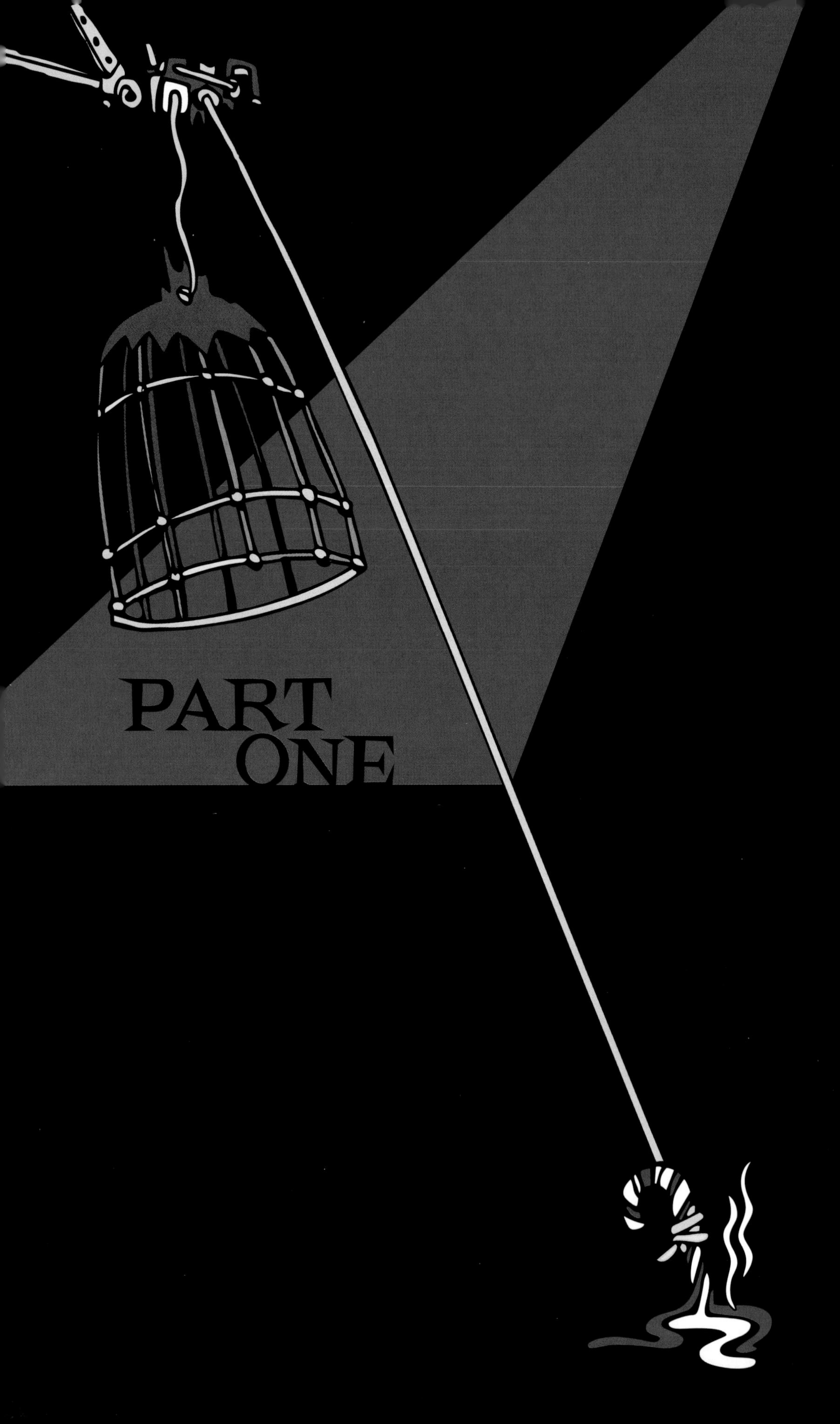
PART
ONE

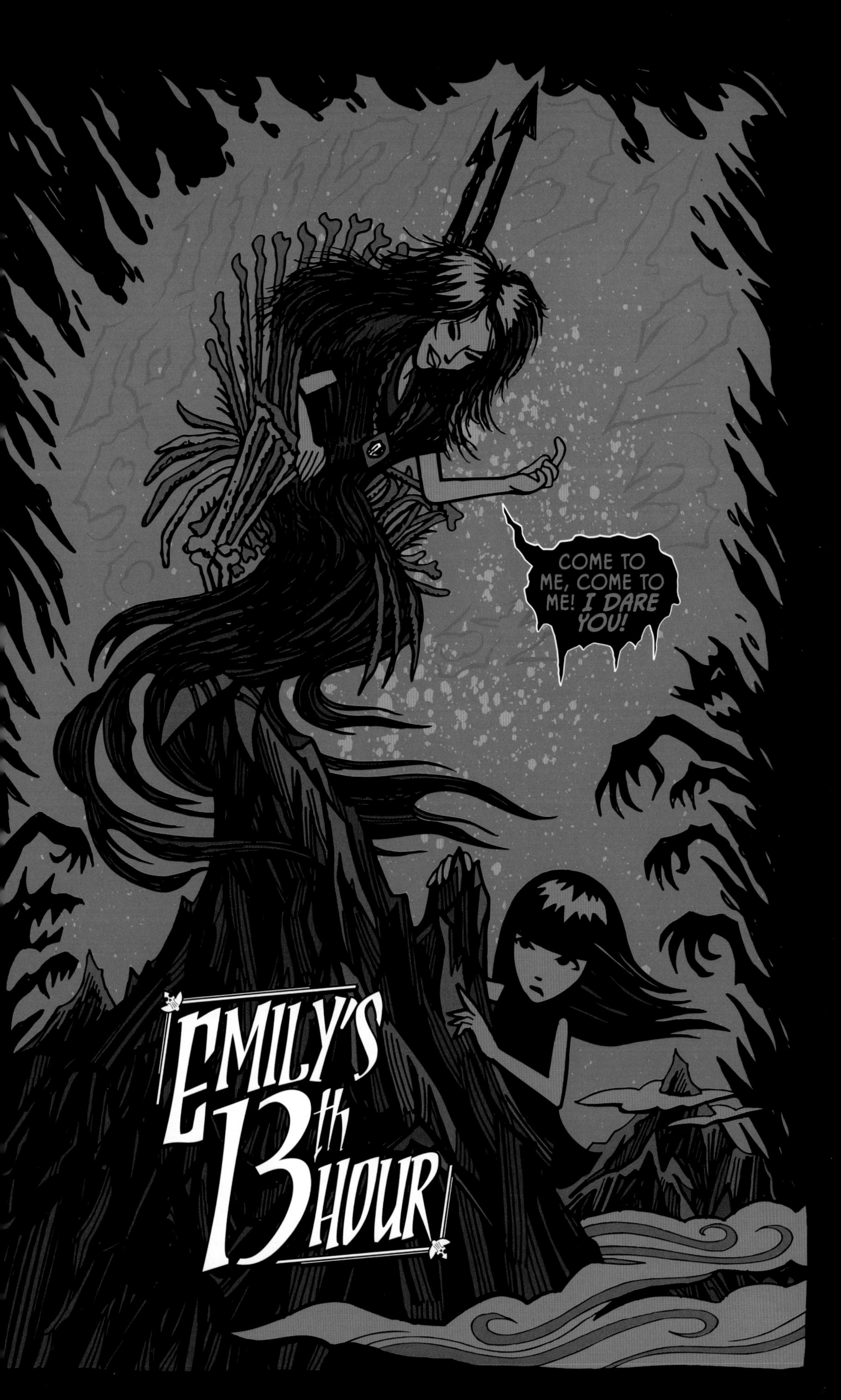
COME TO ME, COME TO ME! I DARE YOU!
EMILY'S 13th HOUR

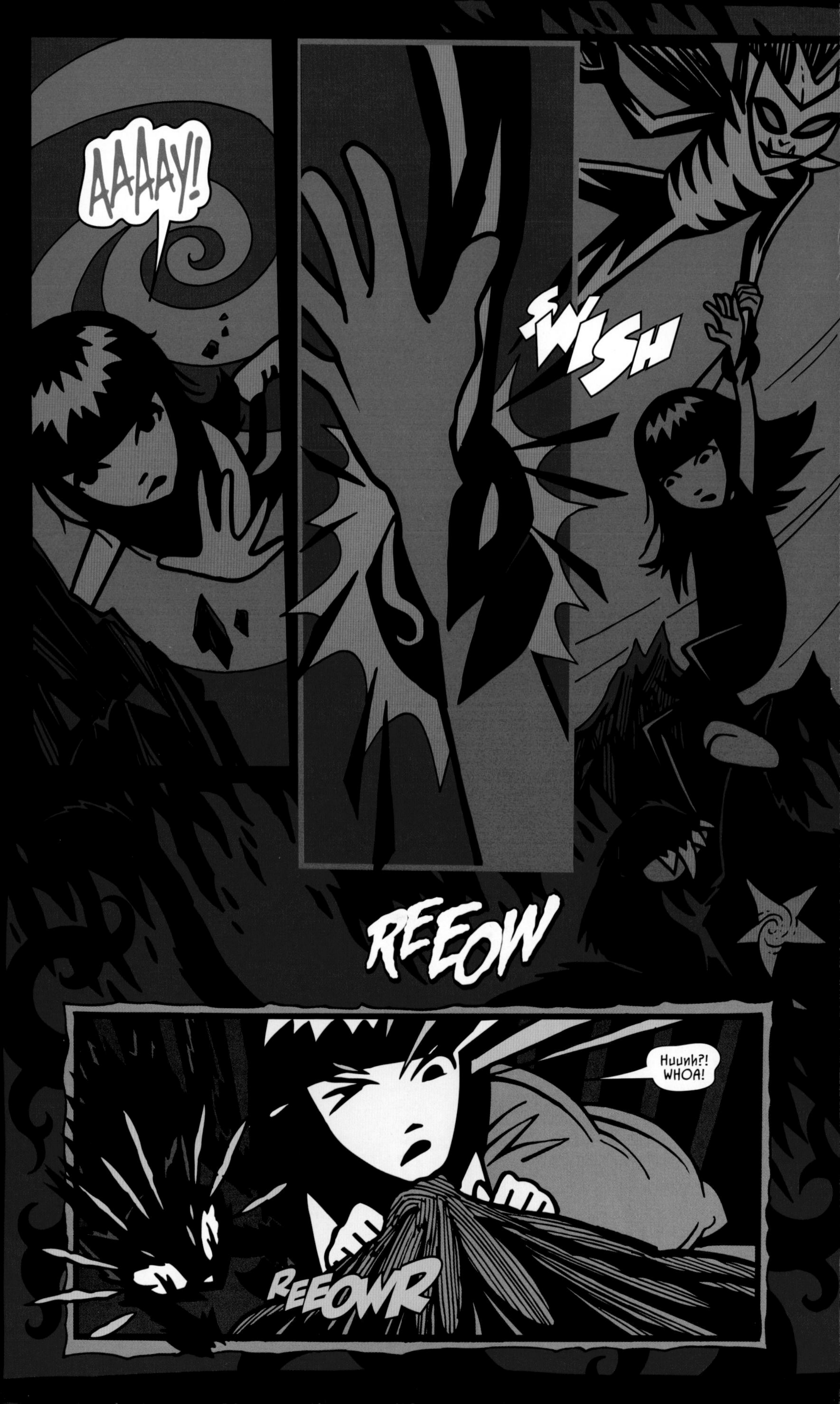
AAAAY!
SWISH
REEOW
Huunh?! WHOA!
REEOWR

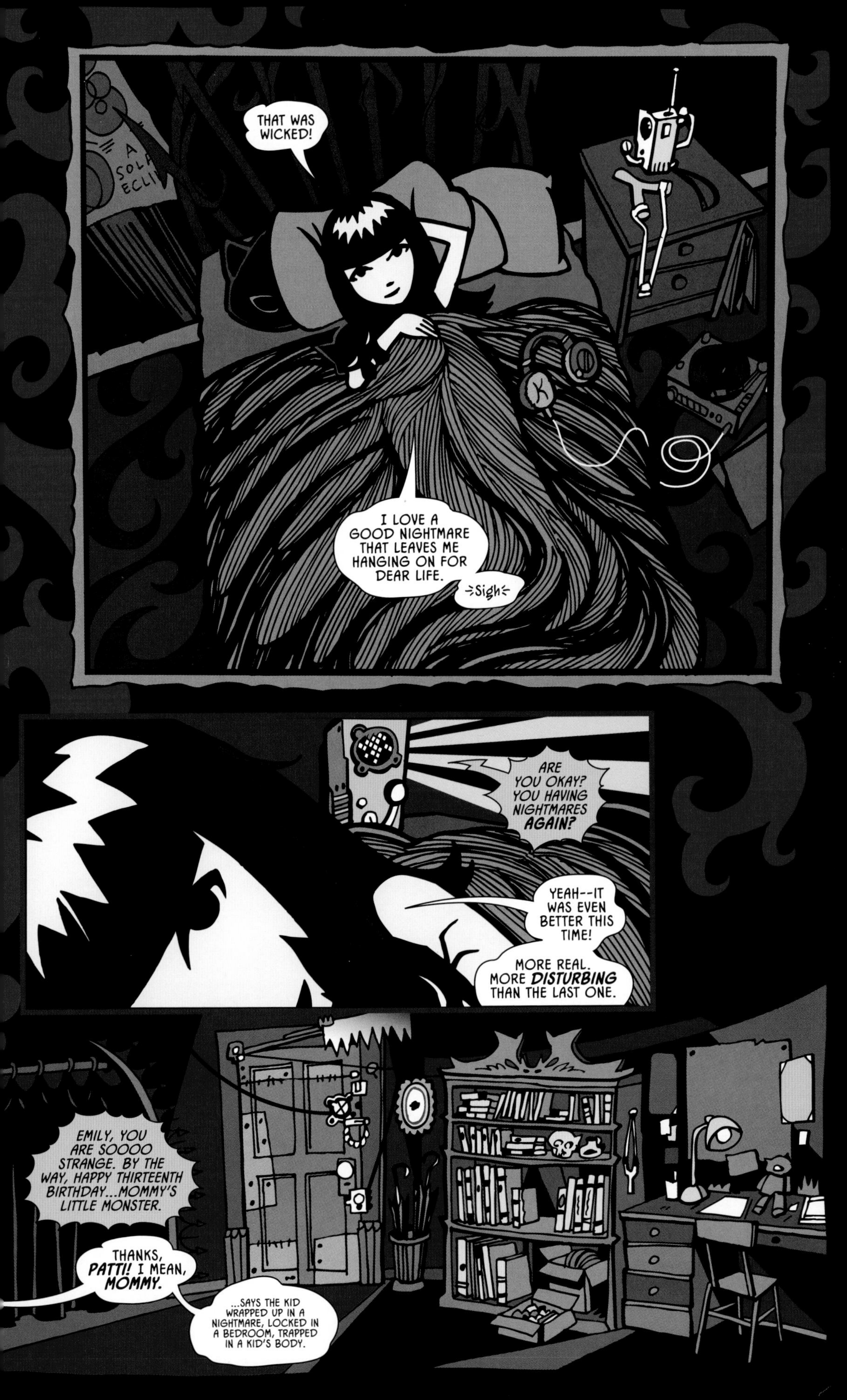
THAT WAS WICKED!
A SOLA ECLI
I LOVE A GOOD NIGHTMARE THAT LEAVES ME HANGING ON FOR DEAR LIFE.
Sigh
ARE YOU OKAY? YOU HAVING NIGHTMARES AGAIN?
YEAH--IT WAS EVEN BETTER THIS TIME!
MORE REAL. MORE DISTURBING THAN THE LAST ONE.
EMILY, YOU ARE SOOOO STRANGE. BY THE WAY, HAPPY THIRTEENTH BIRTHDAY...MOMMY'S LITTLE MONSTER.
THANKS, PATTI! I MEAN, MOMMY.
...SAYS THE KID WRAPPED UP IN A NIGHTMARE, LOCKED IN A BEDROOM, TRAPPED IN A KID'S BODY.

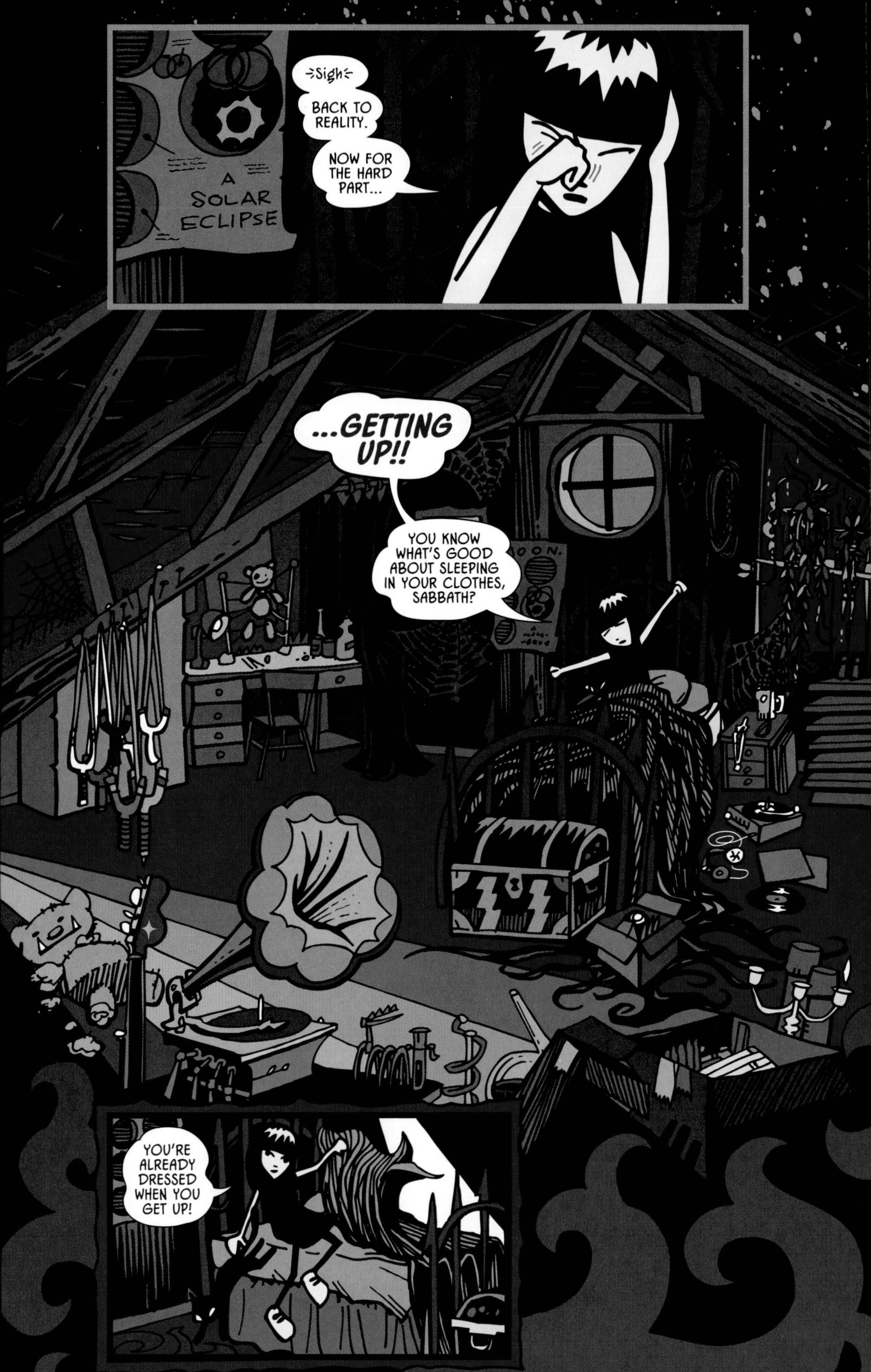
A SOLAR ECLIPSE
=Sigh=
BACK TO REALITY.
NOW FOR THE HARD PART...
...GETTING UP!!
YOU KNOW WHAT'S GOOD ABOUT SLEEPING IN YOUR CLOTHES, SABBATH?
YOU'RE ALREADY DRESSED WHEN YOU GET UP!

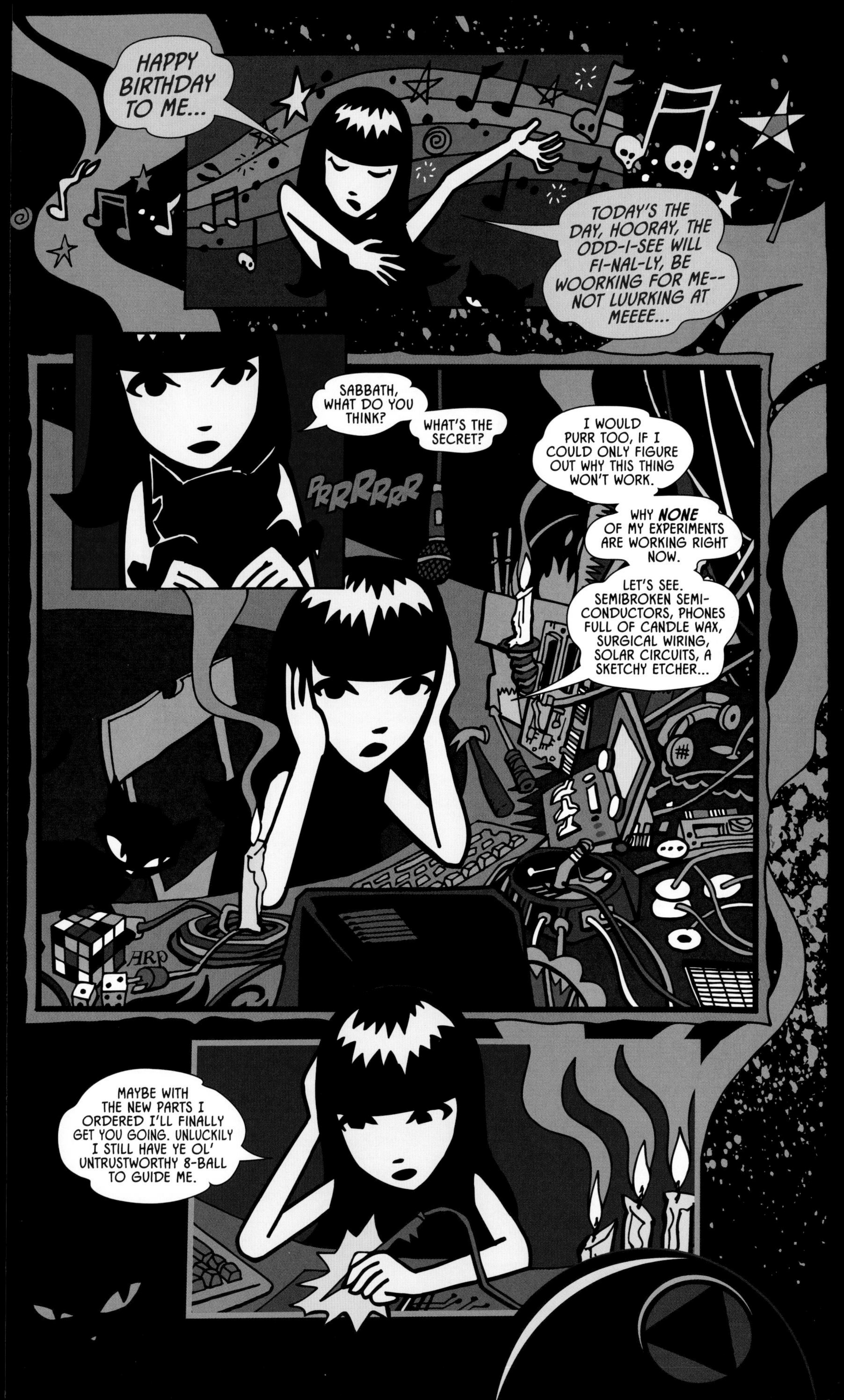
HAPPY BIRTHDAY TO ME...
TODAY'S THE DAY, HOORAY, THE ODD-I-SEE WILL FI-NAL-LY, BE WOORKING FOR ME-- NOT LUURKING AT MEEEE...
SABBATH, WHAT DO YOU THINK?
WHAT'S THE SECRET?
PRRRRRR
I WOULD PURR TOO, IF I COULD ONLY FIGURE OUT WHY THIS THING WON'T WORK.
WHY NONE OF MY EXPERIMENTS ARE WORKING RIGHT NOW.
LET'S SEE. SEMIBROKEN SEMI-CONDUCTORS, PHONES FULL OF CANDLE WAX, SURGICAL WIRING, SOLAR CIRCUITS, A SKETCHY ETCHER...
MAYBE WITH THE NEW PARTS I ORDERED I'LL FINALLY GET YOU GOING. UNLUCKILY I STILL HAVE YE OL' UNTRUSTWORTHY 8-BALL TO GUIDE ME.

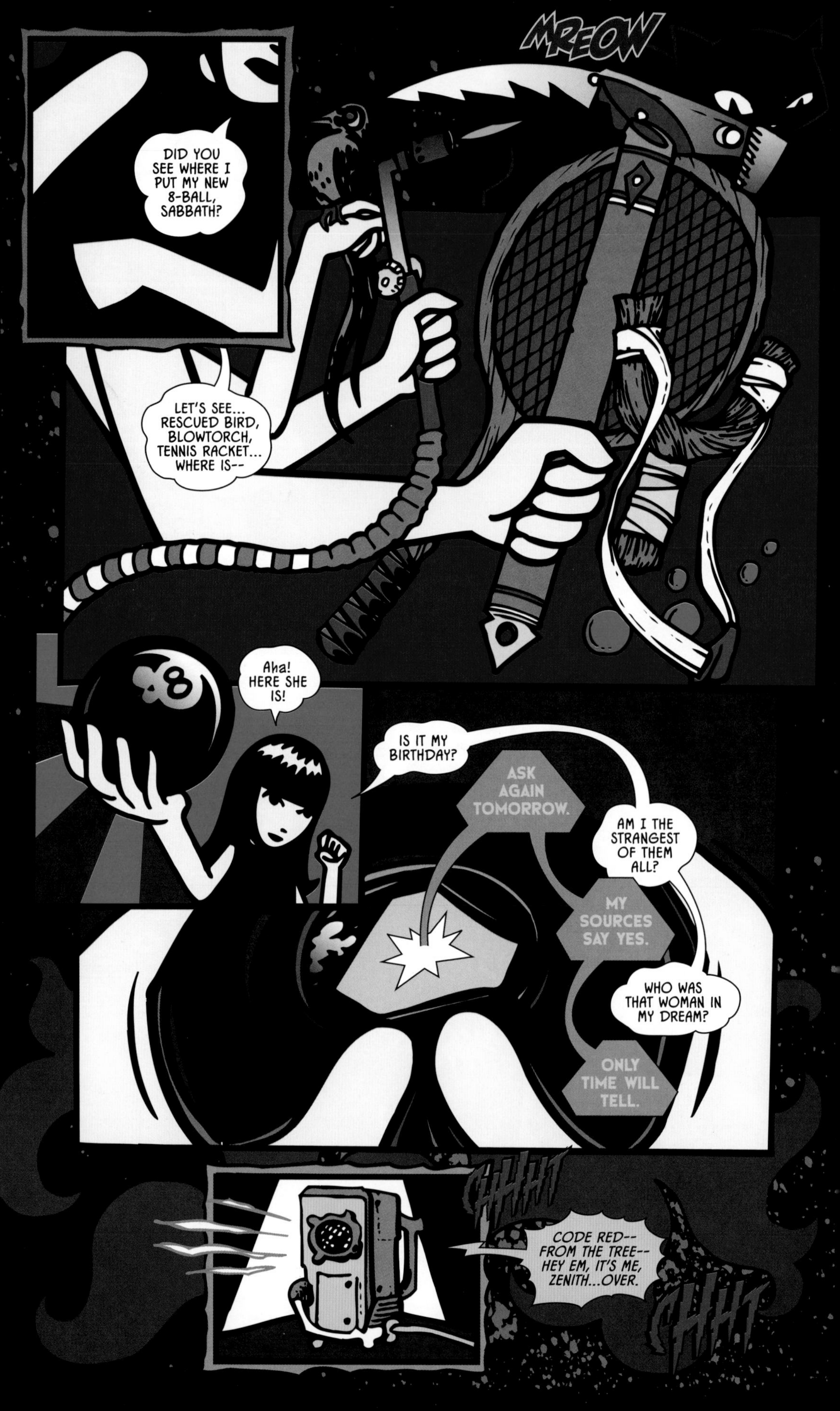
MREOW
DID YOU SEE WHERE I PUT MY NEW 8-BALL, SABBATH?
LET'S SEE... RESCUED BIRD, BLOWTORCH, TENNIS RACKET... WHERE IS--
Aha! HERE SHE IS!
IS IT MY BIRTHDAY?
ASK AGAIN TOMORROW.
AM I THE STRANGEST OF THEM ALL?
MY SOURCES SAY YES.
WHO WAS THAT WOMAN IN MY DREAM?
ONLY TIME WILL TELL.
CHHT
CODE RED-- FROM THE TREE-- HEY EM, IT'S ME, ZENITH...OVER.
CHHT

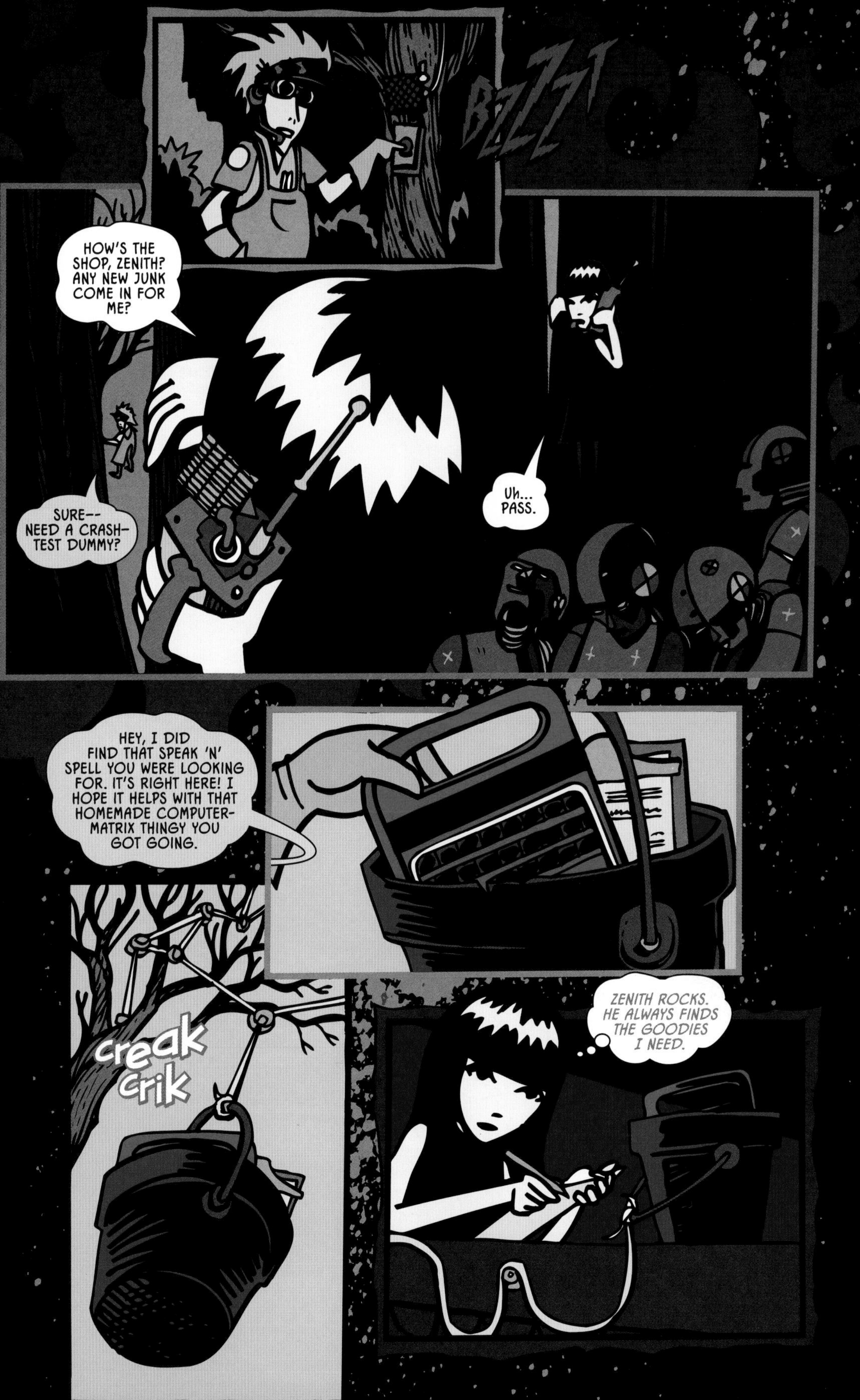
BZZZT
HOW'S THE SHOP, ZENITH? ANY NEW JUNK COME IN FOR ME?
SURE-- NEED A CRASH-TEST DUMMY?
Uh... PASS.
HEY, I DID FIND THAT SPEAK 'N' SPELL YOU WERE LOOKING FOR. IT'S RIGHT HERE! I HOPE IT HELPS WITH THAT HOMEMADE COMPUTER-MATRIX THINGY YOU GOT GOING.
creak
crik
ZENITH ROCKS. HE ALWAYS FINDS THE GOODIES I NEED.

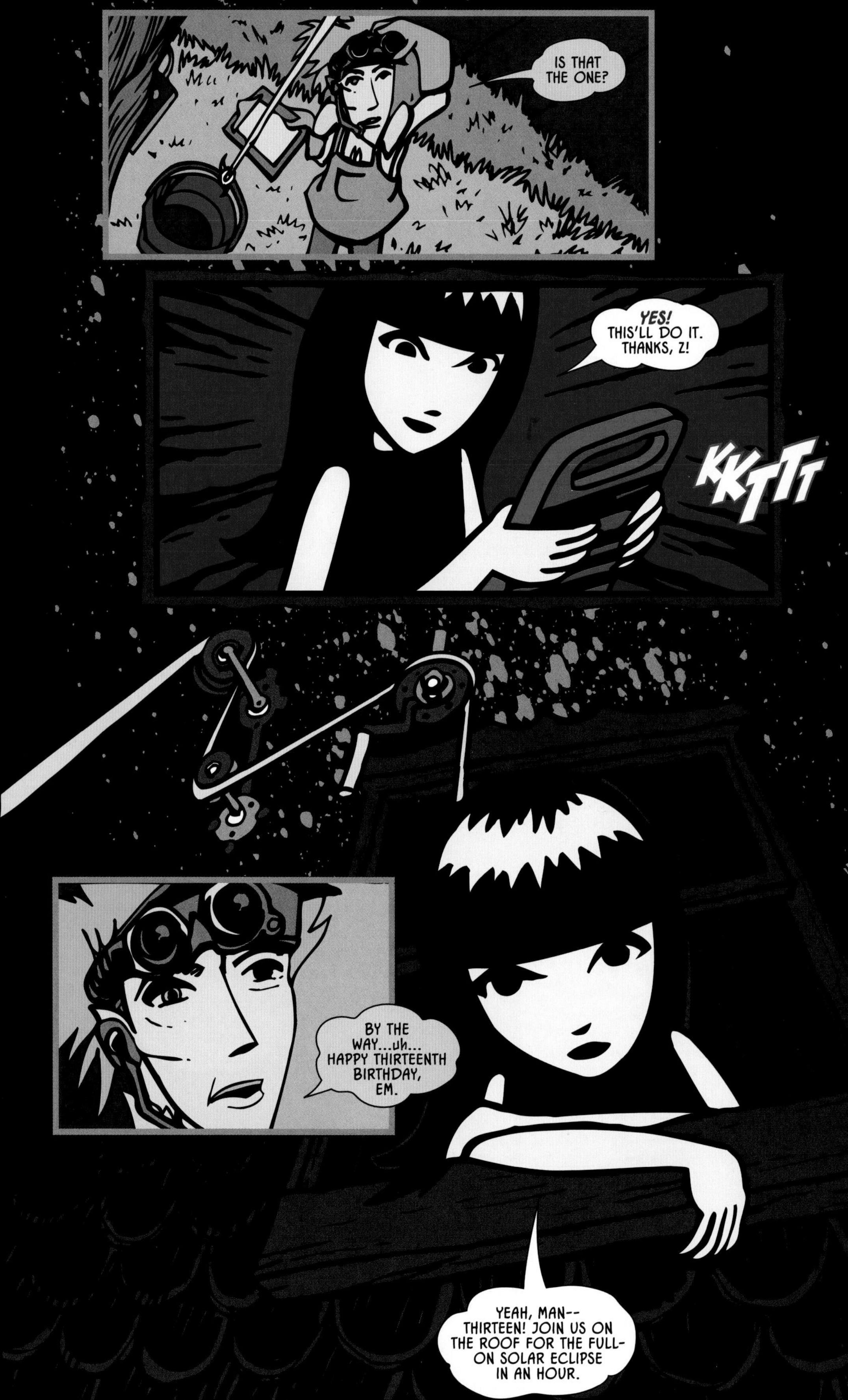
IS THAT THE ONE?
YES! THIS'LL DO IT. THANKS, Z!
KKTTTT
BY THE WAY...uh... HAPPY THIRTEENTH BIRTHDAY, EM.
YEAH, MAN-- THIRTEEN! JOIN US ON THE ROOF FOR THE FULL-ON SOLAR ECLIPSE IN AN HOUR.

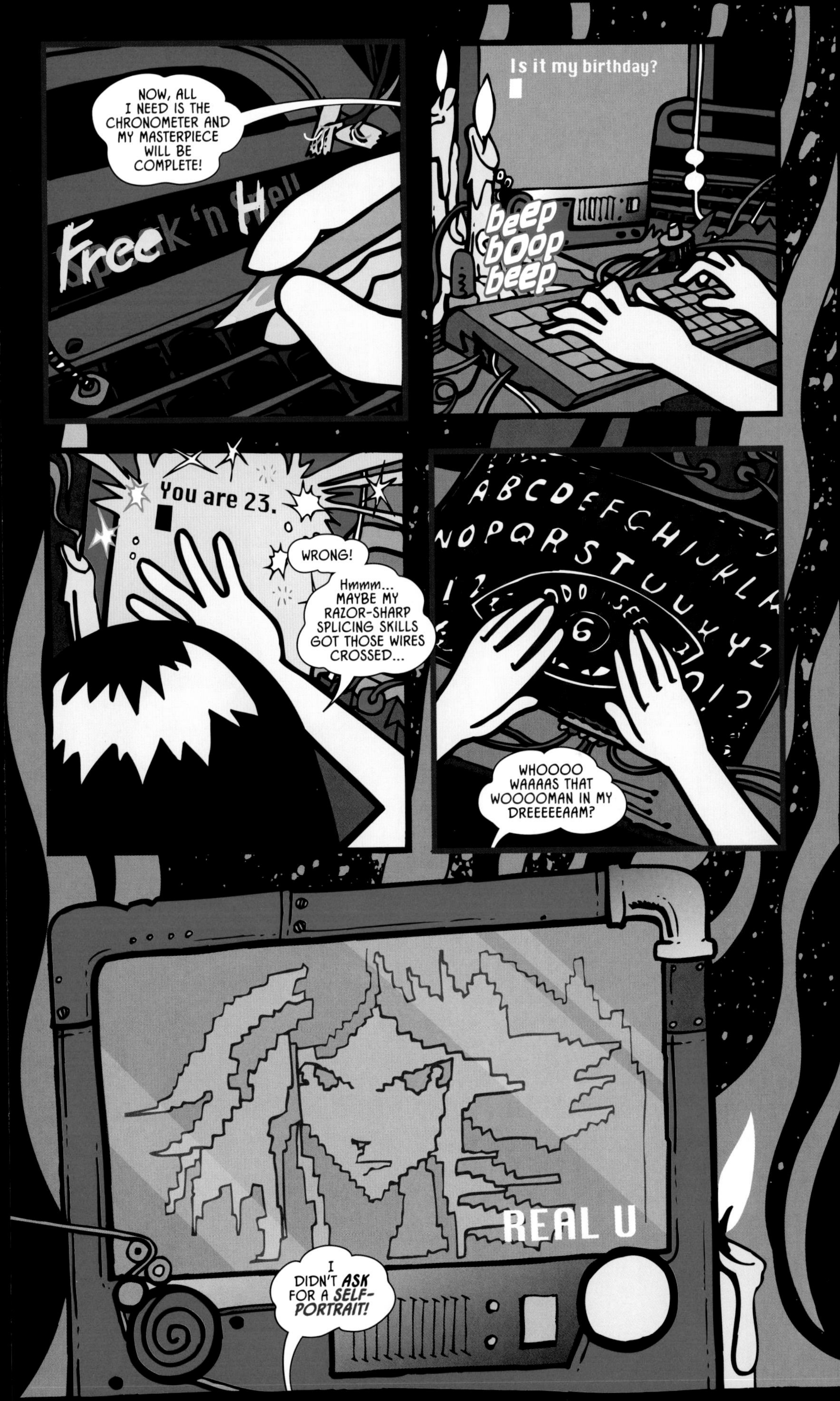
NOW, ALL I NEED IS THE CHRONOMETER AND MY MASTERPIECE WILL BE COMPLETE!
Freek 'n Hell
Is it my birthday?
beep boop beep
You are 23.
WRONG!
Hmmm... MAYBE MY RAZOR-SHARP SPLICING SKILLS GOT THOSE WIRES CROSSED...
ABCDEFGHIJKLM
NOPQRSTUVWXYZ
WHOOOO WAAAAS THAT WOOOOMAN IN MY DREEEEEAAM?
REAL U
I DIDN'T ASK FOR A SELF-PORTRAIT!

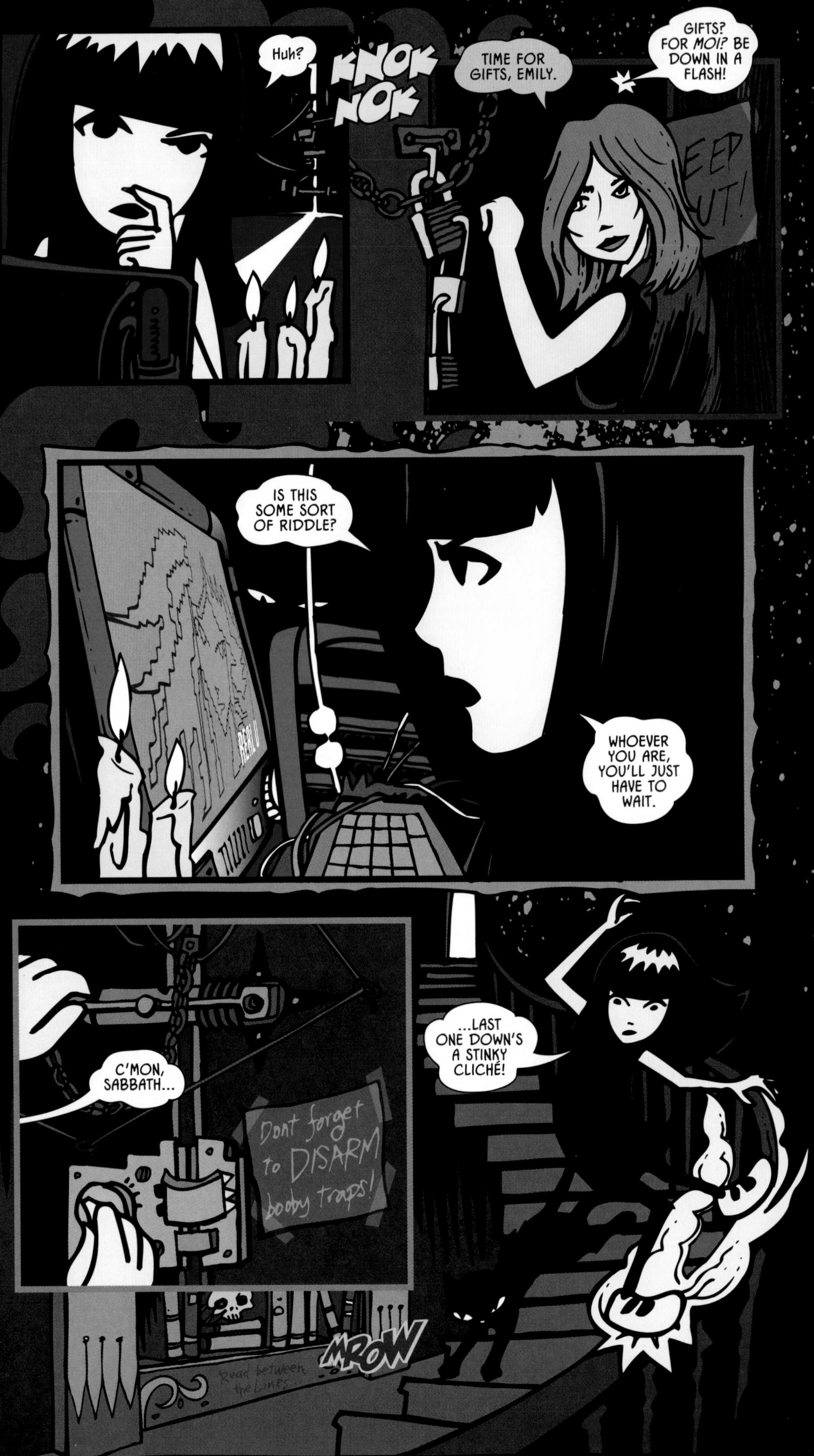
Huh?
KNOK NOK
TIME FOR GIFTS, EMILY.
GIFTS? FOR MOI? BE DOWN IN A FLASH!
IS THIS SOME SORT OF RIDDLE?
WHOEVER YOU ARE, YOU'LL JUST HAVE TO WAIT.
C'MON, SABBATH...
Dont forget to DISARM booby traps!
...LAST ONE DOWN'S A STINKY CLICHÉ!
MROW
Read between the Lines...

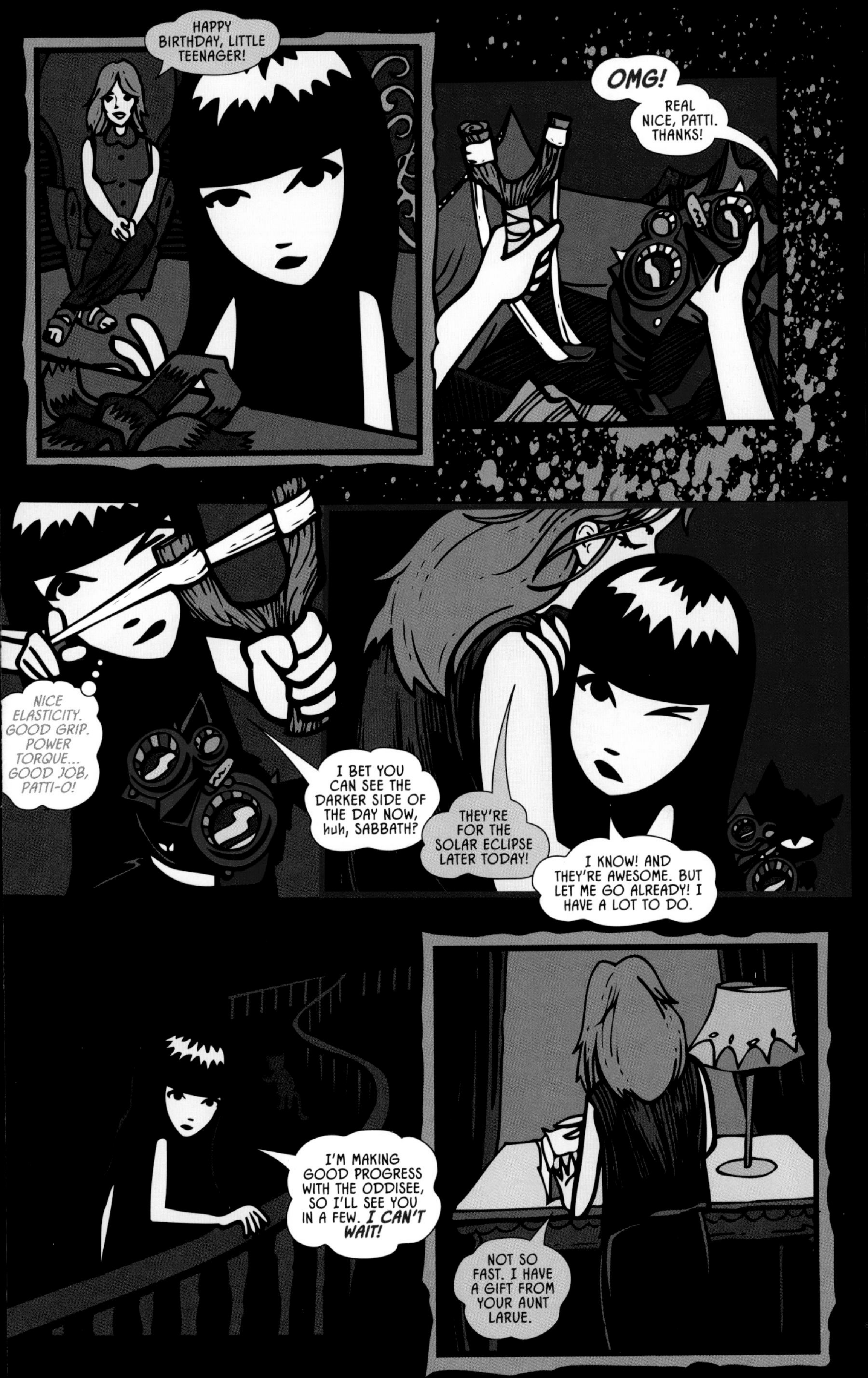
HAPPY BIRTHDAY, LITTLE TEENAGER!
OMG!
REAL NICE, PATTI. THANKS!
NICE ELASTICITY. GOOD GRIP. POWER TORQUE... GOOD JOB, PATTI-O!
I BET YOU CAN SEE THE DARKER SIDE OF THE DAY NOW, huh, SABBATH?
THEY'RE FOR THE SOLAR ECLIPSE LATER TODAY!
I KNOW! AND THEY'RE AWESOME. BUT LET ME GO ALREADY! I HAVE A LOT TO DO.
I'M MAKING GOOD PROGRESS WITH THE ODDISEE, SO I'LL SEE YOU IN A FEW. I CAN'T WAIT!
NOT SO FAST. I HAVE A GIFT FROM YOUR AUNT LARUE.

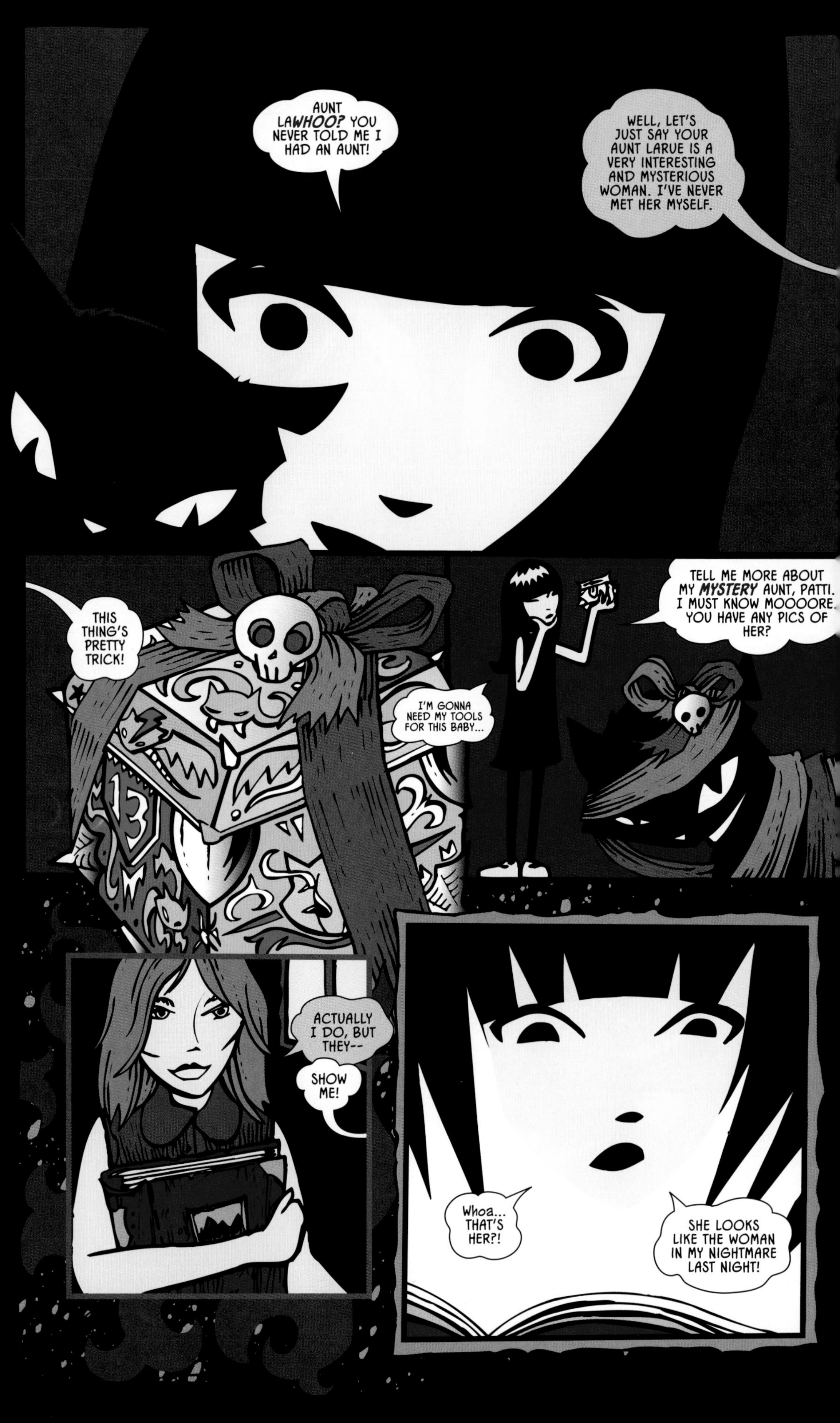

AUNT LA*WHOO?* YOU NEVER TOLD ME I HAD AN AUNT!
WELL, LET'S JUST SAY YOUR AUNT LARUE IS A VERY INTERESTING AND MYSTERIOUS WOMAN. I'VE NEVER MET HER MYSELF.
THIS THING'S PRETTY TRICK!
I'M GONNA NEED MY TOOLS FOR THIS BABY...
TELL ME MORE ABOUT MY *MYSTERY* AUNT, PATTI. I MUST KNOW MOOOORE. YOU HAVE ANY PICS OF HER?
ACTUALLY I DO, BUT THEY--
SHOW ME!
Whoa... THAT'S HER?!
SHE LOOKS LIKE THE WOMAN IN MY NIGHTMARE LAST NIGHT!

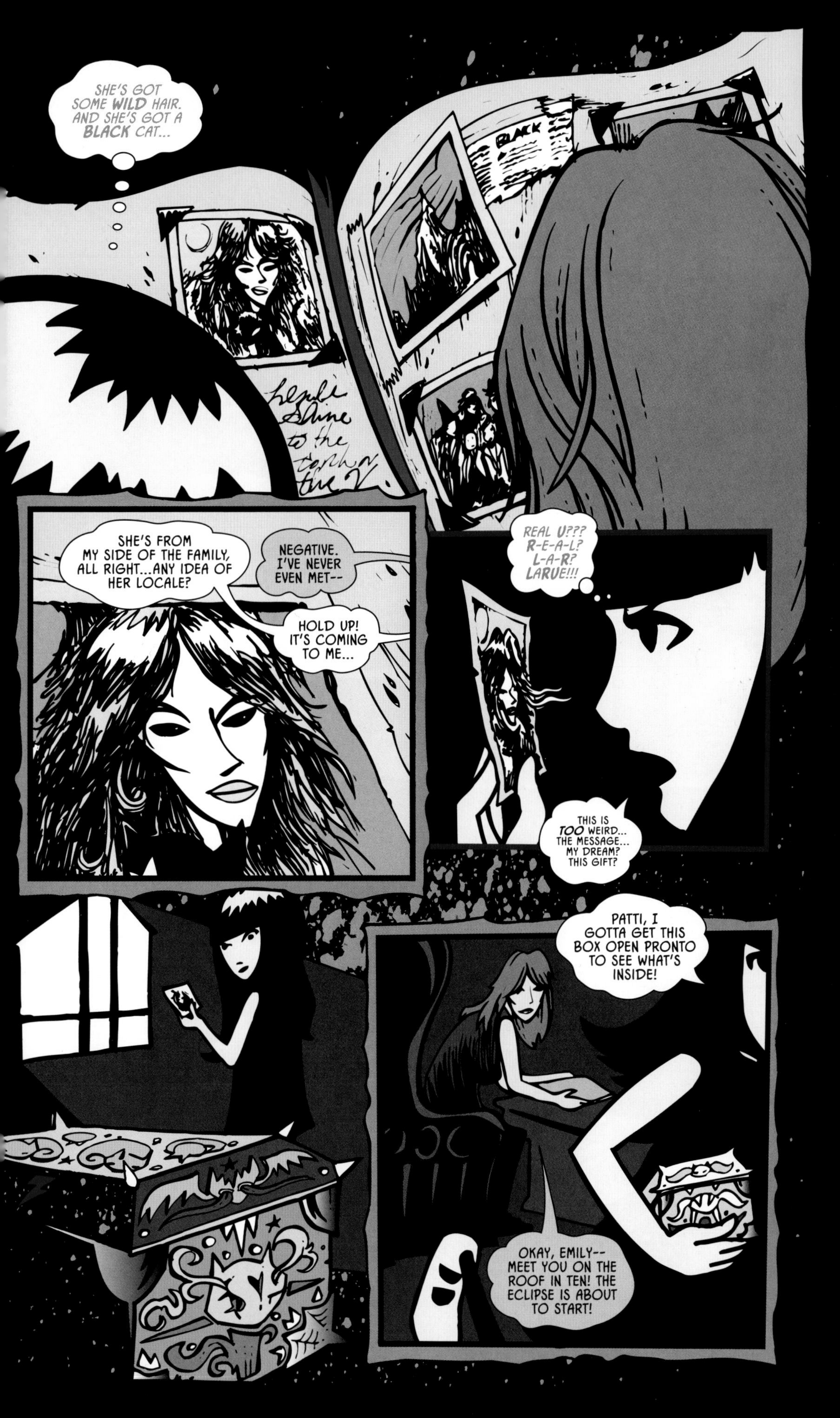
SHE'S GOT SOME WILD HAIR. AND SHE'S GOT A BLACK CAT...
BLACK
SHE'S FROM MY SIDE OF THE FAMILY, ALL RIGHT...ANY IDEA OF HER LOCALE?
NEGATIVE. I'VE NEVER EVEN MET--
HOLD UP! IT'S COMING TO ME...
REAL U??? R-E-A-L? L-A-R? LARUE!!!
THIS IS TOO WEIRD... THE MESSAGE... MY DREAM? THIS GIFT?
PATTI, I GOTTA GET THIS BOX OPEN PRONTO TO SEE WHAT'S INSIDE!
OKAY, EMILY-- MEET YOU ON THE ROOF IN TEN! THE ECLIPSE IS ABOUT TO START!

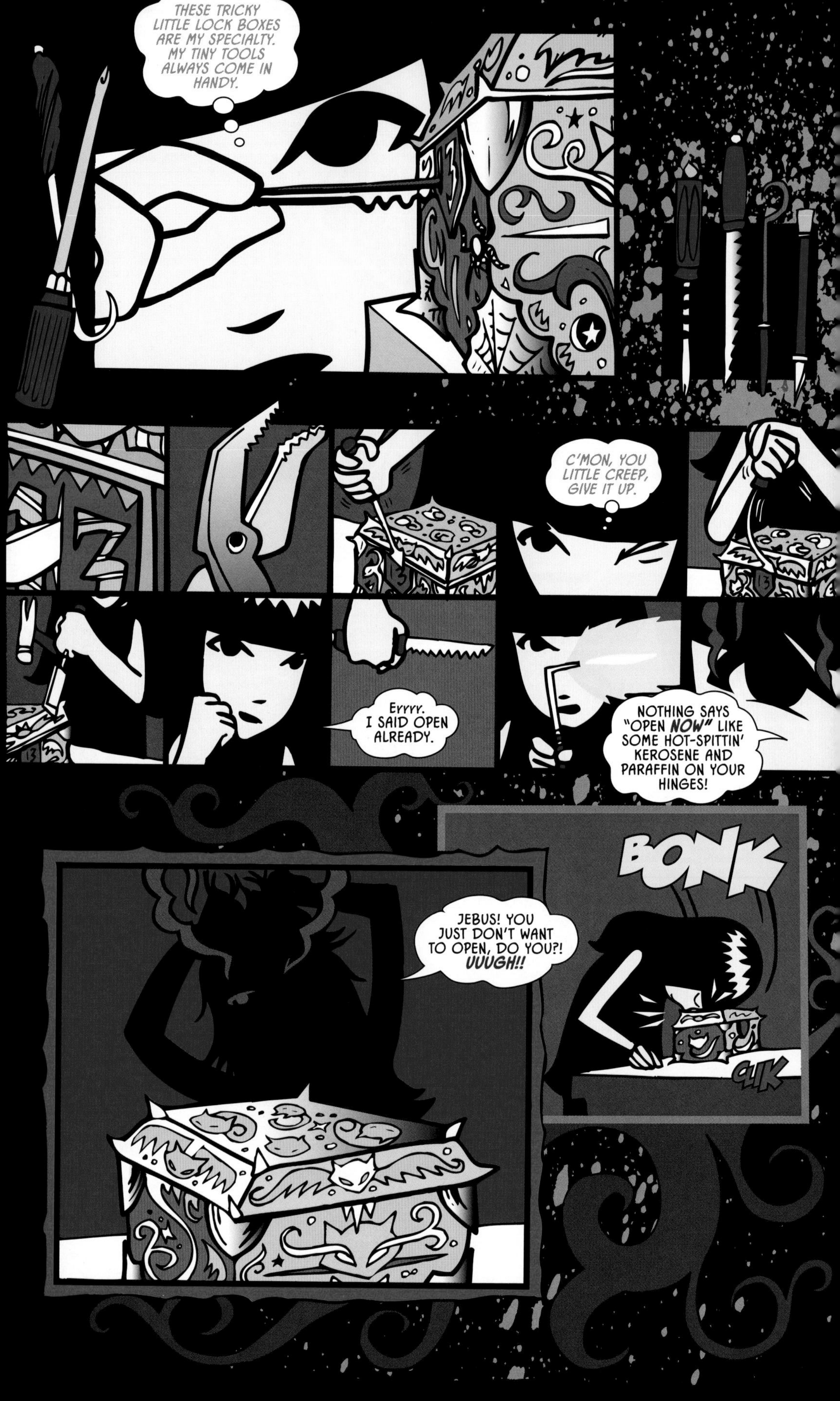
THESE TRICKY LITTLE LOCK BOXES ARE MY SPECIALTY. MY TINY TOOLS ALWAYS COME IN HANDY.
C'MON, YOU LITTLE CREEP, GIVE IT UP.
Erryy. I SAID OPEN ALREADY.
NOTHING SAYS "OPEN NOW" LIKE SOME HOT-SPITTIN' KEROSENE AND PARAFFIN ON YOUR HINGES!
BONK
JEBUS! YOU JUST DON'T WANT TO OPEN, DO YOU?! UUUGH!!
CLIK

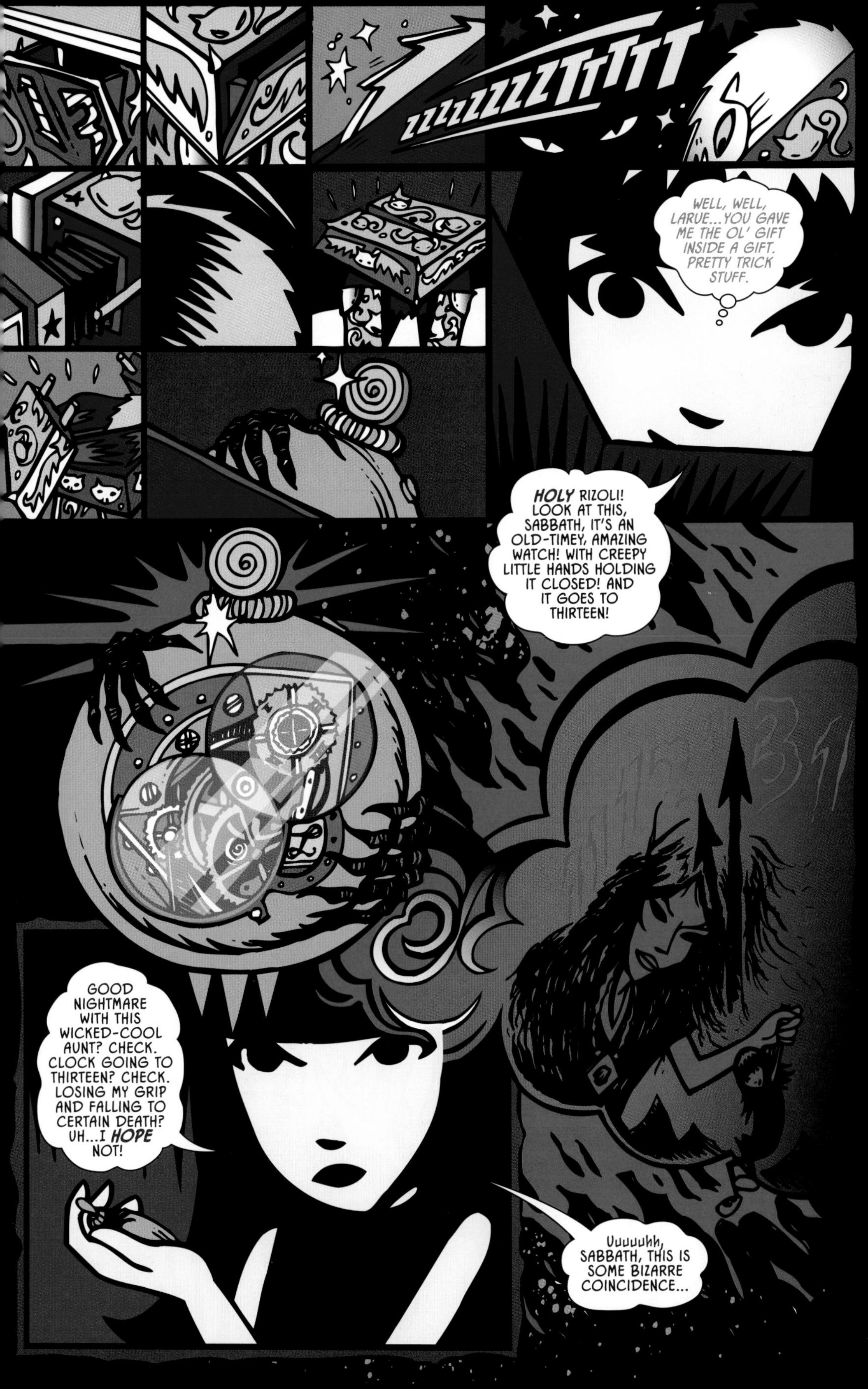

ZZZZZZZZZTTTTTT
WELL, WELL, LARUE...YOU GAVE ME THE OL' GIFT INSIDE A GIFT. PRETTY TRICK STUFF.
HOLY RIZOLI! LOOK AT THIS, SABBATH, IT'S AN OLD-TIMEY, AMAZING WATCH! WITH CREEPY LITTLE HANDS HOLDING IT CLOSED! AND IT GOES TO THIRTEEN!
GOOD NIGHTMARE WITH THIS WICKED-COOL AUNT? CHECK. CLOCK GOING TO THIRTEEN? CHECK. LOSING MY GRIP AND FALLING TO CERTAIN DEATH? UH...I HOPE NOT!
Uuuuuhh, SABBATH, THIS IS SOME BIZARRE COINCIDENCE...

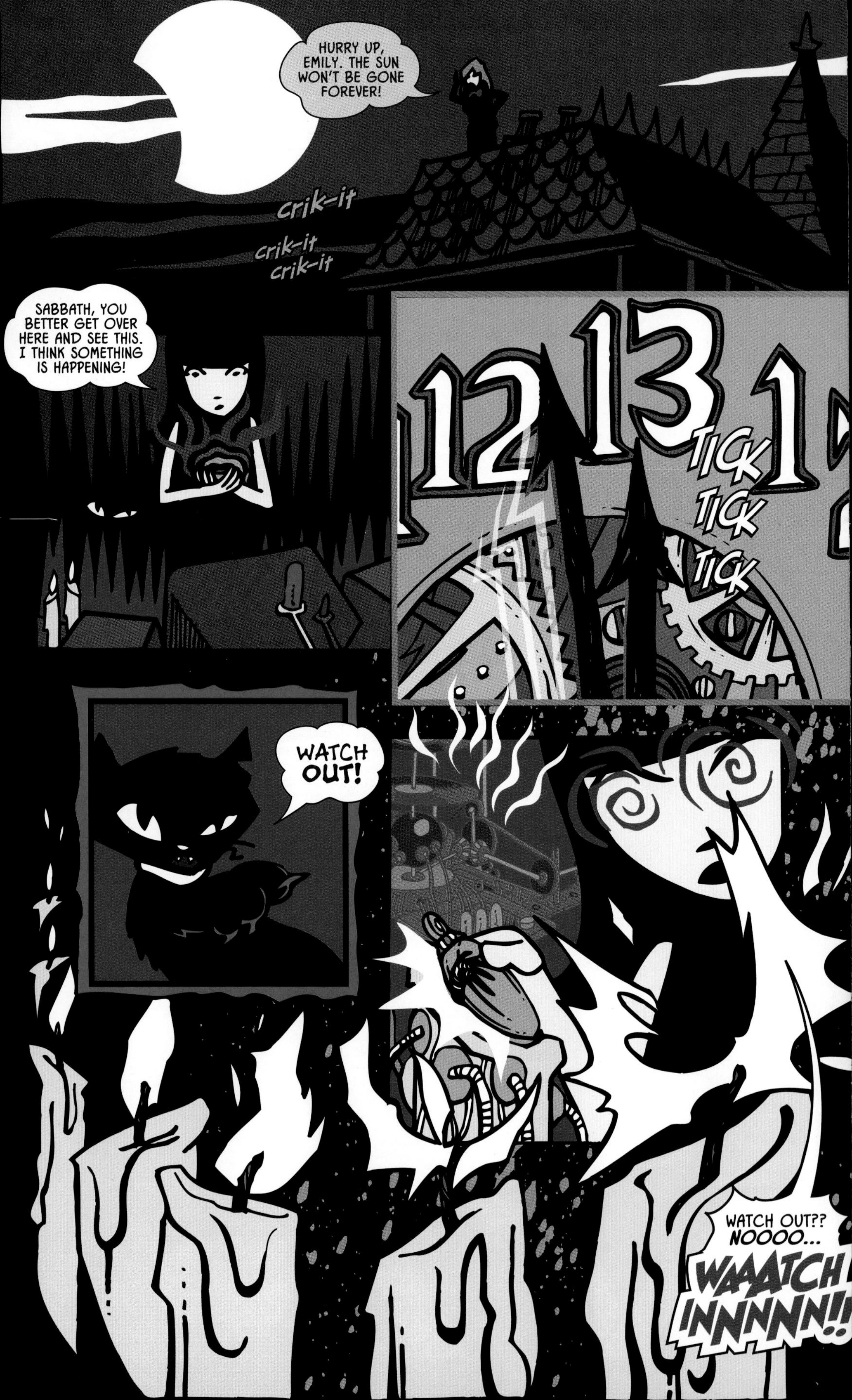
HURRY UP, EMILY. THE SUN WON'T BE GONE FOREVER!
crik-it
crik-it
crik-it
SABBATH, YOU BETTER GET OVER HERE AND SEE THIS. I THINK SOMETHING IS HAPPENING!
12
13
1
TICK
TICK
TICK
WATCH OUT!
WATCH OUT?? NOOOO...
WAAATCH INNNNN!!

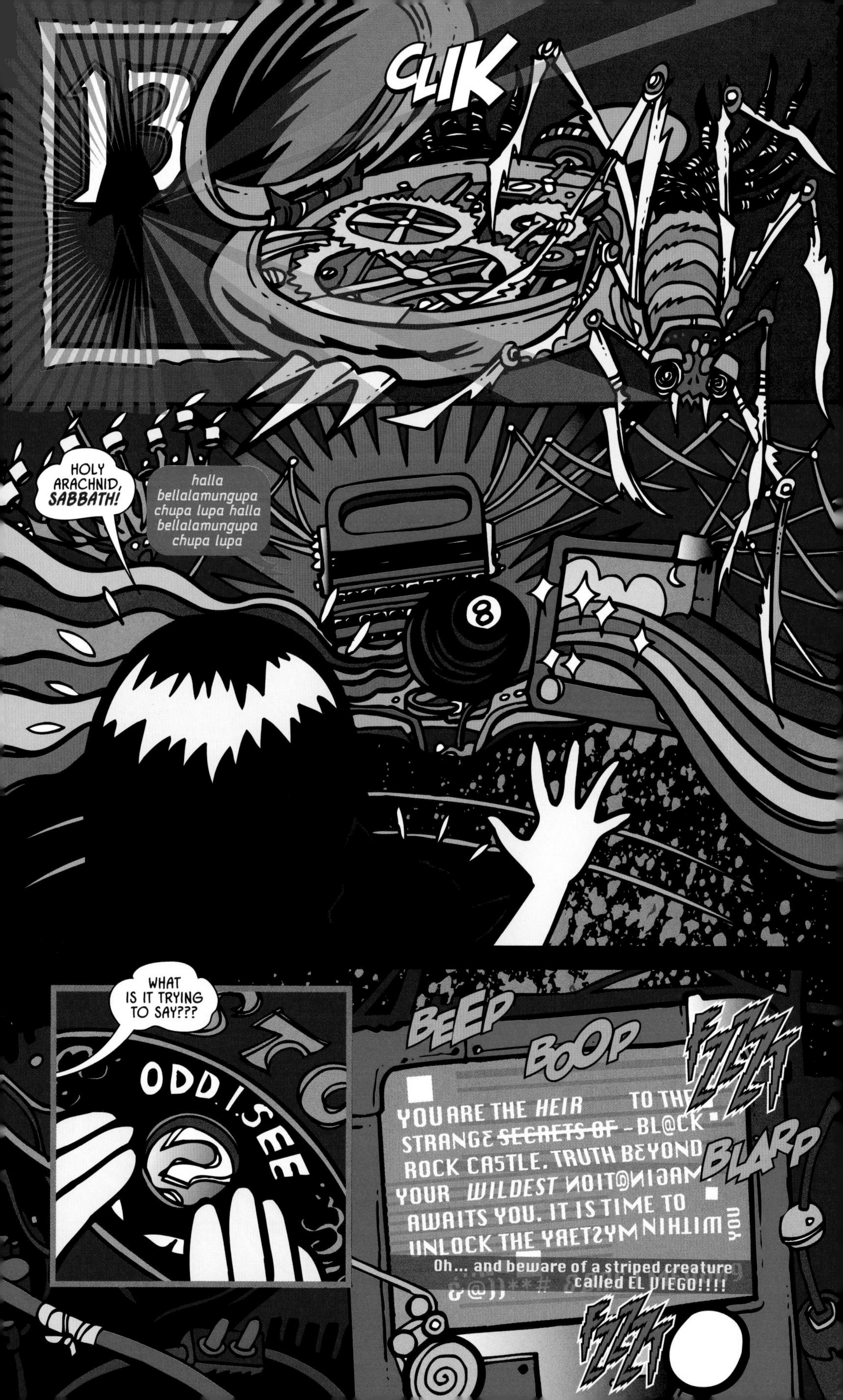
13
CLIK
HOLY ARACHNID, SABBATH!
halla bellalamungupa chupa lupa halla bellalamungupa chupa lupa
8
WHAT IS IT TRYING TO SAY???
ODD.I.SEE
BEEP
BOOP
FZZZT
YOU ARE THE HEIR TO THE STRANGE ~~SECRETS OF~~ - BL@CK ROCK CASTLE. TRUTH BEYOND YOUR WILDEST NOIT@NIGAM AWAITS YOU. IT IS TIME TO UNLOCK THE YRETSYM NIHTIW YOU
BLARP
Oh... and beware of a striped creature called EL VIEGO!!!!
FZZZT

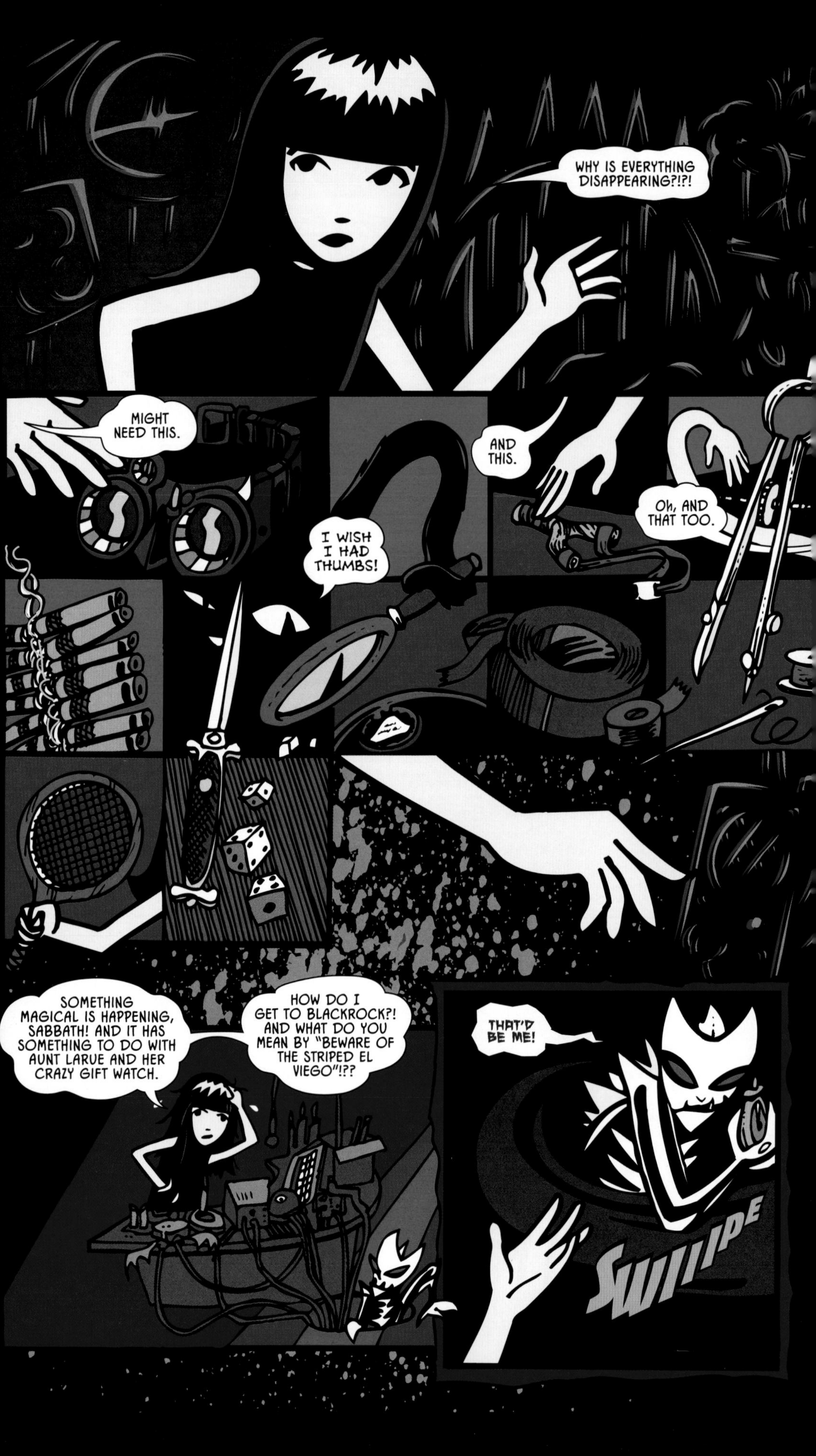
WHY IS EVERYTHING DISAPPEARING?!?!
MIGHT NEED THIS.
I WISH I HAD THUMBS!
AND THIS.
Oh, AND THAT TOO.
SOMETHING MAGICAL IS HAPPENING, SABBATH! AND IT HAS SOMETHING TO DO WITH AUNT LARUE AND HER CRAZY GIFT WATCH.
HOW DO I GET TO BLACKROCK?! AND WHAT DO YOU MEAN BY "BEWARE OF THE STRIPED EL VIEGO"!??
THAT'D BE ME!
SWIIIPE

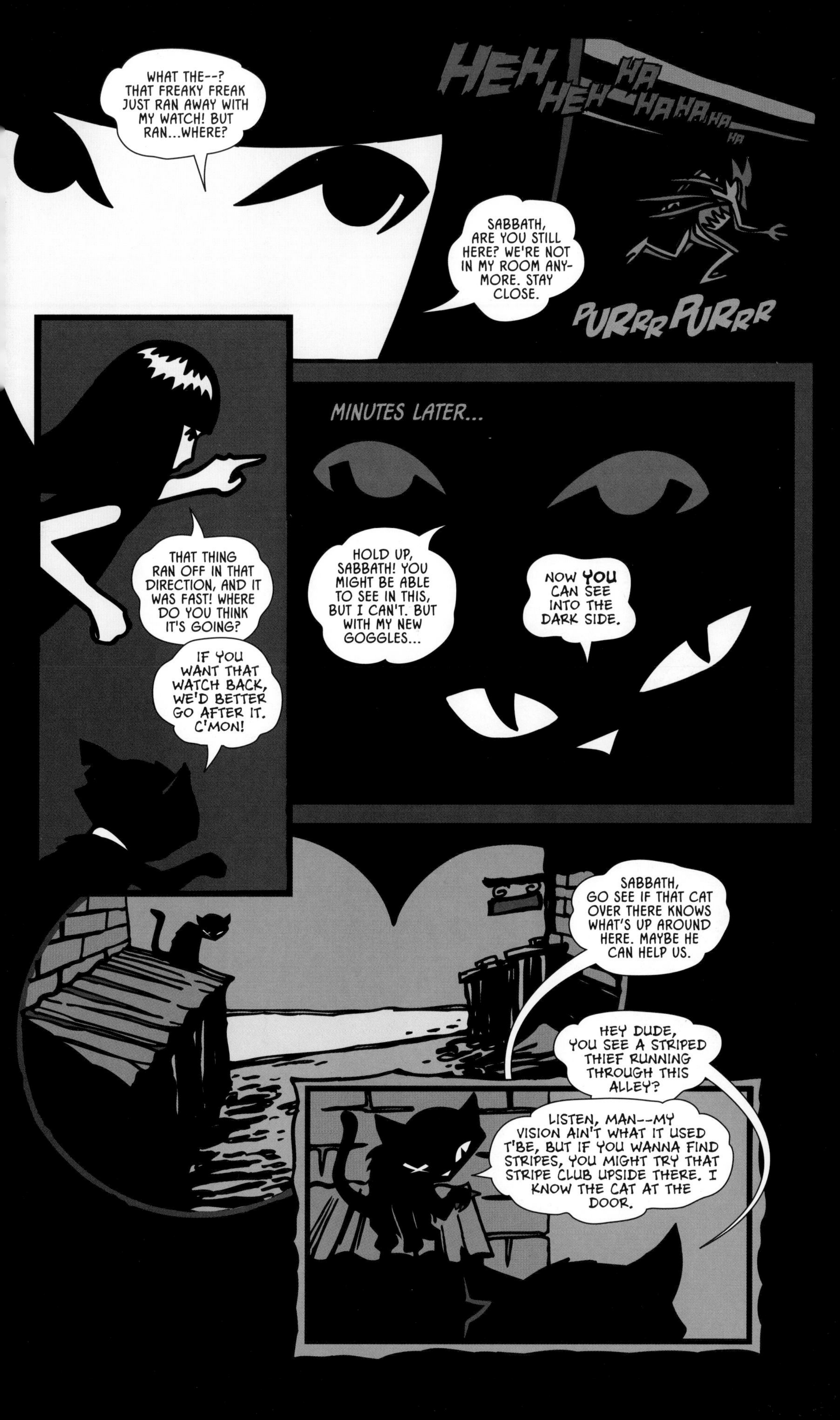
WHAT THE--? THAT FREAKY FREAK JUST RAN AWAY WITH MY WATCH! BUT RAN...WHERE?
HEH HEH HA HA HA HA HA HA
SABBATH, ARE YOU STILL HERE? WE'RE NOT IN MY ROOM ANY-MORE. STAY CLOSE.
PURRR PURRR
THAT THING RAN OFF IN THAT DIRECTION, AND IT WAS FAST! WHERE DO YOU THINK IT'S GOING?
IF YOU WANT THAT WATCH BACK, WE'D BETTER GO AFTER IT. C'MON!
MINUTES LATER...
HOLD UP, SABBATH! YOU MIGHT BE ABLE TO SEE IN THIS, BUT I CAN'T. BUT WITH MY NEW GOGGLES...
NOW YOU CAN SEE INTO THE DARK SIDE.
SABBATH, GO SEE IF THAT CAT OVER THERE KNOWS WHAT'S UP AROUND HERE. MAYBE HE CAN HELP US.
HEY DUDE, YOU SEE A STRIPED THIEF RUNNING THROUGH THIS ALLEY?
LISTEN, MAN--MY VISION AIN'T WHAT IT USED T'BE, BUT IF YOU WANNA FIND STRIPES, YOU MIGHT TRY THAT STRIPE CLUB UPSIDE THERE. I KNOW THE CAT AT THE DOOR.

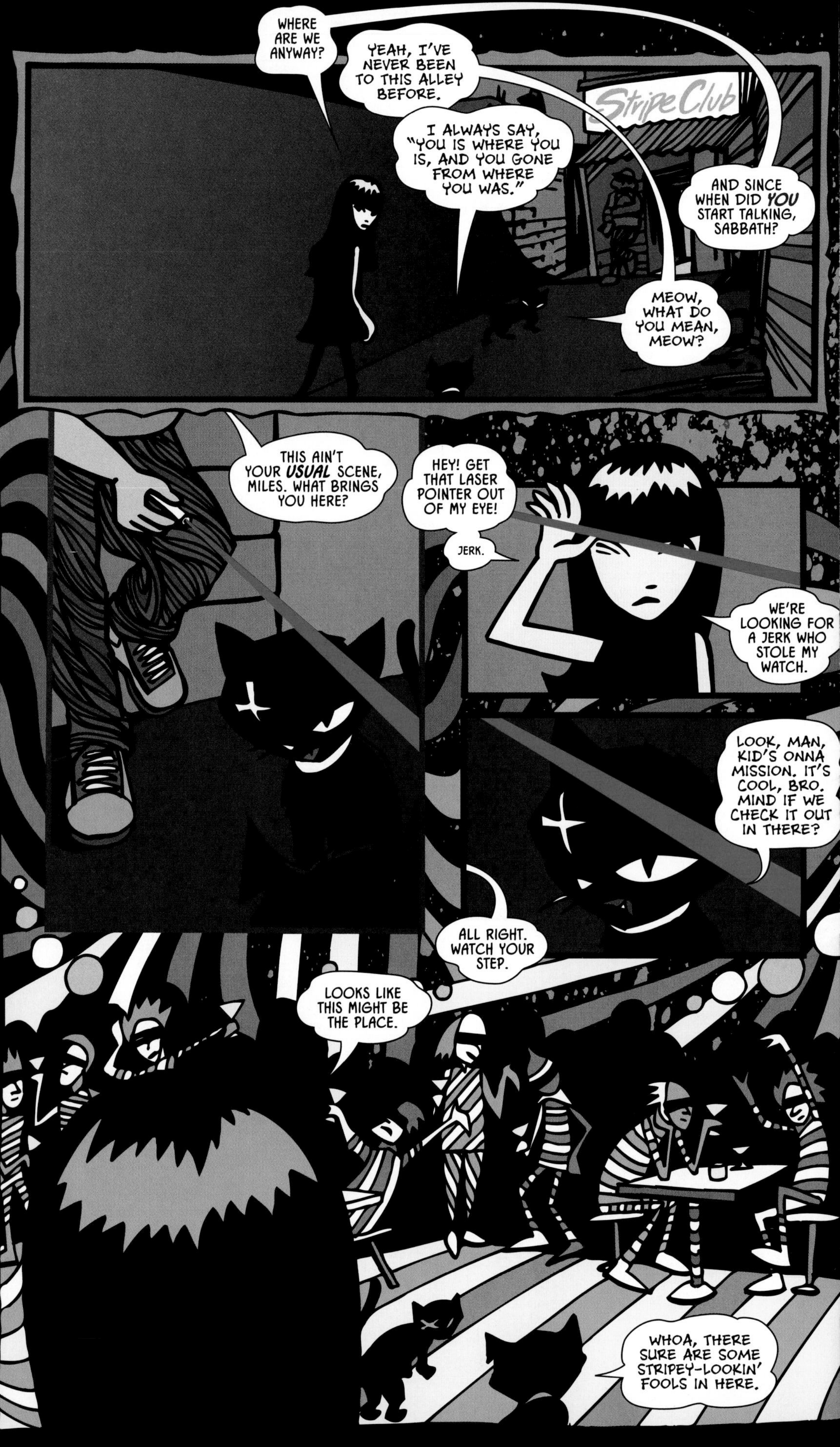

WHERE ARE WE ANYWAY?
YEAH, I'VE NEVER BEEN TO THIS ALLEY BEFORE.
I ALWAYS SAY, "YOU IS WHERE YOU IS, AND YOU GONE FROM WHERE YOU WAS."
Stripe Club
AND SINCE WHEN DID YOU START TALKING, SABBATH?
MEOW, WHAT DO YOU MEAN, MEOW?
THIS AIN'T YOUR USUAL SCENE, MILES. WHAT BRINGS YOU HERE?
HEY! GET THAT LASER POINTER OUT OF MY EYE!
JERK.
WE'RE LOOKING FOR A JERK WHO STOLE MY WATCH.
LOOK, MAN, KID'S ONNA MISSION. IT'S COOL, BRO. MIND IF WE CHECK IT OUT IN THERE?
ALL RIGHT. WATCH YOUR STEP.
LOOKS LIKE THIS MIGHT BE THE PLACE.
WHOA, THERE SURE ARE SOME STRIPEY-LOOKIN' FOOLS IN HERE.

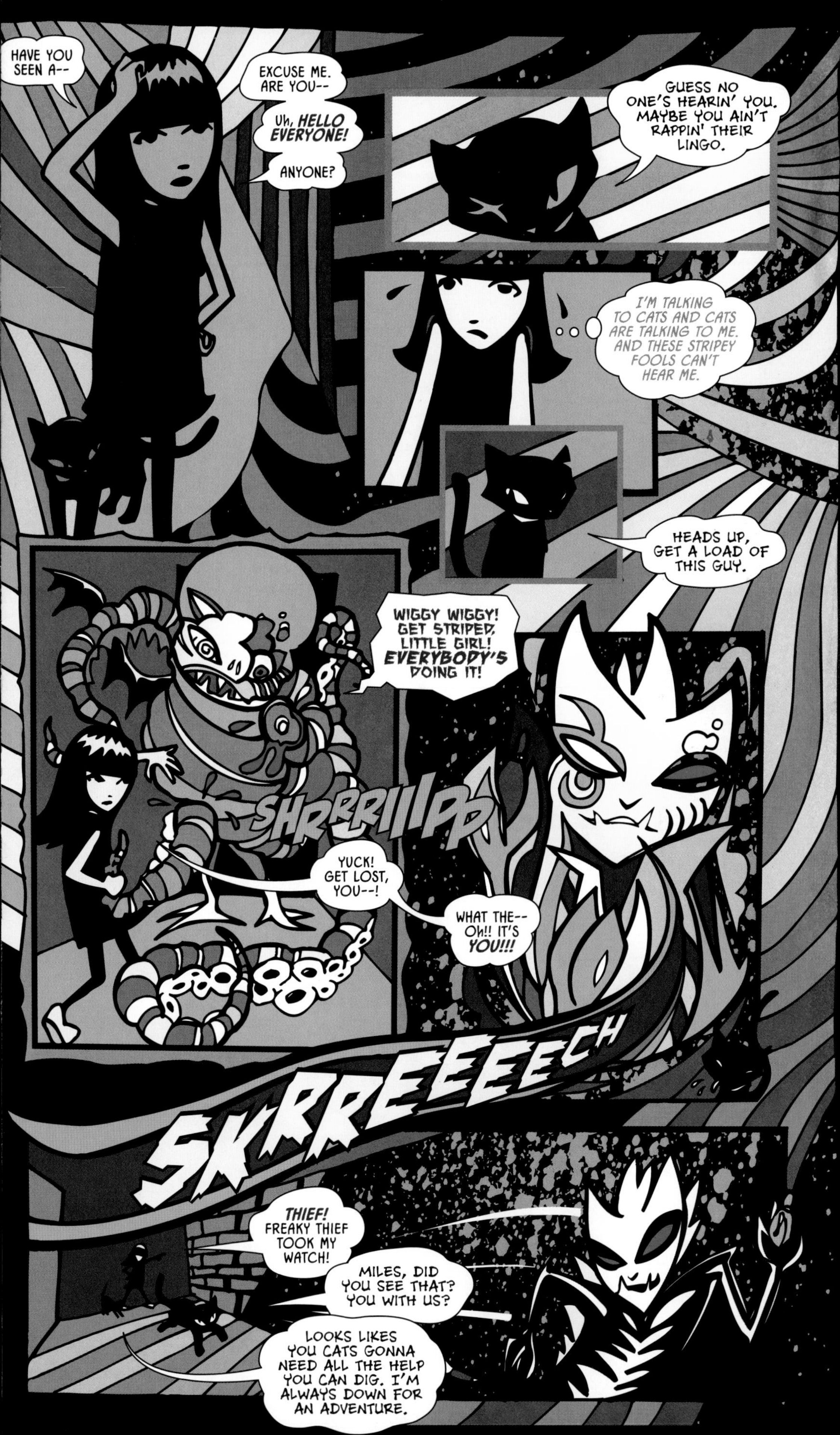
HAVE YOU SEEN A--
EXCUSE ME. ARE YOU--
Uh, HELLO EVERYONE!
ANYONE?
GUESS NO ONE'S HEARIN' YOU. MAYBE YOU AIN'T RAPPIN' THEIR LINGO.
I'M TALKING TO CATS AND CATS ARE TALKING TO ME. AND THESE STRIPEY FOOLS CAN'T HEAR ME.
HEADS UP, GET A LOAD OF THIS GUY.
WIGGY WIGGY! GET STRIPED, LITTLE GIRL! EVERYBODY'S DOING IT!
SHRRRIIIPP
YUCK! GET LOST, YOU--!
WHAT THE-- Oh!! IT'S YOU!!!
SKRREEEEECH
THIEF! FREAKY THIEF TOOK MY WATCH!
MILES, DID YOU SEE THAT? YOU WITH US?
LOOKS LIKES YOU CATS GONNA NEED ALL THE HELP YOU CAN DIG. I'M ALWAYS DOWN FOR AN ADVENTURE.

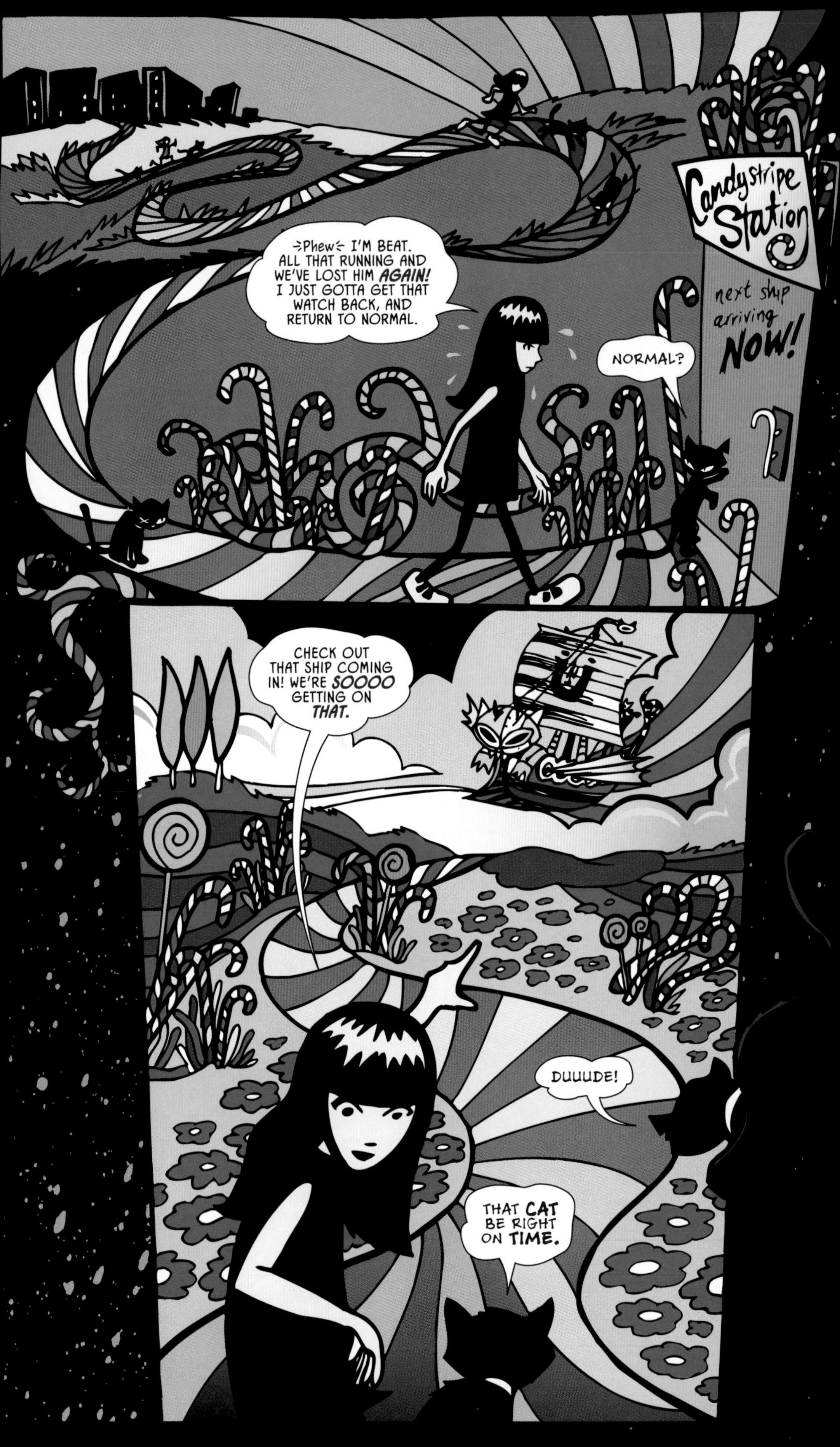
Candystripe Station
⇒Phew⇐ I'M BEAT. ALL THAT RUNNING AND WE'VE LOST HIM AGAIN! I JUST GOTTA GET THAT WATCH BACK, AND RETURN TO NORMAL.
next ship arriving NOW!
NORMAL?
CHECK OUT THAT SHIP COMING IN! WE'RE SOOOO GETTING ON THAT.
DUUUDE!
THAT CAT BE RIGHT ON TIME.

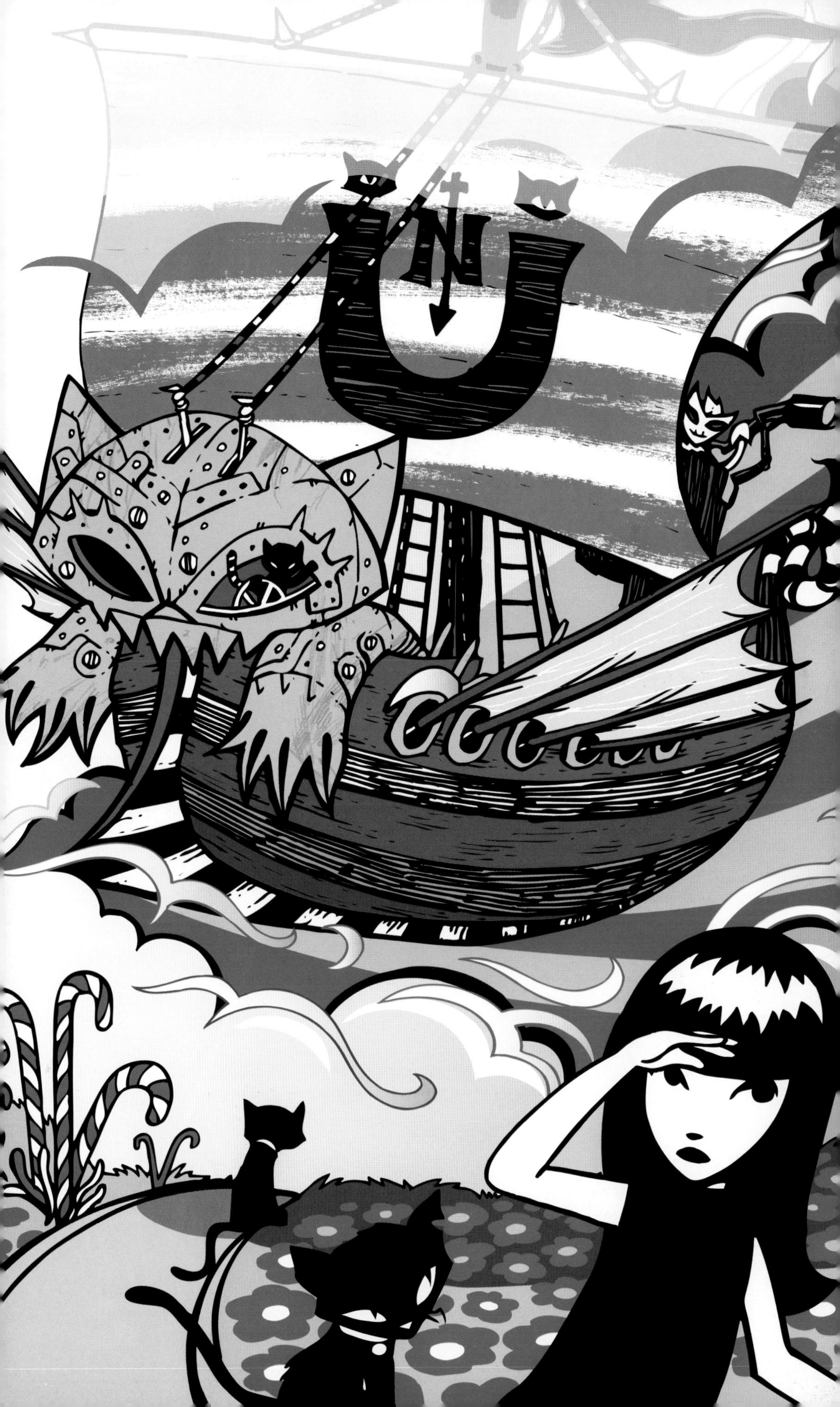

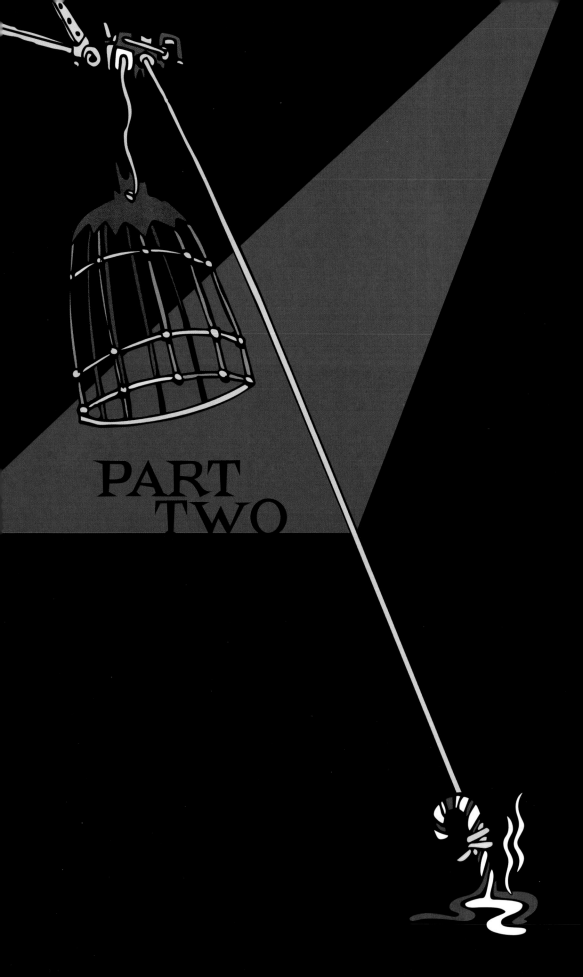

PART
TWO

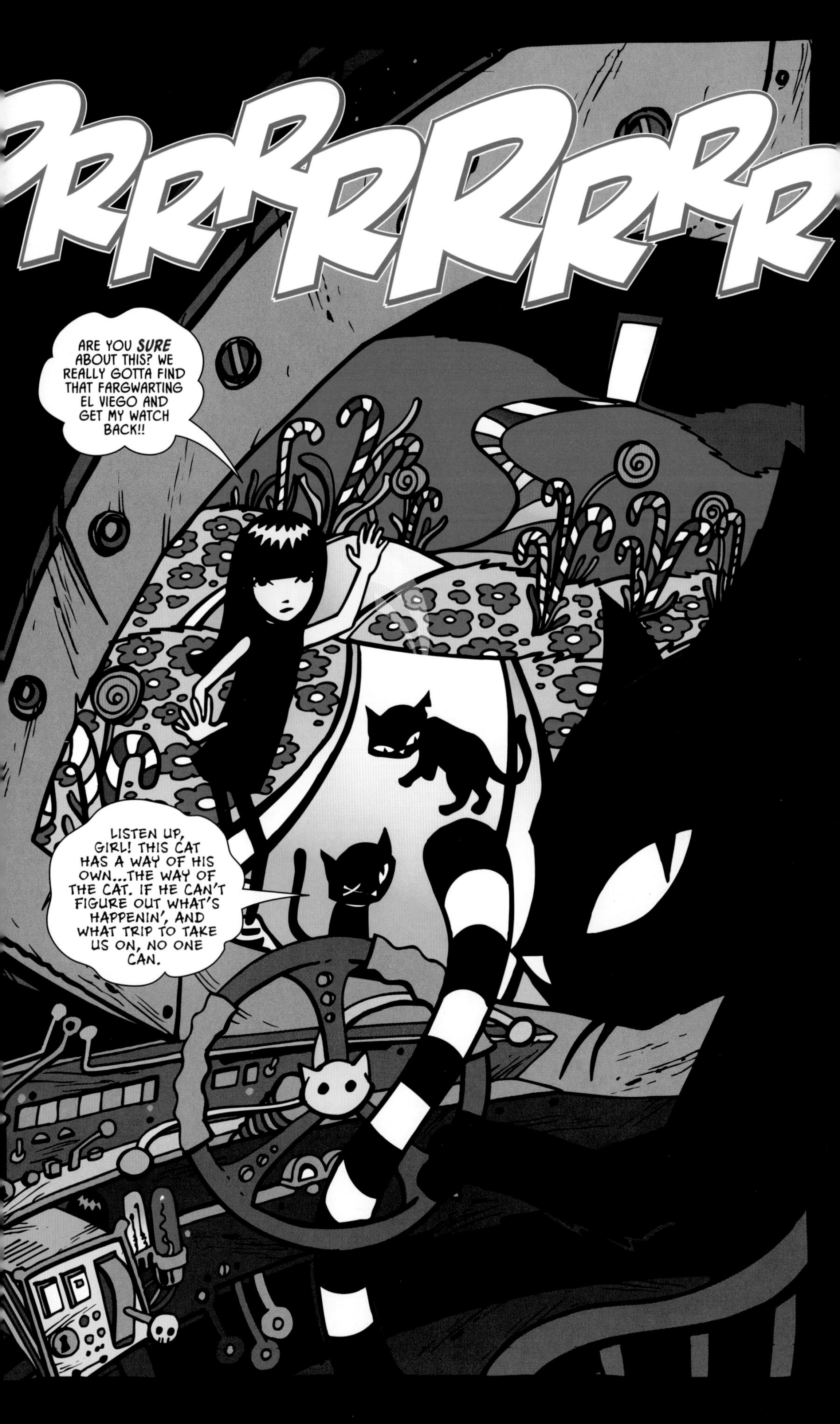
RRRRRRRRR
ARE YOU SURE ABOUT THIS? WE REALLY GOTTA FIND THAT FARGWARTING EL VIEGO AND GET MY WATCH BACK!!
LISTEN UP, GIRL! THIS CAT HAS A WAY OF HIS OWN...THE WAY OF THE CAT. IF HE CAN'T FIGURE OUT WHAT'S HAPPENIN', AND WHAT TRIP TO TAKE US ON, NO ONE CAN.

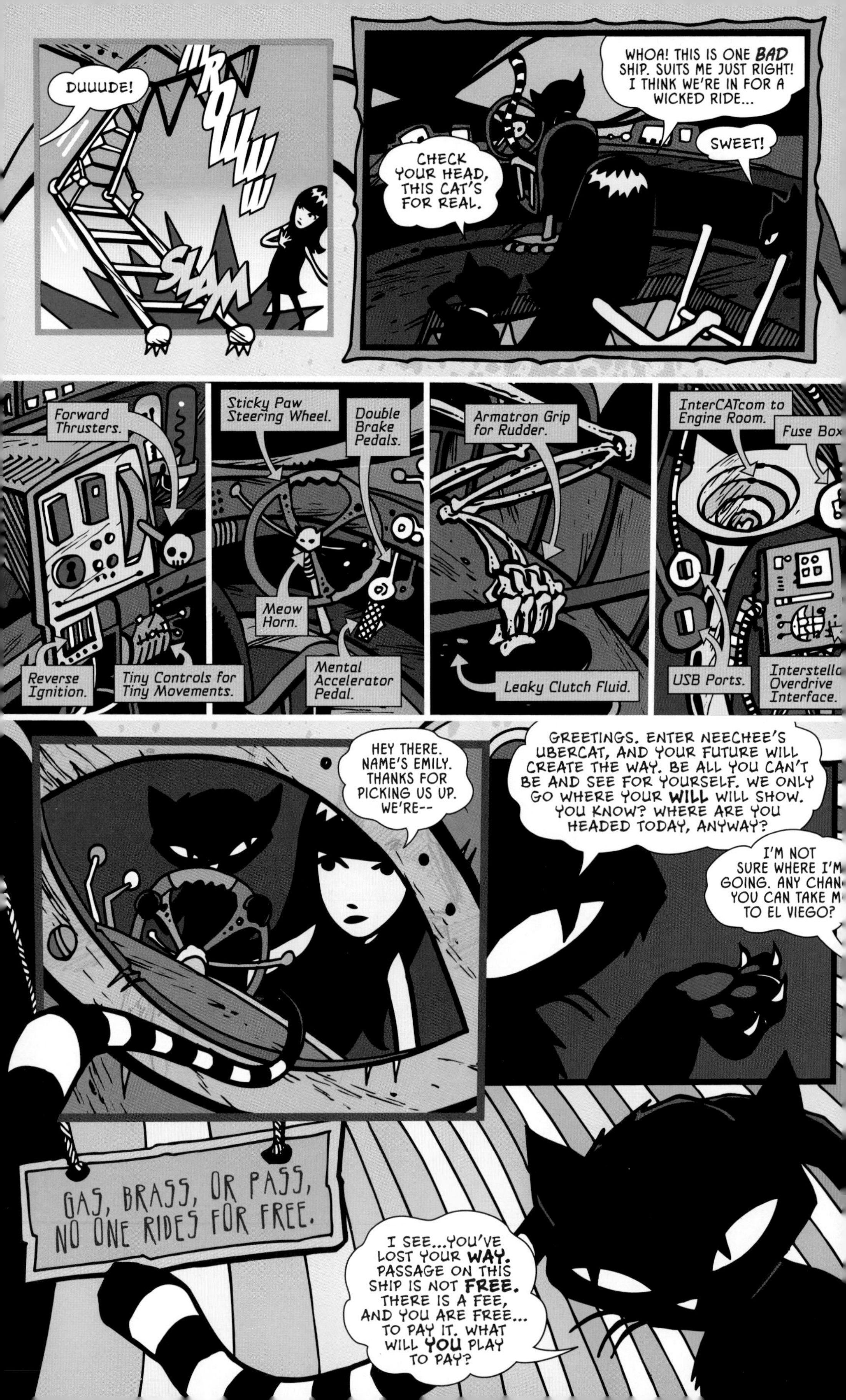
DUUUDE!
VROOUUUW
SLAM
WHOA! THIS IS ONE BAD SHIP. SUITS ME JUST RIGHT! I THINK WE'RE IN FOR A WICKED RIDE...
CHECK YOUR HEAD, THIS CAT'S FOR REAL.
SWEET!
Forward Thrusters.
Reverse Ignition.
Tiny Controls for Tiny Movements.
Sticky Paw Steering Wheel.
Double Brake Pedals.
Meow Horn.
Mental Accelerator Pedal.
Armatron Grip for Rudder.
Leaky Clutch Fluid.
InterCATcom to Engine Room.
Fuse Box
USB Ports.
Interstella Overdrive Interface.
HEY THERE. NAME'S EMILY. THANKS FOR PICKING US UP. WE'RE--
GREETINGS. ENTER NEECHEE'S UBERCAT, AND YOUR FUTURE WILL CREATE THE WAY. BE ALL YOU CAN'T BE AND SEE FOR YOURSELF. WE ONLY GO WHERE YOUR WILL WILL SHOW. YOU KNOW? WHERE ARE YOU HEADED TODAY, ANYWAY?
I'M NOT SURE WHERE I'M GOING. ANY CHAN YOU CAN TAKE M TO EL VIEGO?
GAS, BRASS, OR PASS, NO ONE RIDES FOR FREE.
I SEE...YOU'VE LOST YOUR WAY. PASSAGE ON THIS SHIP IS NOT FREE. THERE IS A FEE, AND YOU ARE FREE... TO PAY IT. WHAT WILL YOU PLAY TO PAY?

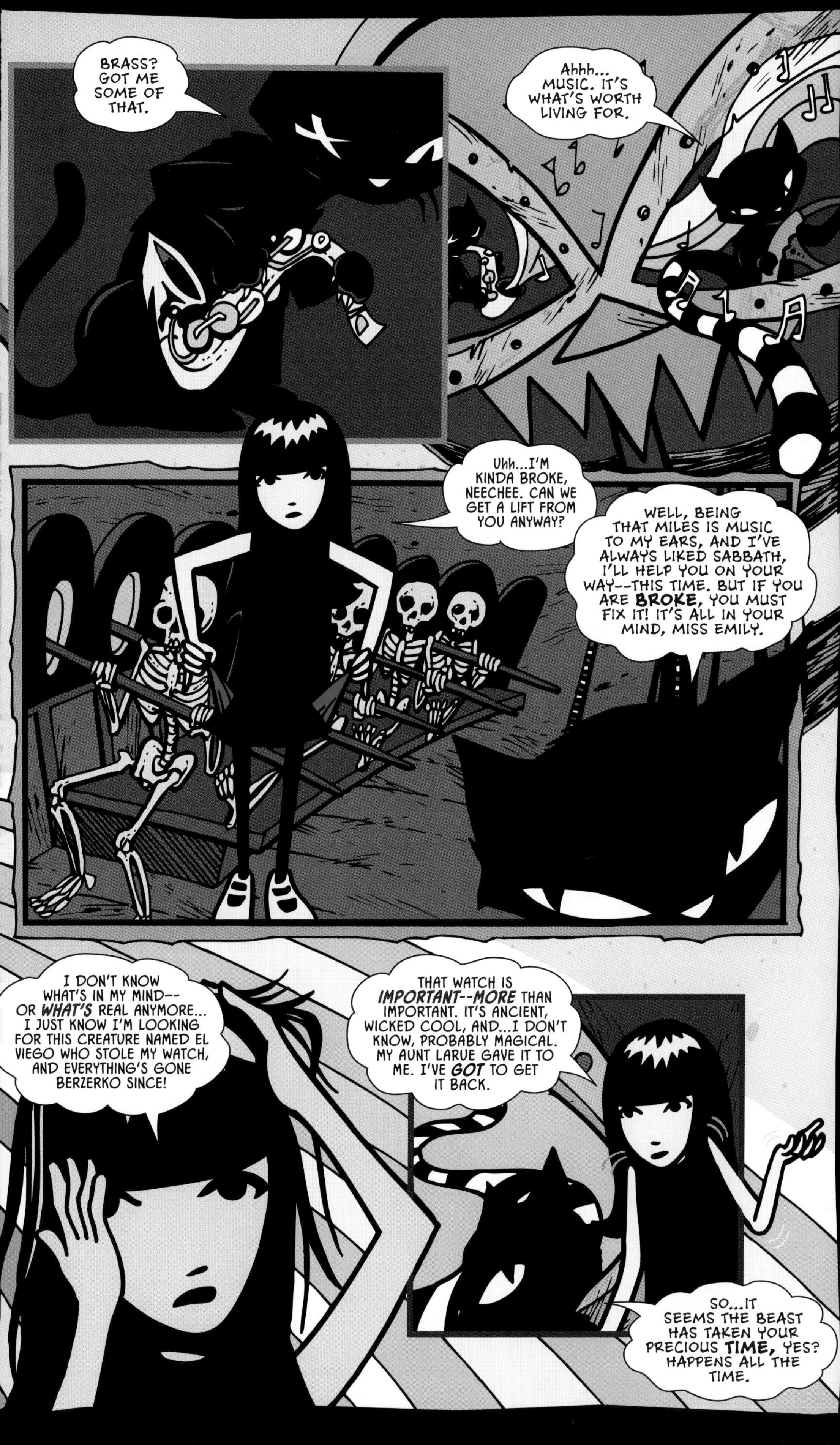
BRASS? GOT ME SOME OF THAT.
Ahhh... MUSIC. IT'S WHAT'S WORTH LIVING FOR.
Uhh...I'M KINDA BROKE, NEECHEE. CAN WE GET A LIFT FROM YOU ANYWAY?
WELL, BEING THAT MILES IS MUSIC TO MY EARS, AND I'VE ALWAYS LIKED SABBATH, I'LL HELP YOU ON YOUR WAY--THIS TIME. BUT IF YOU ARE **BROKE**, YOU MUST FIX IT! IT'S ALL IN YOUR MIND, MISS EMILY.
I DON'T KNOW WHAT'S IN MY MIND-- OR ***WHAT'S*** REAL ANYMORE... I JUST KNOW I'M LOOKING FOR THIS CREATURE NAMED EL VIEGO WHO STOLE MY WATCH, AND EVERYTHING'S GONE BERZERKO SINCE!
THAT WATCH IS ***IMPORTANT--MORE*** THAN IMPORTANT. IT'S ANCIENT, WICKED COOL, AND...I DON'T KNOW, PROBABLY MAGICAL. MY AUNT LARUE GAVE IT TO ME. I'VE ***GOT*** TO GET IT BACK.
SO...IT SEEMS THE BEAST HAS TAKEN YOUR PRECIOUS **TIME,** YES? HAPPENS ALL THE TIME.

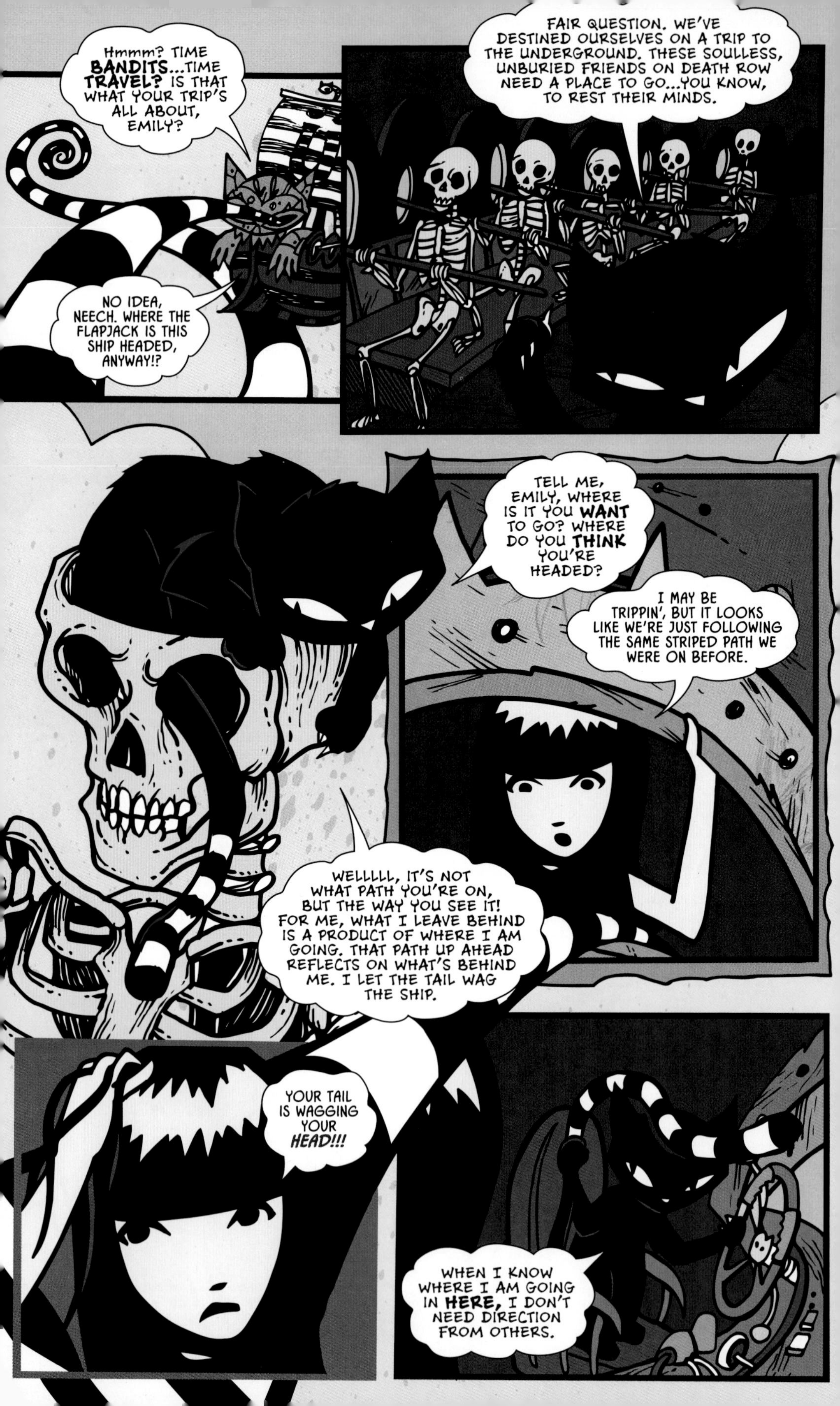
Hmmm? TIME BANDITS...TIME TRAVEL? IS THAT WHAT YOUR TRIP'S ALL ABOUT, EMILY?
NO IDEA, NEECH. WHERE THE FLAPJACK IS THIS SHIP HEADED, ANYWAY!?
FAIR QUESTION. WE'VE DESTINED OURSELVES ON A TRIP TO THE UNDERGROUND. THESE SOULLESS, UNBURIED FRIENDS ON DEATH ROW NEED A PLACE TO GO...YOU KNOW, TO REST THEIR MINDS.
TELL ME, EMILY, WHERE IS IT YOU WANT TO GO? WHERE DO YOU THINK YOU'RE HEADED?
I MAY BE TRIPPIN', BUT IT LOOKS LIKE WE'RE JUST FOLLOWING THE SAME STRIPED PATH WE WERE ON BEFORE.
WELLLLL, IT'S NOT WHAT PATH YOU'RE ON, BUT THE WAY YOU SEE IT! FOR ME, WHAT I LEAVE BEHIND IS A PRODUCT OF WHERE I AM GOING. THAT PATH UP AHEAD REFLECTS ON WHAT'S BEHIND ME. I LET THE TAIL WAG THE SHIP.
YOUR TAIL IS WAGGING YOUR HEAD!!!
WHEN I KNOW WHERE I AM GOING IN HERE, I DON'T NEED DIRECTION FROM OTHERS.

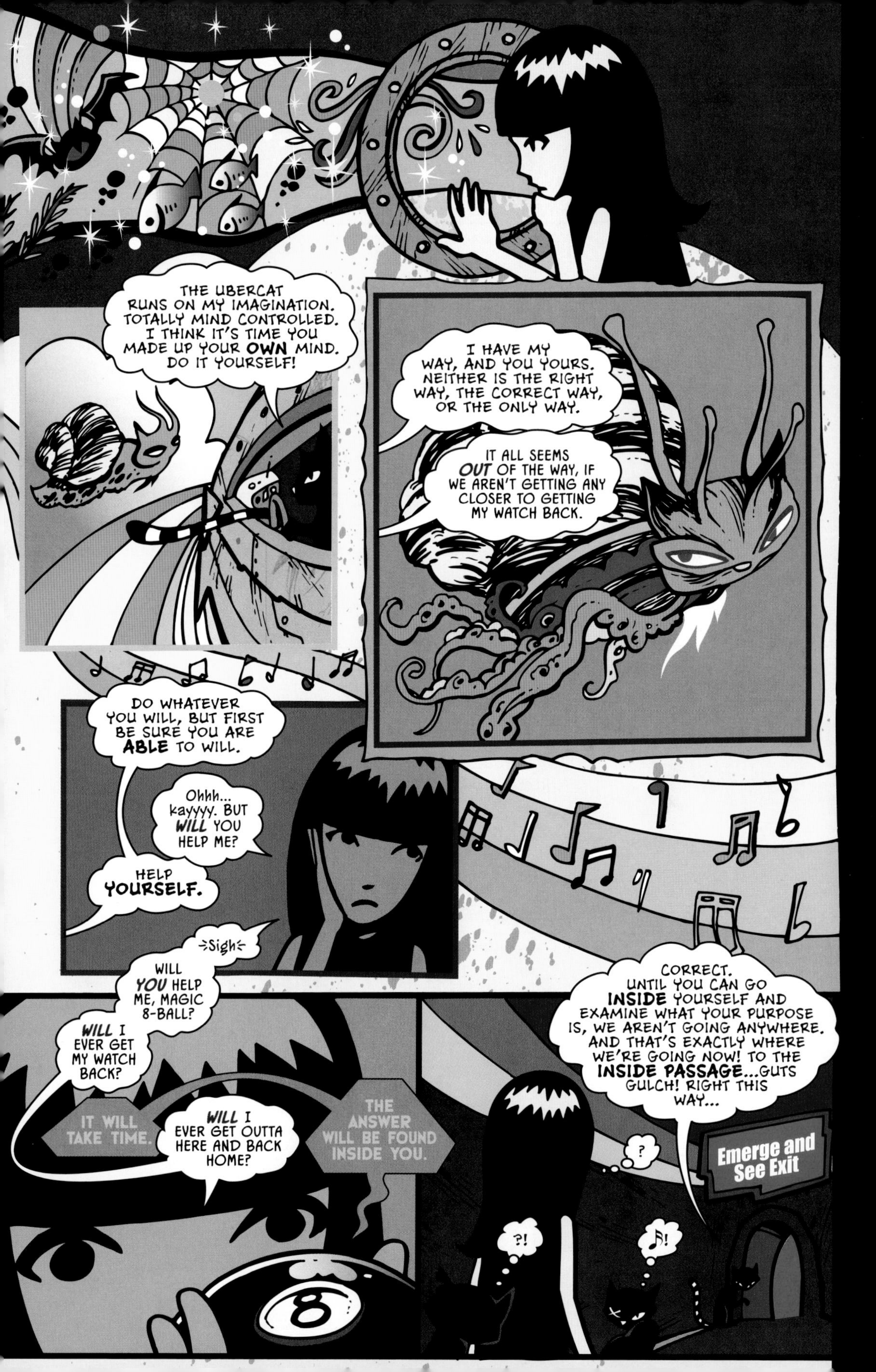
THE UBERCAT RUNS ON MY IMAGINATION. TOTALLY MIND CONTROLLED. I THINK IT'S TIME YOU MADE UP YOUR OWN MIND. DO IT YOURSELF!
I HAVE MY WAY, AND YOU YOURS. NEITHER IS THE RIGHT WAY, THE CORRECT WAY, OR THE ONLY WAY.
IT ALL SEEMS OUT OF THE WAY, IF WE AREN'T GETTING ANY CLOSER TO GETTING MY WATCH BACK.
DO WHATEVER YOU WILL, BUT FIRST BE SURE YOU ARE ABLE TO WILL.
Ohhh... kayyyy. BUT WILL YOU HELP ME?
HELP YOURSELF.
Sigh
WILL YOU HELP ME, MAGIC 8-BALL?
WILL I EVER GET MY WATCH BACK?
IT WILL TAKE TIME.
WILL I EVER GET OUTTA HERE AND BACK HOME?
THE ANSWER WILL BE FOUND INSIDE YOU.
CORRECT. UNTIL YOU CAN GO INSIDE YOURSELF AND EXAMINE WHAT YOUR PURPOSE IS, WE AREN'T GOING ANYWHERE. AND THAT'S EXACTLY WHERE WE'RE GOING NOW! TO THE INSIDE PASSAGE...GUTS GULCH! RIGHT THIS WAY...
?
?!
Emerge and See Exit

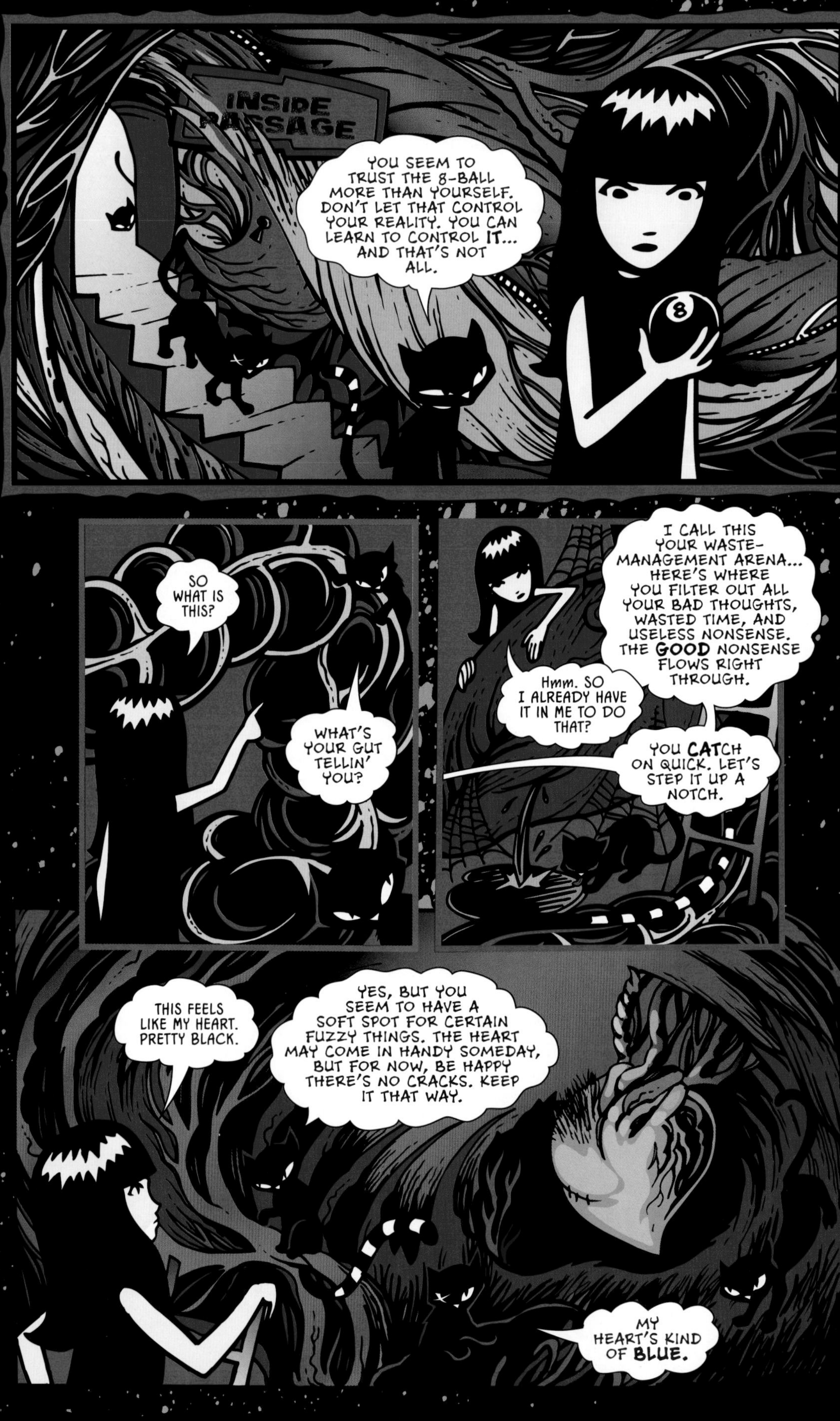
INSIDE PASSAGE
YOU SEEM TO TRUST THE 8-BALL MORE THAN YOURSELF. DON'T LET THAT CONTROL YOUR REALITY. YOU CAN LEARN TO CONTROL IT... AND THAT'S NOT ALL.
8
SO WHAT IS THIS?
WHAT'S YOUR GUT TELLIN' YOU?
I CALL THIS YOUR WASTE-MANAGEMENT ARENA... HERE'S WHERE YOU FILTER OUT ALL YOUR BAD THOUGHTS, WASTED TIME, AND USELESS NONSENSE. THE GOOD NONSENSE FLOWS RIGHT THROUGH.
Hmm. SO I ALREADY HAVE IT IN ME TO DO THAT?
YOU CATCH ON QUICK. LET'S STEP IT UP A NOTCH.
THIS FEELS LIKE MY HEART. PRETTY BLACK.
YES, BUT YOU SEEM TO HAVE A SOFT SPOT FOR CERTAIN FUZZY THINGS. THE HEART MAY COME IN HANDY SOMEDAY, BUT FOR NOW, BE HAPPY THERE'S NO CRACKS. KEEP IT THAT WAY.
MY HEART'S KIND OF BLUE.

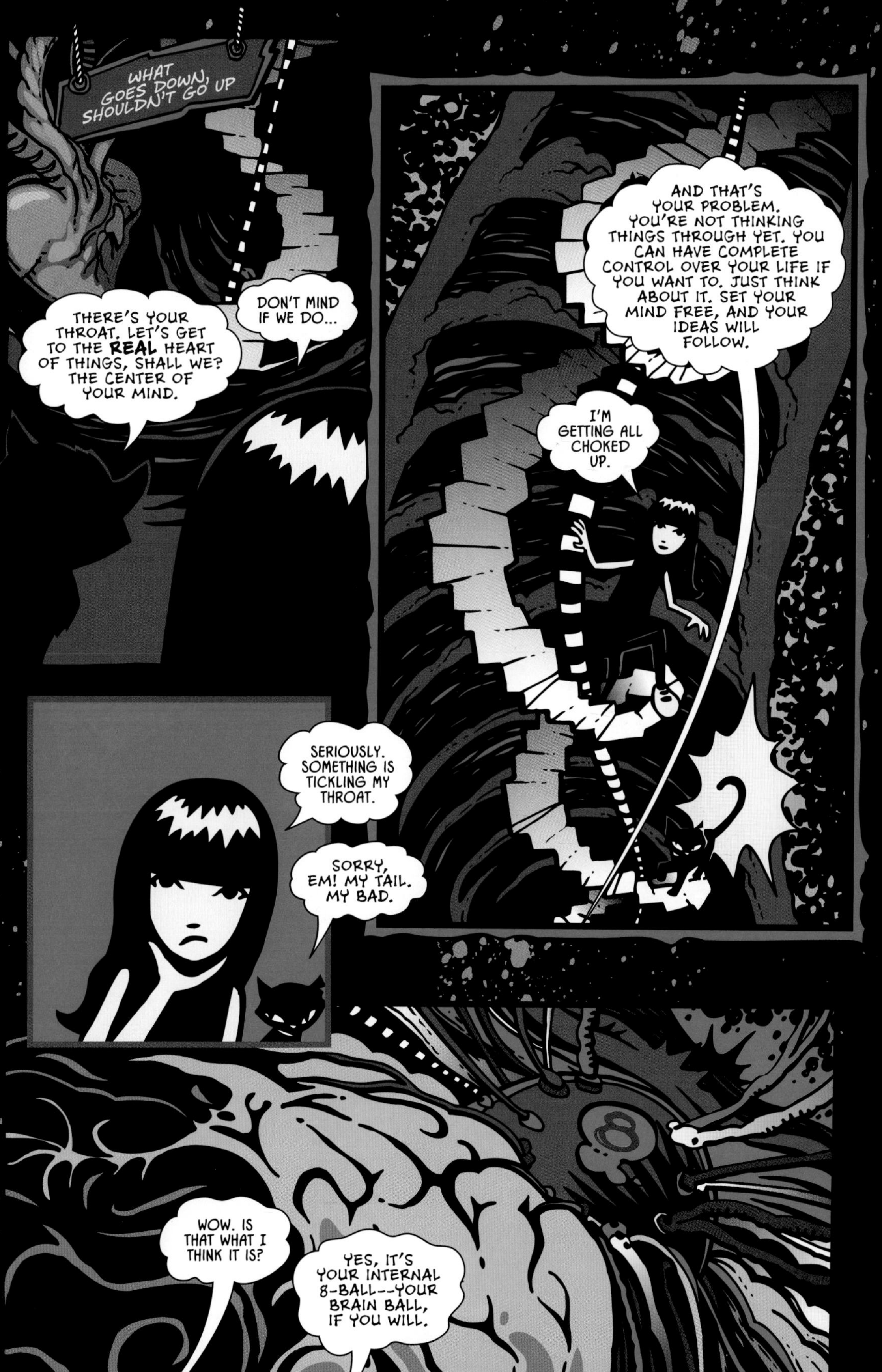
WHAT GOES DOWN, SHOULDN'T GO UP
THERE'S YOUR THROAT. LET'S GET TO THE **REAL** HEART OF THINGS, SHALL WE? THE CENTER OF YOUR MIND.
DON'T MIND IF WE DO...
AND THAT'S YOUR PROBLEM. YOU'RE NOT THINKING THINGS THROUGH YET. YOU CAN HAVE COMPLETE CONTROL OVER YOUR LIFE IF YOU WANT TO. JUST THINK ABOUT IT. SET YOUR MIND FREE, AND YOUR IDEAS WILL FOLLOW.
I'M GETTING ALL CHOKED UP.
SERIOUSLY. SOMETHING IS TICKLING MY THROAT.
SORRY, EM! MY TAIL. MY BAD.
WOW. IS THAT WHAT I THINK IT IS?
YES, IT'S YOUR INTERNAL 8-BALL--YOUR BRAIN BALL, IF YOU WILL.

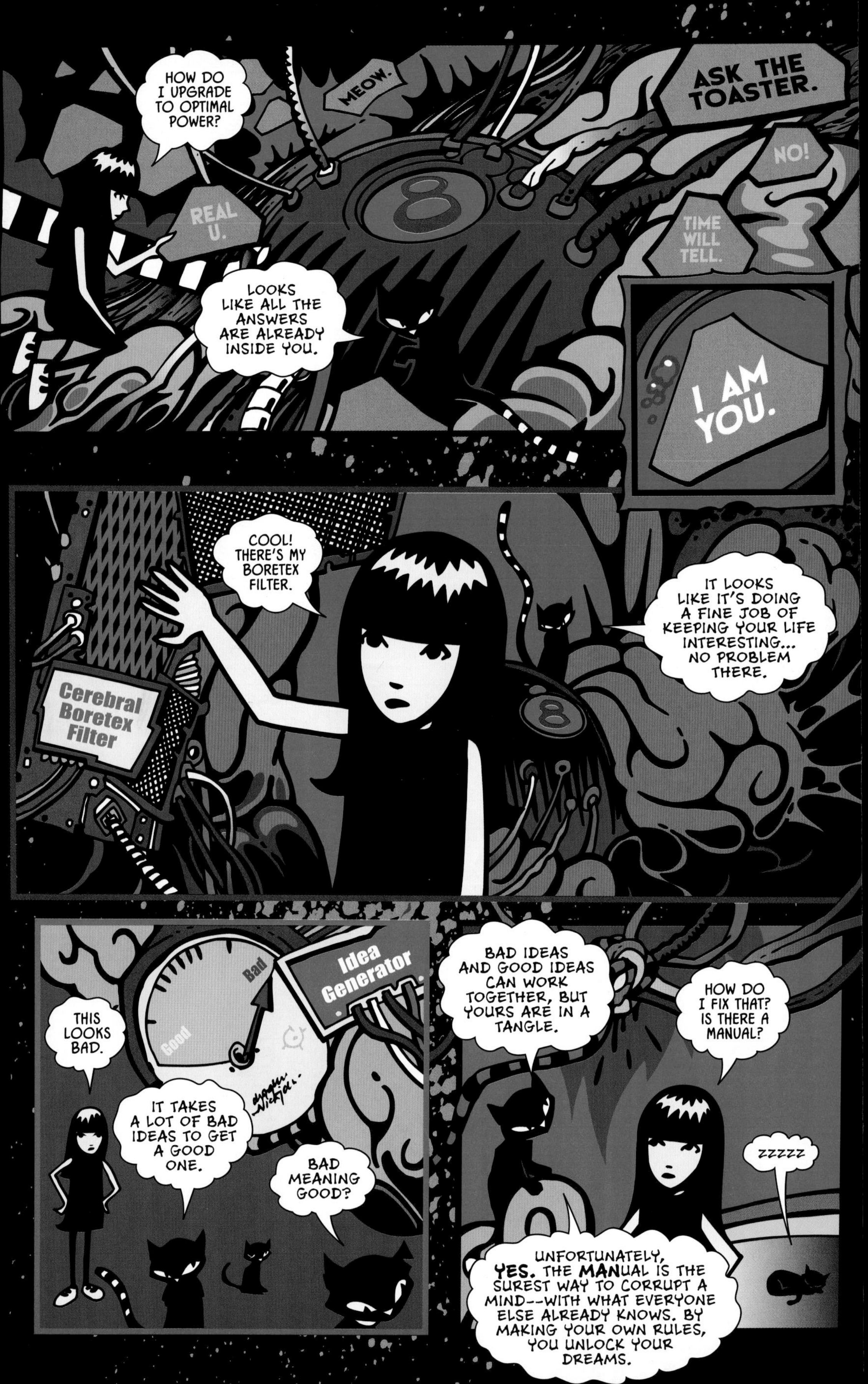
HOW DO I UPGRADE TO OPTIMAL POWER?
MEOW.
ASK THE TOASTER.
NO!
REAL U.
TIME WILL TELL.
LOOKS LIKE ALL THE ANSWERS ARE ALREADY INSIDE YOU.
I AM YOU.
COOL! THERE'S MY BORETEX FILTER.
IT LOOKS LIKE IT'S DOING A FINE JOB OF KEEPING YOUR LIFE INTERESTING... NO PROBLEM THERE.
Cerebral Boretex Filter
Idea Generator
Bad
Good
THIS LOOKS BAD.
IT TAKES A LOT OF BAD IDEAS TO GET A GOOD ONE.
BAD MEANING GOOD?
BAD IDEAS AND GOOD IDEAS CAN WORK TOGETHER, BUT YOURS ARE IN A TANGLE.
HOW DO I FIX THAT? IS THERE A MANUAL?
ZZZZZ
UNFORTUNATELY, YES. THE MANUAL IS THE SUREST WAY TO CORRUPT A MIND--WITH WHAT EVERYONE ELSE ALREADY KNOWS. BY MAKING YOUR OWN RULES, YOU UNLOCK YOUR DREAMS.

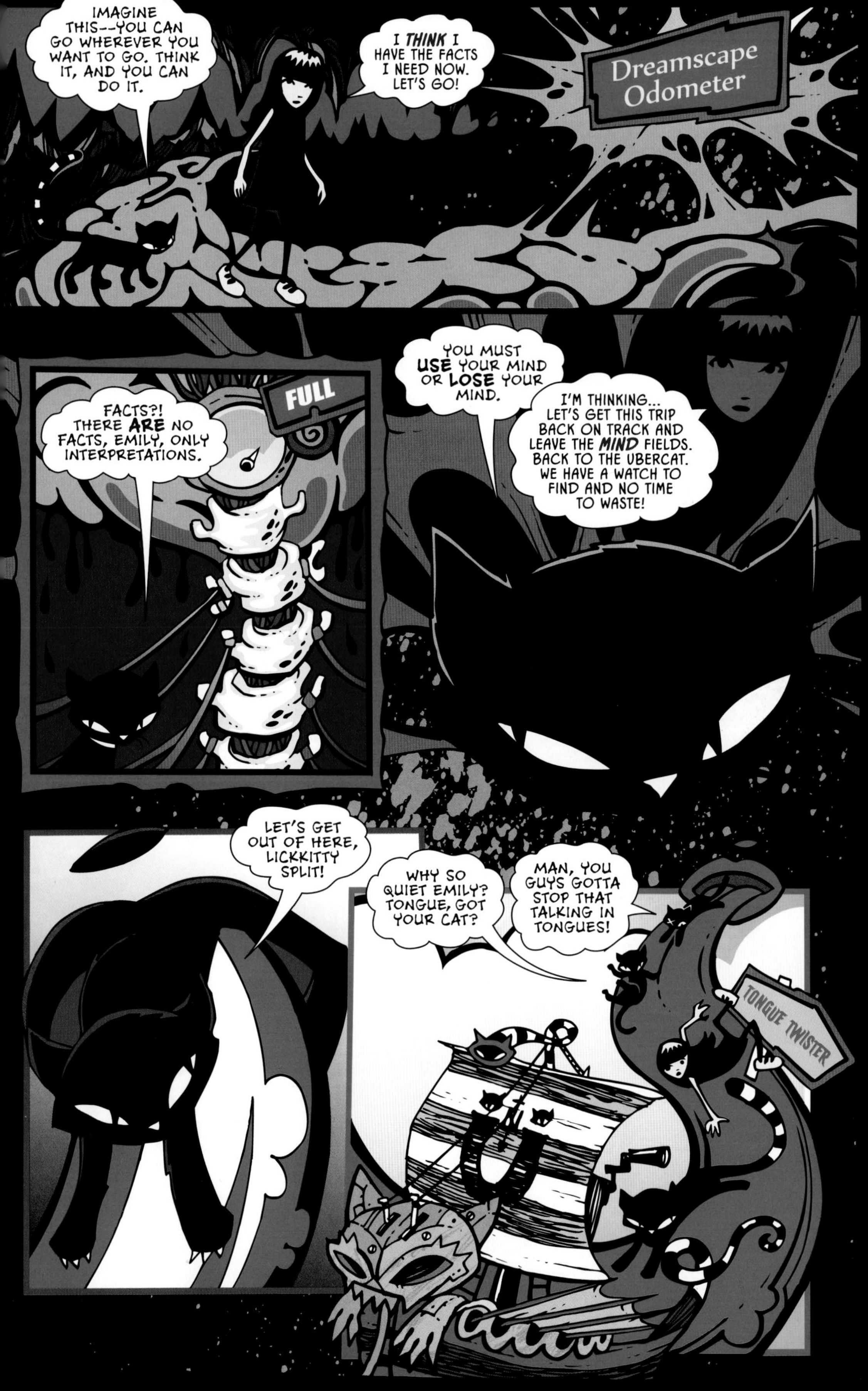
IMAGINE THIS--YOU CAN GO WHEREVER YOU WANT TO GO. THINK IT, AND YOU CAN DO IT.
I *THINK* I HAVE THE FACTS I NEED NOW. LET'S GO!
Dreamscape Odometer
FULL
FACTS?! THERE **ARE** NO FACTS, EMILY, ONLY INTERPRETATIONS.
YOU MUST **USE** YOUR MIND OR **LOSE** YOUR MIND.
I'M THINKING... LET'S GET THIS TRIP BACK ON TRACK AND LEAVE THE *MIND* FIELDS. BACK TO THE UBERCAT. WE HAVE A WATCH TO FIND AND NO TIME TO WASTE!
LET'S GET OUT OF HERE, LICKKITTY SPLIT!
WHY SO QUIET EMILY? TONGUE, GOT YOUR CAT?
MAN, YOU GUYS GOTTA STOP THAT TALKING IN TONGUES!
TONGUE TWISTER

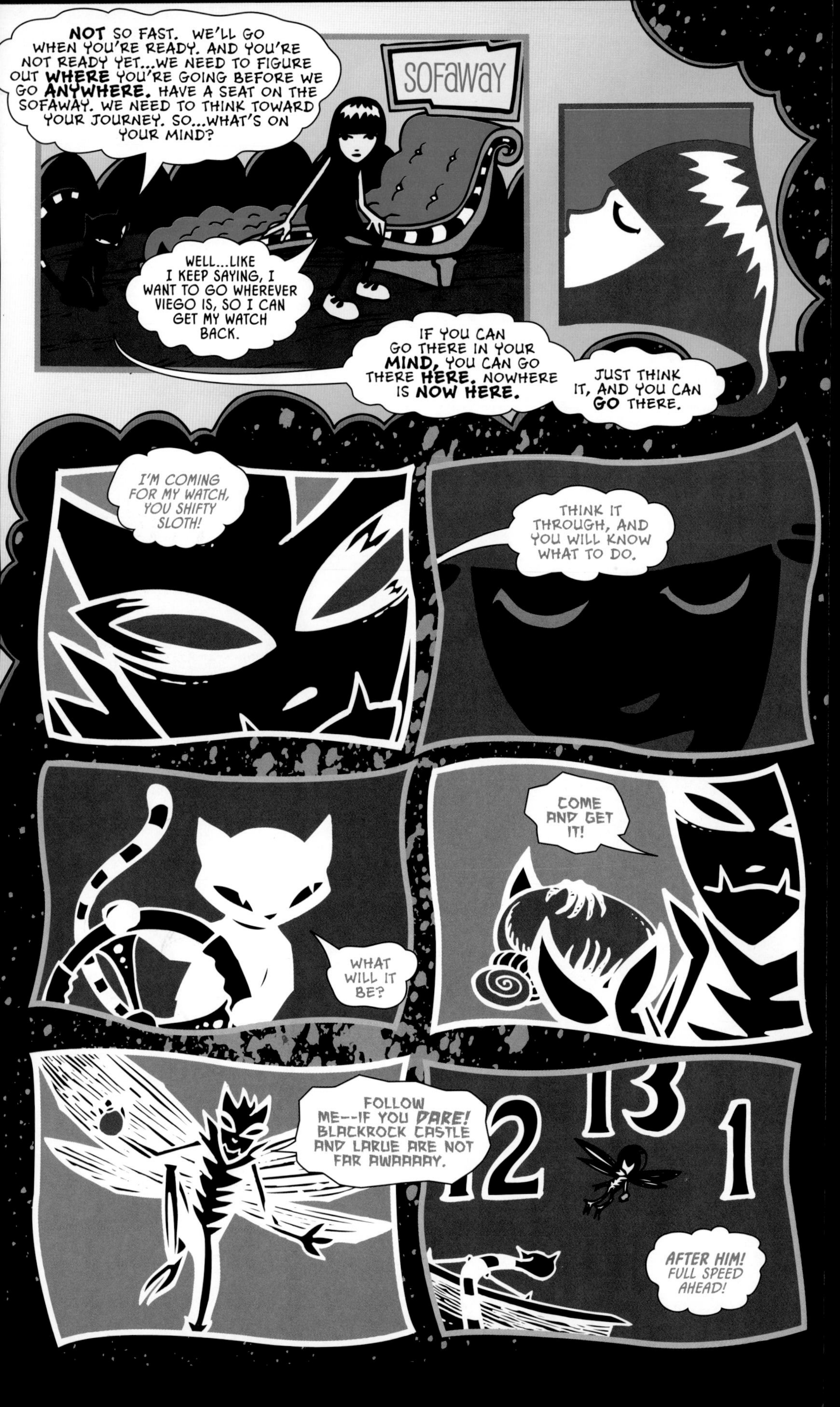

SOFAWAY
NOT SO FAST. WE'LL GO WHEN YOU'RE READY. AND YOU'RE NOT READY YET...WE NEED TO FIGURE OUT WHERE YOU'RE GOING BEFORE WE GO ANYWHERE. HAVE A SEAT ON THE SOFAWAY. WE NEED TO THINK TOWARD YOUR JOURNEY. SO...WHAT'S ON YOUR MIND?
WELL...LIKE I KEEP SAYING, I WANT TO GO WHEREVER VIEGO IS, SO I CAN GET MY WATCH BACK.
IF YOU CAN GO THERE IN YOUR MIND, YOU CAN GO THERE HERE. NOWHERE IS NOW HERE.
JUST THINK IT, AND YOU CAN GO THERE.
I'M COMING FOR MY WATCH, YOU SHIFTY SLOTH!
THINK IT THROUGH, AND YOU WILL KNOW WHAT TO DO.
WHAT WILL IT BE?
COME AND GET IT!
FOLLOW ME--IF YOU DARE! BLACKROCK CASTLE AND LARUE ARE NOT FAR AWAAAAY.
12
13
1
AFTER HIM! FULL SPEED AHEAD!

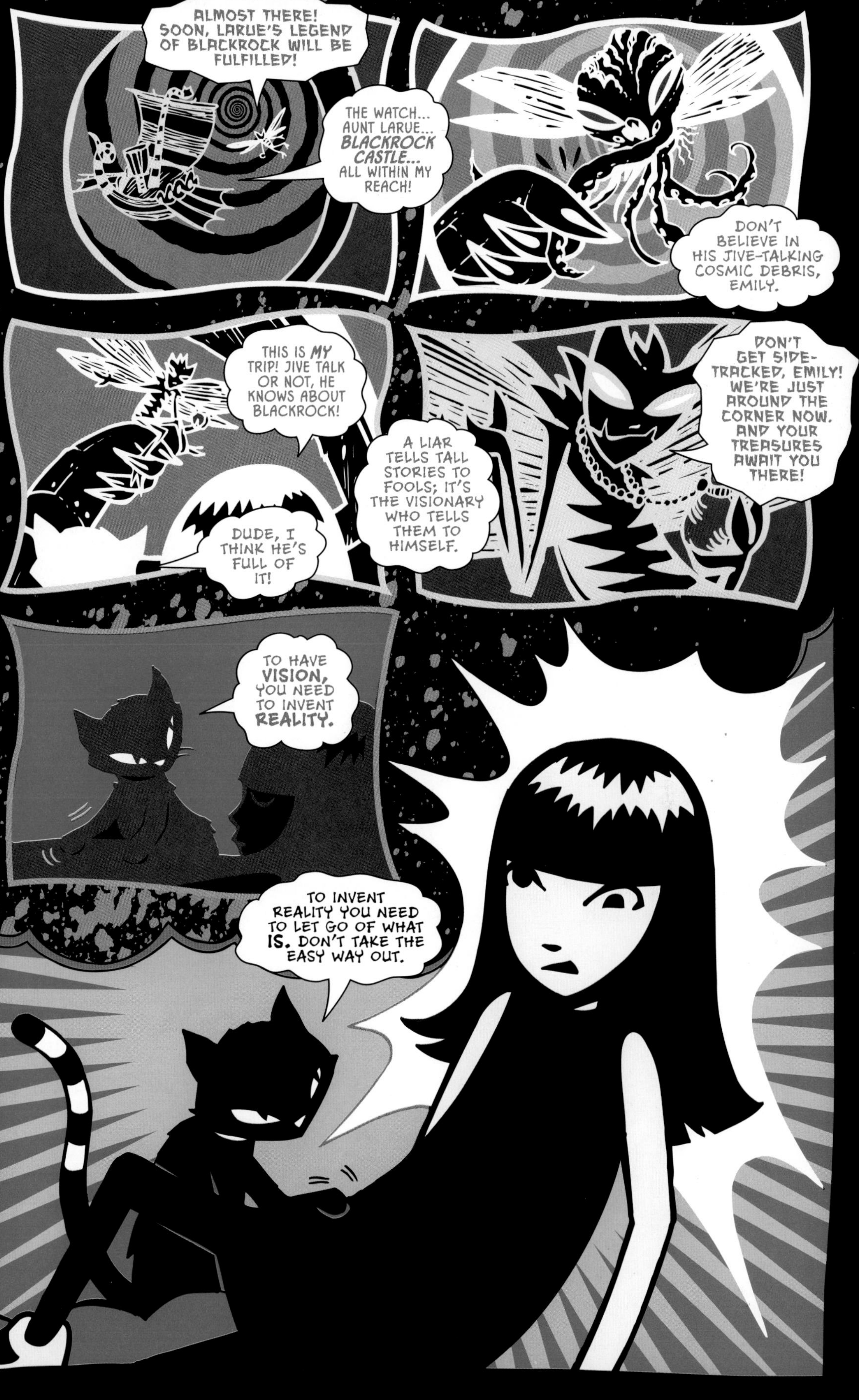

ALMOST THERE! SOON, LARUE'S LEGEND OF BLACKROCK WILL BE FULFILLED!
THE WATCH... AUNT LARUE... BLACKROCK CASTLE... ALL WITHIN MY REACH!
DON'T BELIEVE IN HIS JIVE-TALKING COSMIC DEBRIS, EMILY.
THIS IS MY TRIP! JIVE TALK OR NOT, HE KNOWS ABOUT BLACKROCK!
DUDE, I THINK HE'S FULL OF IT!
A LIAR TELLS TALL STORIES TO FOOLS; IT'S THE VISIONARY WHO TELLS THEM TO HIMSELF.
DON'T GET SIDE-TRACKED, EMILY! WE'RE JUST AROUND THE CORNER NOW. AND YOUR TREASURES AWAIT YOU THERE!
TO HAVE VISION, YOU NEED TO INVENT REALITY.
TO INVENT REALITY YOU NEED TO LET GO OF WHAT IS. DON'T TAKE THE EASY WAY OUT.

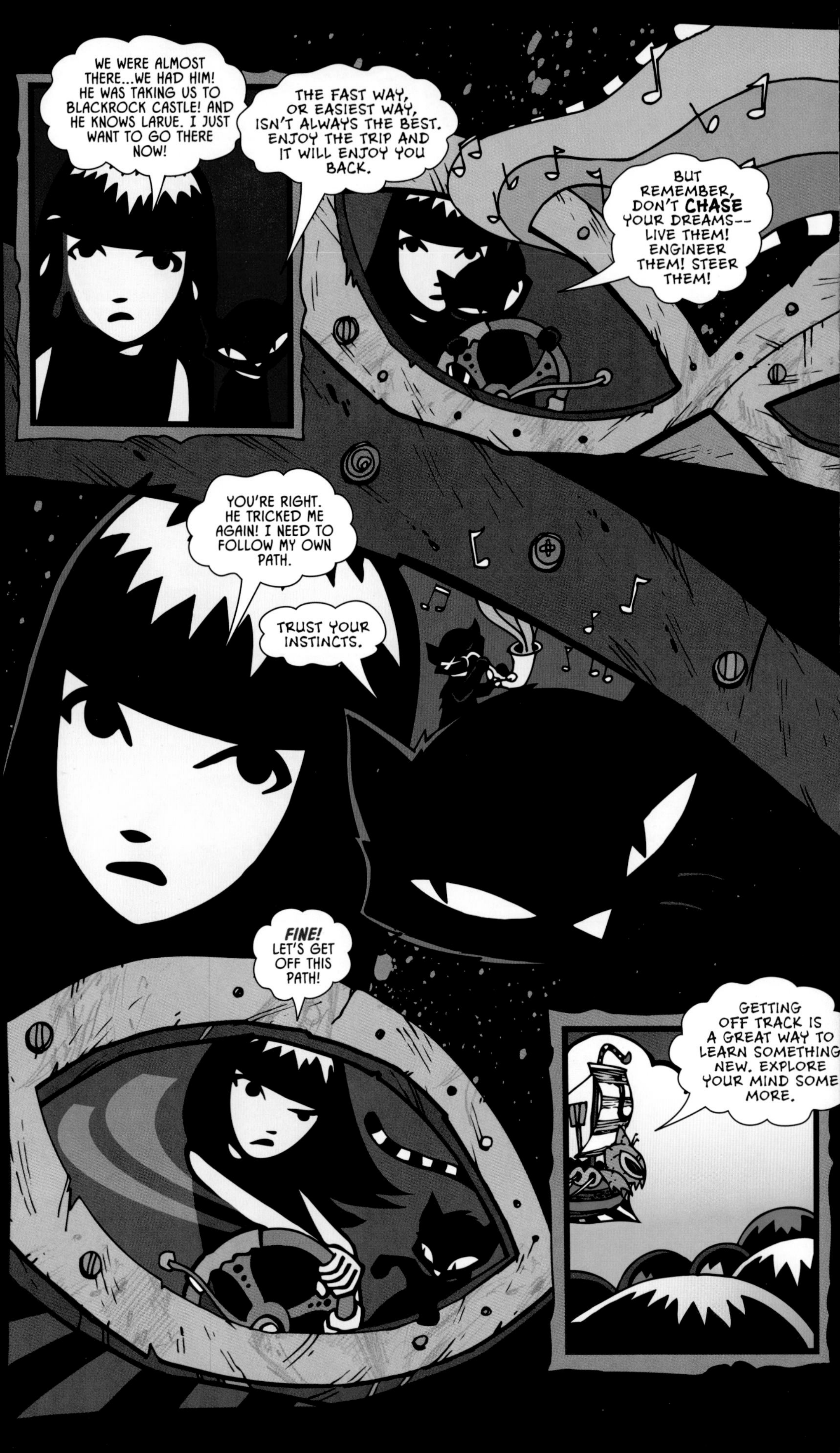

WE WERE ALMOST THERE...WE HAD HIM! HE WAS TAKING US TO BLACKROCK CASTLE! AND HE KNOWS LARUE. I JUST WANT TO GO THERE NOW!
THE FAST WAY, OR EASIEST WAY, ISN'T ALWAYS THE BEST. ENJOY THE TRIP AND IT WILL ENJOY YOU BACK.
BUT REMEMBER, DON'T **CHASE** YOUR DREAMS--LIVE THEM! ENGINEER THEM! STEER THEM!
YOU'RE RIGHT. HE TRICKED ME AGAIN! I NEED TO FOLLOW MY OWN PATH.
TRUST YOUR INSTINCTS.
FINE! LET'S GET OFF THIS PATH!
GETTING OFF TRACK IS A GREAT WAY TO LEARN SOMETHING NEW. EXPLORE YOUR MIND SOME MORE.

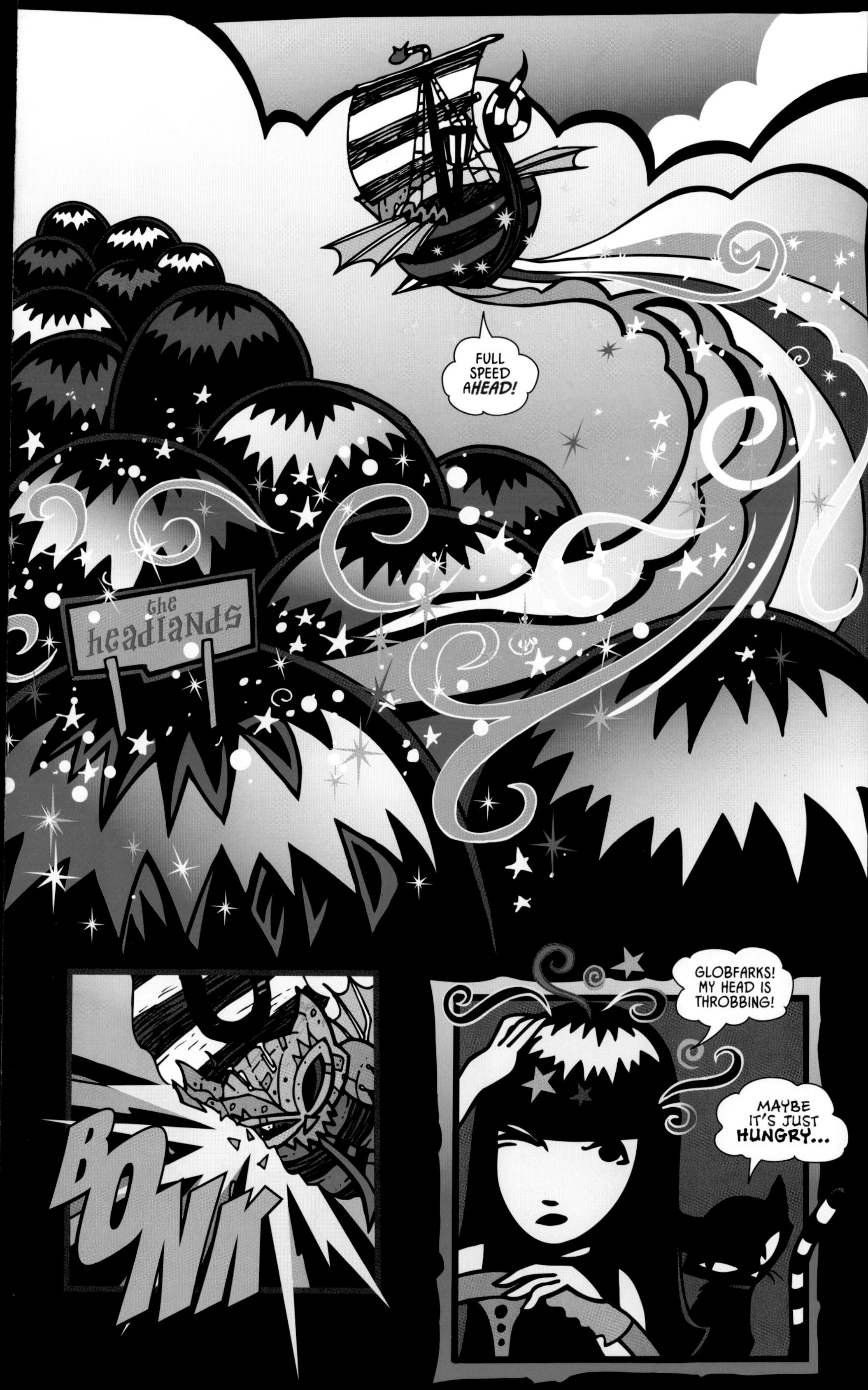
FULL SPEED AHEAD!
the headlands
BONK
GLOBFARKS! MY HEAD IS THROBBING!
MAYBE IT'S JUST HUNGRY...

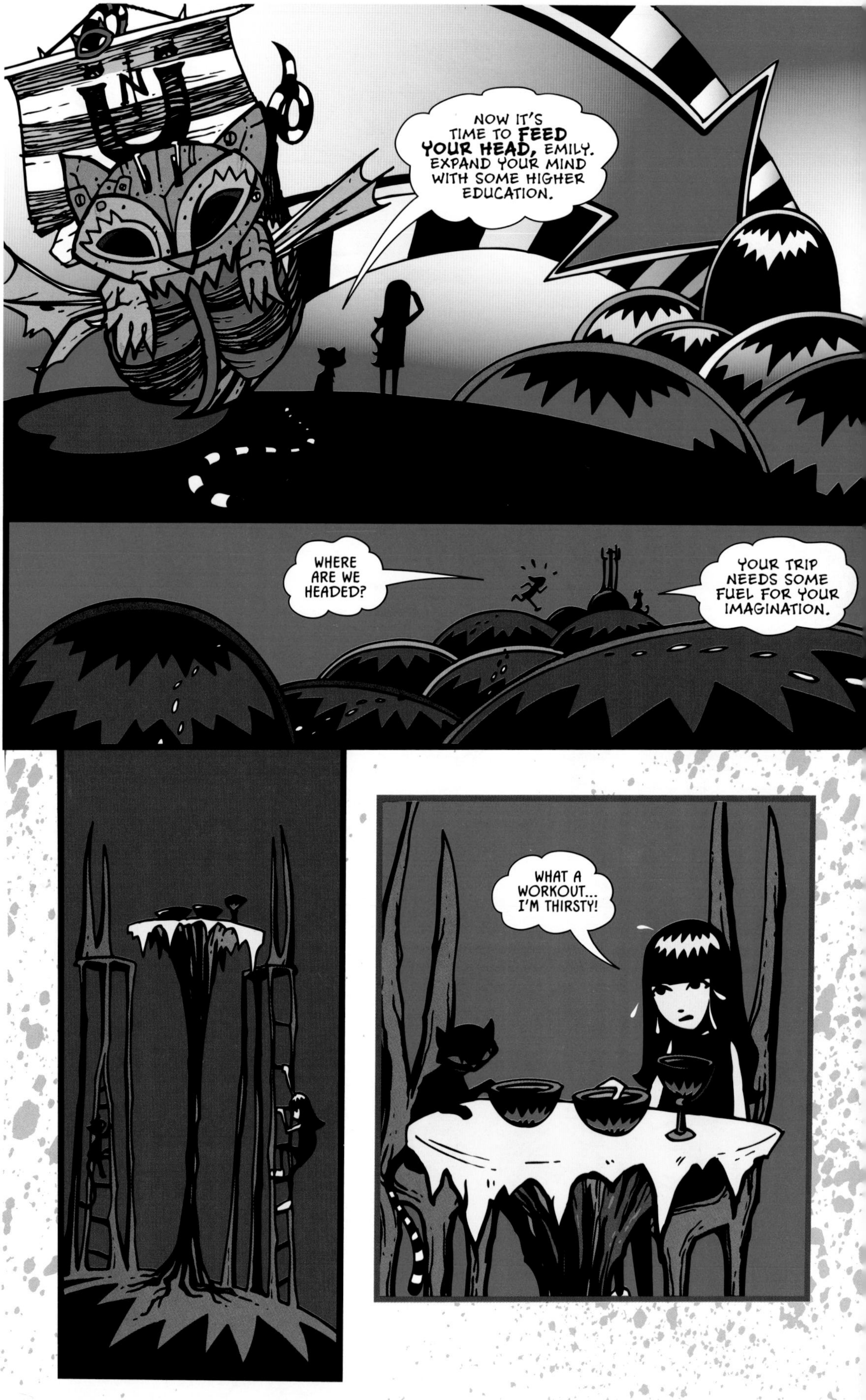
NOW IT'S TIME TO **FEED YOUR HEAD,** EMILY. EXPAND YOUR MIND WITH SOME HIGHER EDUCATION.
WHERE ARE WE HEADED?
YOUR TRIP NEEDS SOME FUEL FOR YOUR IMAGINATION.
WHAT A WORKOUT... I'M THIRSTY!

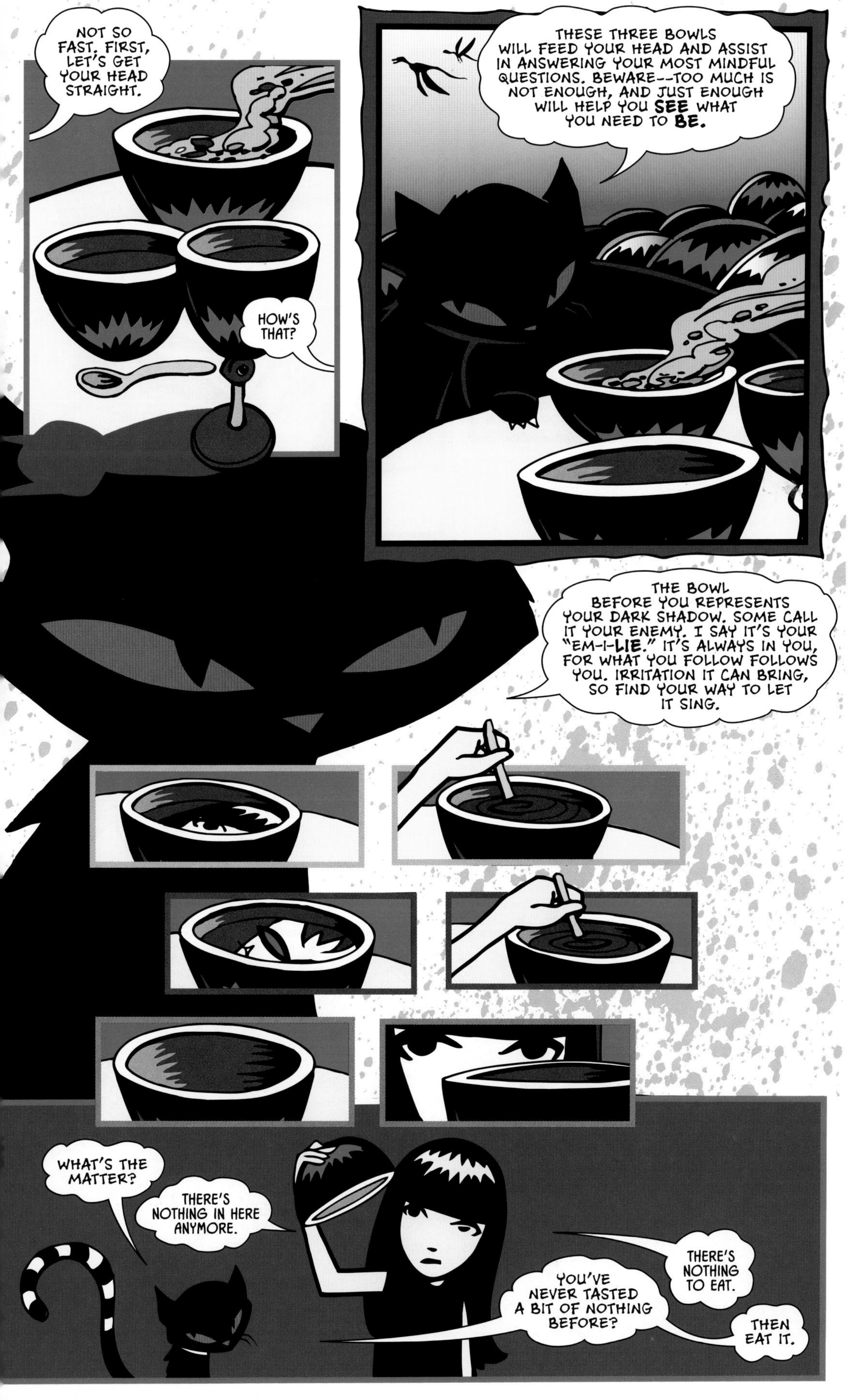
NOT SO FAST. FIRST, LET'S GET YOUR HEAD STRAIGHT.
HOW'S THAT?
THESE THREE BOWLS WILL FEED YOUR HEAD AND ASSIST IN ANSWERING YOUR MOST MINDFUL QUESTIONS. BEWARE--TOO MUCH IS NOT ENOUGH, AND JUST ENOUGH WILL HELP YOU **SEE** WHAT YOU NEED TO **BE.**
THE BOWL BEFORE YOU REPRESENTS YOUR DARK SHADOW. SOME CALL IT YOUR ENEMY. I SAY IT'S YOUR "EM-I-**LIE**." IT'S ALWAYS IN YOU, FOR WHAT YOU FOLLOW FOLLOWS YOU. IRRITATION IT CAN BRING, SO FIND YOUR WAY TO LET IT SING.
WHAT'S THE MATTER?
THERE'S NOTHING IN HERE ANYMORE.
THERE'S NOTHING TO EAT.
YOU'VE NEVER TASTED A BIT OF NOTHING BEFORE?
THEN EAT IT.

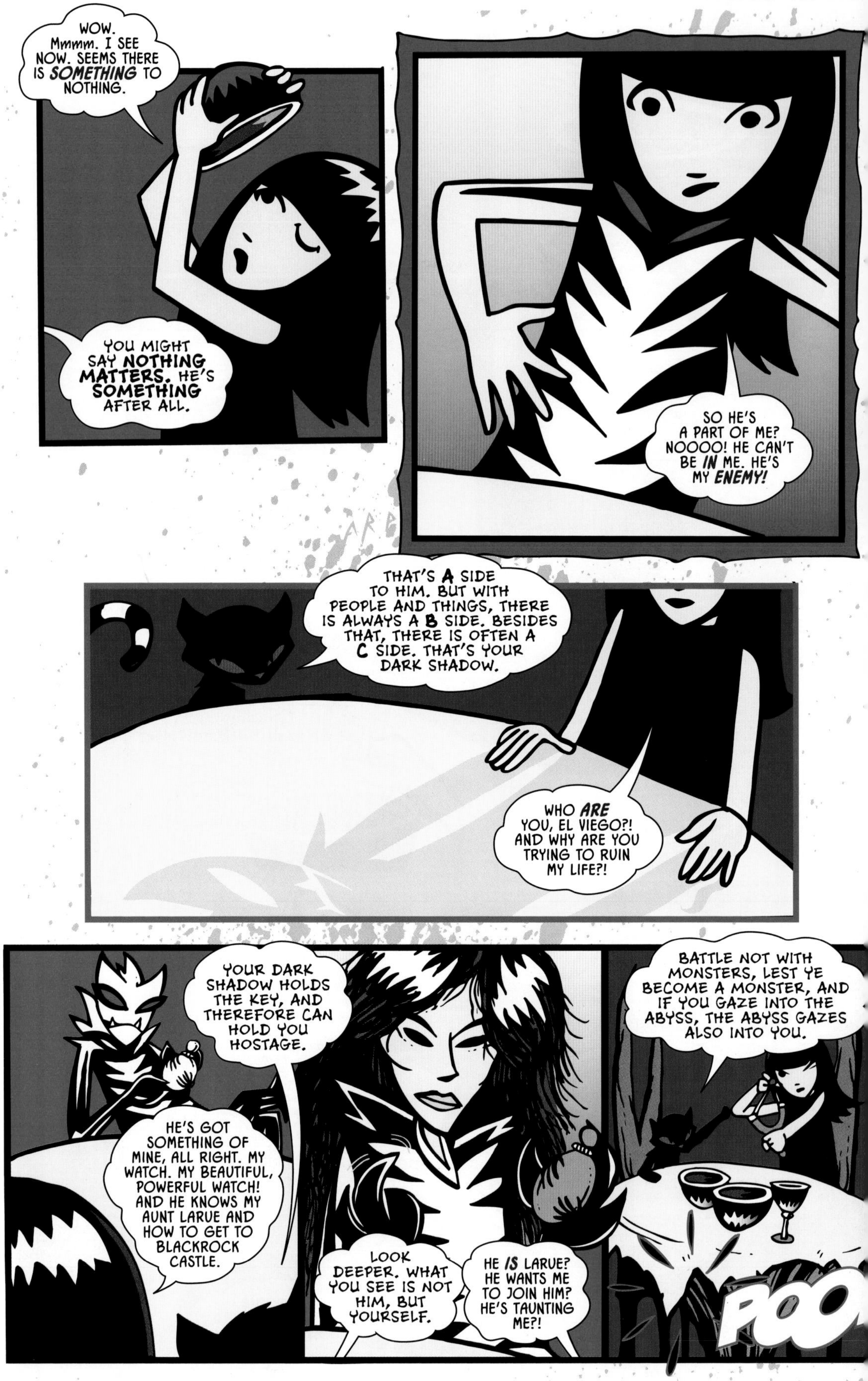

WOW. Mmmm. I SEE NOW. SEEMS THERE IS SOMETHING TO NOTHING.
YOU MIGHT SAY NOTHING MATTERS. HE'S SOMETHING AFTER ALL.
SO HE'S A PART OF ME? NOOOO! HE CAN'T BE IN ME. HE'S MY ENEMY!
THAT'S A SIDE TO HIM. BUT WITH PEOPLE AND THINGS, THERE IS ALWAYS A B SIDE. BESIDES THAT, THERE IS OFTEN A C SIDE. THAT'S YOUR DARK SHADOW.
WHO ARE YOU, EL VIEGO?! AND WHY ARE YOU TRYING TO RUIN MY LIFE?!
YOUR DARK SHADOW HOLDS THE KEY, AND THEREFORE CAN HOLD YOU HOSTAGE.
HE'S GOT SOMETHING OF MINE, ALL RIGHT. MY WATCH. MY BEAUTIFUL, POWERFUL WATCH! AND HE KNOWS MY AUNT LARUE AND HOW TO GET TO BLACKROCK CASTLE.
LOOK DEEPER. WHAT YOU SEE IS NOT HIM, BUT YOURSELF.
HE IS LARUE? HE WANTS ME TO JOIN HIM? HE'S TAUNTING ME?!
BATTLE NOT WITH MONSTERS, LEST YE BECOME A MONSTER, AND IF YOU GAZE INTO THE ABYSS, THE ABYSS GAZES ALSO INTO YOU.
POO

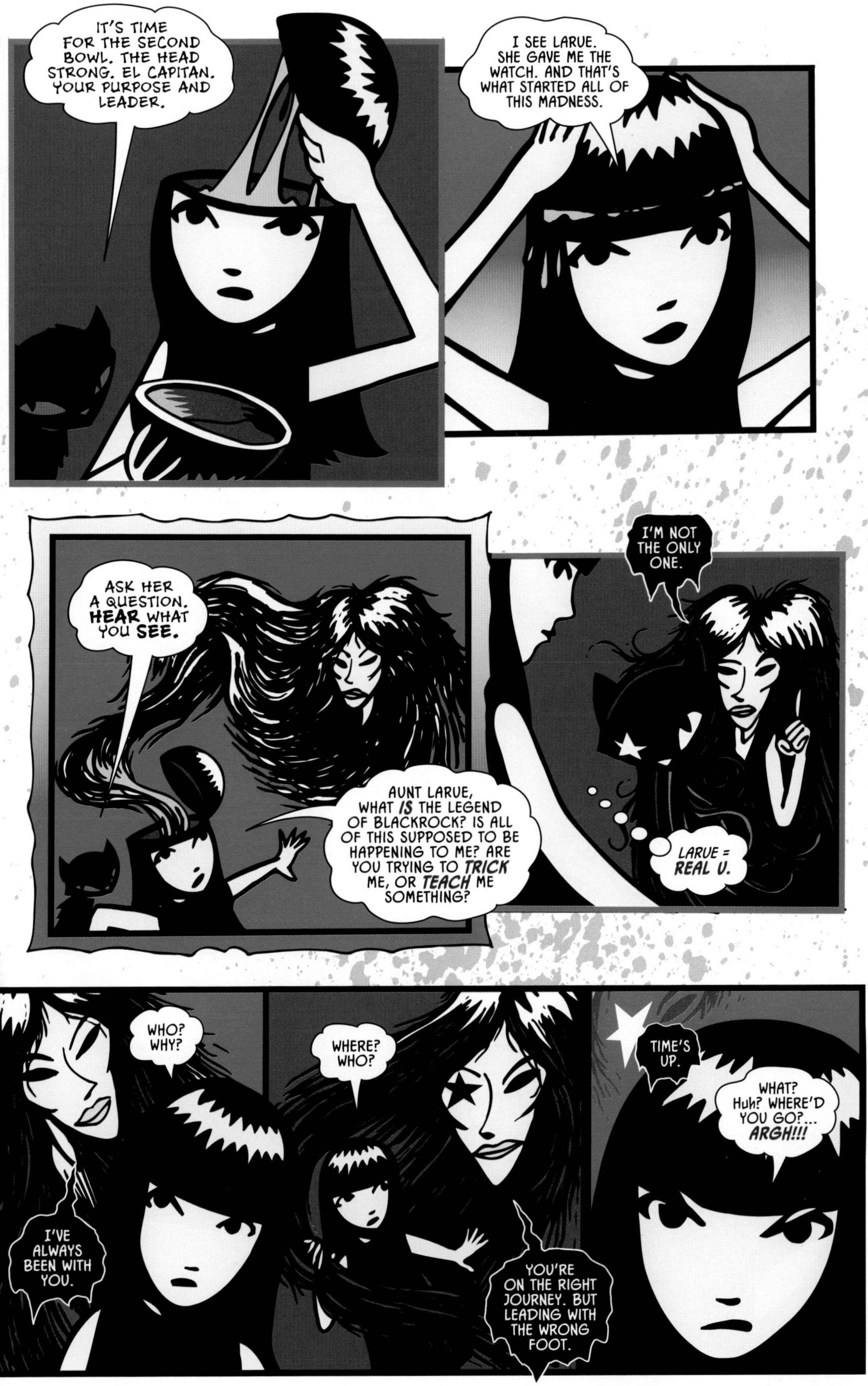
IT'S TIME FOR THE SECOND BOWL. THE HEAD STRONG. EL CAPITAN. YOUR PURPOSE AND LEADER.
I SEE LARUE. SHE GAVE ME THE WATCH. AND THAT'S WHAT STARTED ALL OF THIS MADNESS.
ASK HER A QUESTION. HEAR WHAT YOU SEE.
AUNT LARUE, WHAT IS THE LEGEND OF BLACKROCK? IS ALL OF THIS SUPPOSED TO BE HAPPENING TO ME? ARE YOU TRYING TO TRICK ME, OR TEACH ME SOMETHING?
I'M NOT THE ONLY ONE.
LARUE = REAL U.
WHO? WHY?
I'VE ALWAYS BEEN WITH YOU.
WHERE? WHO?
YOU'RE ON THE RIGHT JOURNEY. BUT LEADING WITH THE WRONG FOOT.
TIME'S UP.
WHAT? Huh? WHERE'D YOU GO?... ARGH!!!

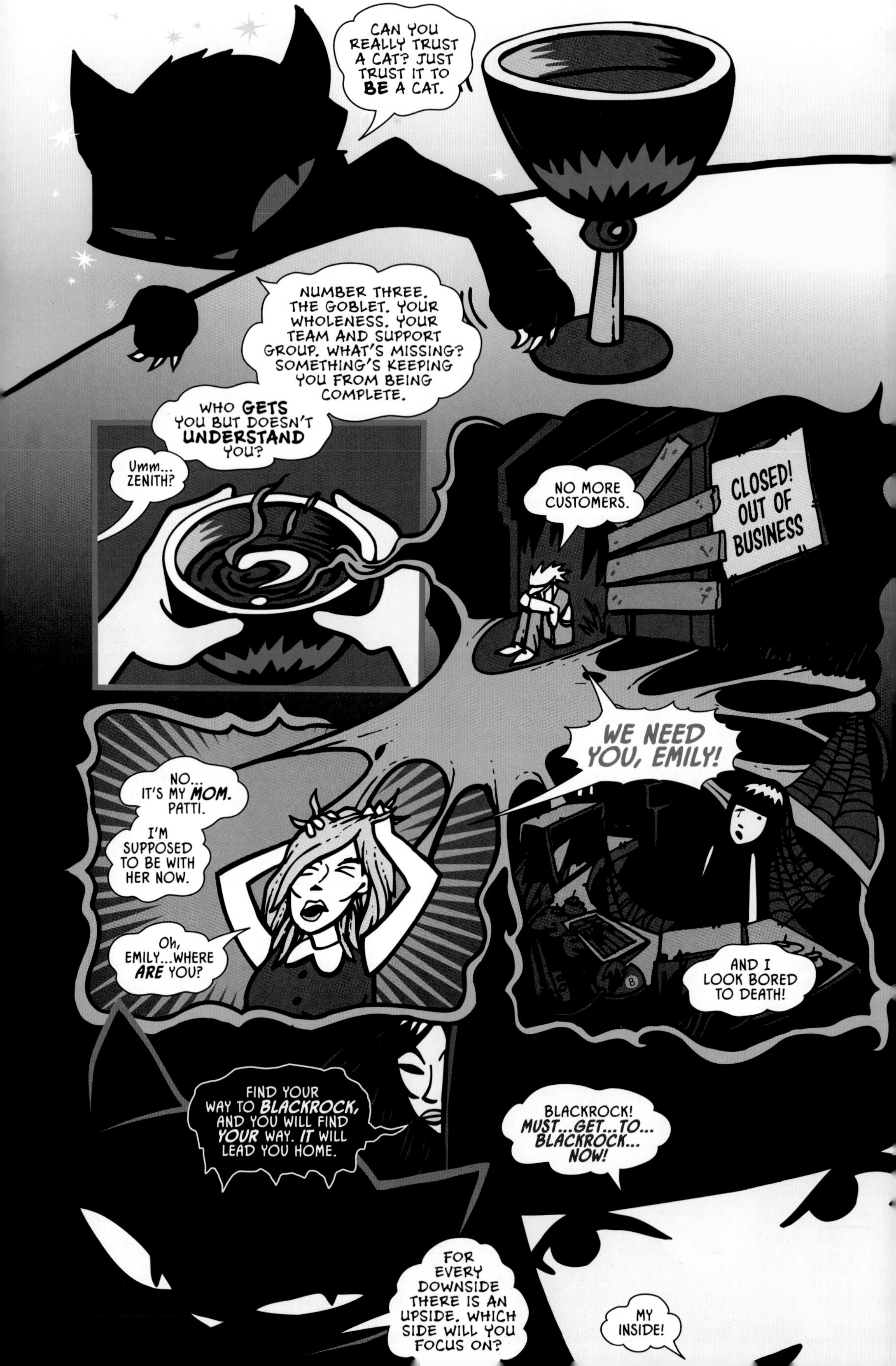
CAN YOU REALLY TRUST A CAT? JUST TRUST IT TO BE A CAT.
NUMBER THREE. THE GOBLET. YOUR WHOLENESS. YOUR TEAM AND SUPPORT GROUP. WHAT'S MISSING? SOMETHING'S KEEPING YOU FROM BEING COMPLETE.
WHO GETS YOU BUT DOESN'T UNDERSTAND YOU?
Umm... ZENITH?
NO MORE CUSTOMERS.
CLOSED! OUT OF BUSINESS
NO... IT'S MY MOM. PATTI.
I'M SUPPOSED TO BE WITH HER NOW.
Oh, EMILY...WHERE ARE YOU?
WE NEED YOU, EMILY!
AND I LOOK BORED TO DEATH!
FIND YOUR WAY TO BLACKROCK, AND YOU WILL FIND YOUR WAY. IT WILL LEAD YOU HOME.
BLACKROCK! MUST...GET...TO... BLACKROCK... NOW!
FOR EVERY DOWNSIDE THERE IS AN UPSIDE. WHICH SIDE WILL YOU FOCUS ON?
MY INSIDE!

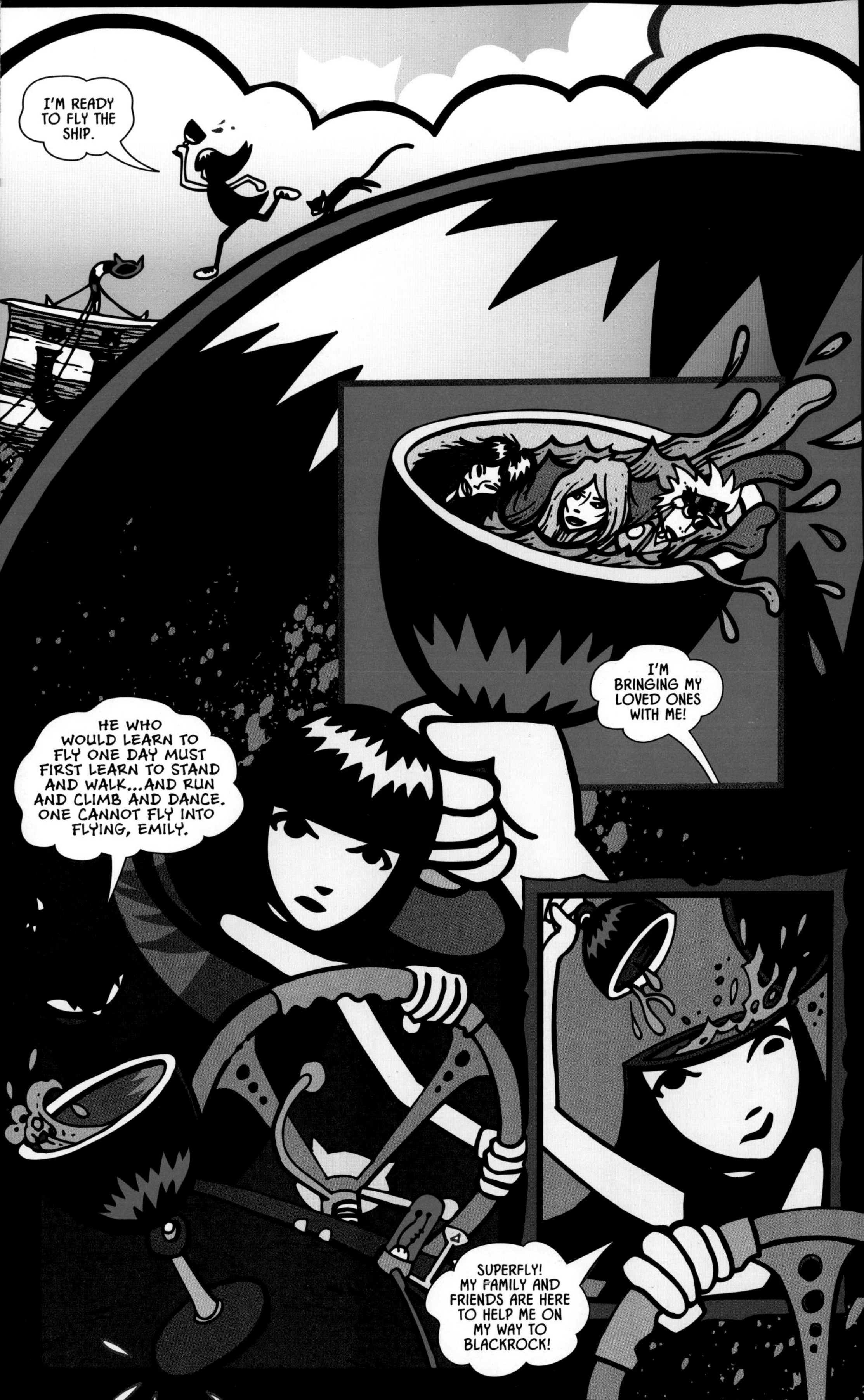
I'M READY TO FLY THE SHIP.
I'M BRINGING MY LOVED ONES WITH ME!
HE WHO WOULD LEARN TO FLY ONE DAY MUST FIRST LEARN TO STAND AND WALK...AND RUN AND CLIMB AND DANCE. ONE CANNOT FLY INTO FLYING, EMILY.
SUPERFLY! MY FAMILY AND FRIENDS ARE HERE TO HELP ME ON MY WAY TO BLACKROCK!

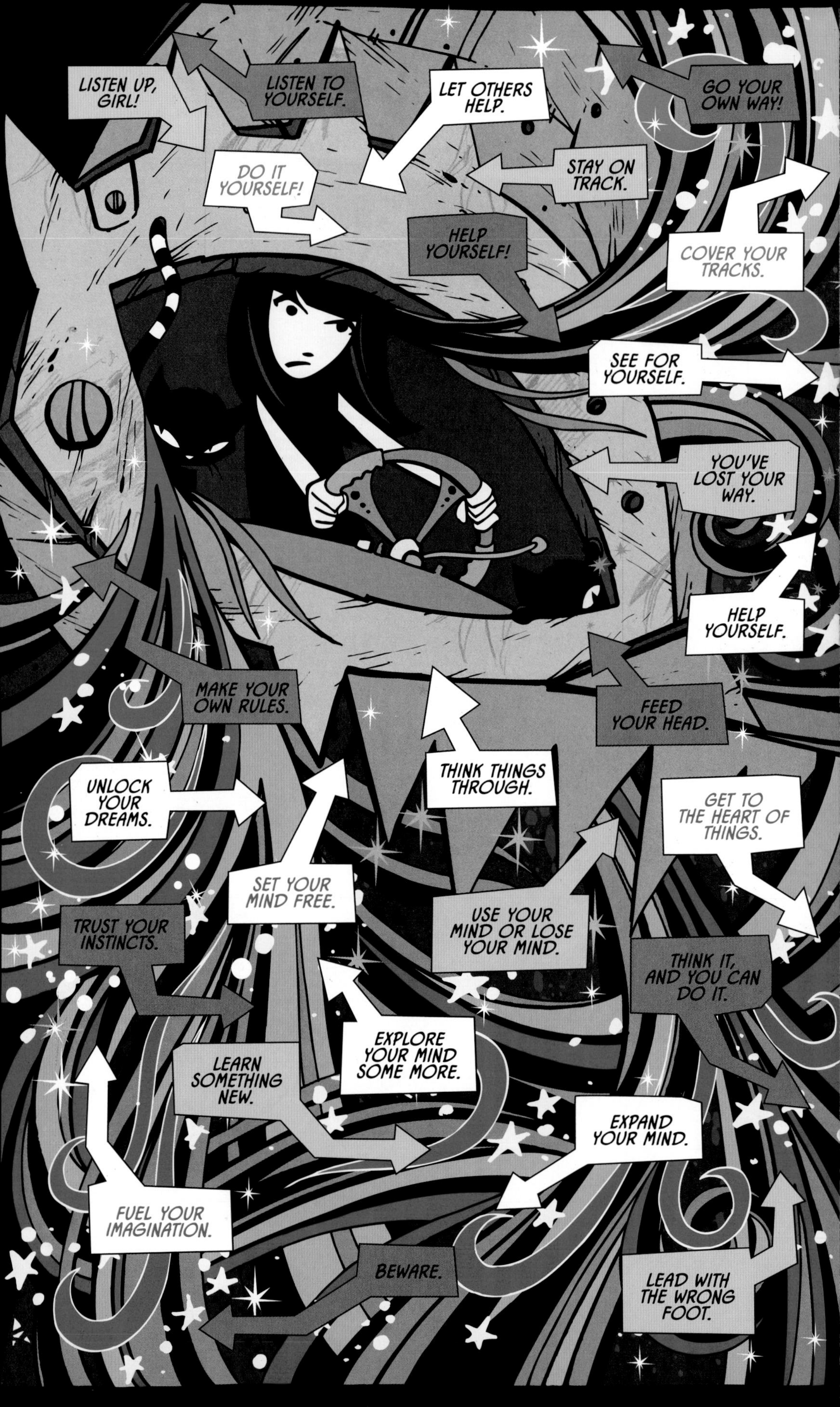

LISTEN UP, GIRL!
LISTEN TO YOURSELF.
LET OTHERS HELP.
GO YOUR OWN WAY!
DO IT YOURSELF!
STAY ON TRACK.
HELP YOURSELF!
COVER YOUR TRACKS.
SEE FOR YOURSELF.
YOU'VE LOST YOUR WAY.
HELP YOURSELF.
MAKE YOUR OWN RULES.
FEED YOUR HEAD.
THINK THINGS THROUGH.
UNLOCK YOUR DREAMS.
GET TO THE HEART OF THINGS.
SET YOUR MIND FREE.
USE YOUR MIND OR LOSE YOUR MIND.
TRUST YOUR INSTINCTS.
THINK IT, AND YOU CAN DO IT.
EXPLORE YOUR MIND SOME MORE.
LEARN SOMETHING NEW.
EXPAND YOUR MIND.
FUEL YOUR IMAGINATION.
BEWARE.
LEAD WITH THE WRONG FOOT.

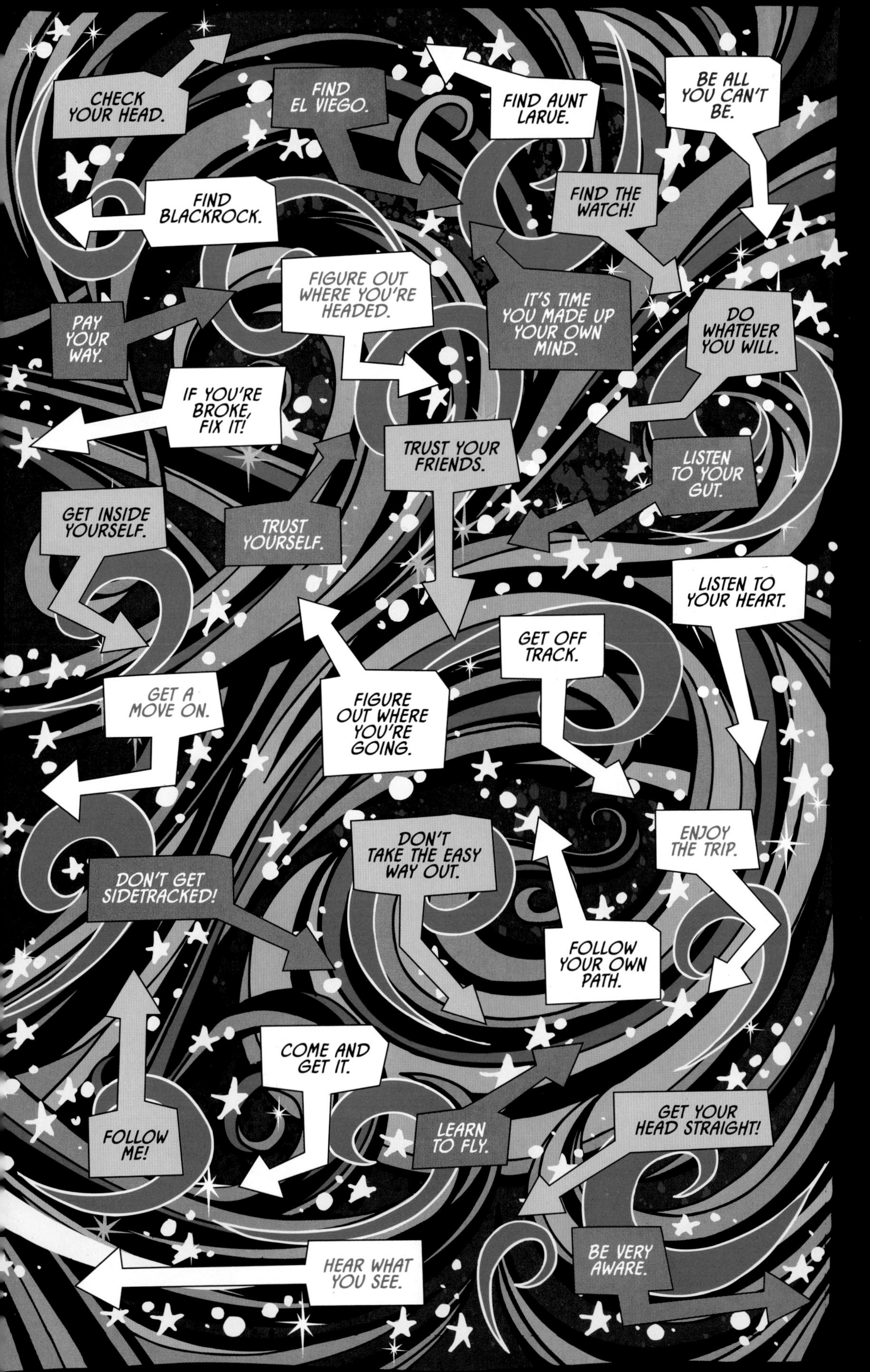

CHECK YOUR HEAD.
FIND EL VIEGO.
FIND AUNT LARUE.
BE ALL YOU CAN'T BE.
FIND BLACKROCK.
FIND THE WATCH!
PAY YOUR WAY.
FIGURE OUT WHERE YOU'RE HEADED.
IT'S TIME YOU MADE UP YOUR OWN MIND.
DO WHATEVER YOU WILL.
IF YOU'RE BROKE, FIX IT!
TRUST YOUR FRIENDS.
LISTEN TO YOUR GUT.
GET INSIDE YOURSELF.
TRUST YOURSELF.
LISTEN TO YOUR HEART.
GET OFF TRACK.
GET A MOVE ON.
FIGURE OUT WHERE YOU'RE GOING.
DON'T TAKE THE EASY WAY OUT.
ENJOY THE TRIP.
DON'T GET SIDETRACKED!
FOLLOW YOUR OWN PATH.
COME AND GET IT.
GET YOUR HEAD STRAIGHT!
FOLLOW ME!
LEARN TO FLY.
HEAR WHAT YOU SEE.
BE VERY AWARE.

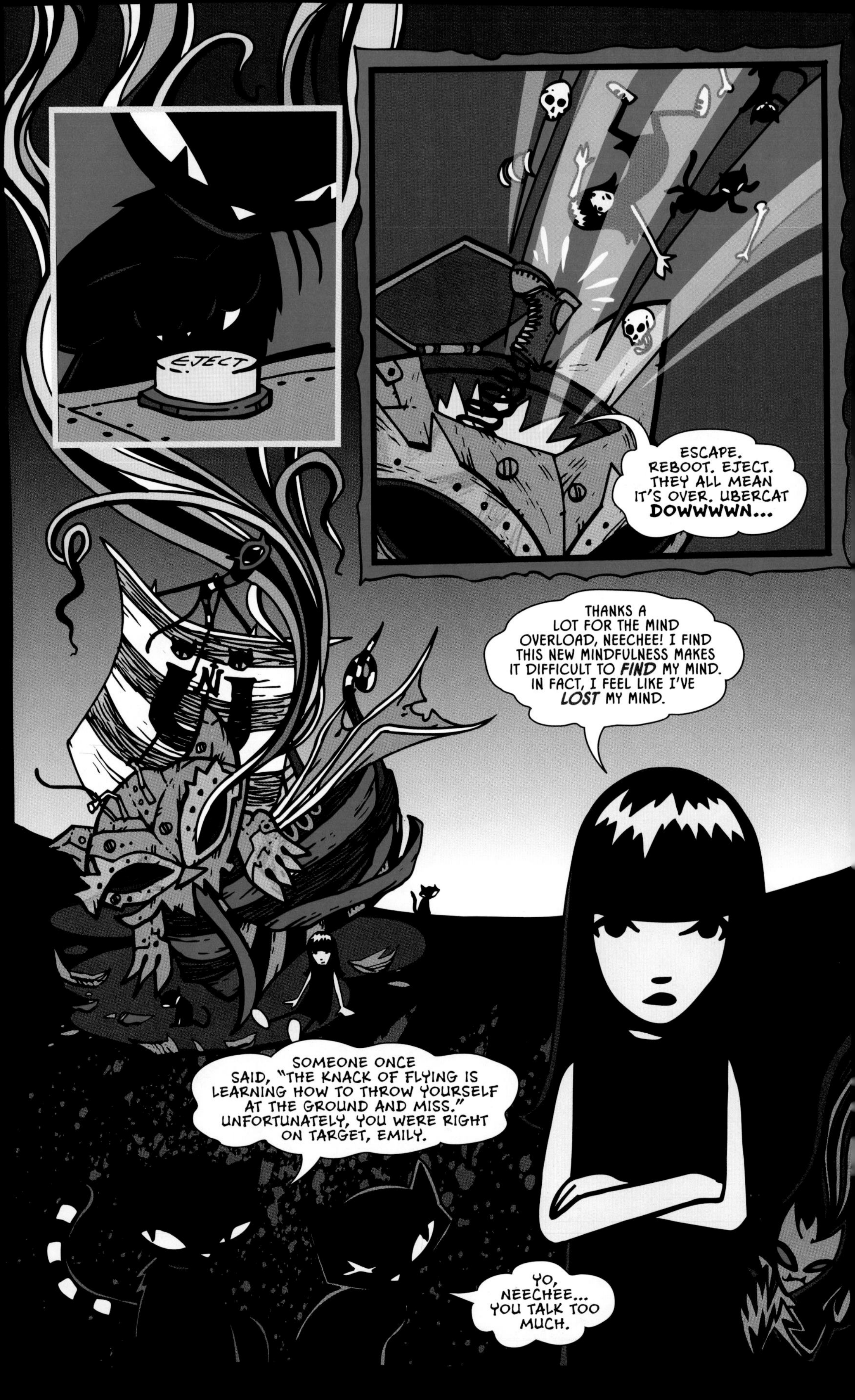
EJECT
ESCAPE. REBOOT. EJECT. THEY ALL MEAN IT'S OVER. UBERCAT DOWWWWN...
THANKS A LOT FOR THE MIND OVERLOAD, NEECHEE! I FIND THIS NEW MINDFULNESS MAKES IT DIFFICULT TO FIND MY MIND. IN FACT, I FEEL LIKE I'VE LOST MY MIND.
SOMEONE ONCE SAID, "THE KNACK OF FLYING IS LEARNING HOW TO THROW YOURSELF AT THE GROUND AND MISS." UNFORTUNATELY, YOU WERE RIGHT ON TARGET, EMILY.
YO, NEECHEE... YOU TALK TOO MUCH.

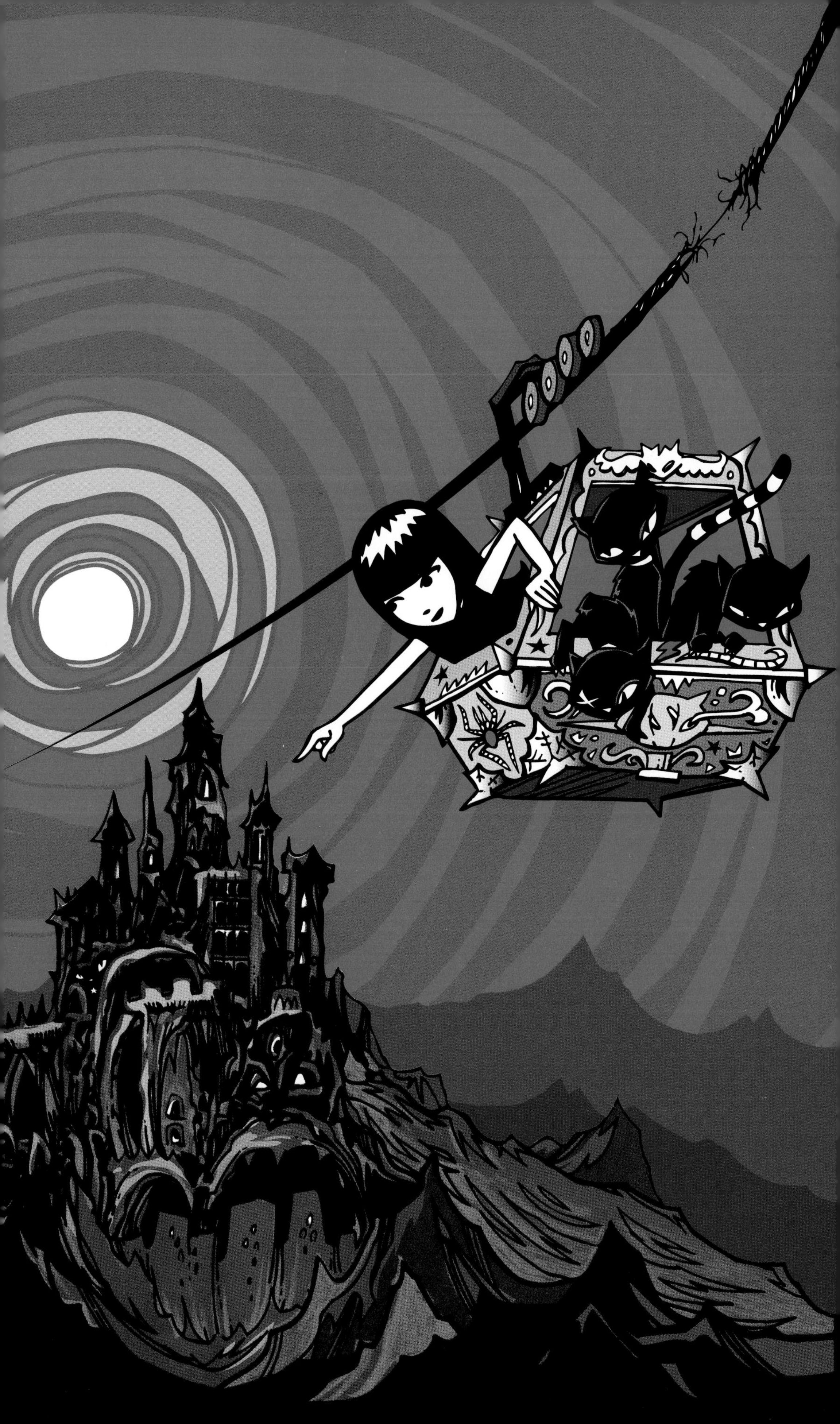

PART THREE

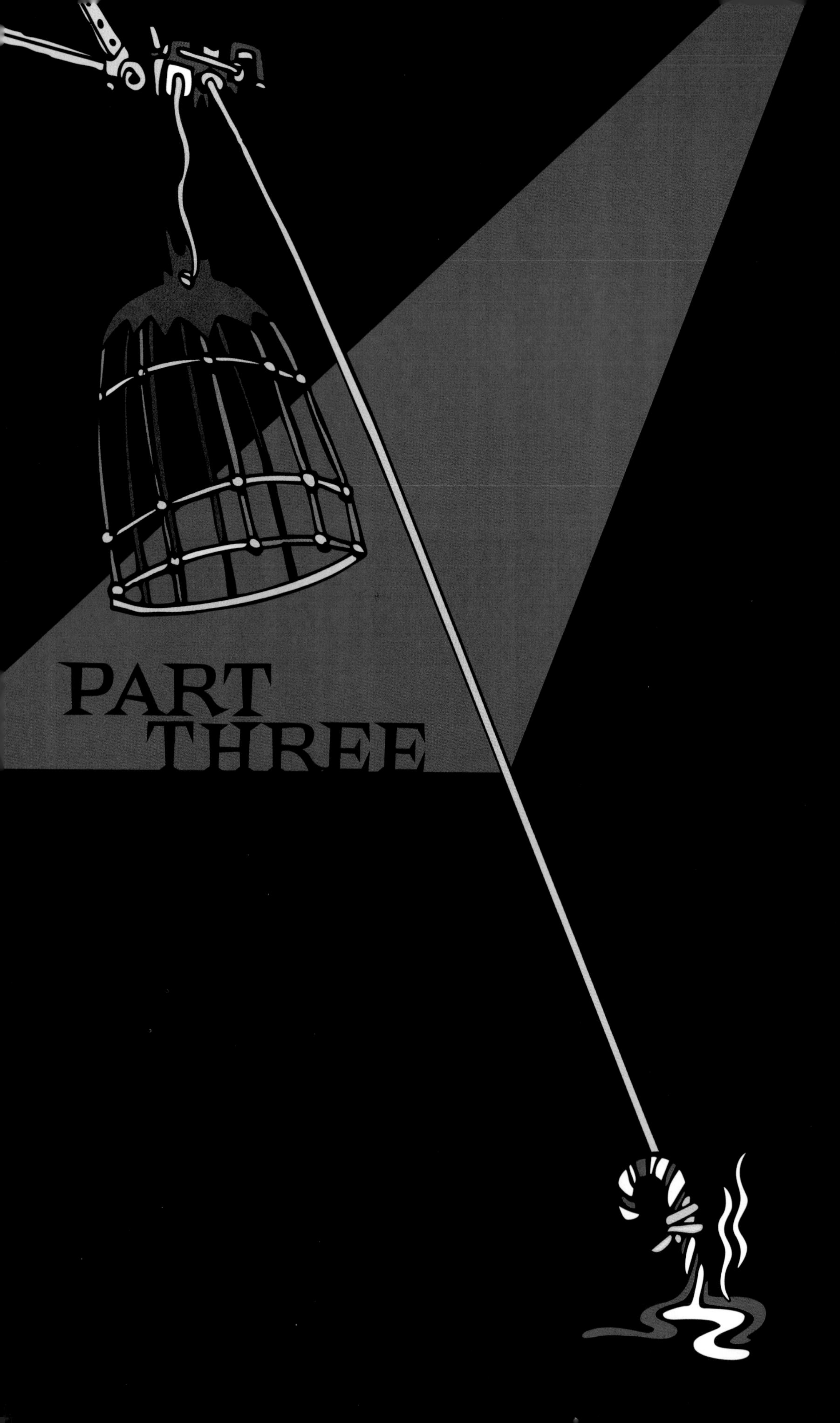

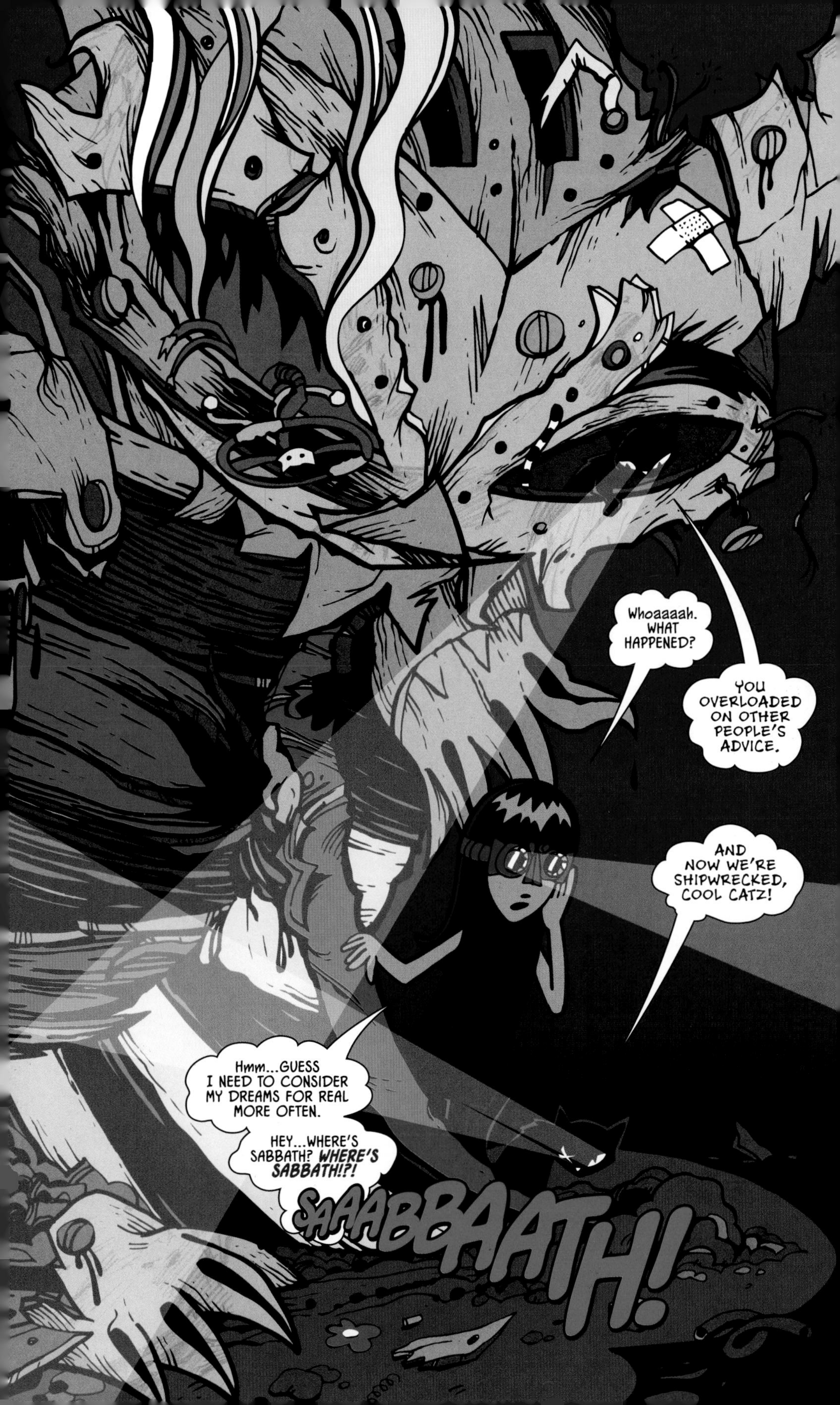
Whoaaaah. WHAT HAPPENED?
YOU OVERLOADED ON OTHER PEOPLE'S ADVICE.
AND NOW WE'RE SHIPWRECKED, COOL CATZ!
Hmm...GUESS I NEED TO CONSIDER MY DREAMS FOR REAL MORE OFTEN.
HEY...WHERE'S SABBATH? *WHERE'S SABBATH!?!*
SAAABBAATH!

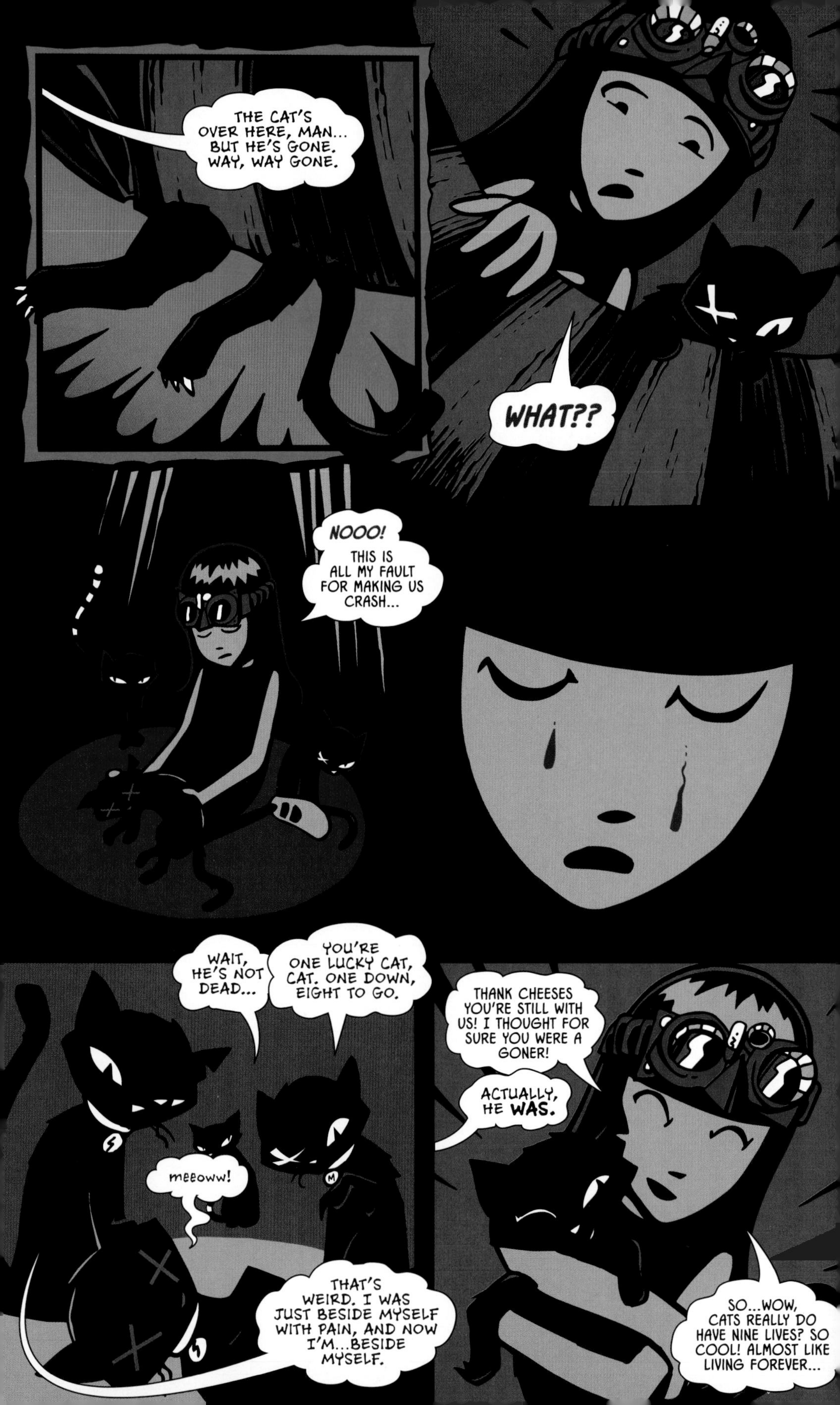
THE CAT'S OVER HERE, MAN... BUT HE'S GONE. WAY, WAY GONE.
WHAT??
NOOO! THIS IS ALL MY FAULT FOR MAKING US CRASH...
WAIT, HE'S NOT DEAD...
YOU'RE ONE LUCKY CAT, CAT. ONE DOWN, EIGHT TO GO.
meeoww!
THAT'S WEIRD. I WAS JUST BESIDE MYSELF WITH PAIN, AND NOW I'M...BESIDE MYSELF.
THANK CHEESES YOU'RE STILL WITH US! I THOUGHT FOR SURE YOU WERE A GONER!
ACTUALLY, HE **WAS.**
SO...WOW, CATS REALLY DO HAVE NINE LIVES? SO COOL! ALMOST LIKE LIVING FOREVER...

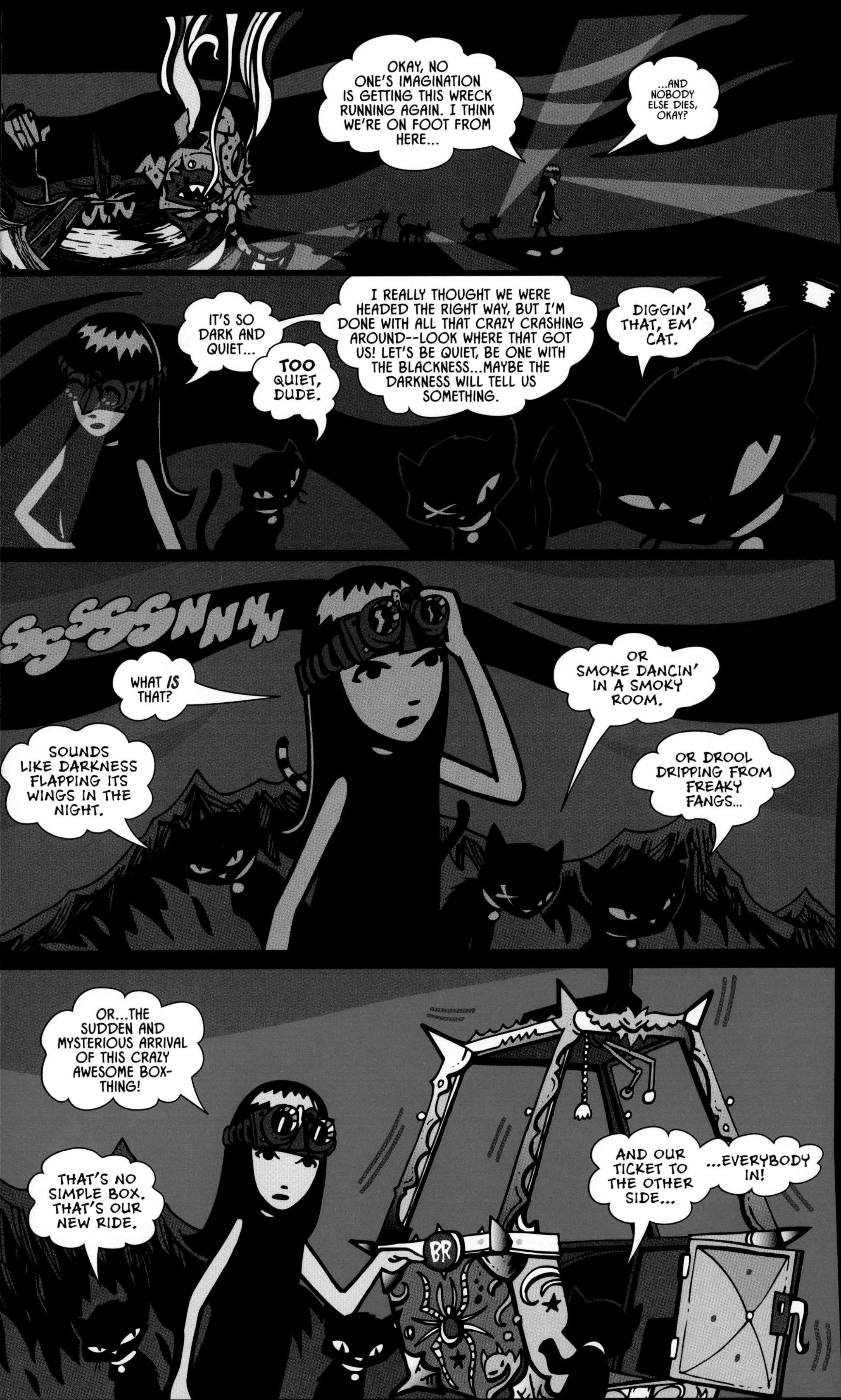

OKAY, NO ONE'S IMAGINATION IS GETTING THIS WRECK RUNNING AGAIN. I THINK WE'RE ON FOOT FROM HERE...
...AND NOBODY ELSE DIES, OKAY?
IT'S SO DARK AND QUIET...
TOO QUIET, DUDE.
I REALLY THOUGHT WE WERE HEADED THE RIGHT WAY, BUT I'M DONE WITH ALL THAT CRAZY CRASHING AROUND--LOOK WHERE THAT GOT US! LET'S BE QUIET, BE ONE WITH THE BLACKNESS...MAYBE THE DARKNESS WILL TELL US SOMETHING.
DIGGIN' THAT, EM' CAT.
SSSSSNNNN
WHAT IS THAT?
OR SMOKE DANCIN' IN A SMOKY ROOM.
SOUNDS LIKE DARKNESS FLAPPING ITS WINGS IN THE NIGHT.
OR DROOL DRIPPING FROM FREAKY FANGS...
OR...THE SUDDEN AND MYSTERIOUS ARRIVAL OF THIS CRAZY AWESOME BOX-THING!
THAT'S NO SIMPLE BOX. THAT'S OUR NEW RIDE.
AND OUR TICKET TO THE OTHER SIDE...
...EVERYBODY IN!
BR

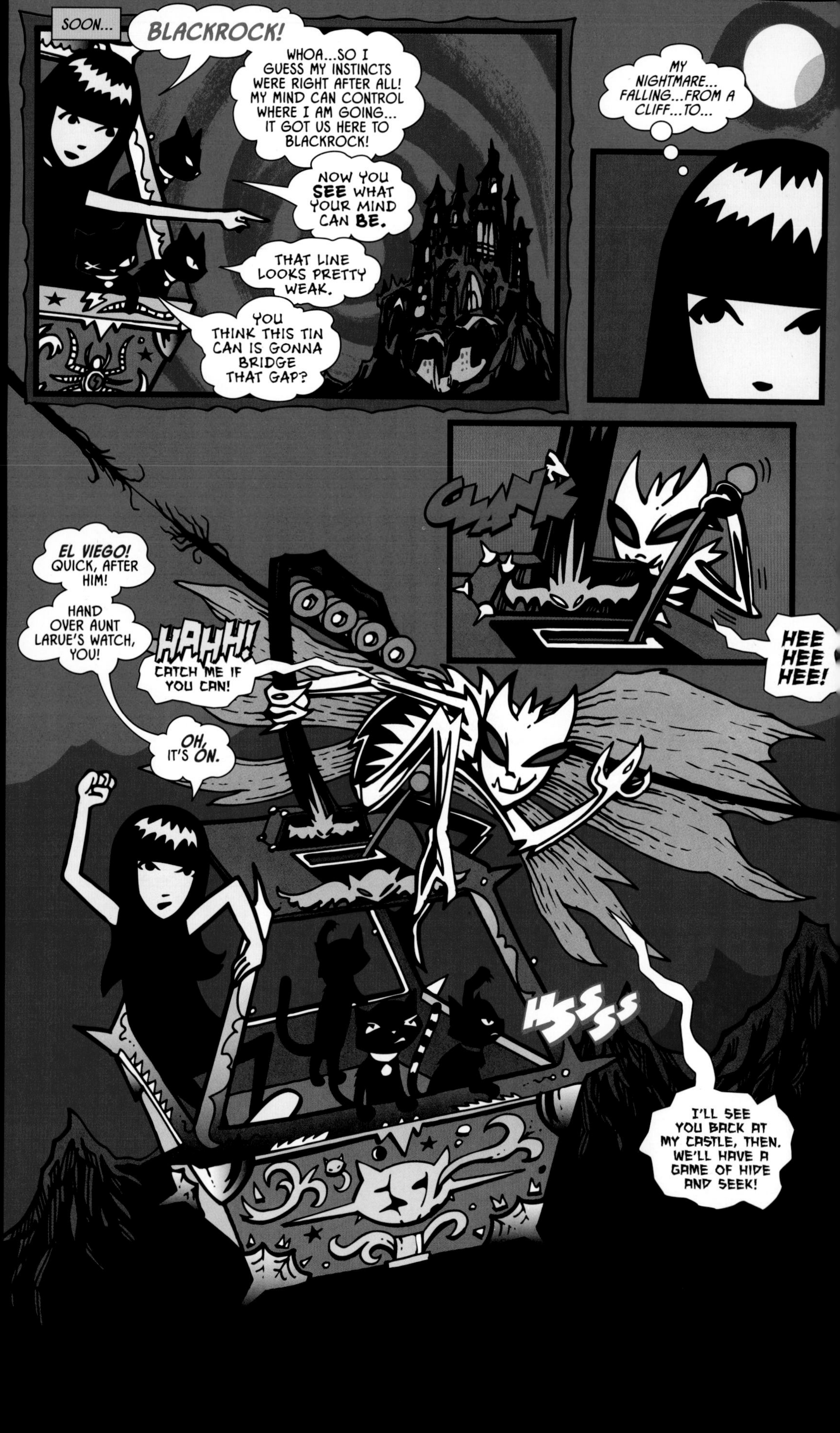
SOON...
BLACKROCK!
WHOA...SO I GUESS MY INSTINCTS WERE RIGHT AFTER ALL! MY MIND CAN CONTROL WHERE I AM GOING... IT GOT US HERE TO BLACKROCK!
NOW YOU SEE WHAT YOUR MIND CAN BE.
THAT LINE LOOKS PRETTY WEAK.
YOU THINK THIS TIN CAN IS GONNA BRIDGE THAT GAP?
MY NIGHTMARE... FALLING...FROM A CLIFF...TO...
CLANK
HEE HEE HEE!
EL VIEGO! QUICK, AFTER HIM!
HAND OVER AUNT LARUE'S WATCH, YOU!
HAHH! CATCH ME IF YOU CAN!
OH, IT'S ON.
HSSSS
I'LL SEE YOU BACK AT MY CASTLE, THEN. WE'LL HAVE A GAME OF HIDE AND SEEK!

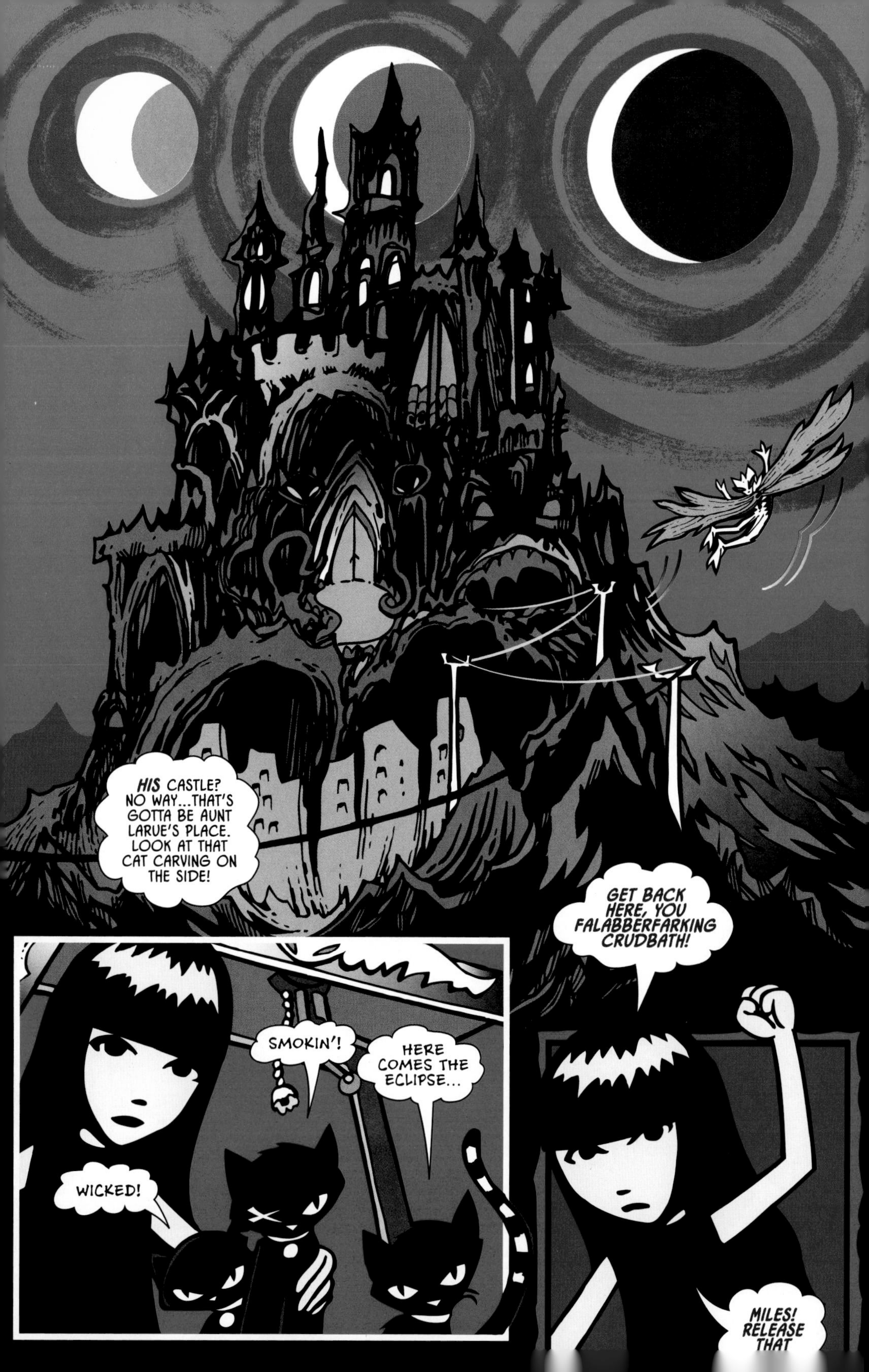

HIS CASTLE? NO WAY...THAT'S GOTTA BE AUNT LARUE'S PLACE. LOOK AT THAT CAT CARVING ON THE SIDE!
SMOKIN'!
HERE COMES THE ECLIPSE...
WICKED!
GET BACK HERE, YOU FALABBERFARKING CRUDBATH!
MILES! RELEASE THAT

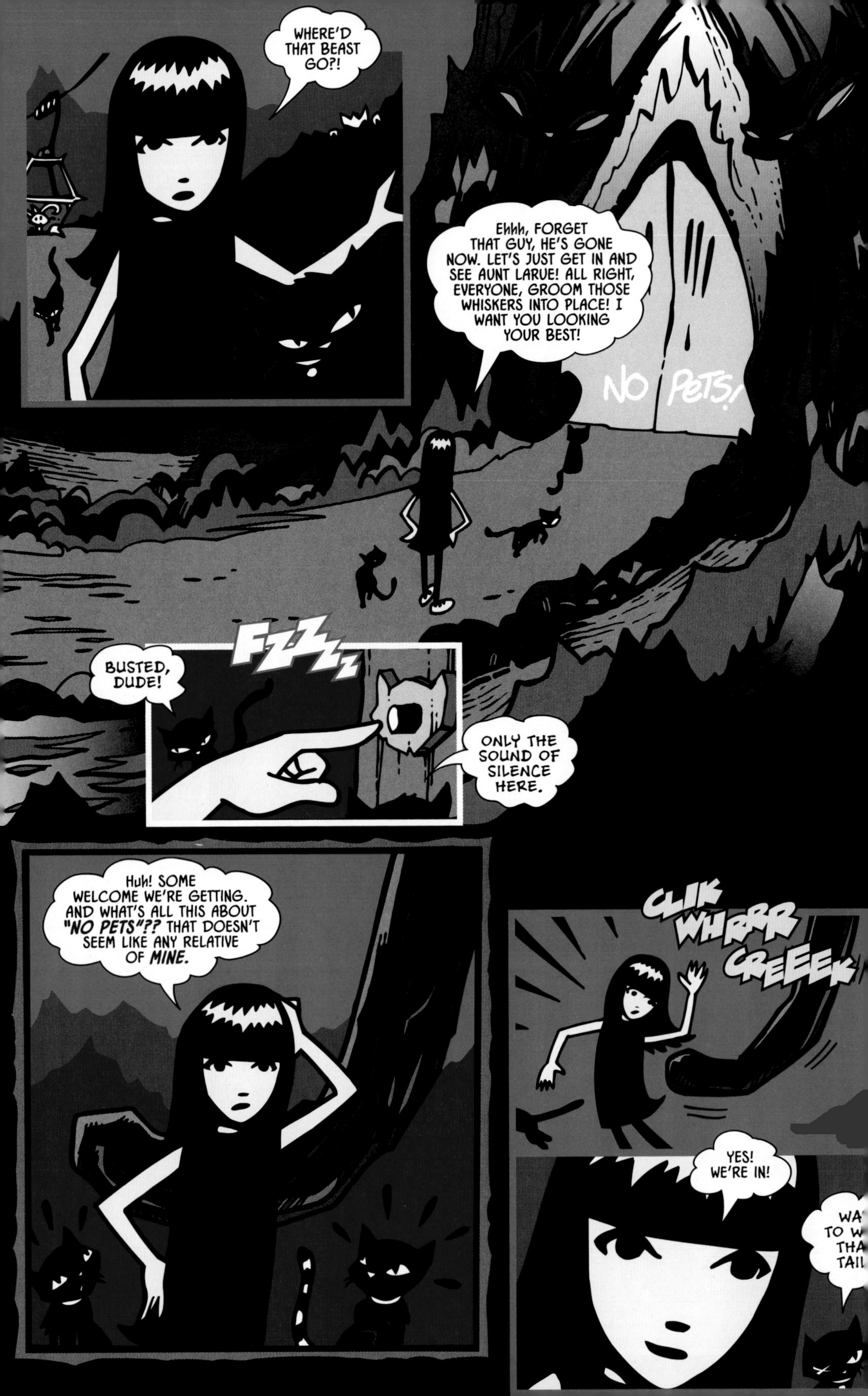
WHERE'D THAT BEAST GO?!
Ehhh, FORGET THAT GUY, HE'S GONE NOW. LET'S JUST GET IN AND SEE AUNT LARUE! ALL RIGHT, EVERYONE, GROOM THOSE WHISKERS INTO PLACE! I WANT YOU LOOKING YOUR BEST!
NO PETS!
FZZZZ
BUSTED, DUDE!
ONLY THE SOUND OF SILENCE HERE.
Huh! SOME WELCOME WE'RE GETTING. AND WHAT'S ALL THIS ABOUT "NO PETS"?? THAT DOESN'T SEEM LIKE ANY RELATIVE OF MINE.
CLIK WHRRR CREEEK
YES! WE'RE IN!

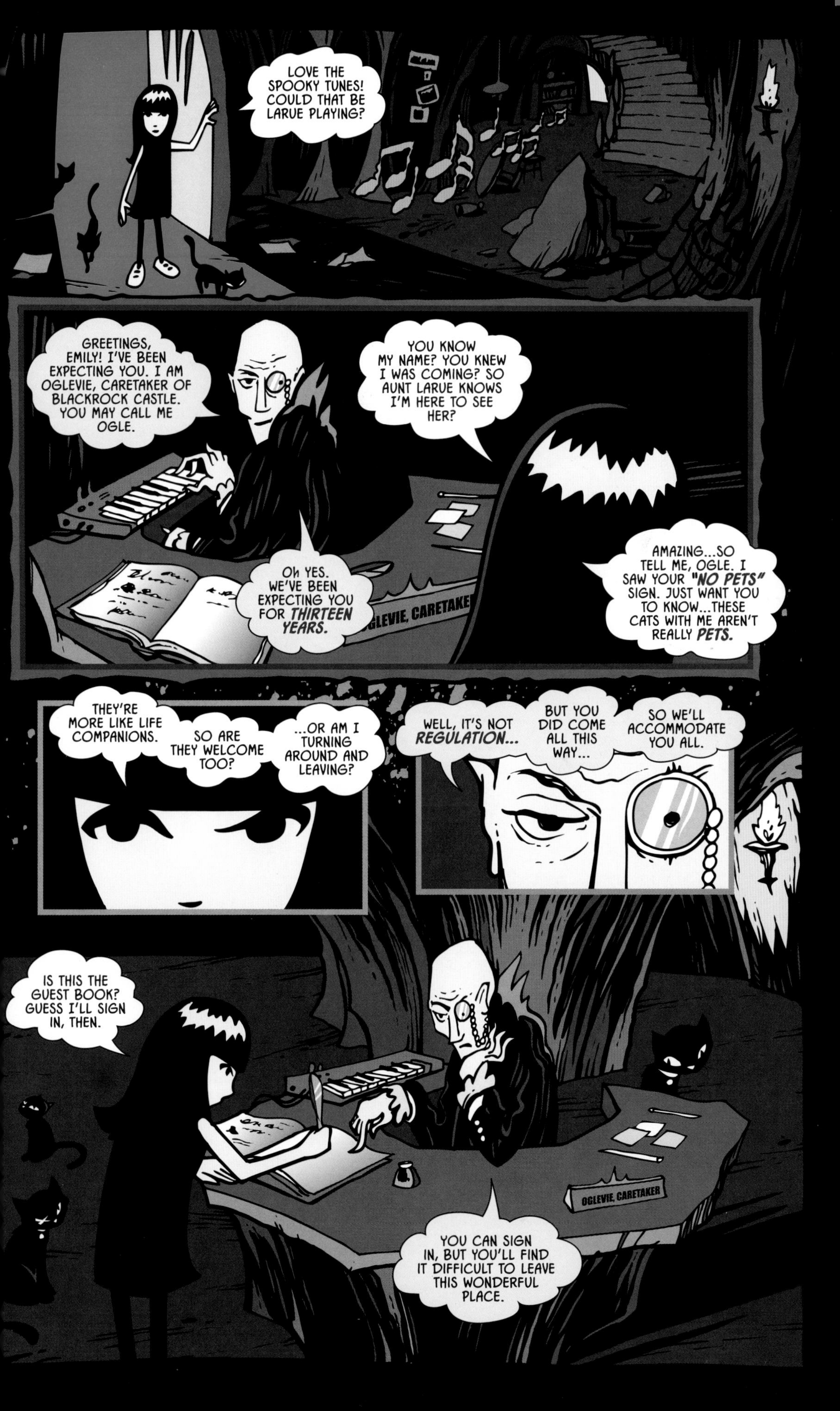

LOVE THE SPOOKY TUNES! COULD THAT BE LARUE PLAYING?
GREETINGS, EMILY! I'VE BEEN EXPECTING YOU. I AM OGLEVIE, CARETAKER OF BLACKROCK CASTLE. YOU MAY CALL ME OGLE.
YOU KNOW MY NAME? YOU KNEW I WAS COMING? SO AUNT LARUE KNOWS I'M HERE TO SEE HER?
Oh YES. WE'VE BEEN EXPECTING YOU FOR *THIRTEEN YEARS.*
OGLEVIE, CARETAKER
AMAZING...SO TELL ME, OGLE. I SAW YOUR ***"NO PETS"*** SIGN. JUST WANT YOU TO KNOW...THESE CATS WITH ME AREN'T REALLY ***PETS.***
THEY'RE MORE LIKE LIFE COMPANIONS.
SO ARE THEY WELCOME TOO?
...OR AM I TURNING AROUND AND LEAVING?
WELL, IT'S NOT ***REGULATION...***
BUT YOU DID COME ALL THIS WAY...
SO WE'LL ACCOMMODATE YOU ALL.
IS THIS THE GUEST BOOK? GUESS I'LL SIGN IN, THEN.
OGLEVIE, CARETAKER
YOU CAN SIGN IN, BUT YOU'LL FIND IT DIFFICULT TO LEAVE THIS WONDERFUL PLACE.

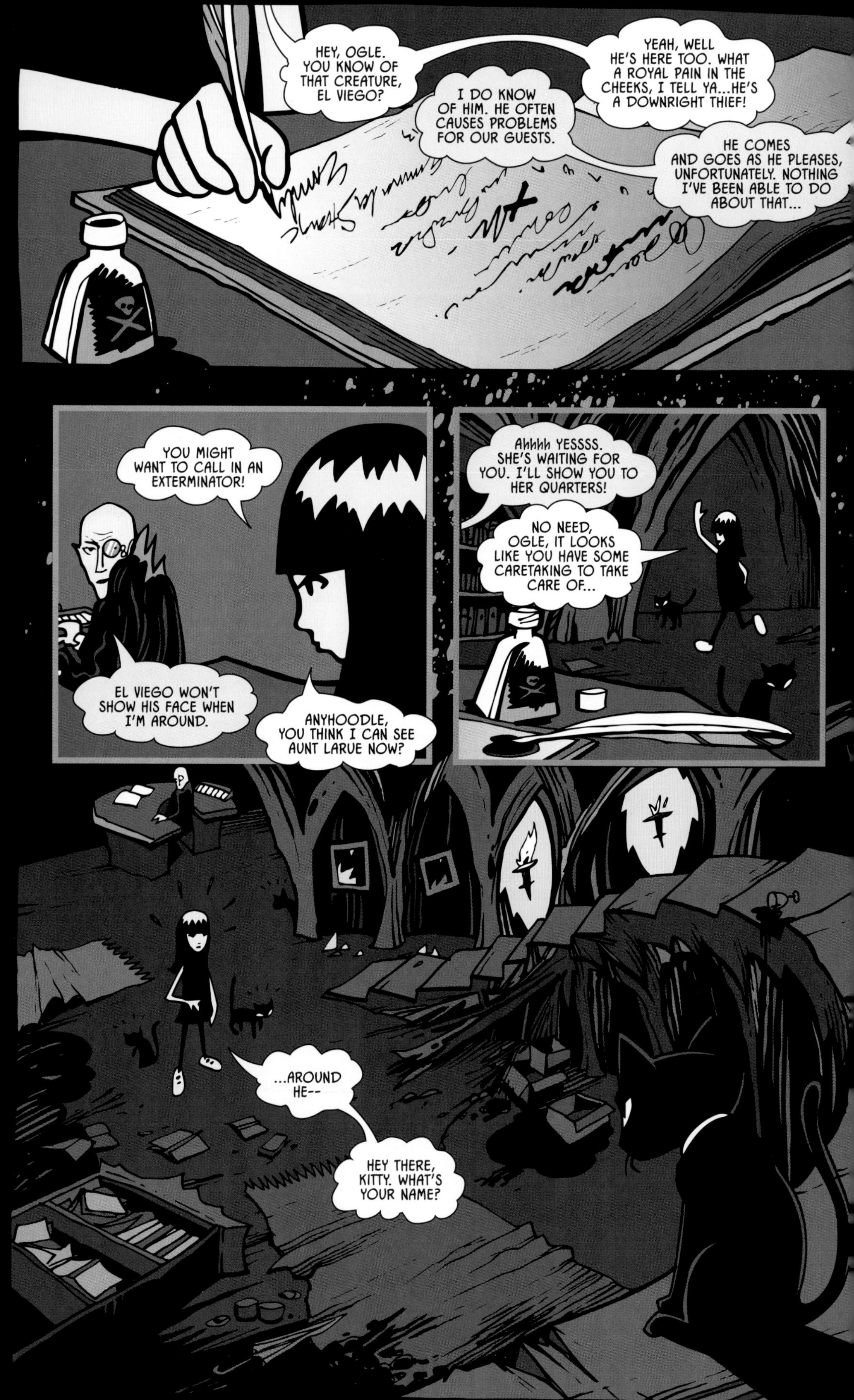
HEY, OGLE. YOU KNOW OF THAT CREATURE, EL VIEGO?
I DO KNOW OF HIM. HE OFTEN CAUSES PROBLEMS FOR OUR GUESTS.
YEAH, WELL HE'S HERE TOO. WHAT A ROYAL PAIN IN THE CHEEKS, I TELL YA...HE'S A DOWNRIGHT THIEF!
HE COMES AND GOES AS HE PLEASES, UNFORTUNATELY. NOTHING I'VE BEEN ABLE TO DO ABOUT THAT...
YOU MIGHT WANT TO CALL IN AN EXTERMINATOR!
EL VIEGO WON'T SHOW HIS FACE WHEN I'M AROUND.
ANYHOODLE, YOU THINK I CAN SEE AUNT LARUE NOW?
Ahhhh YESSSS. SHE'S WAITING FOR YOU. I'LL SHOW YOU TO HER QUARTERS!
NO NEED, OGLE, IT LOOKS LIKE YOU HAVE SOME CARETAKING TO TAKE CARE OF...
...AROUND HE--
HEY THERE, KITTY. WHAT'S YOUR NAME?

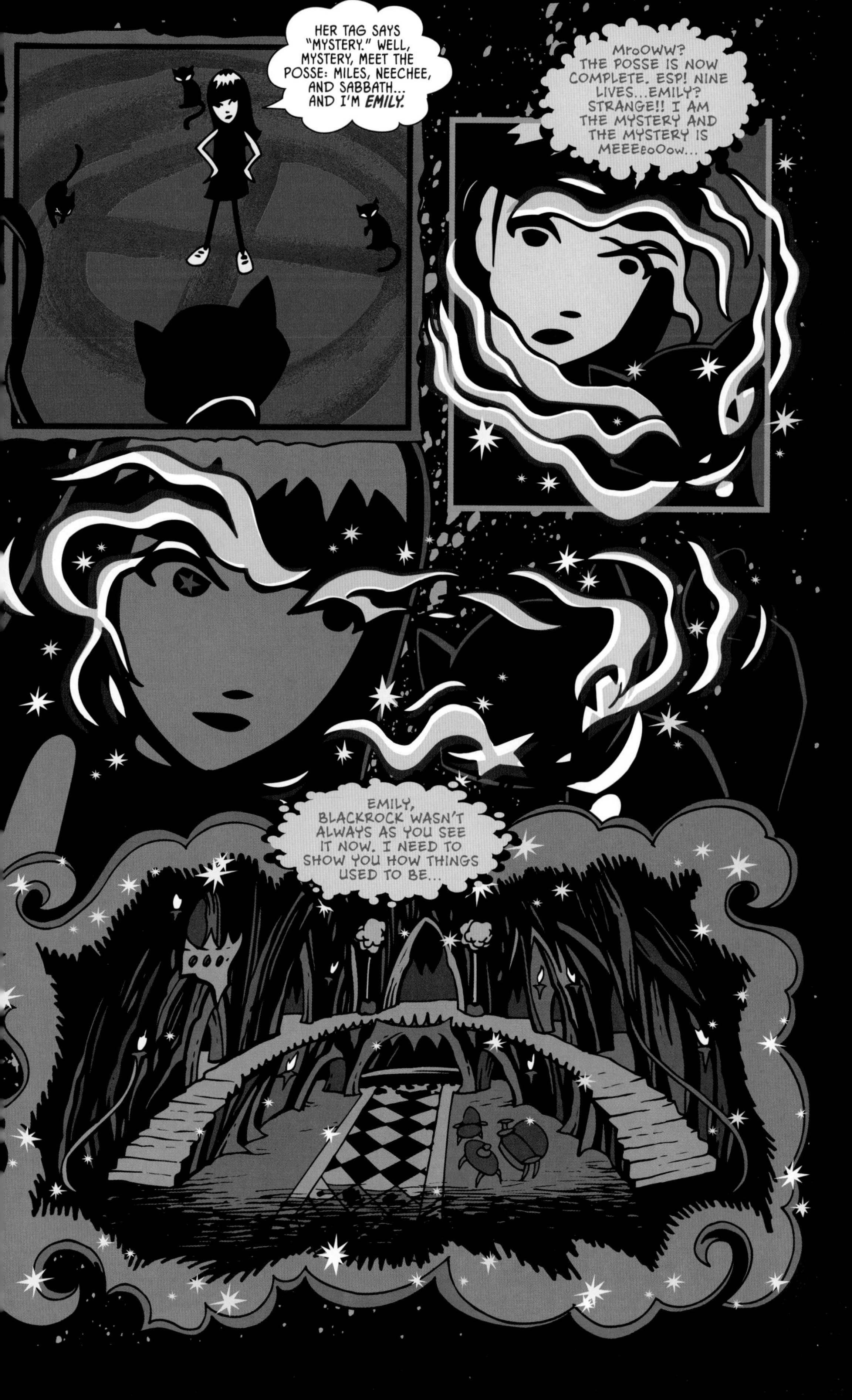
HER TAG SAYS "MYSTERY." WELL, MYSTERY, MEET THE POSSE: MILES, NEECHEE, AND SABBATH... AND I'M *EMILY.*
MroOWW? THE POSSE IS NOW COMPLETE. ESP! NINE LIVES...EMILY? STRANGE!! I AM THE MYSTERY AND THE MYSTERY IS MEEEeoOow...
EMILY, BLACKROCK WASN'T ALWAYS AS YOU SEE IT NOW. I NEED TO SHOW YOU HOW THINGS USED TO BE...

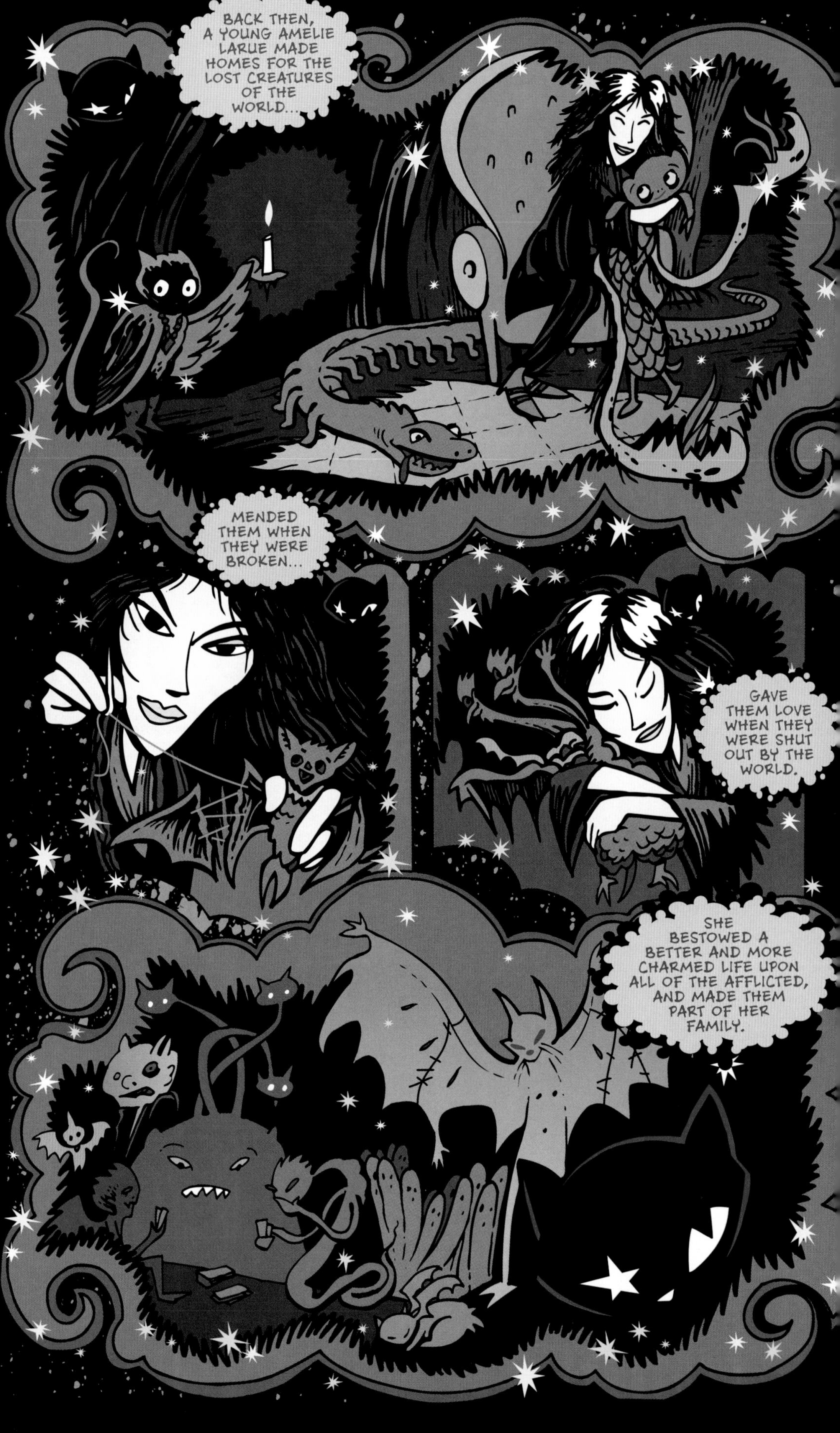
BACK THEN, A YOUNG AMELIE LARUE MADE HOMES FOR THE LOST CREATURES OF THE WORLD...
MENDED THEM WHEN THEY WERE BROKEN...
GAVE THEM LOVE WHEN THEY WERE SHUT OUT BY THE WORLD.
SHE BESTOWED A BETTER AND MORE CHARMED LIFE UPON ALL OF THE AFFLICTED, AND MADE THEM PART OF HER FAMILY.

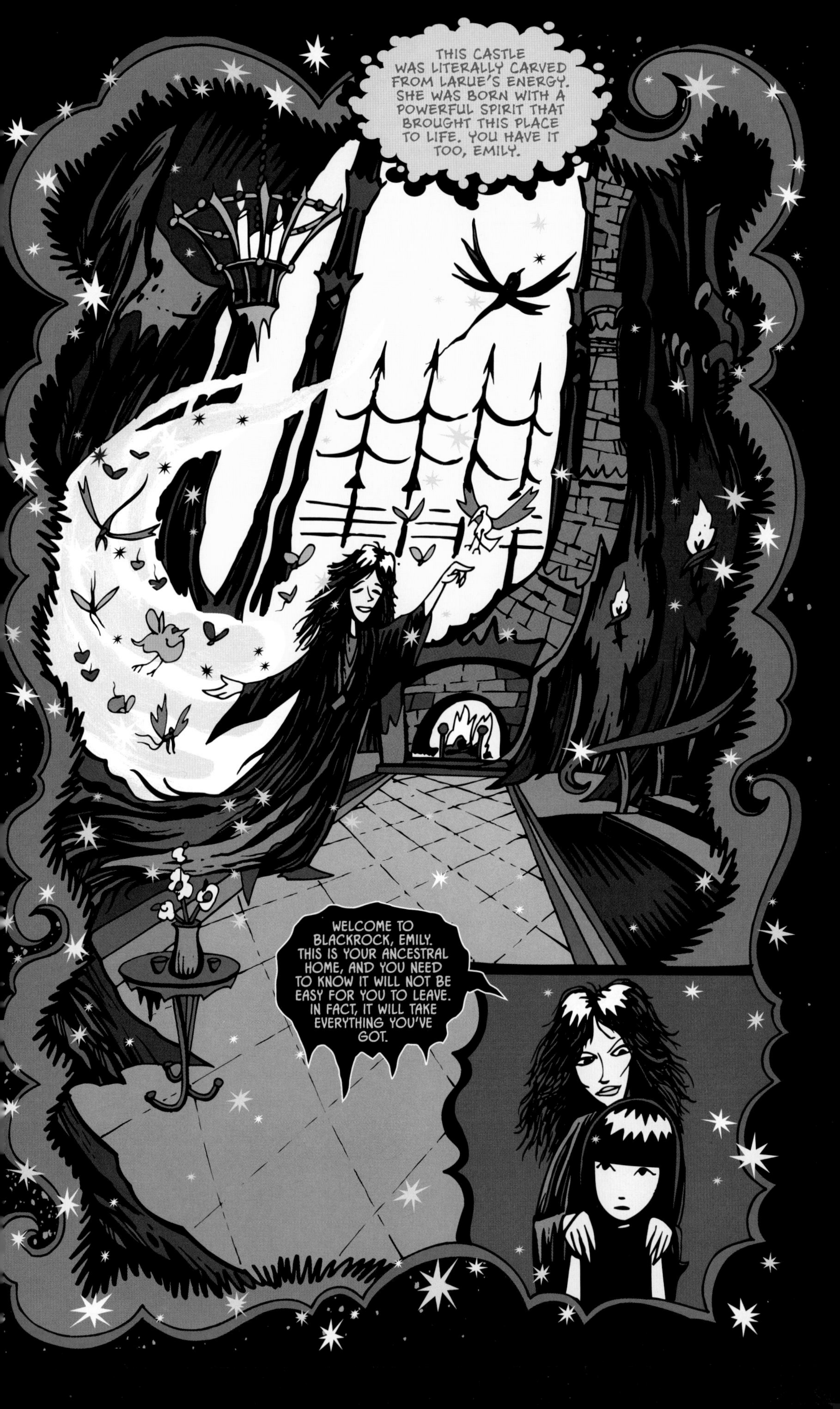
THIS CASTLE WAS LITERALLY CARVED FROM LARUE'S ENERGY. SHE WAS BORN WITH A POWERFUL SPIRIT THAT BROUGHT THIS PLACE TO LIFE. YOU HAVE IT TOO, EMILY.
WELCOME TO BLACKROCK, EMILY. THIS IS YOUR ANCESTRAL HOME, AND YOU NEED TO KNOW IT WILL NOT BE EASY FOR YOU TO LEAVE. IN FACT, IT WILL TAKE EVERYTHING YOU'VE GOT.

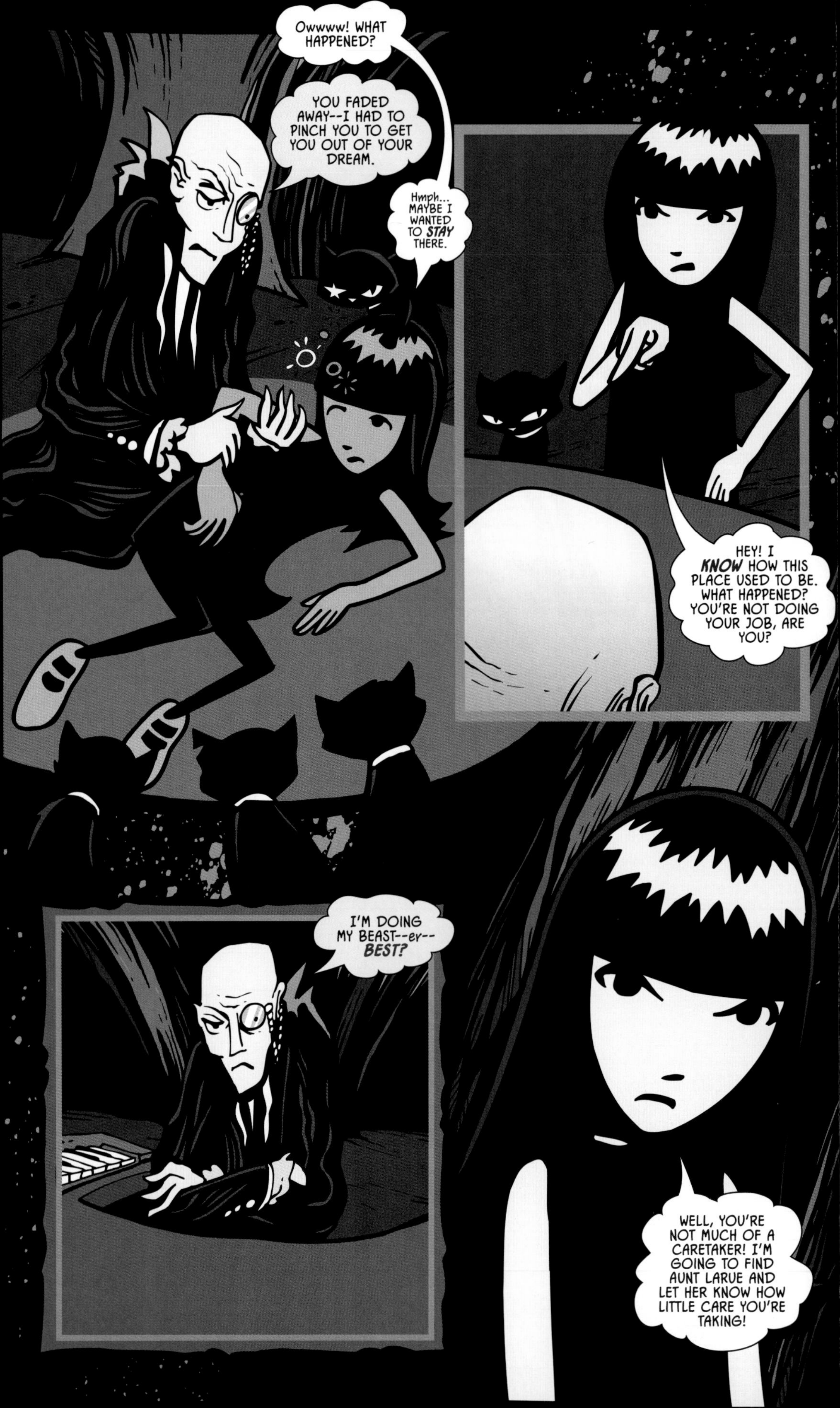

Owwww! WHAT HAPPENED?
YOU FADED AWAY--I HAD TO PINCH YOU TO GET YOU OUT OF YOUR DREAM.
Hmph... MAYBE I WANTED TO STAY THERE.
HEY! I KNOW HOW THIS PLACE USED TO BE. WHAT HAPPENED? YOU'RE NOT DOING YOUR JOB, ARE YOU?
I'M DOING MY BEAST--er--BEST?
WELL, YOU'RE NOT MUCH OF A CARETAKER! I'M GOING TO FIND AUNT LARUE AND LET HER KNOW HOW LITTLE CARE YOU'RE TAKING!

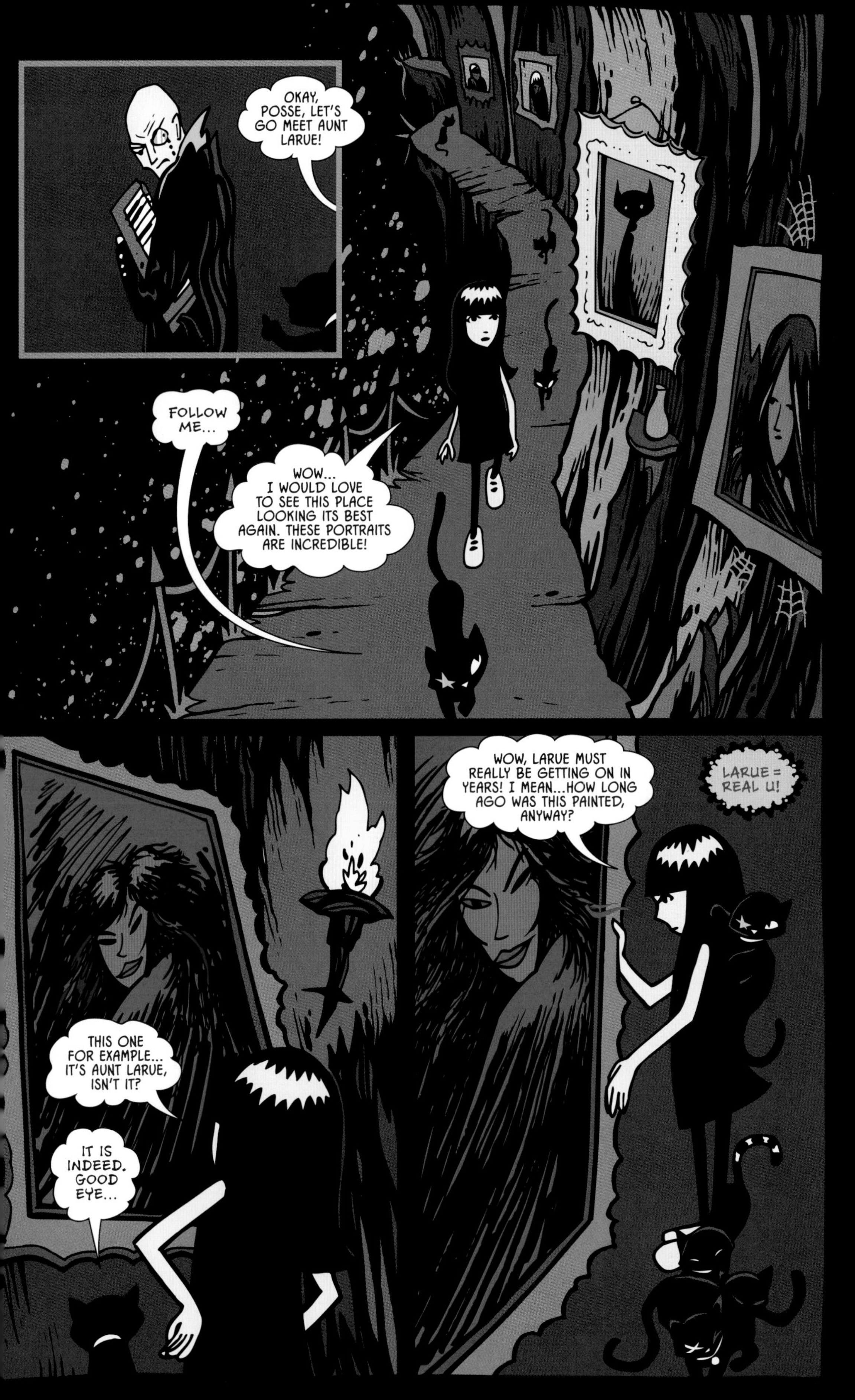
OKAY, POSSE, LET'S GO MEET AUNT LARUE!
FOLLOW ME...
WOW... I WOULD LOVE TO SEE THIS PLACE LOOKING ITS BEST AGAIN. THESE PORTRAITS ARE INCREDIBLE!
THIS ONE FOR EXAMPLE... IT'S AUNT LARUE, ISN'T IT?
IT IS INDEED. GOOD EYE...
WOW, LARUE MUST REALLY BE GETTING ON IN YEARS! I MEAN...HOW LONG AGO WAS THIS PAINTED, ANYWAY?
LARUE = REAL U!

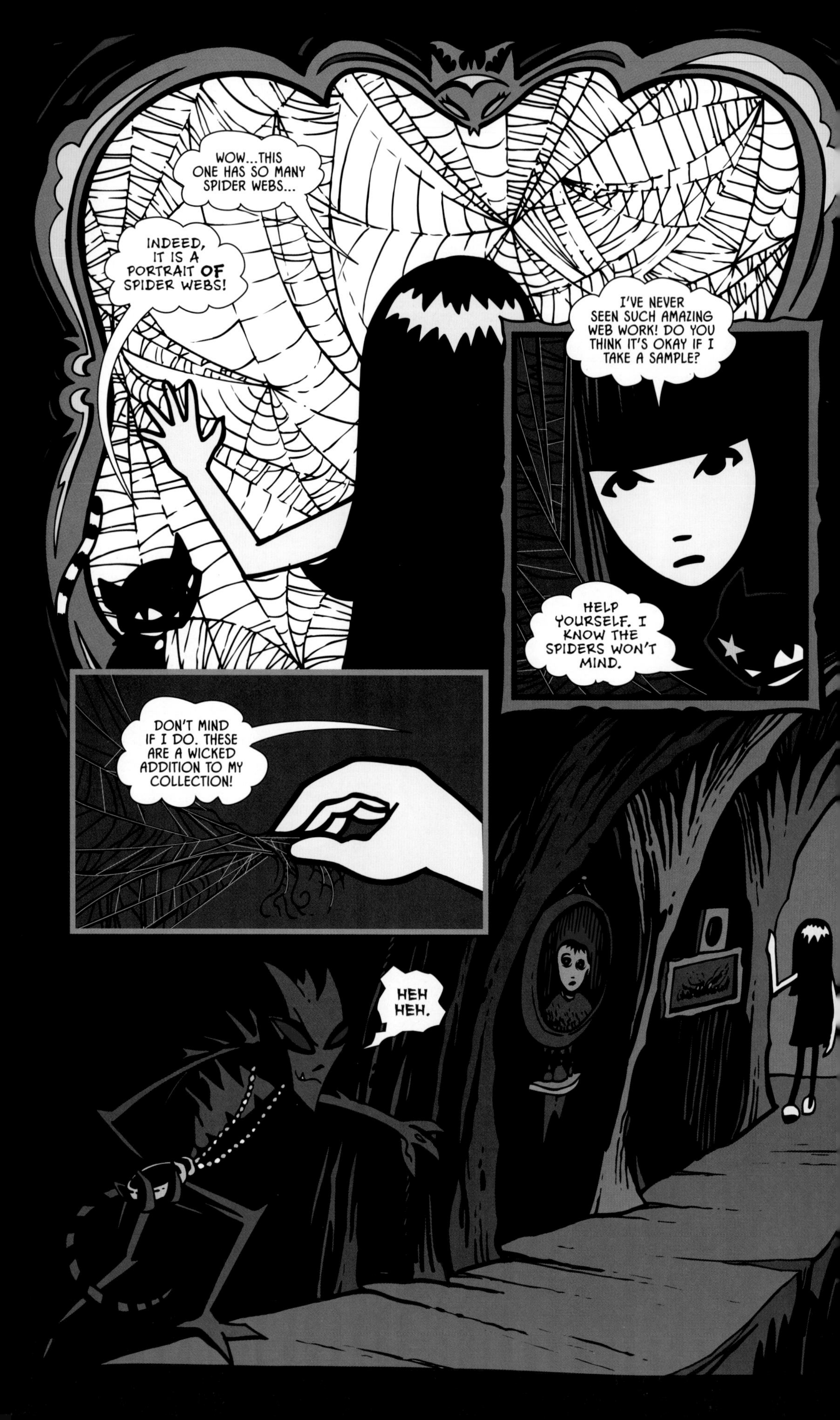
WOW...THIS ONE HAS SO MANY SPIDER WEBS...
INDEED, IT IS A PORTRAIT OF SPIDER WEBS!
I'VE NEVER SEEN SUCH AMAZING WEB WORK! DO YOU THINK IT'S OKAY IF I TAKE A SAMPLE?
HELP YOURSELF. I KNOW THE SPIDERS WON'T MIND.
DON'T MIND IF I DO. THESE ARE A WICKED ADDITION TO MY COLLECTION!
HEH HEH.

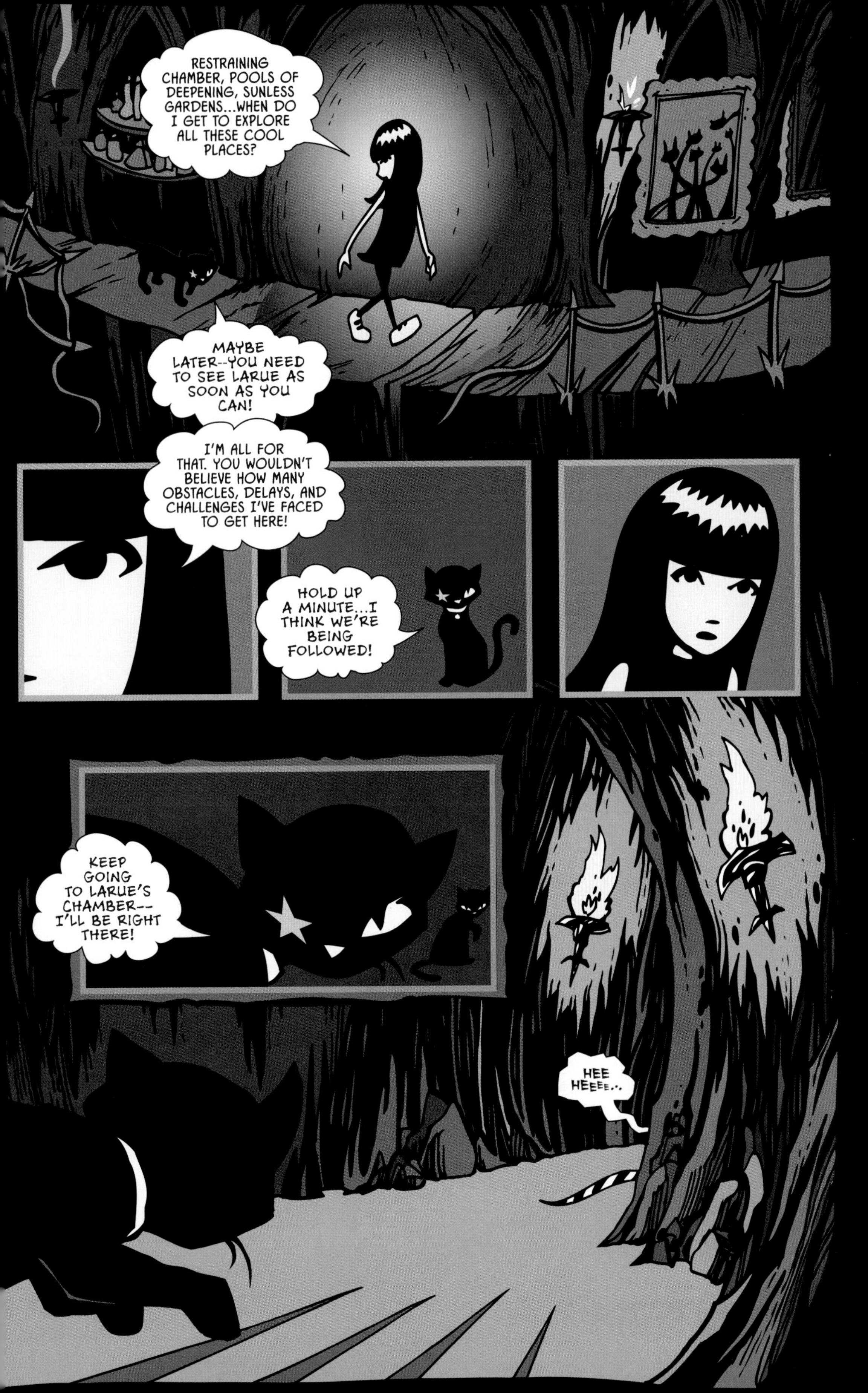
RESTRAINING CHAMBER, POOLS OF DEEPENING, SUNLESS GARDENS...WHEN DO I GET TO EXPLORE ALL THESE COOL PLACES?
MAYBE LATER--YOU NEED TO SEE LARUE AS SOON AS YOU CAN!
I'M ALL FOR THAT. YOU WOULDN'T BELIEVE HOW MANY OBSTACLES, DELAYS, AND CHALLENGES I'VE FACED TO GET HERE!
HOLD UP A MINUTE...I THINK WE'RE BEING FOLLOWED!
KEEP GOING TO LARUE'S CHAMBER-- I'LL BE RIGHT THERE!
HEE HEEEE...

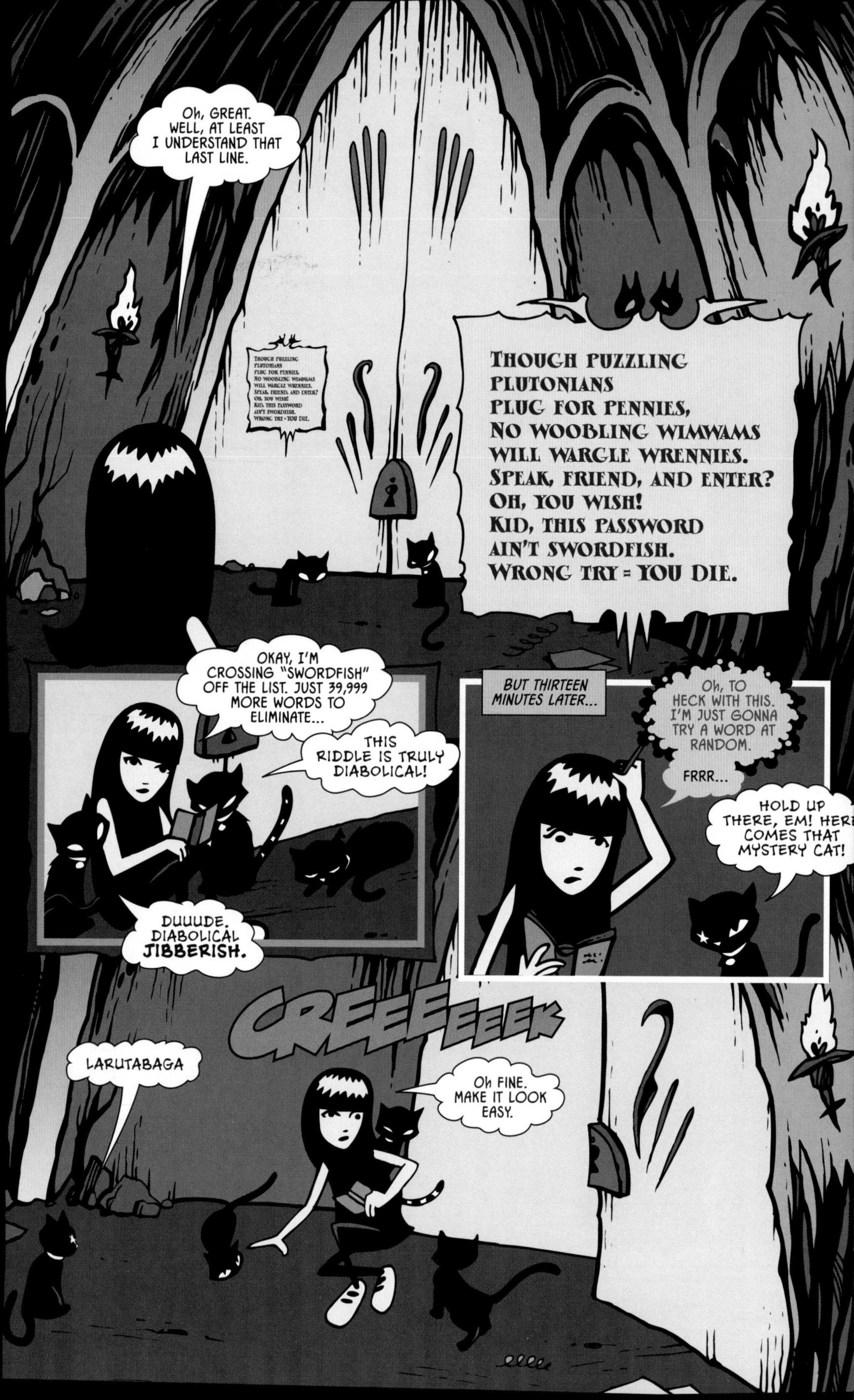
Oh, GREAT. WELL, AT LEAST I UNDERSTAND THAT LAST LINE.
THOUGH PUZZLING PLUTONIANS PLUG FOR PENNIES, NO WOOBLING WIMWAMS WILL WARGLE WRENNIES. SPEAK, FRIEND, AND ENTER? OH, YOU WISH! KID, THIS PASSWORD AIN'T SWORDFISH. WRONG TRY = YOU DIE.
OKAY, I'M CROSSING "SWORDFISH" OFF THE LIST. JUST 39,999 MORE WORDS TO ELIMINATE...
THIS RIDDLE IS TRULY DIABOLICAL!
DUUUDE. DIABOLICAL JIBBERISH.
BUT THIRTEEN MINUTES LATER...
Oh, TO HECK WITH THIS. I'M JUST GONNA TRY A WORD AT RANDOM.
FRRR...
HOLD UP THERE, EM! HERE COMES THAT MYSTERY CAT!
CREEEEEEK
LARUTABAGA
Oh FINE. MAKE IT LOOK EASY.

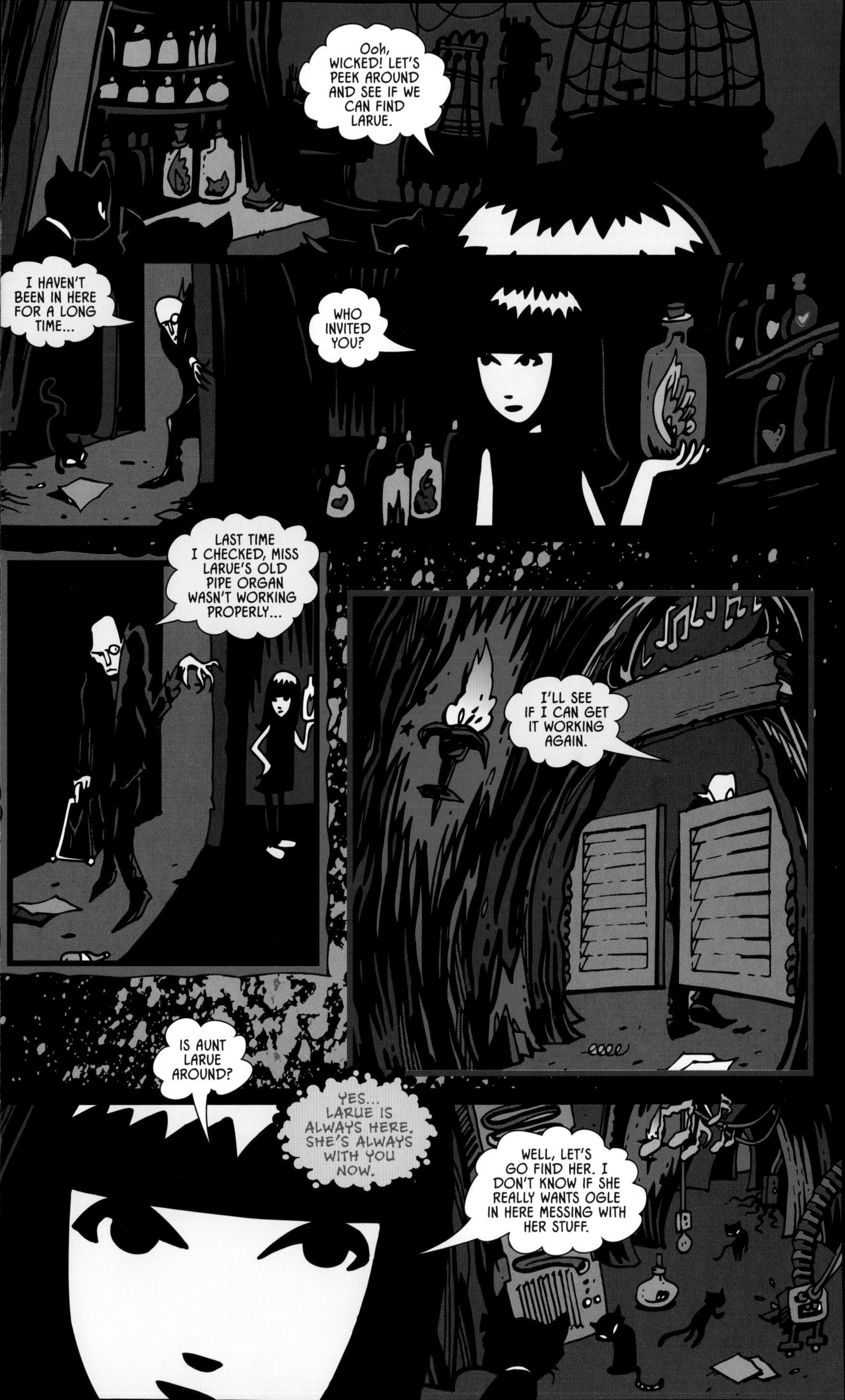
Ooh, WICKED! LET'S PEEK AROUND AND SEE IF WE CAN FIND LARUE.
I HAVEN'T BEEN IN HERE FOR A LONG TIME...
WHO INVITED YOU?
LAST TIME I CHECKED, MISS LARUE'S OLD PIPE ORGAN WASN'T WORKING PROPERLY...
I'LL SEE IF I CAN GET IT WORKING AGAIN.
IS AUNT LARUE AROUND?
YES... LARUE IS ALWAYS HERE. SHE'S ALWAYS WITH YOU NOW.
WELL, LET'S GO FIND HER. I DON'T KNOW IF SHE REALLY WANTS OGLE IN HERE MESSING WITH HER STUFF.

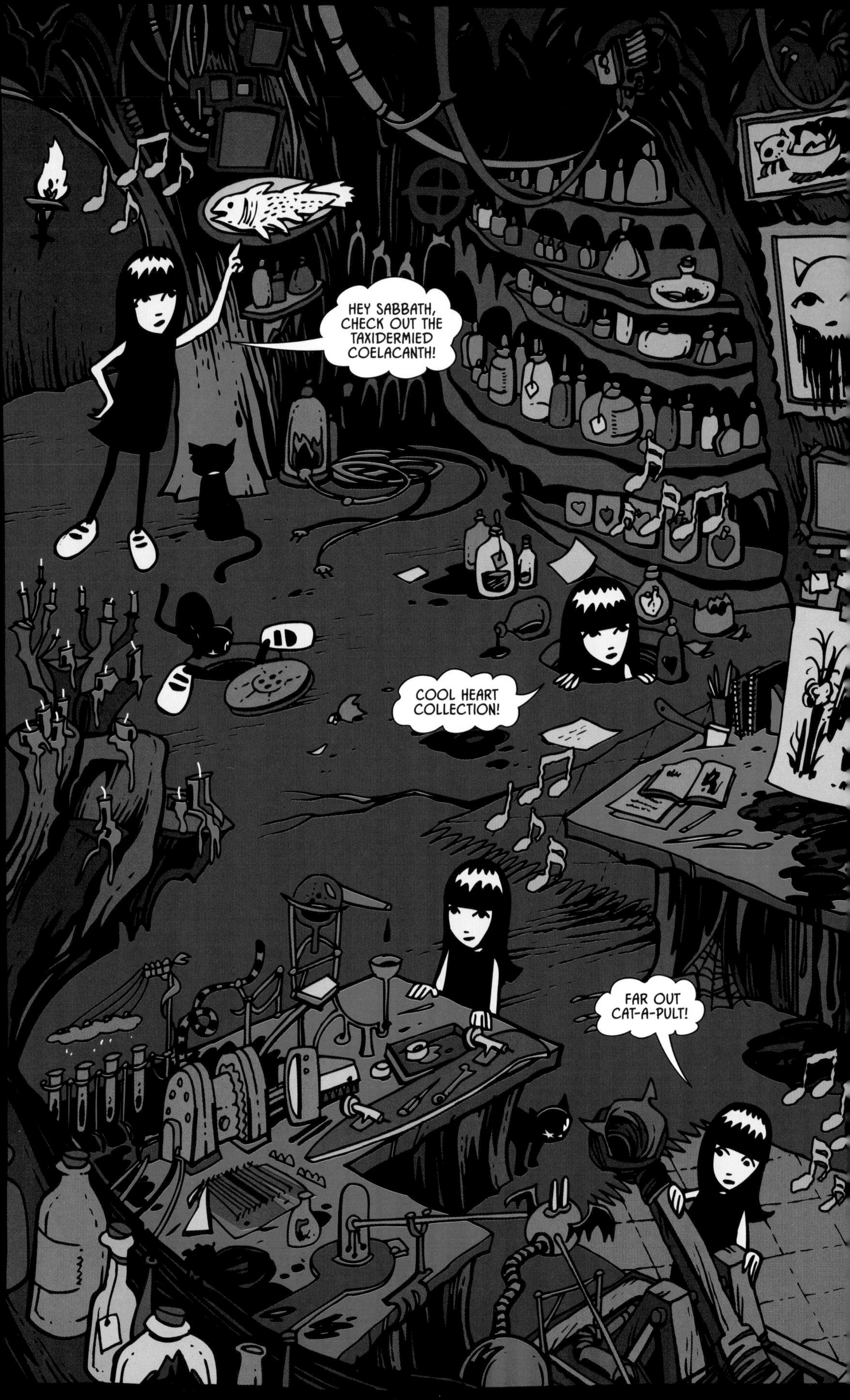
HEY SABBATH, CHECK OUT THE TAXIDERMIED COELACANTH!
COOL HEART COLLECTION!
FAR OUT CAT-A-PULT!

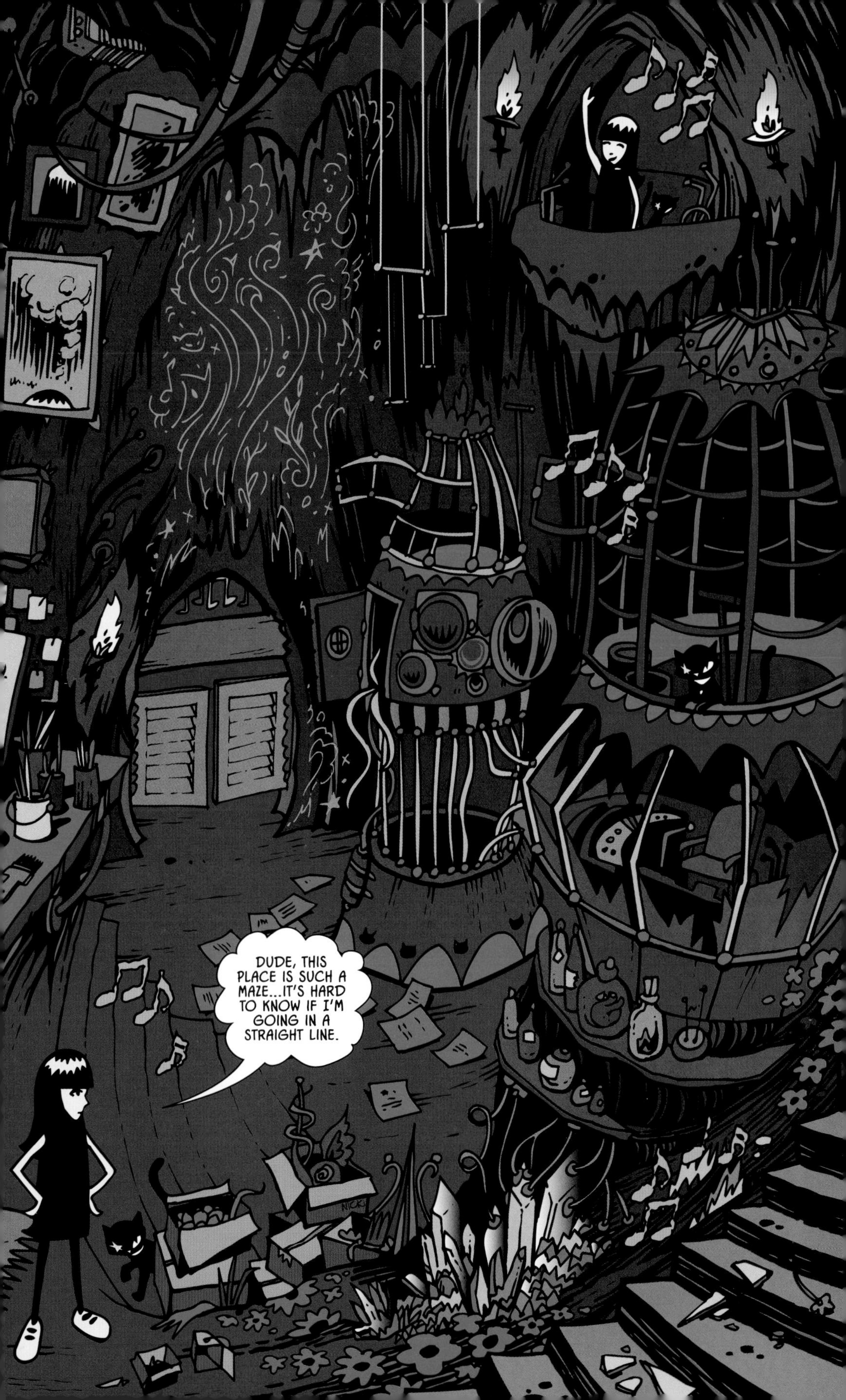
DUDE, THIS PLACE IS SUCH A MAZE...IT'S HARD TO KNOW IF I'M GOING IN A STRAIGHT LINE.

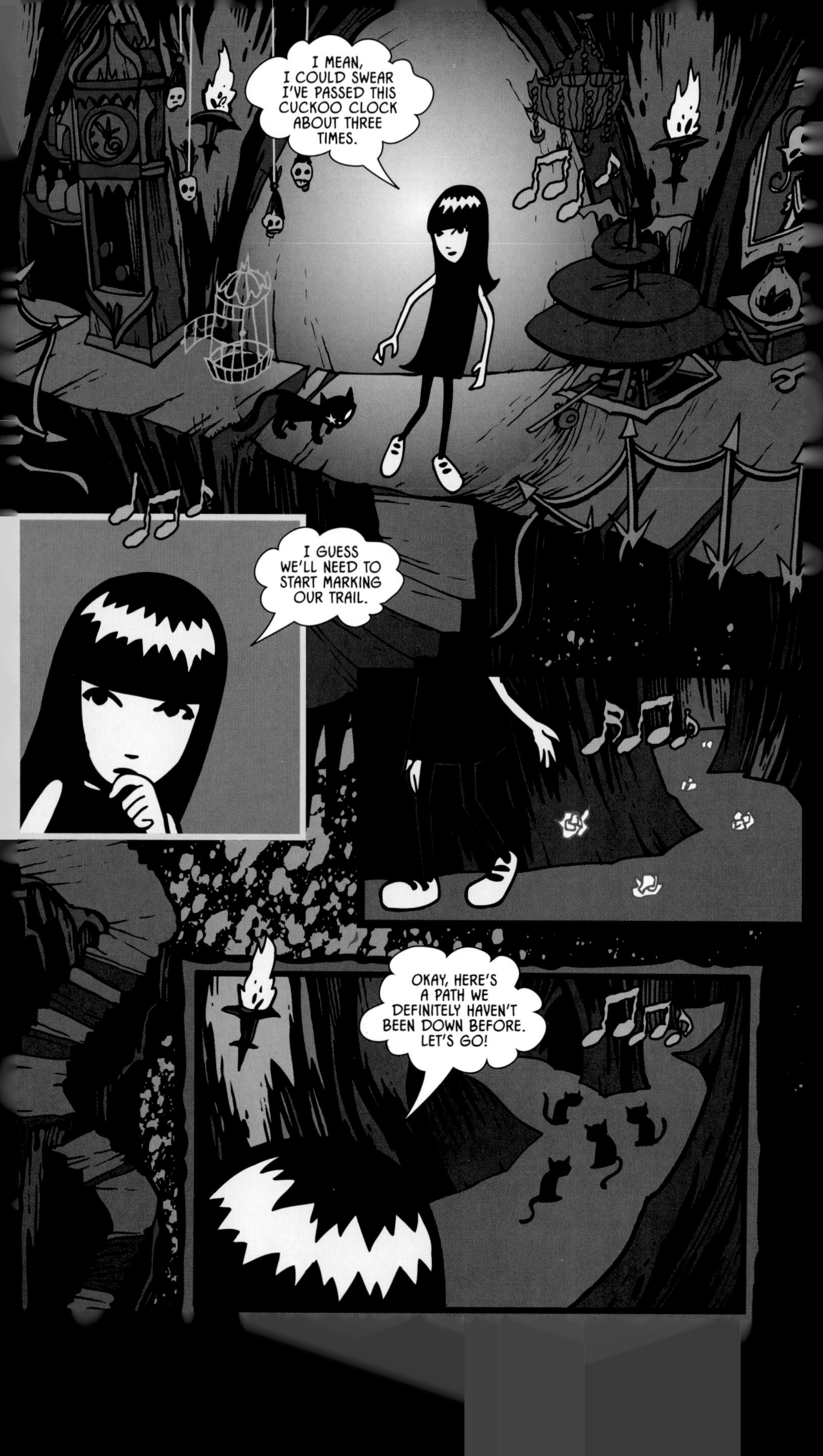
I MEAN, I COULD SWEAR I'VE PASSED THIS CUCKOO CLOCK ABOUT THREE TIMES.
I GUESS WE'LL NEED TO START MARKING OUR TRAIL.
OKAY, HERE'S A PATH WE DEFINITELY HAVEN'T BEEN DOWN BEFORE. LET'S GO!

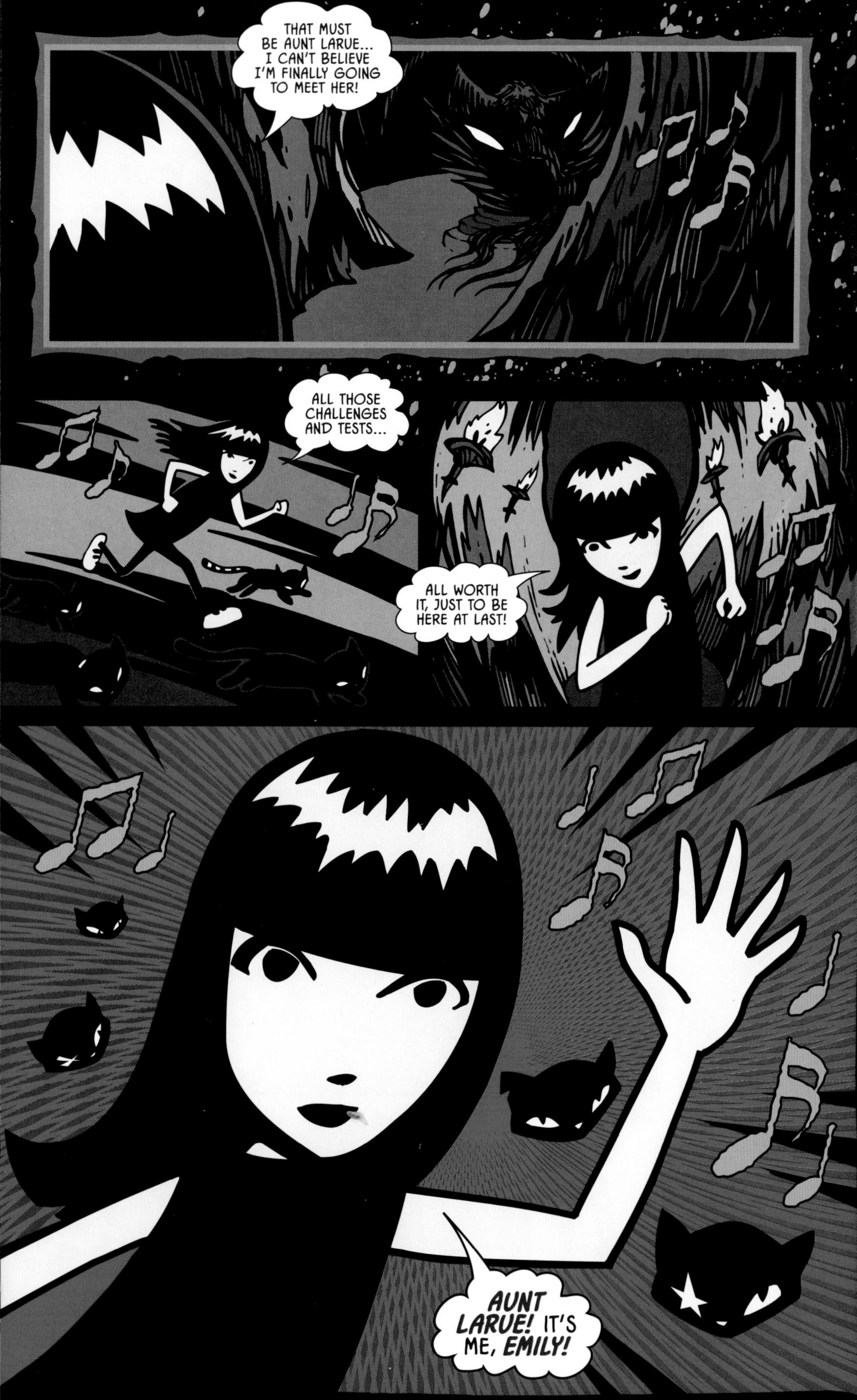
THAT MUST BE AUNT LARUE... I CAN'T BELIEVE I'M FINALLY GOING TO MEET HER!
ALL THOSE CHALLENGES AND TESTS...
ALL WORTH IT, JUST TO BE HERE AT LAST!
AUNT LARUE! IT'S ME, EMILY!

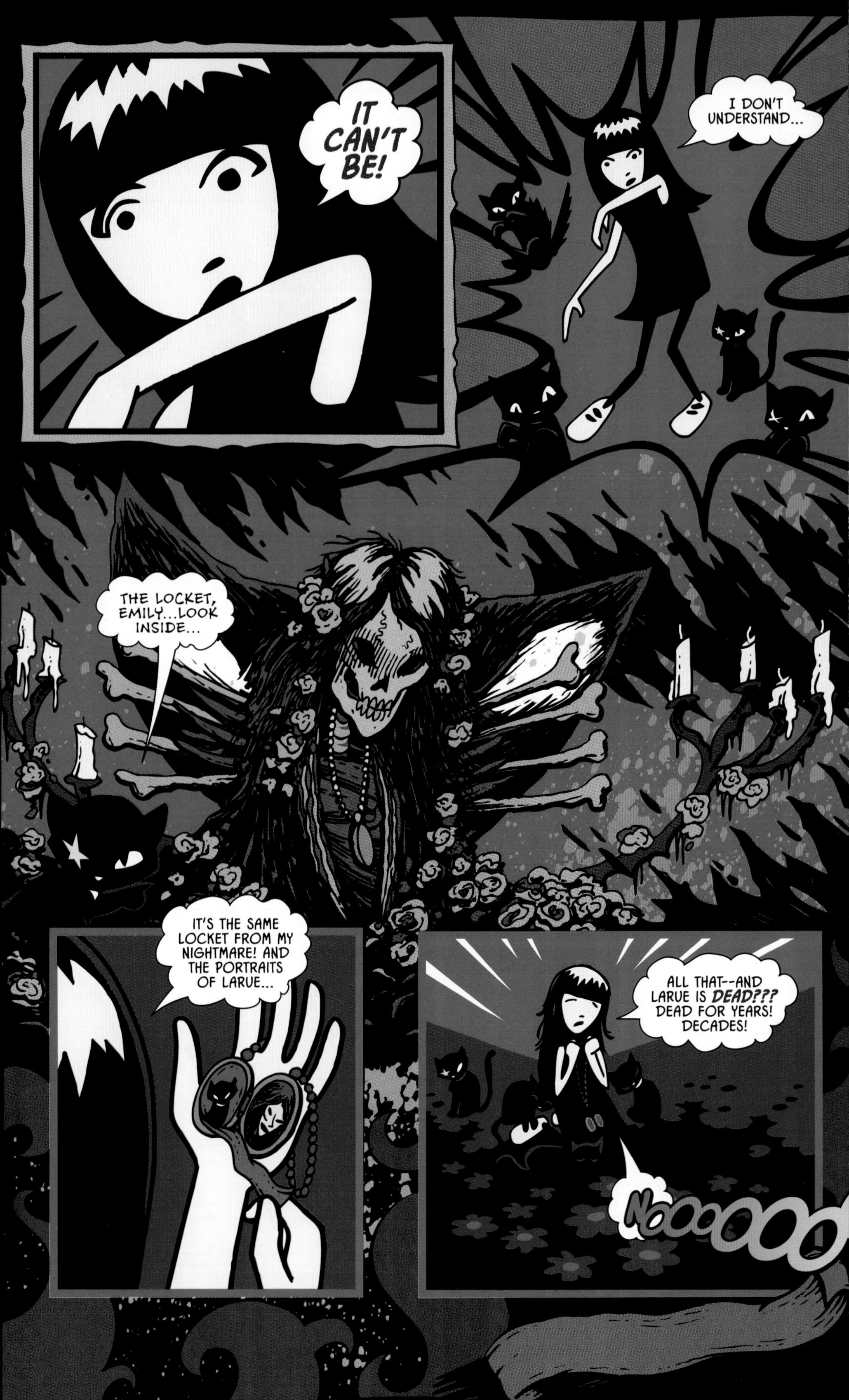
IT CAN'T BE!
I DON'T UNDERSTAND...
THE LOCKET, EMILY...LOOK INSIDE...
IT'S THE SAME LOCKET FROM MY NIGHTMARE! AND THE PORTRAITS OF LARUE...
ALL THAT--AND LARUE IS DEAD??? DEAD FOR YEARS! DECADES!
NOOOOOO

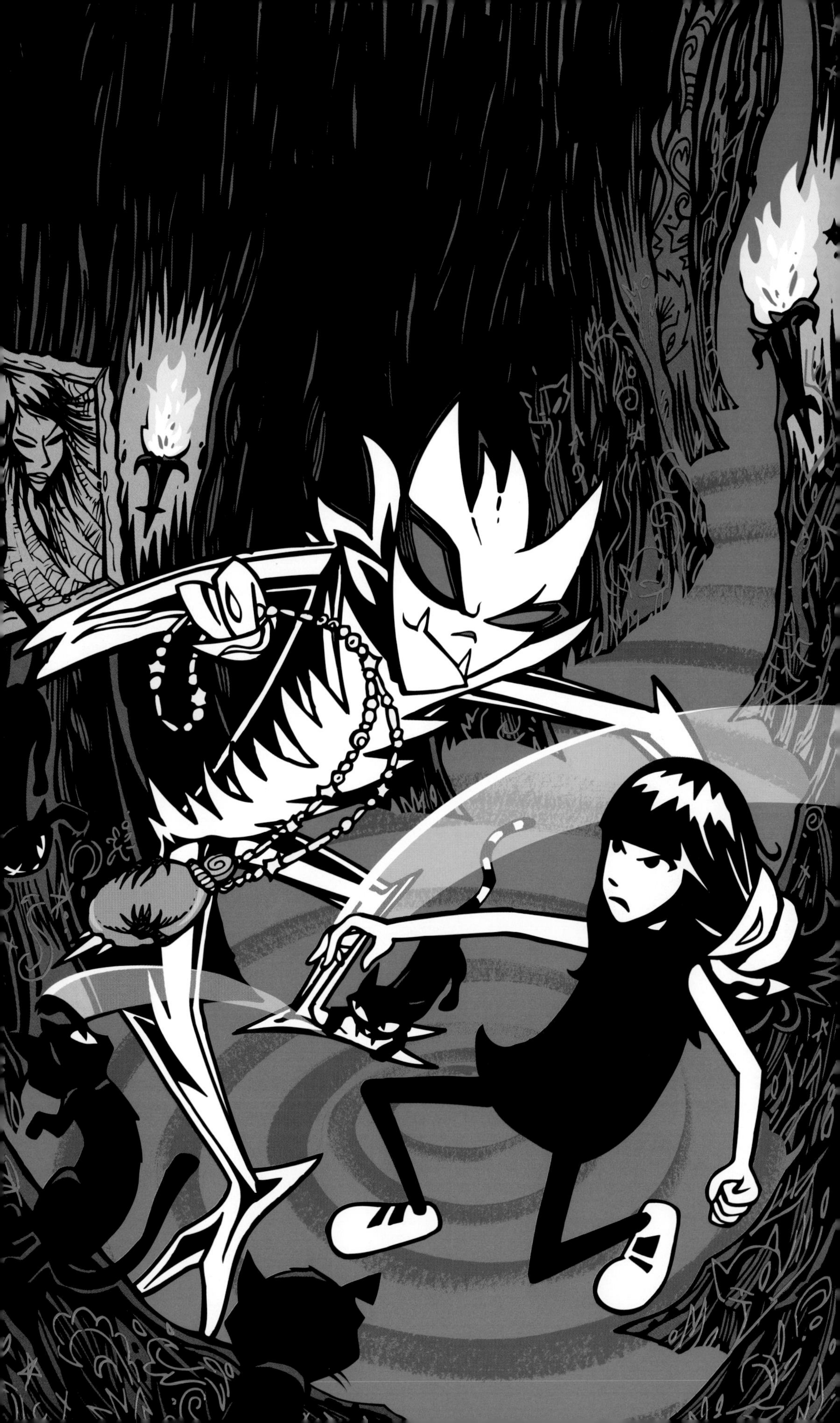

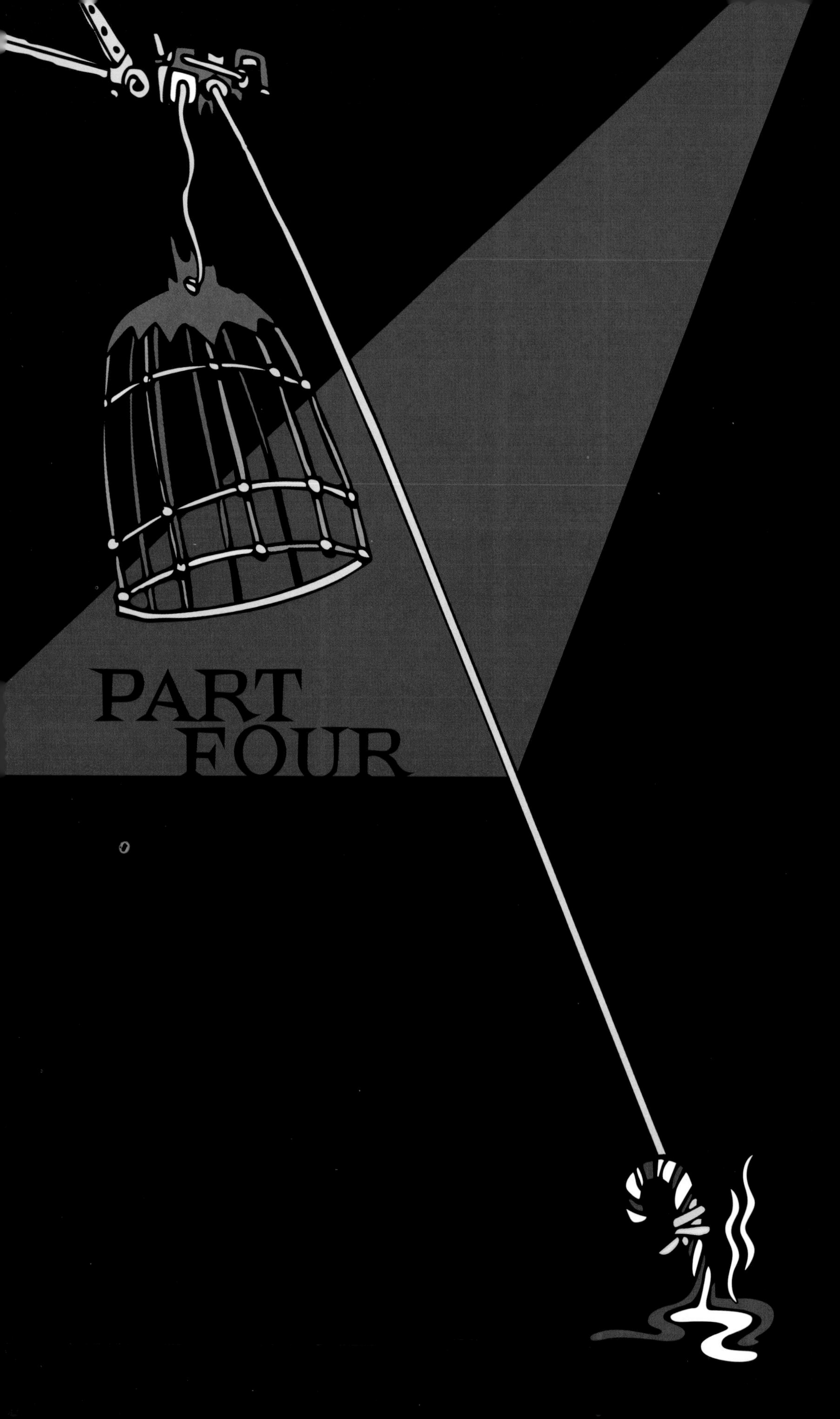
PART
FOUR

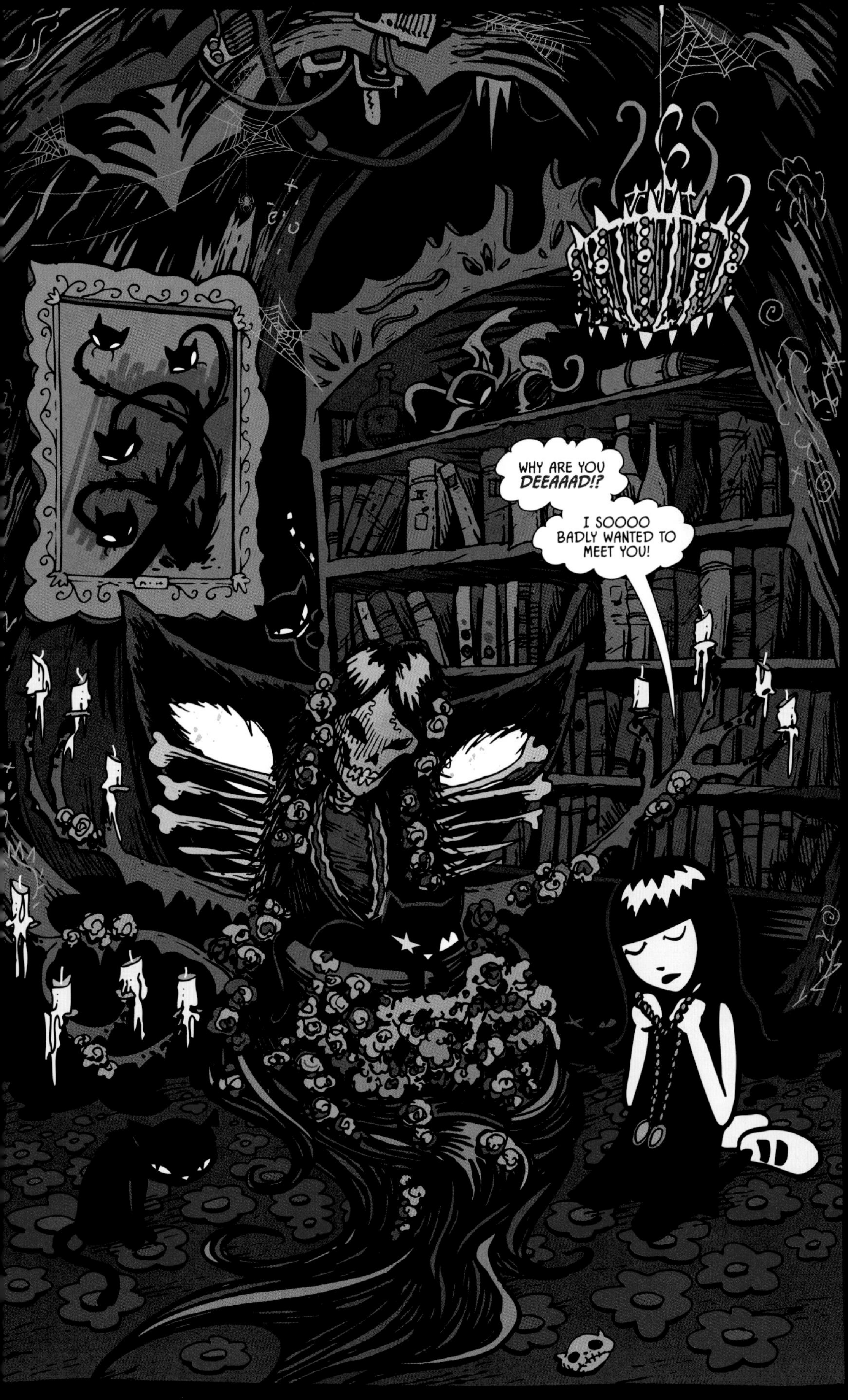
WHY ARE YOU *DEEAAAD!?*
I SOOOO BADLY WANTED TO MEET YOU!

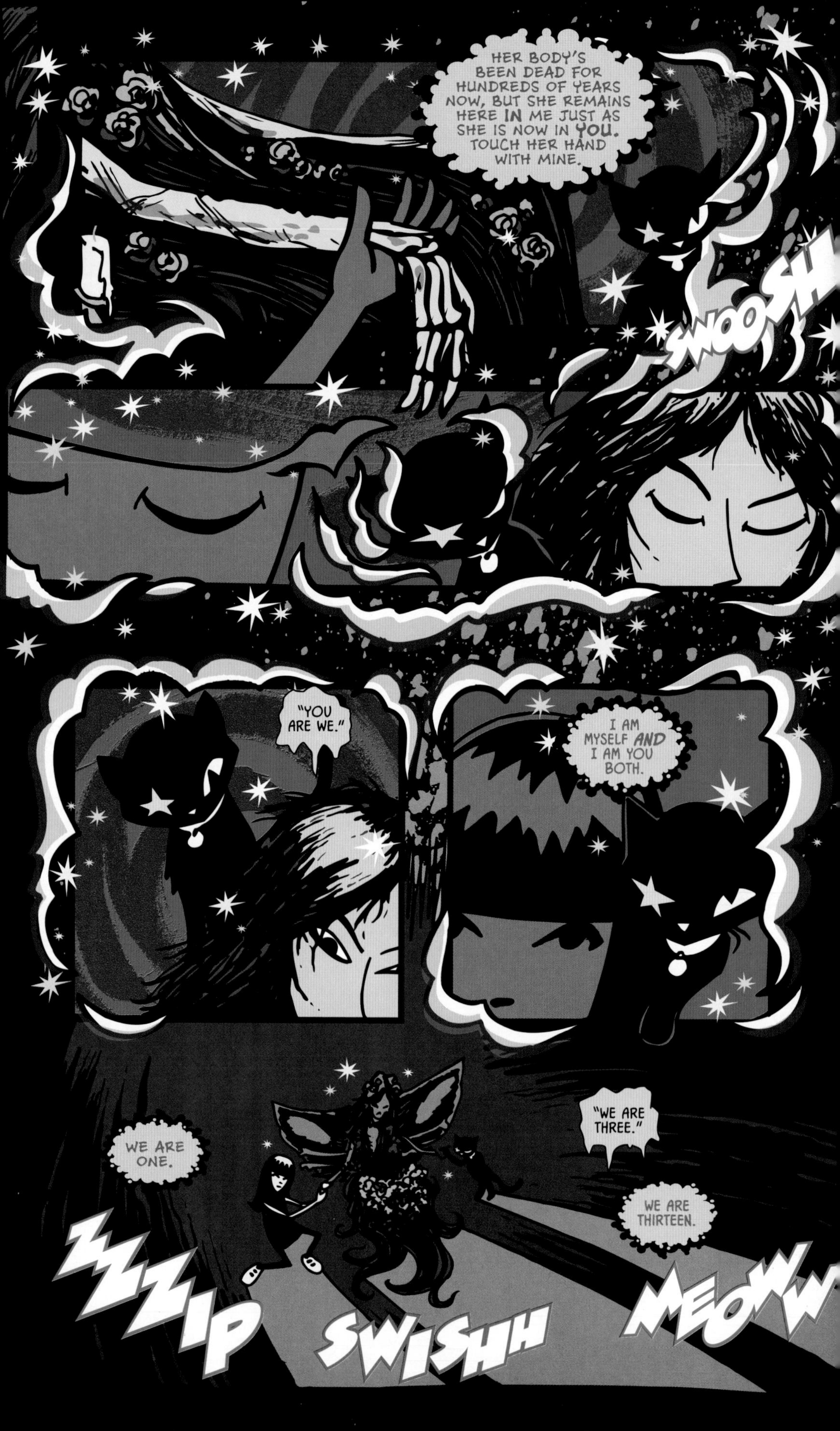
HER BODY'S BEEN DEAD FOR HUNDREDS OF YEARS NOW, BUT SHE REMAINS HERE IN ME JUST AS SHE IS NOW IN YOU. TOUCH HER HAND WITH MINE.
SWOOSH
"YOU ARE WE."
I AM MYSELF AND I AM YOU BOTH.
WE ARE ONE.
"WE ARE THREE."
WE ARE THIRTEEN.
ZZZIP
SWISHH
MEOWW

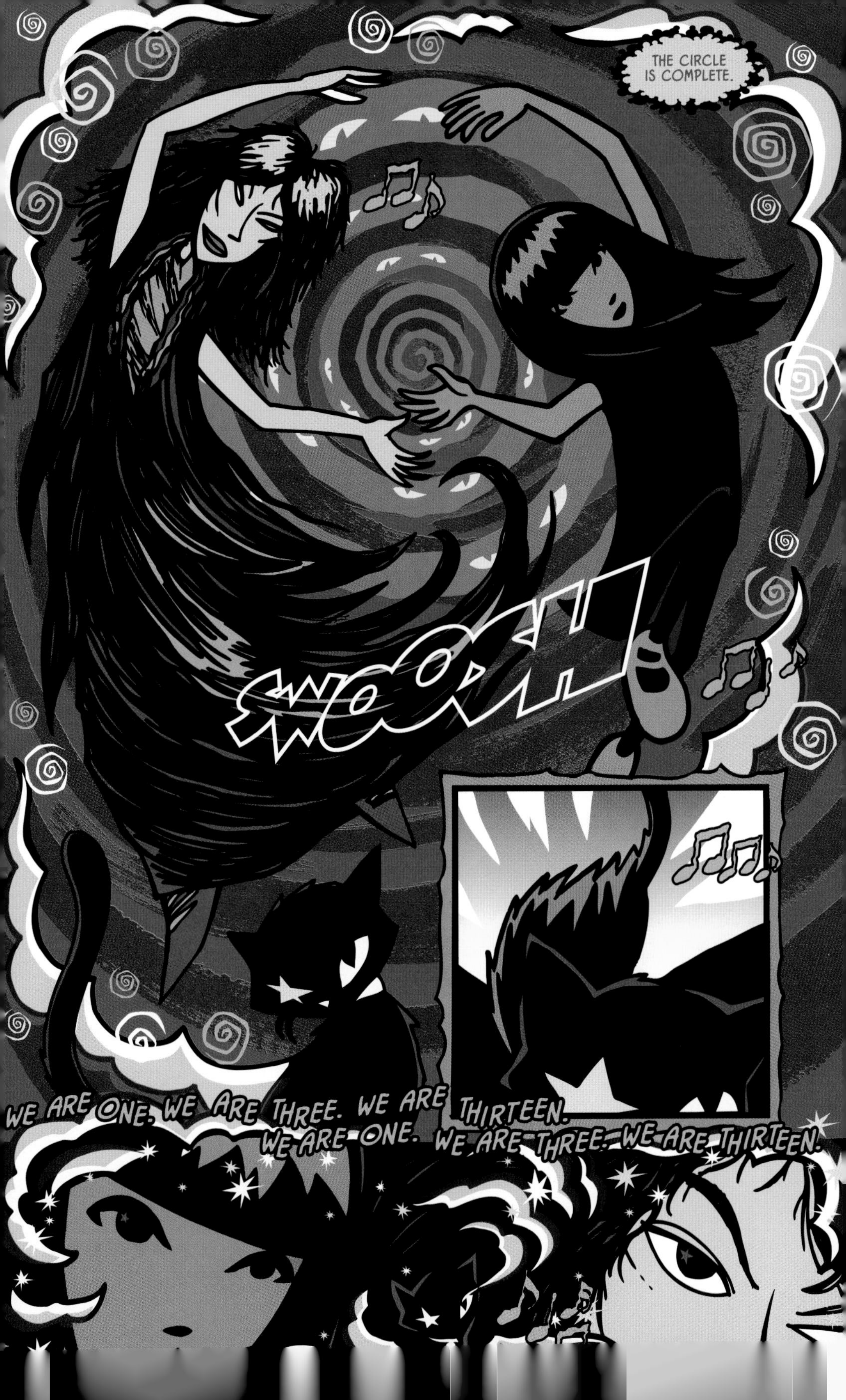

THE CIRCLE IS COMPLETE.
SWOOSH
WE ARE ONE. WE ARE THREE. WE ARE THIRTEEN.
WE ARE ONE. WE ARE THREE. WE ARE THIRTEEN.

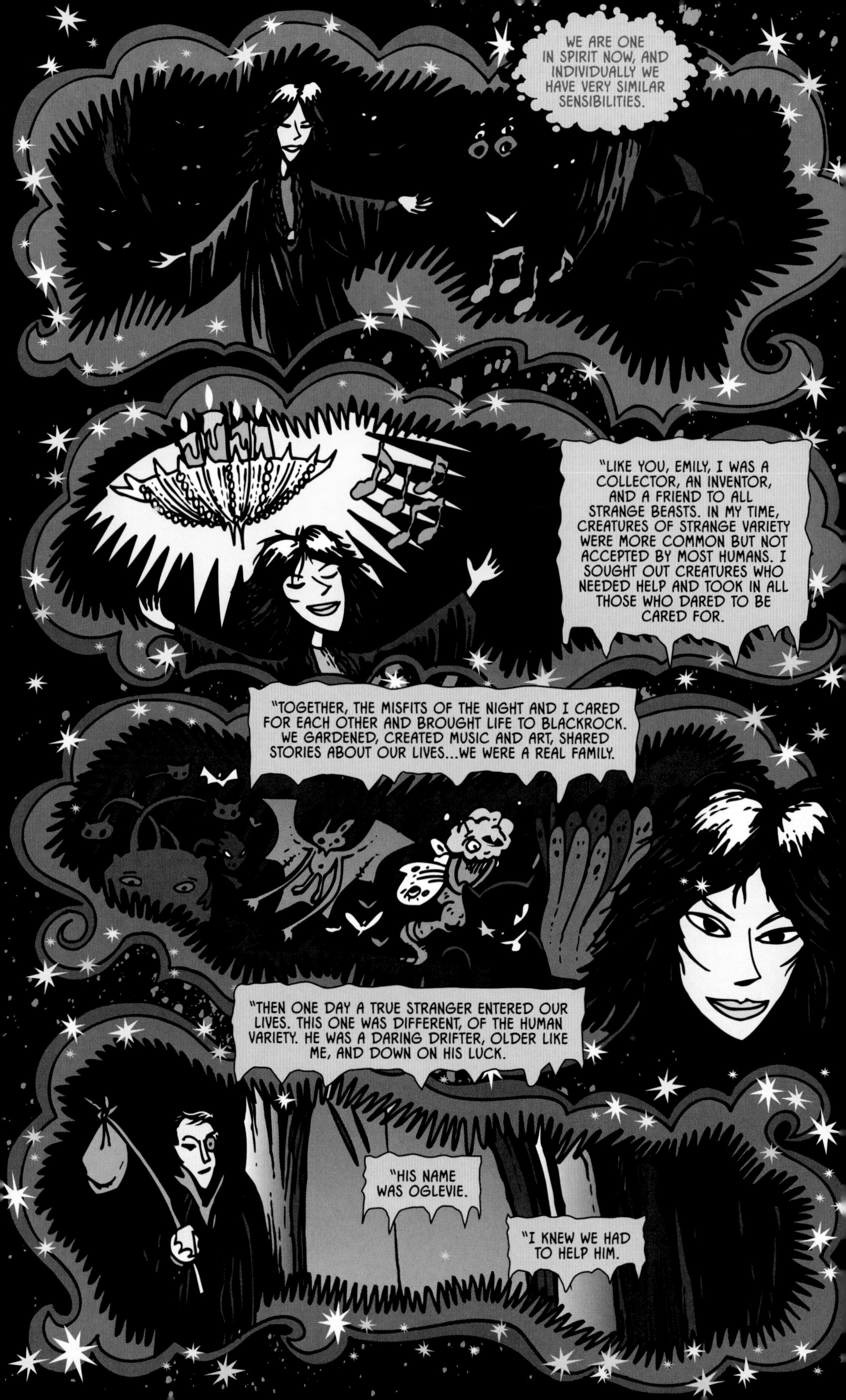
WE ARE ONE IN SPIRIT NOW, AND INDIVIDUALLY WE HAVE VERY SIMILAR SENSIBILITIES.
"LIKE YOU, EMILY, I WAS A COLLECTOR, AN INVENTOR, AND A FRIEND TO ALL STRANGE BEASTS. IN MY TIME, CREATURES OF STRANGE VARIETY WERE MORE COMMON BUT NOT ACCEPTED BY MOST HUMANS. I SOUGHT OUT CREATURES WHO NEEDED HELP AND TOOK IN ALL THOSE WHO DARED TO BE CARED FOR.
"TOGETHER, THE MISFITS OF THE NIGHT AND I CARED FOR EACH OTHER AND BROUGHT LIFE TO BLACKROCK. WE GARDENED, CREATED MUSIC AND ART, SHARED STORIES ABOUT OUR LIVES...WE WERE A REAL FAMILY.
"THEN ONE DAY A TRUE STRANGER ENTERED OUR LIVES. THIS ONE WAS DIFFERENT, OF THE HUMAN VARIETY. HE WAS A DARING DRIFTER, OLDER LIKE ME, AND DOWN ON HIS LUCK.
"HIS NAME WAS OGLEVIE.
"I KNEW WE HAD TO HELP HIM.

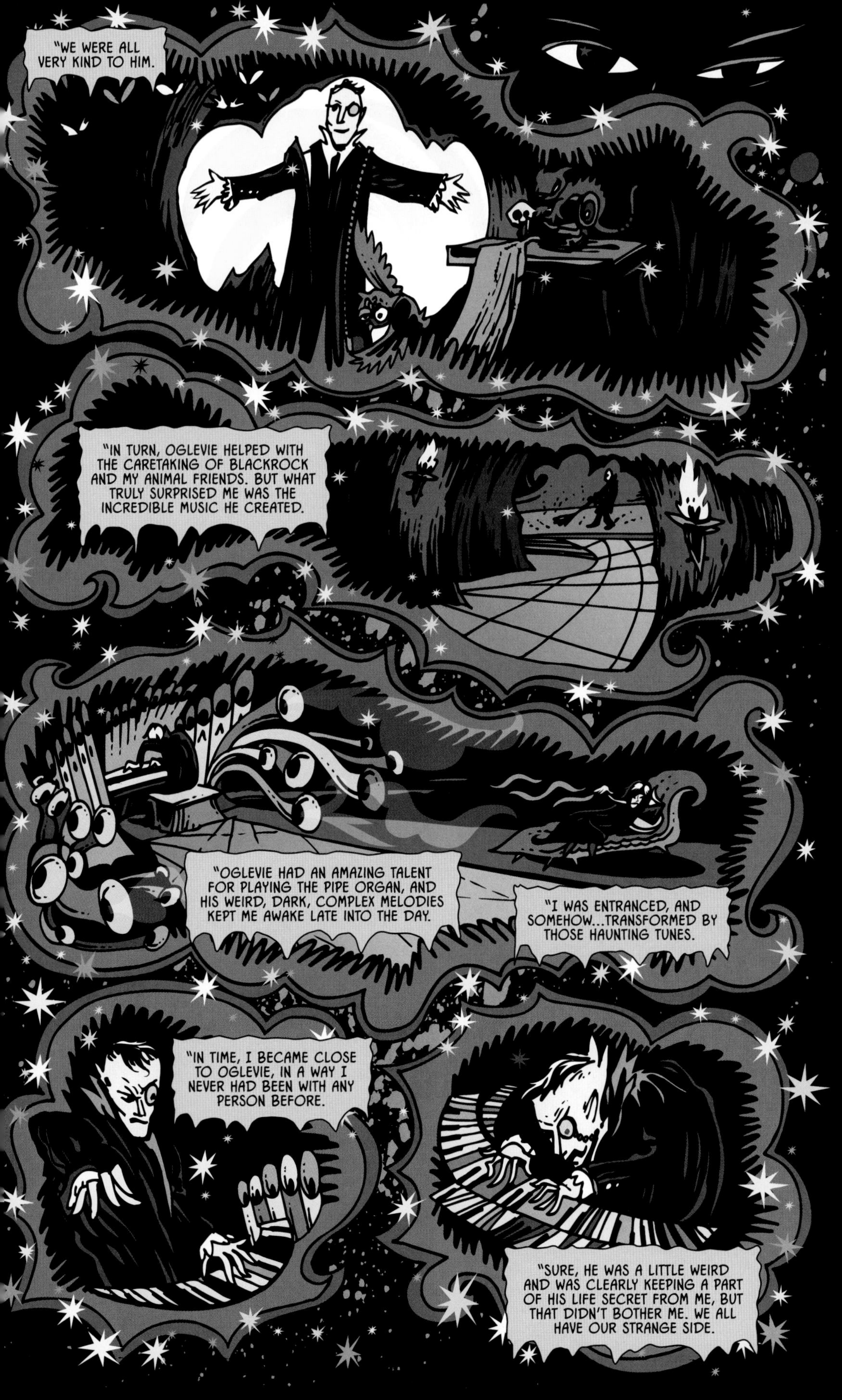
"WE WERE ALL VERY KIND TO HIM.
"IN TURN, OGLEVIE HELPED WITH THE CARETAKING OF BLACKROCK AND MY ANIMAL FRIENDS. BUT WHAT TRULY SURPRISED ME WAS THE INCREDIBLE MUSIC HE CREATED.
"OGLEVIE HAD AN AMAZING TALENT FOR PLAYING THE PIPE ORGAN, AND HIS WEIRD, DARK, COMPLEX MELODIES KEPT ME AWAKE LATE INTO THE DAY.
"I WAS ENTRANCED, AND SOMEHOW...TRANSFORMED BY THOSE HAUNTING TUNES.
"IN TIME, I BECAME CLOSE TO OGLEVIE, IN A WAY I NEVER HAD BEEN WITH ANY PERSON BEFORE.
"SURE, HE WAS A LITTLE WEIRD AND WAS CLEARLY KEEPING A PART OF HIS LIFE SECRET FROM ME, BUT THAT DIDN'T BOTHER ME. WE ALL HAVE OUR STRANGE SIDE.

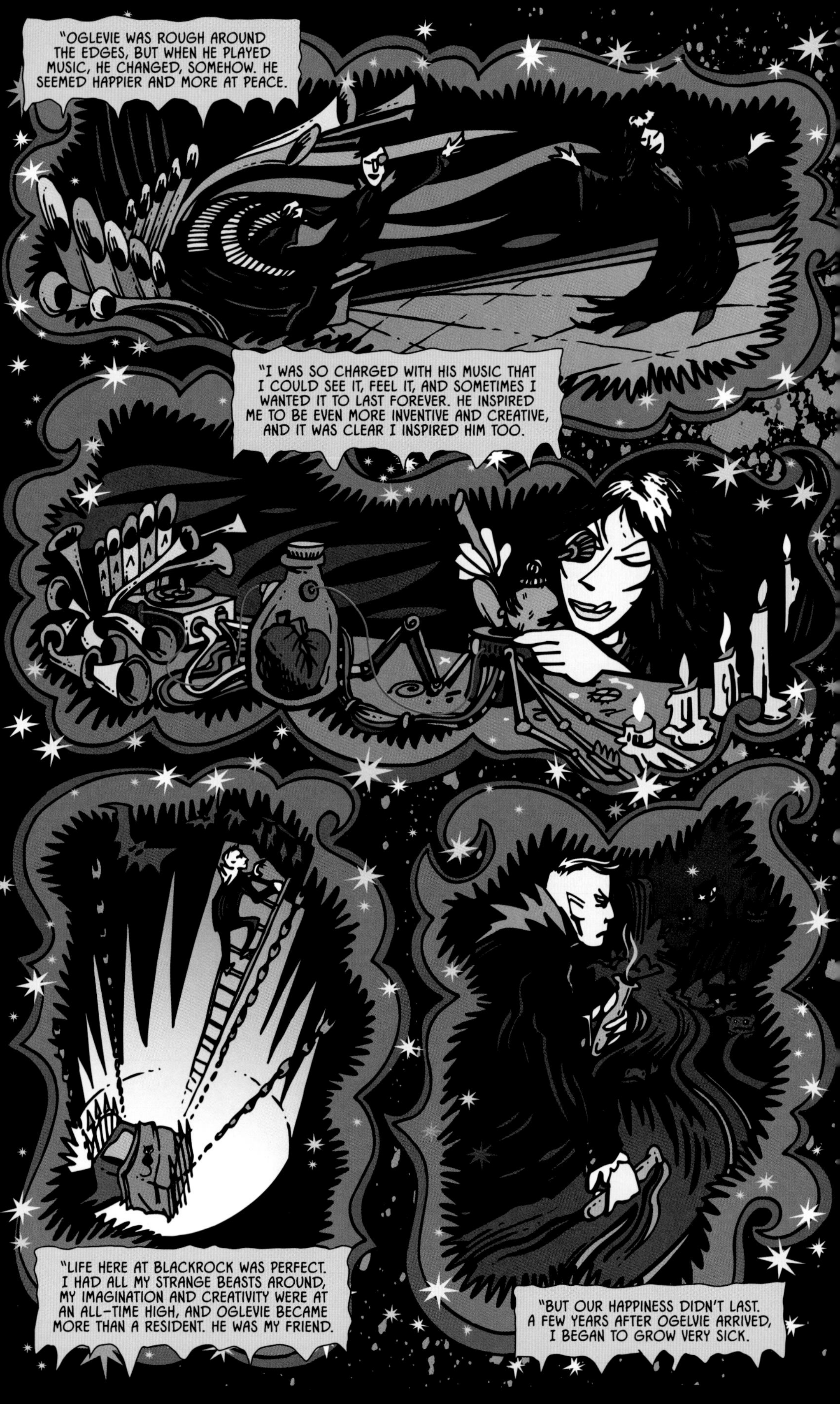
"OGLEVIE WAS ROUGH AROUND THE EDGES, BUT WHEN HE PLAYED MUSIC, HE CHANGED, SOMEHOW. HE SEEMED HAPPIER AND MORE AT PEACE.
"I WAS SO CHARGED WITH HIS MUSIC THAT I COULD SEE IT, FEEL IT, AND SOMETIMES I WANTED IT TO LAST FOREVER. HE INSPIRED ME TO BE EVEN MORE INVENTIVE AND CREATIVE, AND IT WAS CLEAR I INSPIRED HIM TOO.
"LIFE HERE AT BLACKROCK WAS PERFECT. I HAD ALL MY STRANGE BEASTS AROUND, MY IMAGINATION AND CREATIVITY WERE AT AN ALL-TIME HIGH, AND OGLEVIE BECAME MORE THAN A RESIDENT. HE WAS MY FRIEND.
"BUT OUR HAPPINESS DIDN'T LAST. A FEW YEARS AFTER OGELVIE ARRIVED, I BEGAN TO GROW VERY SICK.

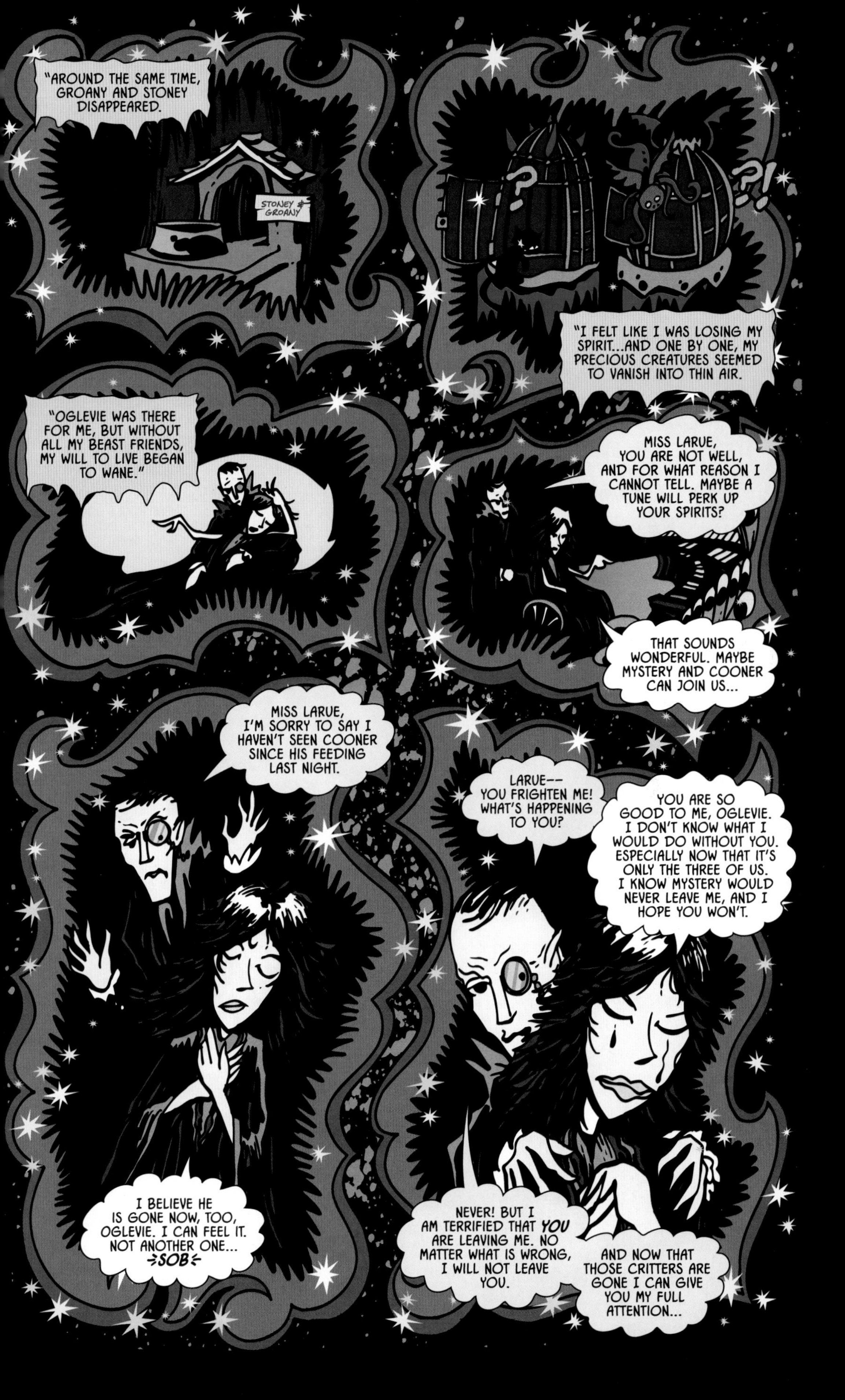
"AROUND THE SAME TIME, GROANY AND STONEY DISAPPEARED.
STONEY & GROANY
?
?!
"I FELT LIKE I WAS LOSING MY SPIRIT...AND ONE BY ONE, MY PRECIOUS CREATURES SEEMED TO VANISH INTO THIN AIR.
"OGLEVIE WAS THERE FOR ME, BUT WITHOUT ALL MY BEAST FRIENDS, MY WILL TO LIVE BEGAN TO WANE."
MISS LARUE, YOU ARE NOT WELL, AND FOR WHAT REASON I CANNOT TELL. MAYBE A TUNE WILL PERK UP YOUR SPIRITS?
THAT SOUNDS WONDERFUL. MAYBE MYSTERY AND COONER CAN JOIN US...
MISS LARUE, I'M SORRY TO SAY I HAVEN'T SEEN COONER SINCE HIS FEEDING LAST NIGHT.
I BELIEVE HE IS GONE NOW, TOO, OGLEVIE. I CAN FEEL IT. NOT ANOTHER ONE... SOB
LARUE-- YOU FRIGHTEN ME! WHAT'S HAPPENING TO YOU?
YOU ARE SO GOOD TO ME, OGLEVIE. I DON'T KNOW WHAT I WOULD DO WITHOUT YOU. ESPECIALLY NOW THAT IT'S ONLY THE THREE OF US. I KNOW MYSTERY WOULD NEVER LEAVE ME, AND I HOPE YOU WON'T.
NEVER! BUT I AM TERRIFIED THAT YOU ARE LEAVING ME. NO MATTER WHAT IS WRONG, I WILL NOT LEAVE YOU.
AND NOW THAT THOSE CRITTERS ARE GONE I CAN GIVE YOU MY FULL ATTENTION...

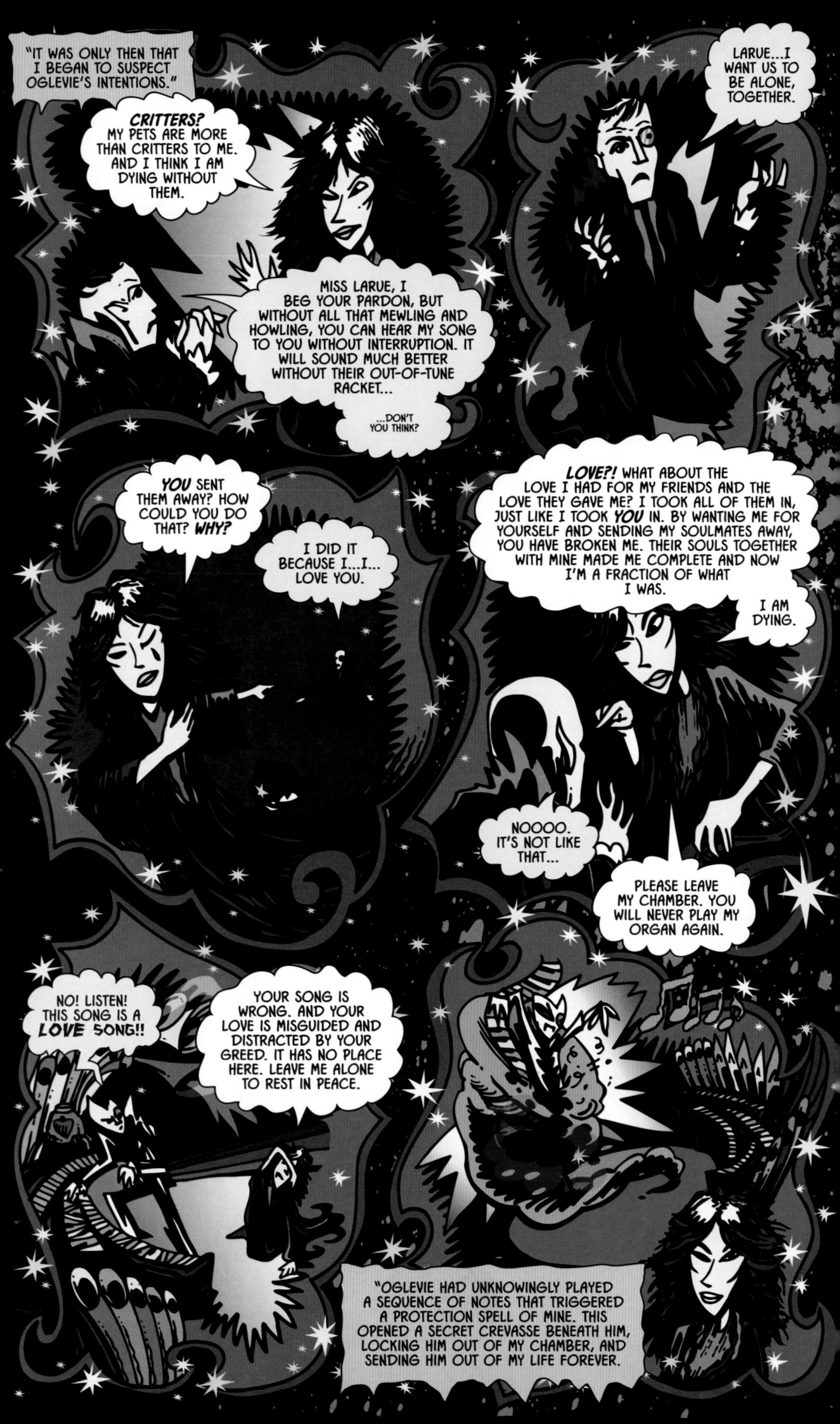
"IT WAS ONLY THEN THAT I BEGAN TO SUSPECT OGLEVIE'S INTENTIONS."
CRITTERS? MY PETS ARE MORE THAN CRITTERS TO ME. AND I THINK I AM DYING WITHOUT THEM.
MISS LARUE, I BEG YOUR PARDON, BUT WITHOUT ALL THAT MEWLING AND HOWLING, YOU CAN HEAR MY SONG TO YOU WITHOUT INTERRUPTION. IT WILL SOUND MUCH BETTER WITHOUT THEIR OUT-OF-TUNE RACKET...
...DON'T YOU THINK?
LARUE...I WANT US TO BE ALONE, TOGETHER.
YOU SENT THEM AWAY? HOW COULD YOU DO THAT? WHY?
I DID IT BECAUSE I...I... LOVE YOU.
LOVE?! WHAT ABOUT THE LOVE I HAD FOR MY FRIENDS AND THE LOVE THEY GAVE ME? I TOOK ALL OF THEM IN, JUST LIKE I TOOK YOU IN. BY WANTING ME FOR YOURSELF AND SENDING MY SOULMATES AWAY, YOU HAVE BROKEN ME. THEIR SOULS TOGETHER WITH MINE MADE ME COMPLETE AND NOW I'M A FRACTION OF WHAT I WAS.
I AM DYING.
NOOOO. IT'S NOT LIKE THAT...
PLEASE LEAVE MY CHAMBER. YOU WILL NEVER PLAY MY ORGAN AGAIN.
NO! LISTEN! THIS SONG IS A LOVE SONG!!
YOUR SONG IS WRONG. AND YOUR LOVE IS MISGUIDED AND DISTRACTED BY YOUR GREED. IT HAS NO PLACE HERE. LEAVE ME ALONE TO REST IN PEACE.
"OGLEVIE HAD UNKNOWINGLY PLAYED A SEQUENCE OF NOTES THAT TRIGGERED A PROTECTION SPELL OF MINE. THIS OPENED A SECRET CREVASSE BENEATH HIM, LOCKING HIM OUT OF MY CHAMBER, AND SENDING HIM OUT OF MY LIFE FOREVER.

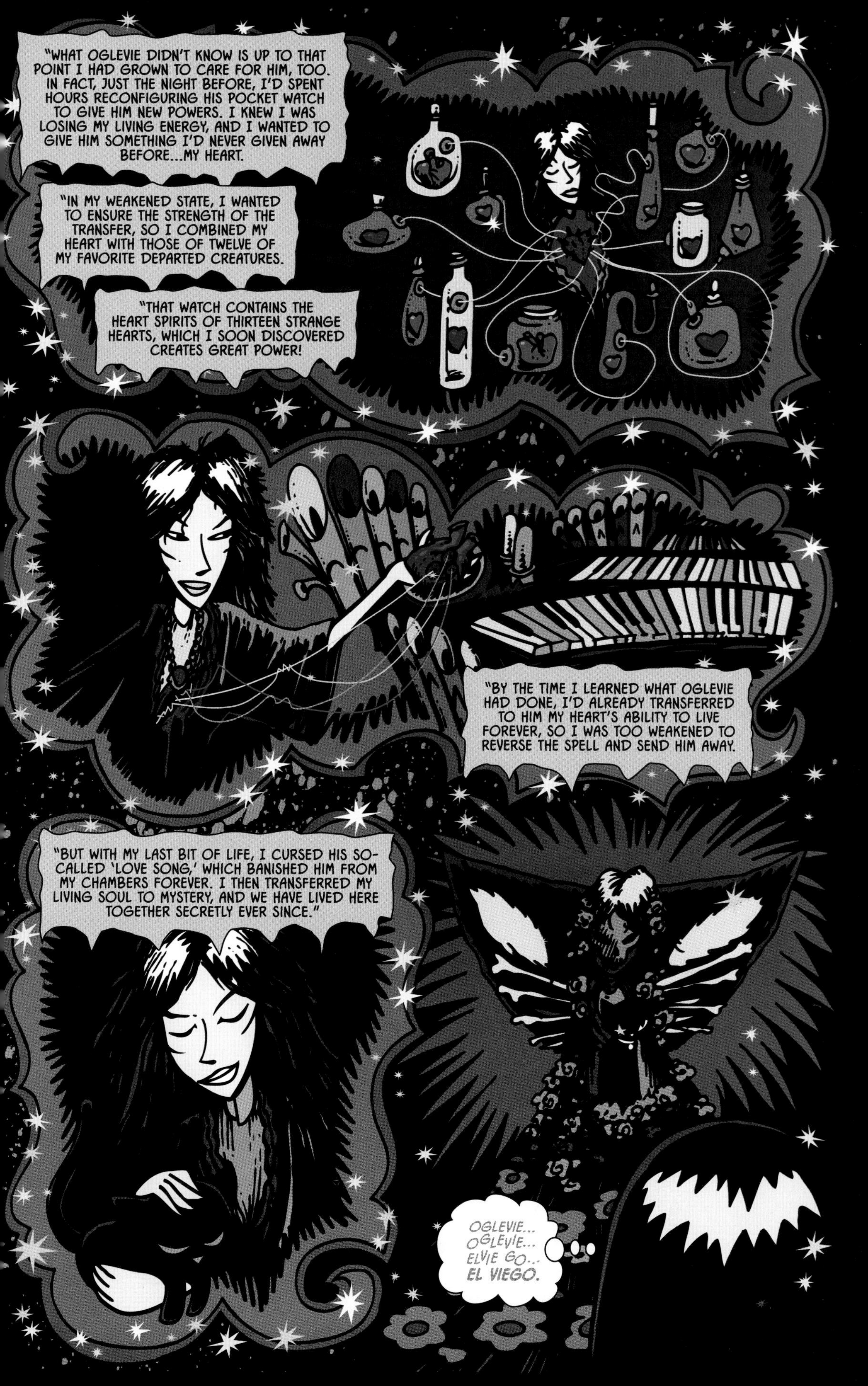
"WHAT OGLEVIE DIDN'T KNOW IS UP TO THAT POINT I HAD GROWN TO CARE FOR HIM, TOO. IN FACT, JUST THE NIGHT BEFORE, I'D SPENT HOURS RECONFIGURING HIS POCKET WATCH TO GIVE HIM NEW POWERS. I KNEW I WAS LOSING MY LIVING ENERGY, AND I WANTED TO GIVE HIM SOMETHING I'D NEVER GIVEN AWAY BEFORE...MY HEART.
"IN MY WEAKENED STATE, I WANTED TO ENSURE THE STRENGTH OF THE TRANSFER, SO I COMBINED MY HEART WITH THOSE OF TWELVE OF MY FAVORITE DEPARTED CREATURES.
"THAT WATCH CONTAINS THE HEART SPIRITS OF THIRTEEN STRANGE HEARTS, WHICH I SOON DISCOVERED CREATES GREAT POWER!
"BY THE TIME I LEARNED WHAT OGLEVIE HAD DONE, I'D ALREADY TRANSFERRED TO HIM MY HEART'S ABILITY TO LIVE FOREVER, SO I WAS TOO WEAKENED TO REVERSE THE SPELL AND SEND HIM AWAY.
"BUT WITH MY LAST BIT OF LIFE, I CURSED HIS SO-CALLED 'LOVE SONG,' WHICH BANISHED HIM FROM MY CHAMBERS FOREVER. I THEN TRANSFERRED MY LIVING SOUL TO MYSTERY, AND WE HAVE LIVED HERE TOGETHER SECRETLY EVER SINCE."
OGLEVIE... OGLEVIE... ELVIE GO... EL VIEGO.

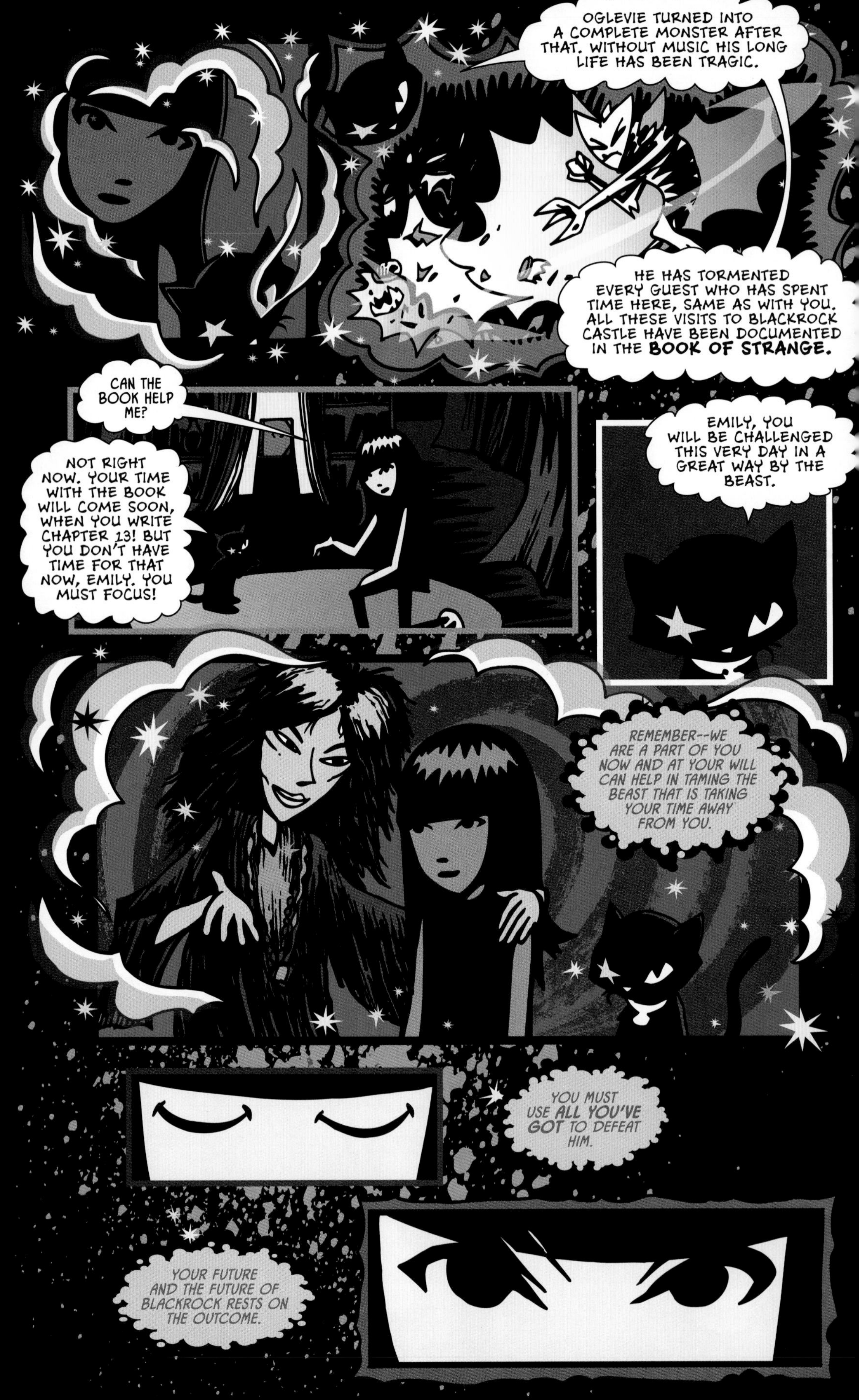
OGLEVIE TURNED INTO A COMPLETE MONSTER AFTER THAT. WITHOUT MUSIC HIS LONG LIFE HAS BEEN TRAGIC.
HE HAS TORMENTED EVERY GUEST WHO HAS SPENT TIME HERE, SAME AS WITH YOU. ALL THESE VISITS TO BLACKROCK CASTLE HAVE BEEN DOCUMENTED IN THE **BOOK OF STRANGE.**
CAN THE BOOK HELP ME?
NOT RIGHT NOW. YOUR TIME WITH THE BOOK WILL COME SOON, WHEN YOU WRITE CHAPTER 13! BUT YOU DON'T HAVE TIME FOR THAT NOW, EMILY. YOU MUST FOCUS!
EMILY, YOU WILL BE CHALLENGED THIS VERY DAY IN A GREAT WAY BY THE BEAST.
REMEMBER--WE ARE A PART OF YOU NOW AND AT YOUR WILL CAN HELP IN TAMING THE BEAST THAT IS TAKING YOUR TIME AWAY FROM YOU.
YOU MUST USE **ALL YOU'VE GOT** TO DEFEAT HIM.
YOUR FUTURE AND THE FUTURE OF BLACKROCK RESTS ON THE OUTCOME.

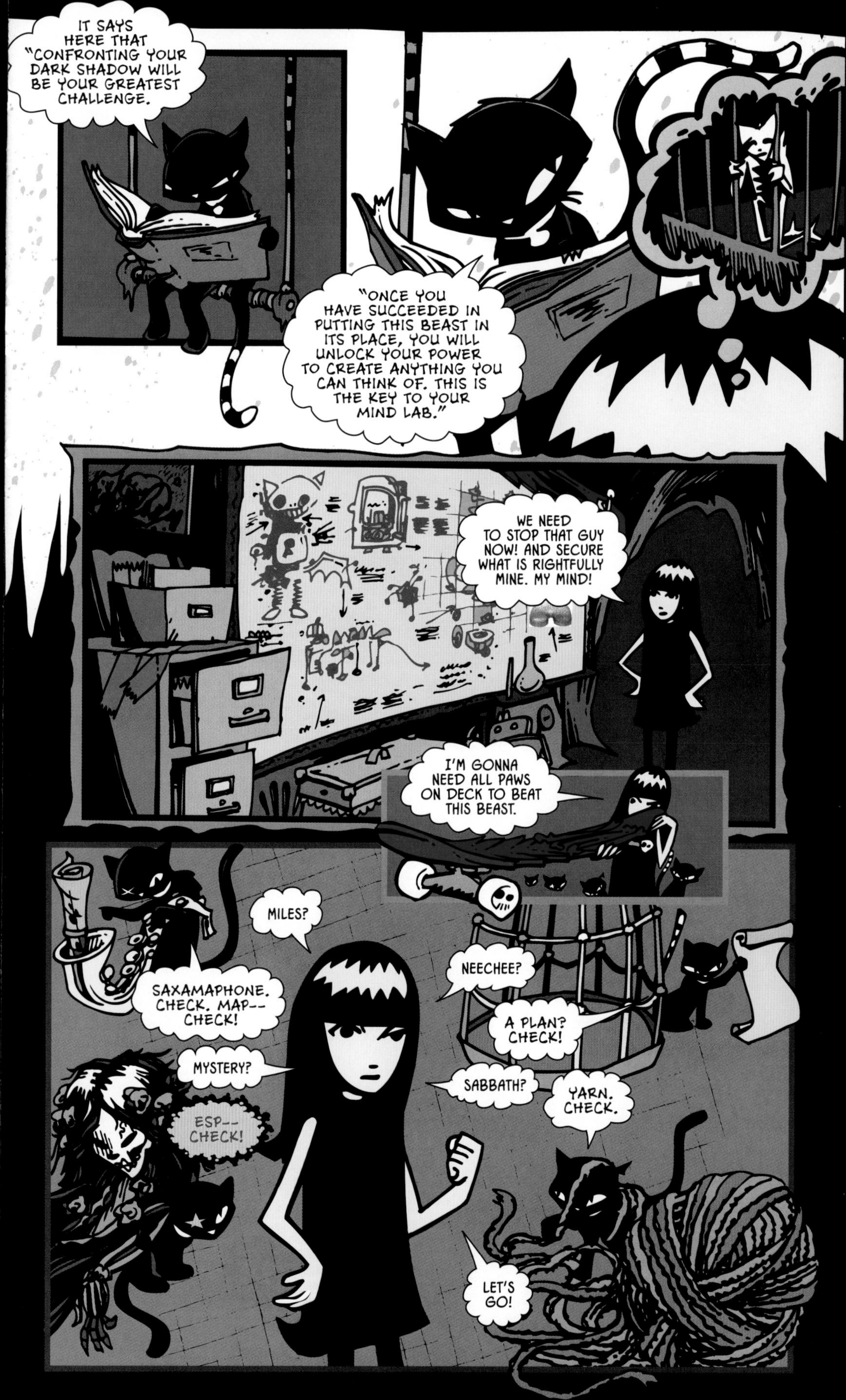
IT SAYS HERE THAT "CONFRONTING YOUR DARK SHADOW WILL BE YOUR GREATEST CHALLENGE.
"ONCE YOU HAVE SUCCEEDED IN PUTTING THIS BEAST IN ITS PLACE, YOU WILL UNLOCK YOUR POWER TO CREATE ANYTHING YOU CAN THINK OF. THIS IS THE KEY TO YOUR MIND LAB."
WE NEED TO STOP THAT GUY NOW! AND SECURE WHAT IS RIGHTFULLY MINE. MY MIND!
I'M GONNA NEED ALL PAWS ON DECK TO BEAT THIS BEAST.
MILES?
SAXAMAPHONE. CHECK. MAP-- CHECK!
NEECHEE?
A PLAN? CHECK!
MYSTERY?
ESP-- CHECK!
SABBATH?
YARN. CHECK.
LET'S GO!

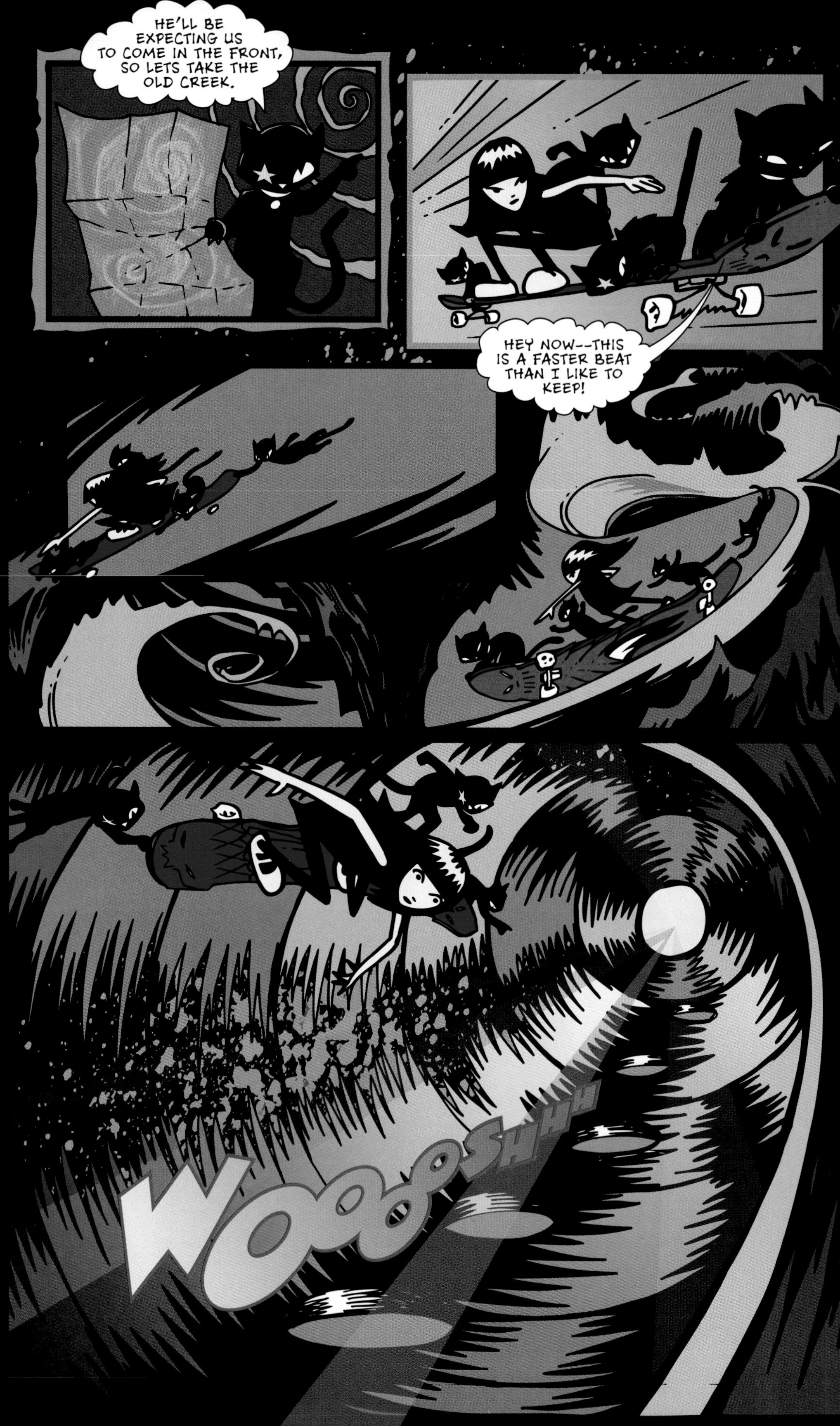
HE'LL BE EXPECTING US TO COME IN THE FRONT, SO LETS TAKE THE OLD CREEK.
HEY NOW--THIS IS A FASTER BEAT THAN I LIKE TO KEEP!
WOOOOSHHH

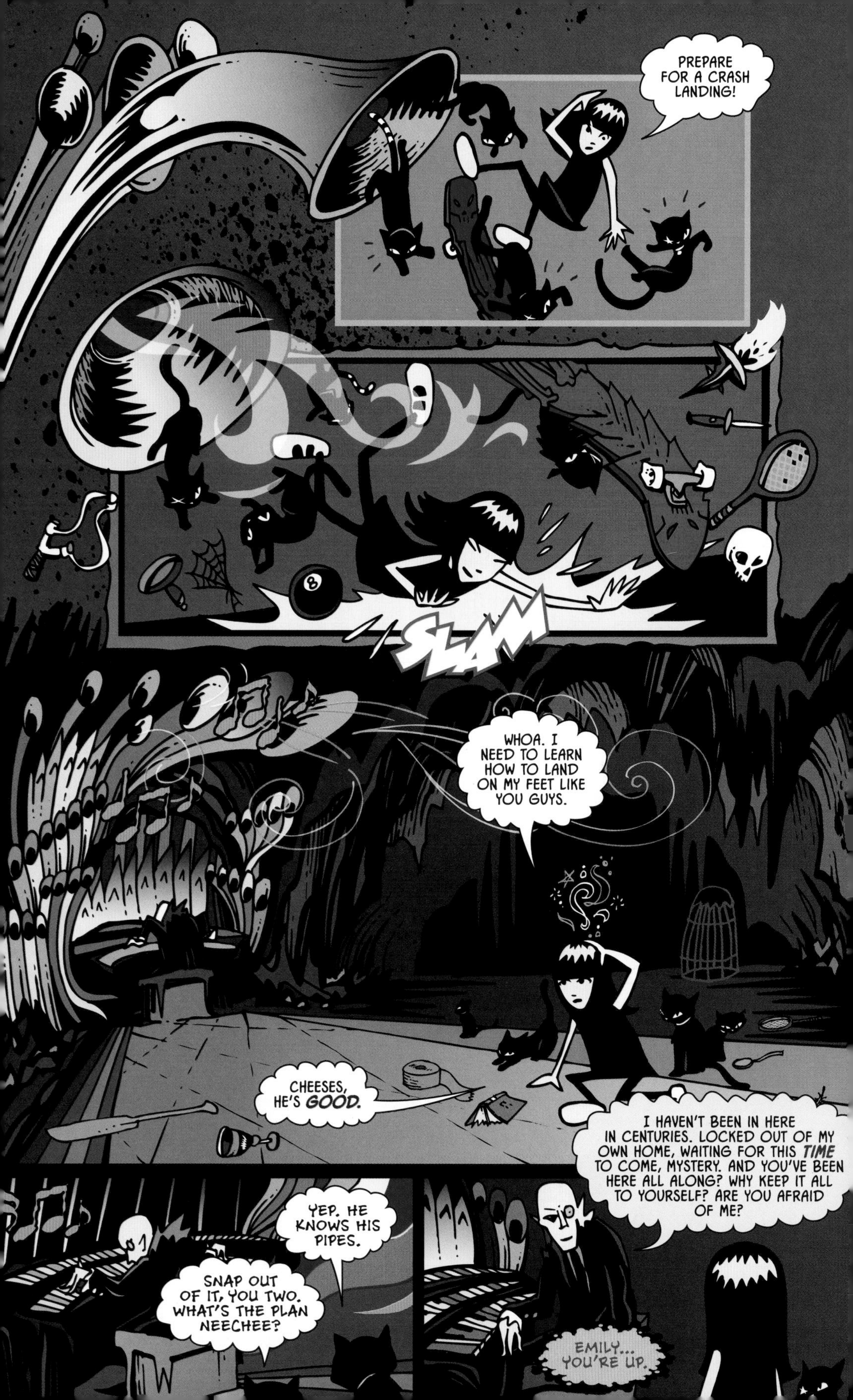
PREPARE FOR A CRASH LANDING!
SLAM
WHOA. I NEED TO LEARN HOW TO LAND ON MY FEET LIKE YOU GUYS.
CHEESES, HE'S GOOD.
I HAVEN'T BEEN IN HERE IN CENTURIES. LOCKED OUT OF MY OWN HOME, WAITING FOR THIS TIME TO COME, MYSTERY. AND YOU'VE BEEN HERE ALL ALONG? WHY KEEP IT ALL TO YOURSELF? ARE YOU AFRAID OF ME?
YEP. HE KNOWS HIS PIPES.
SNAP OUT OF IT, YOU TWO. WHAT'S THE PLAN NEECHEE?
EMILY... YOU'RE UP.

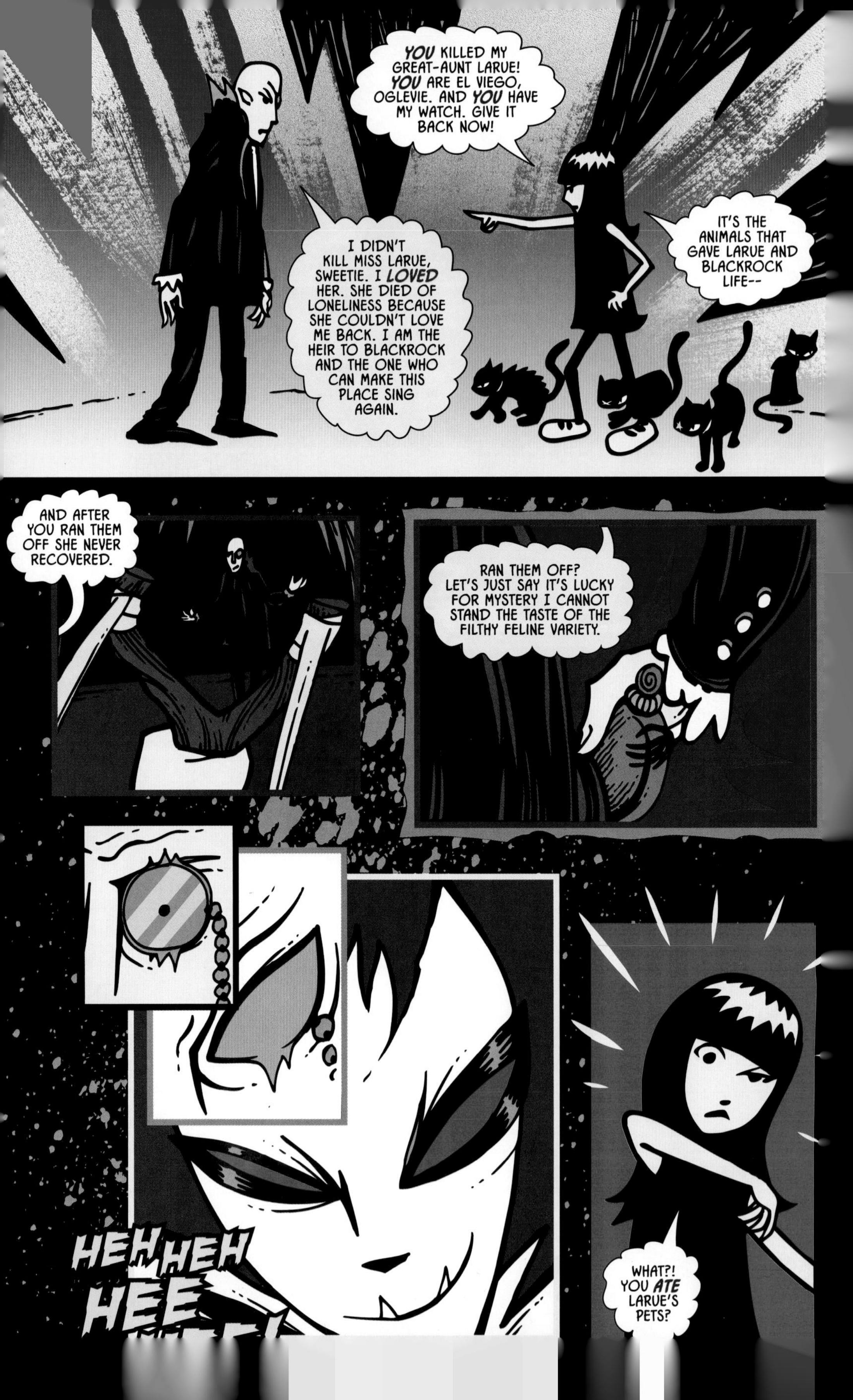
YOU KILLED MY GREAT-AUNT LARUE! YOU ARE EL VIEGO, OGLEVIE. AND YOU HAVE MY WATCH. GIVE IT BACK NOW!
I DIDN'T KILL MISS LARUE, SWEETIE. I LOVED HER. SHE DIED OF LONELINESS BECAUSE SHE COULDN'T LOVE ME BACK. I AM THE HEIR TO BLACKROCK AND THE ONE WHO CAN MAKE THIS PLACE SING AGAIN.
IT'S THE ANIMALS THAT GAVE LARUE AND BLACKROCK LIFE--
AND AFTER YOU RAN THEM OFF SHE NEVER RECOVERED.
RAN THEM OFF? LET'S JUST SAY IT'S LUCKY FOR MYSTERY I CANNOT STAND THE TASTE OF THE FILTHY FELINE VARIETY.
HEH HEH HEE
WHAT?! YOU ATE LARUE'S PETS?

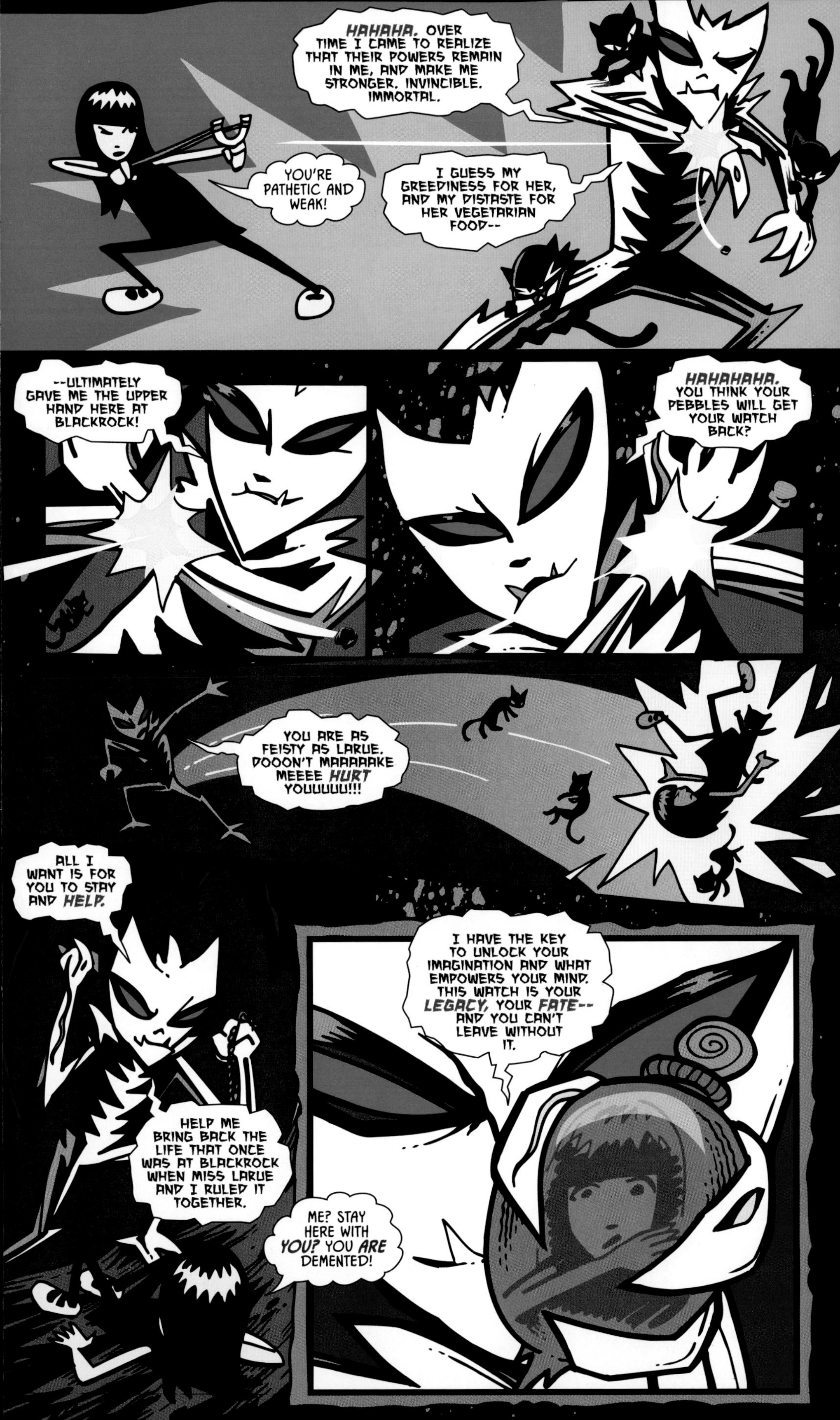
HAHAHA. OVER TIME I CAME TO REALIZE THAT THEIR POWERS REMAIN IN ME, AND MAKE ME STRONGER. INVINCIBLE. IMMORTAL.
YOU'RE PATHETIC AND WEAK!
I GUESS MY GREEDINESS FOR HER, AND MY DISTASTE FOR HER VEGETARIAN FOOD--
--ULTIMATELY GAVE ME THE UPPER HAND HERE AT BLACKROCK!
HAHAHAHA. YOU THINK YOUR PEBBLES WILL GET YOUR WATCH BACK?
YOU ARE AS FEISTY AS LARUE. DOOON'T MAAAAAKE MEEEE HURT YOUUUUU!!!
ALL I WANT IS FOR YOU TO STAY AND HELP.
HELP ME BRING BACK THE LIFE THAT ONCE WAS AT BLACKROCK WHEN MISS LARUE AND I RULED IT TOGETHER.
ME? STAY HERE WITH YOU? YOU ARE DEMENTED!
I HAVE THE KEY TO UNLOCK YOUR IMAGINATION AND WHAT EMPOWERS YOUR MIND. THIS WATCH IS YOUR LEGACY, YOUR FATE-- AND YOU CAN'T LEAVE WITHOUT IT.

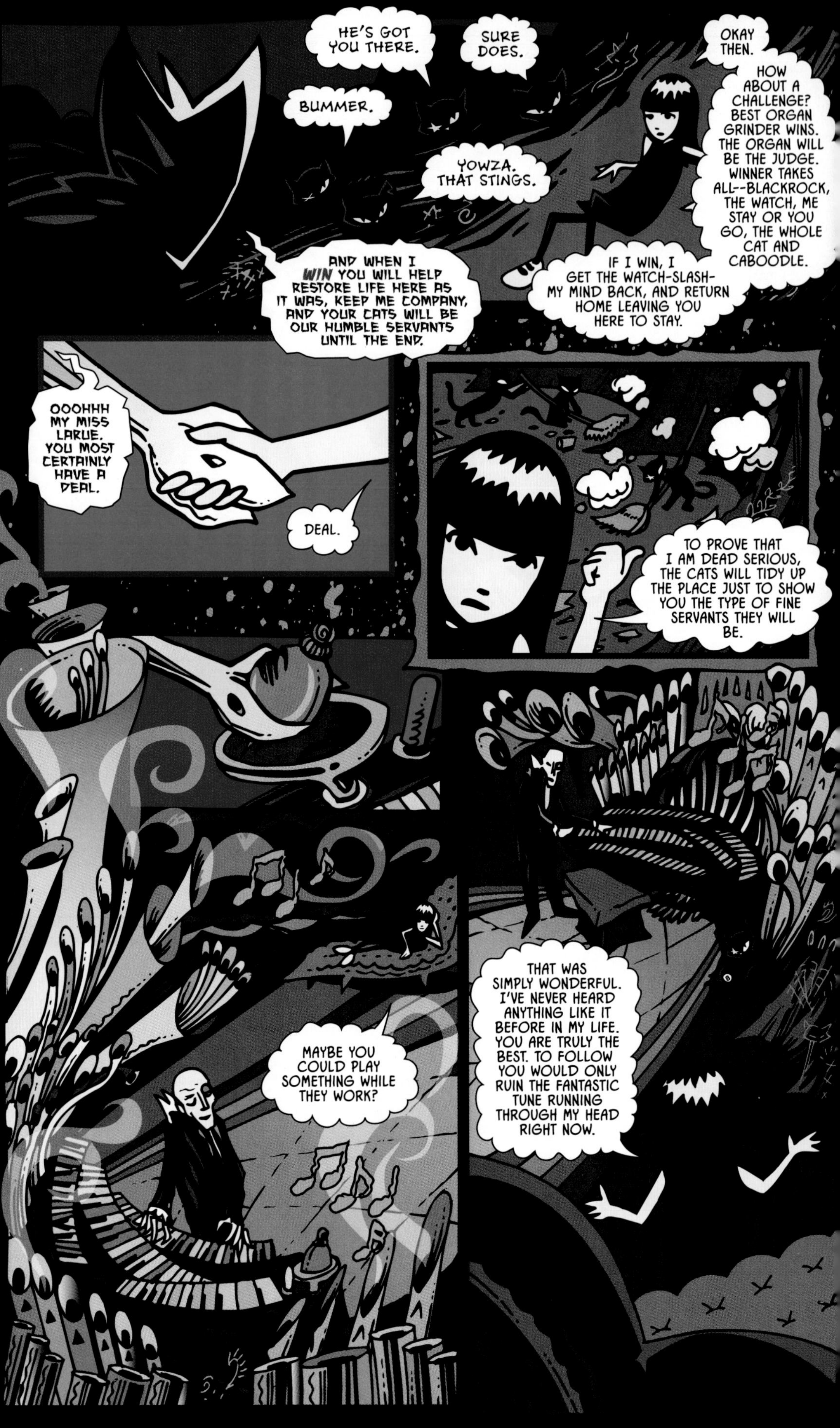
HE'S GOT YOU THERE.
SURE DOES.
BUMMER.
YOWZA. THAT STINGS.
OKAY THEN.
HOW ABOUT A CHALLENGE? BEST ORGAN GRINDER WINS. THE ORGAN WILL BE THE JUDGE. WINNER TAKES ALL--BLACKROCK, THE WATCH, ME STAY OR YOU GO, THE WHOLE CAT AND CABOODLE.
IF I WIN, I GET THE WATCH-SLASH-MY MIND BACK, AND RETURN HOME LEAVING YOU HERE TO STAY.
AND WHEN I WIN YOU WILL HELP RESTORE LIFE HERE AS IT WAS, KEEP ME COMPANY, AND YOUR CATS WILL BE OUR HUMBLE SERVANTS UNTIL THE END.
OOOHHH MY MISS LARUE. YOU MOST CERTAINLY HAVE A DEAL.
DEAL.
TO PROVE THAT I AM DEAD SERIOUS, THE CATS WILL TIDY UP THE PLACE JUST TO SHOW YOU THE TYPE OF FINE SERVANTS THEY WILL BE.
MAYBE YOU COULD PLAY SOMETHING WHILE THEY WORK?
THAT WAS SIMPLY WONDERFUL. I'VE NEVER HEARD ANYTHING LIKE IT BEFORE IN MY LIFE. YOU ARE TRULY THE BEST. TO FOLLOW YOU WOULD ONLY RUIN THE FANTASTIC TUNE RUNNING THROUGH MY HEAD RIGHT NOW.

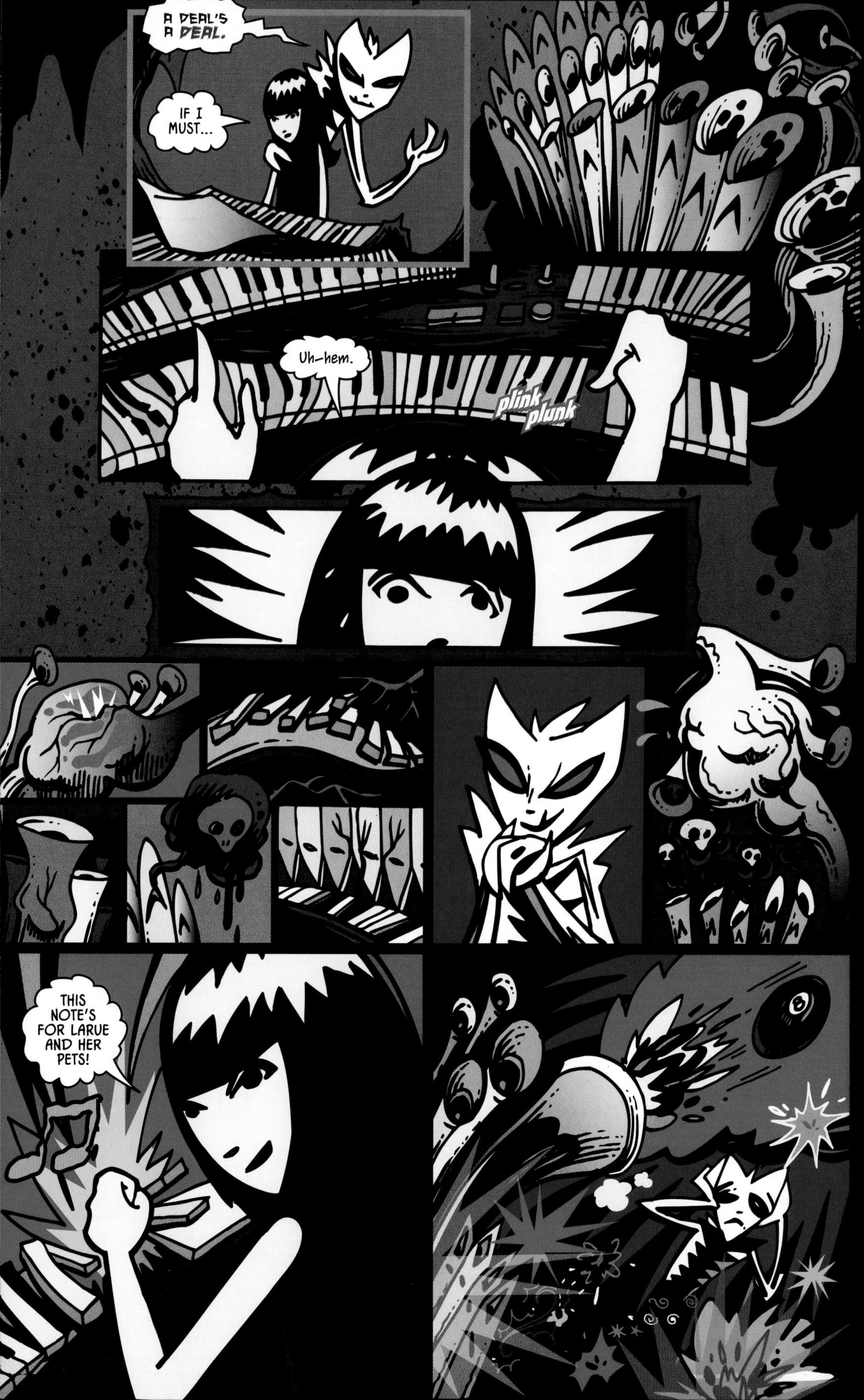
A DEAL'S A DEAL.
IF I MUST...
Uh-hem.
plink plunk
THIS NOTE'S FOR LARUE AND HER PETS!

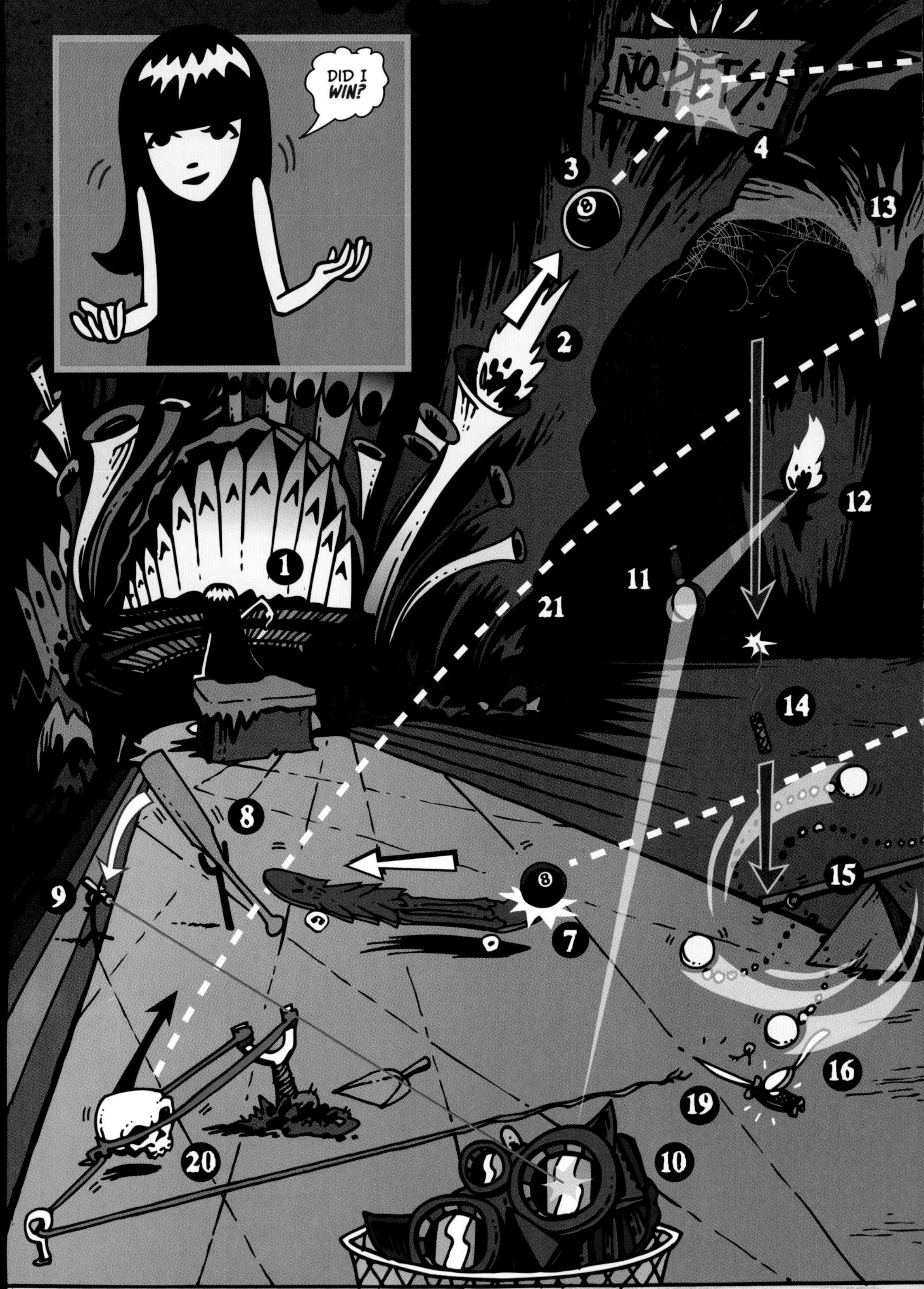

DID I WIN?
1
2
3
4
7
8
9
10
11
12
13
14
15
16
19
20
21

1. During song, play a specific KEY on organ
2. Which activates PIPE, which
3. Shoots lodged 8-BALL out of pipe,
4. Ricocheting off of SIGN
5. Toward a TENNIS RACKET,
6. Which NEECHEE uses to hit 8-ball over
7. To land on SKATEBOARD, which rolls to
8. Knock over ROWING OAR, which
9. Presses down on LASER POINTER, which
10. Points to and is magnified through NIGHT-VISION GOGGLES
11. And heated by MAGNIFYING GLASS aimed
12. To burn TORCH, which catches fire and
13. Lights SPIDER-WEB fuse attached to a
14. FIRECRACKER that explodes and
15. Causes MONOCLE to swing back and forth
16. Simultaneously knocking over SPOON
17. And hypnotizing Miles to play horrible SAX solo
18. Causing THIEF to cover ears and close eyes

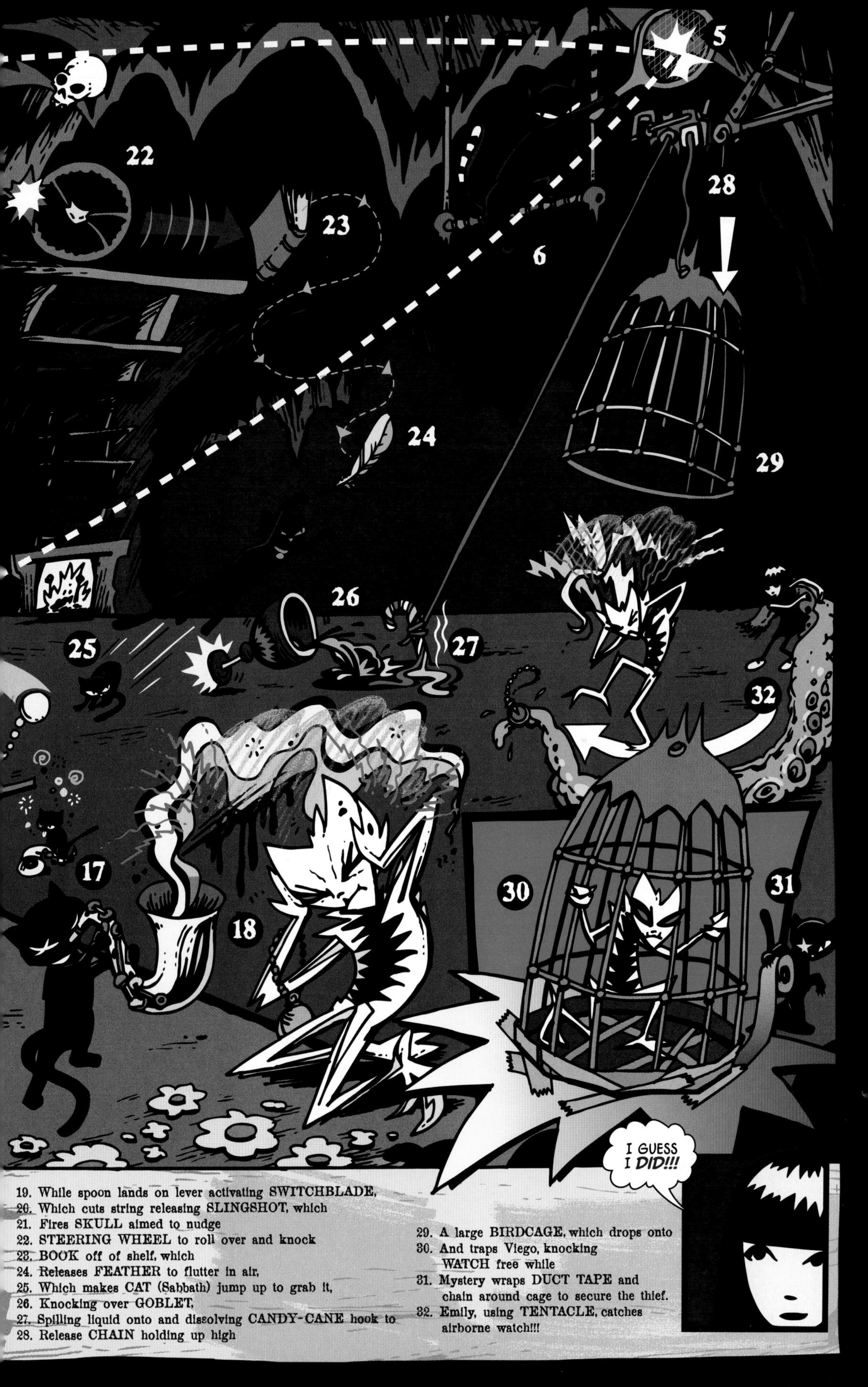
5
22
23
6
28
24
29
26
25
27
32
17
30
31
18
I GUESS I *DID!!!*
19. While spoon lands on lever activating SWITCHBLADE,
20. Which cuts string releasing SLINGSHOT, which
21. Fires SKULL aimed to nudge
22. STEERING WHEEL to roll over and knock
23. BOOK off of shelf, which
24. Releases FEATHER to flutter in air,
25. Which makes CAT (Sabbath) jump up to grab it,
26. Knocking over GOBLET,
27. Spilling liquid onto and dissolving CANDY-CANE hook to
28. Release CHAIN holding up high
29. A large BIRDCAGE, which drops onto
30. And traps Viego, knocking WATCH free while
31. Mystery wraps DUCT TAPE and chain around cage to secure the thief.
32. Emily, using TENTACLE, catches airborne watch!!!

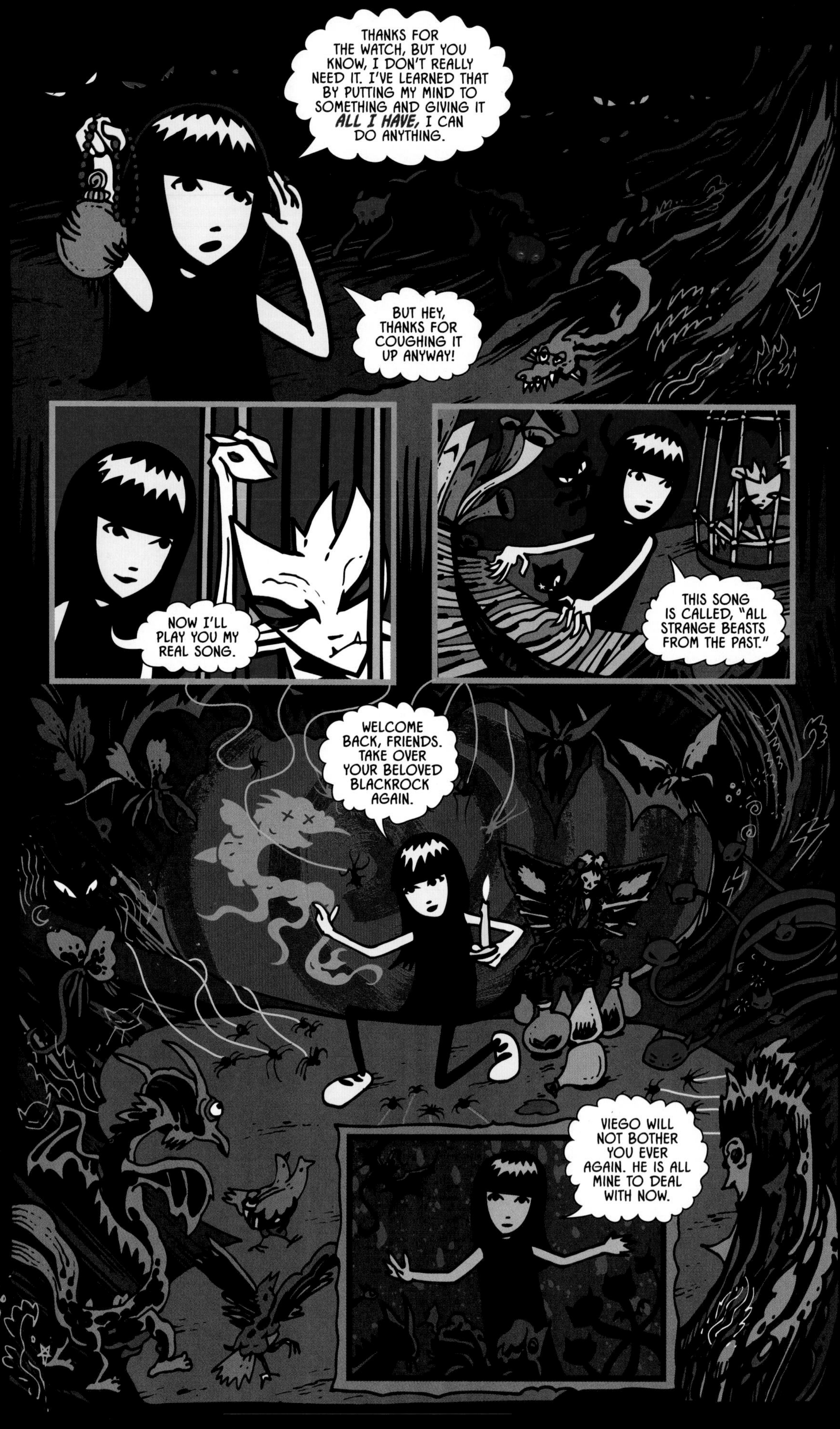
THANKS FOR THE WATCH, BUT YOU KNOW, I DON'T REALLY NEED IT. I'VE LEARNED THAT BY PUTTING MY MIND TO SOMETHING AND GIVING IT ***ALL I HAVE,*** I CAN DO ANYTHING.
BUT HEY, THANKS FOR COUGHING IT UP ANYWAY!
NOW I'LL PLAY YOU MY REAL SONG.
THIS SONG IS CALLED, "ALL STRANGE BEASTS FROM THE PAST."
WELCOME BACK, FRIENDS. TAKE OVER YOUR BELOVED BLACKROCK AGAIN.
VIEGO WILL NOT BOTHER YOU EVER AGAIN. HE IS ALL MINE TO DEAL WITH NOW.

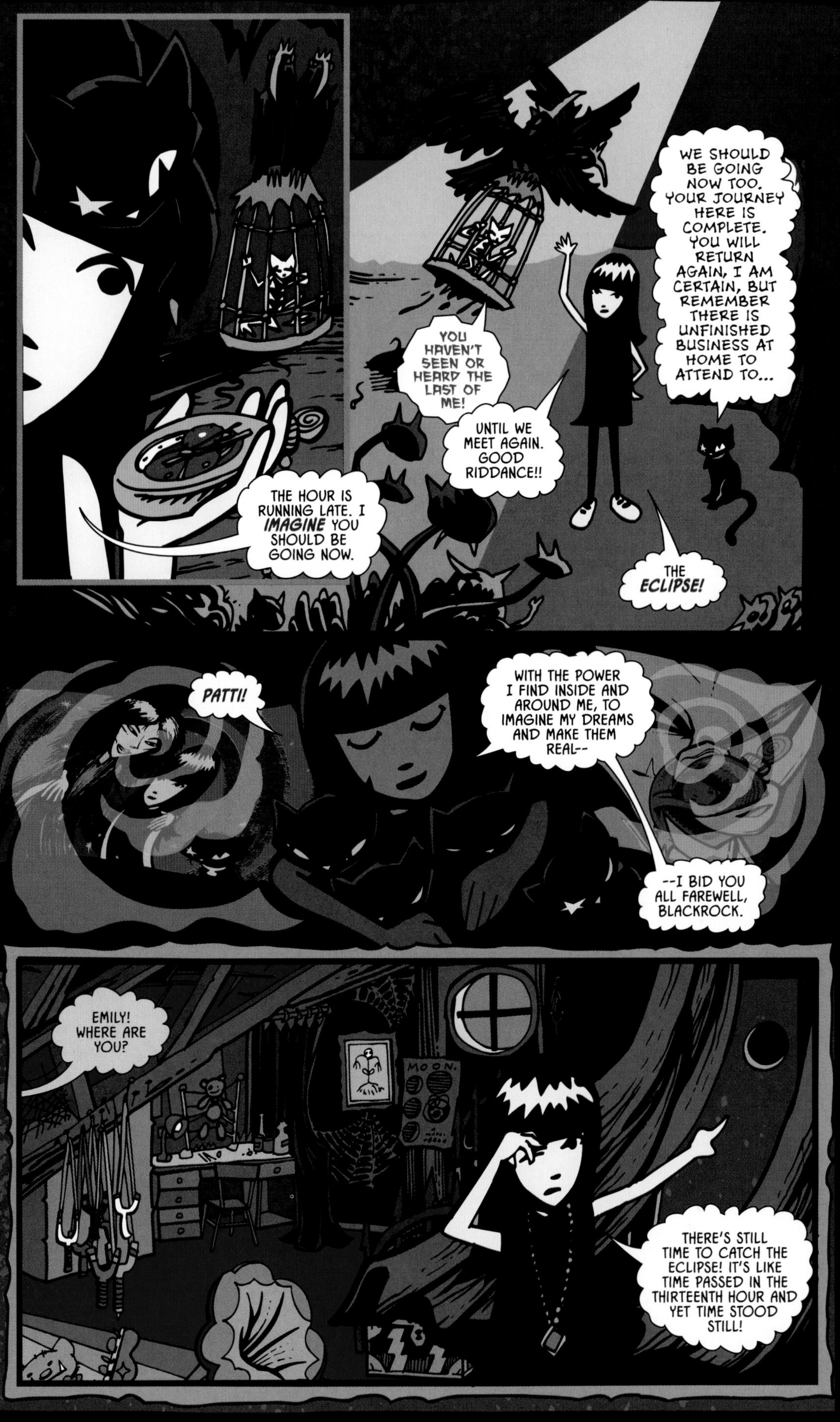
THE HOUR IS RUNNING LATE. I *IMAGINE* YOU SHOULD BE GOING NOW.
YOU HAVEN'T SEEN OR HEARD THE LAST OF ME!
UNTIL WE MEET AGAIN. GOOD RIDDANCE!!
WE SHOULD BE GOING NOW TOO. YOUR JOURNEY HERE IS COMPLETE. YOU WILL RETURN AGAIN, I AM CERTAIN, BUT REMEMBER THERE IS UNFINISHED BUSINESS AT HOME TO ATTEND TO...
THE *ECLIPSE!*
PATTI!
WITH THE POWER I FIND INSIDE AND AROUND ME, TO IMAGINE MY DREAMS AND MAKE THEM REAL--
--I BID YOU ALL FAREWELL, BLACKROCK.
EMILY! WHERE ARE YOU?
MOON.
THERE'S STILL TIME TO CATCH THE ECLIPSE! IT'S LIKE TIME PASSED IN THE THIRTEENTH HOUR AND YET TIME STOOD STILL!

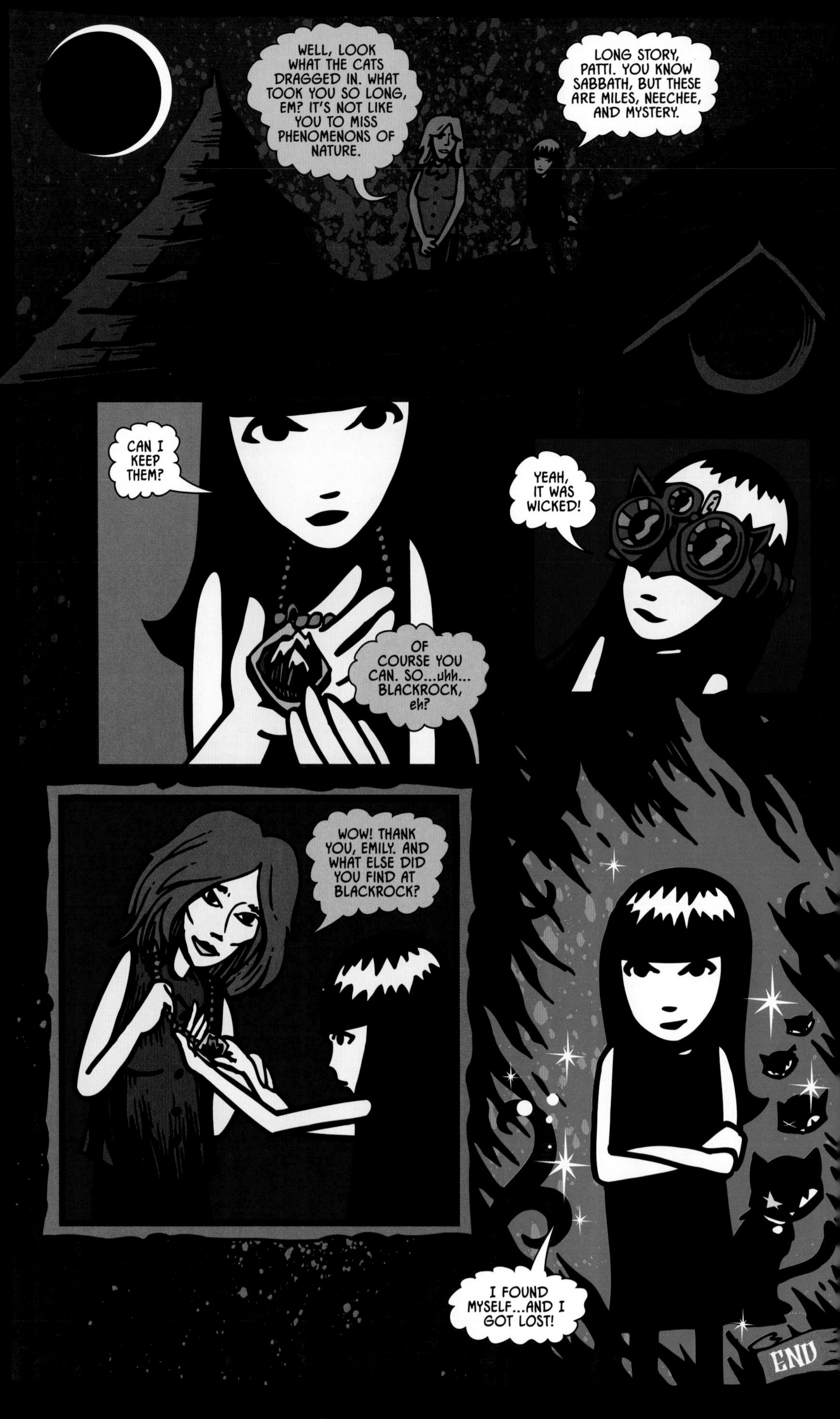
WELL, LOOK WHAT THE CATS DRAGGED IN. WHAT TOOK YOU SO LONG, EM? IT'S NOT LIKE YOU TO MISS PHENOMENONS OF NATURE.
LONG STORY, PATTI. YOU KNOW SABBATH, BUT THESE ARE MILES, NEECHEE, AND MYSTERY.
CAN I KEEP THEM?
YEAH, IT WAS WICKED!
OF COURSE YOU CAN. SO...uhh... BLACKROCK, eh?
WOW! THANK YOU, EMILY. AND WHAT ELSE DID YOU FIND AT BLACKROCK?
I FOUND MYSELF...AND I GOT LOST!
END

Emily® the Strange
The 13th Hour sketchbook selections by BUZZ and RoB

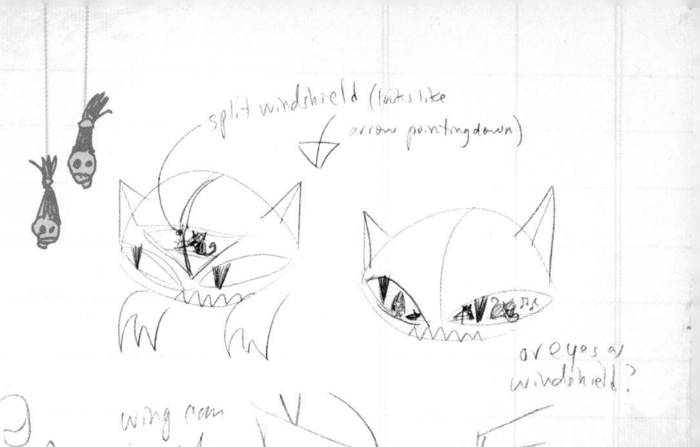

split windshield (looks like arrow pointing down)
or eyes as windshield?

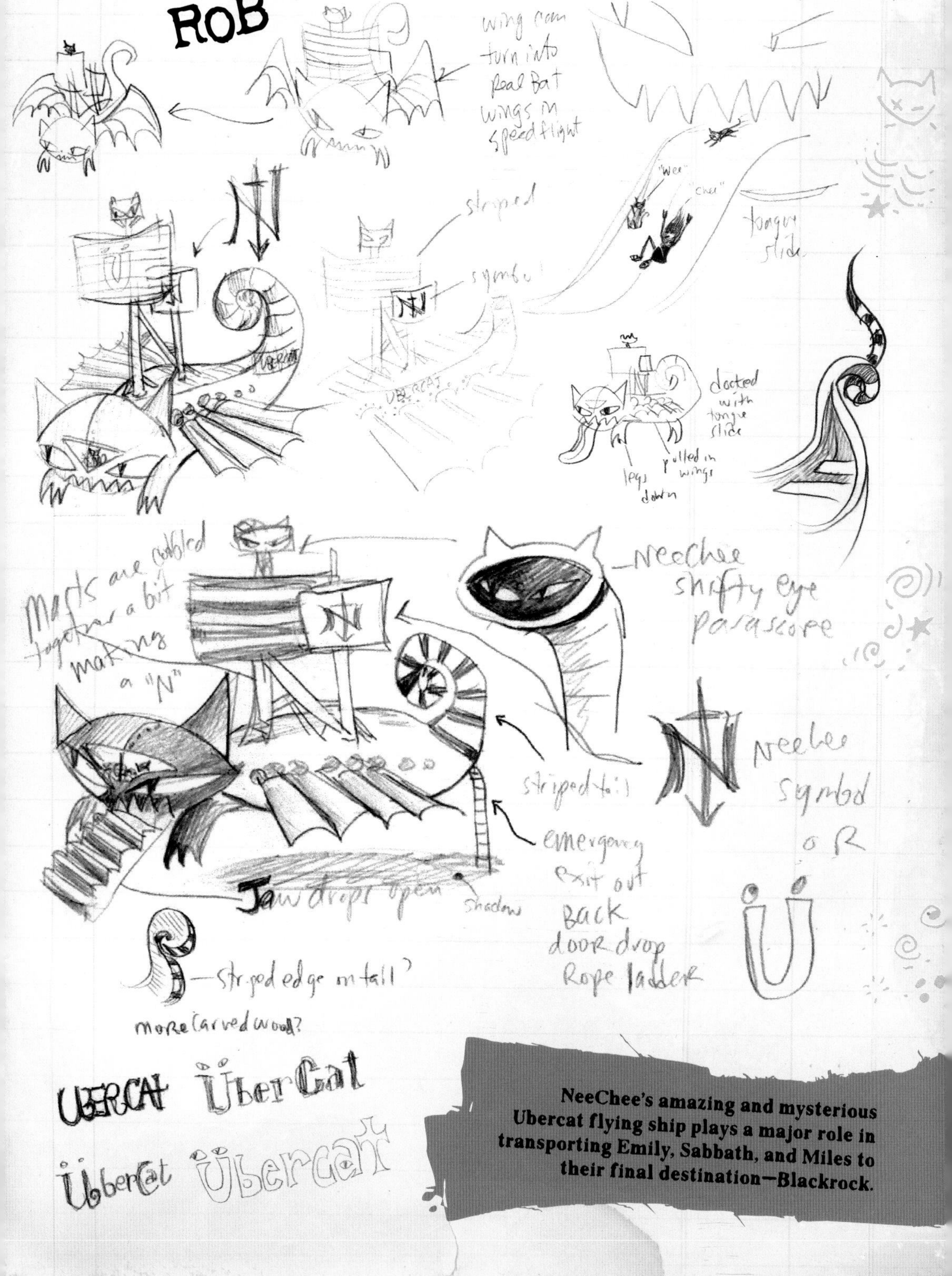

wing can turn into real bat wings in speed flight
striped
symbol
"wee"
"chee"
tongue slide
docked with tongue slide
legs down
pulled in wings
masts are cobbled together a bit making a "N"
NeeChee shifty eye parascope
striped tail
emergency exit out back door drop rope ladder
Neechee symbol or
Jaw drops open
shadow
striped edge on tail?
more carved wood?
UBERCAT
ÜberCat
Übercat
Übercat

NeeChee's amazing and mysterious Ubercat flying ship plays a major role in transporting Emily, Sabbath, and Miles to their final destination—Blackrock.

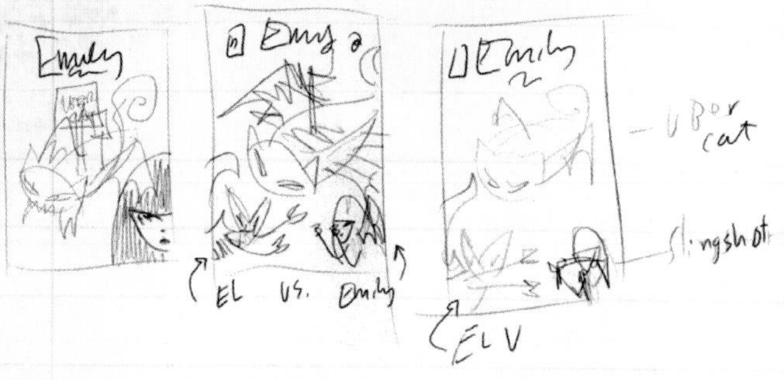
Uber cat
slingshot
EL vs. Emily
ELV

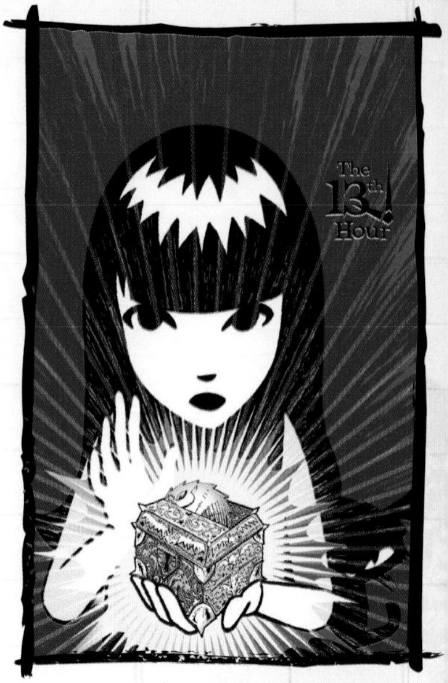
The 13th Hour

Designing the covers for each issue is really fun and a lot of work. We have to make sure we're giving the readers an accurate idea of what is in each issue without giving too much away, so Rob and Buzz will often do multiple sketches building off each other's ideas for each cover until we find the perfect image.

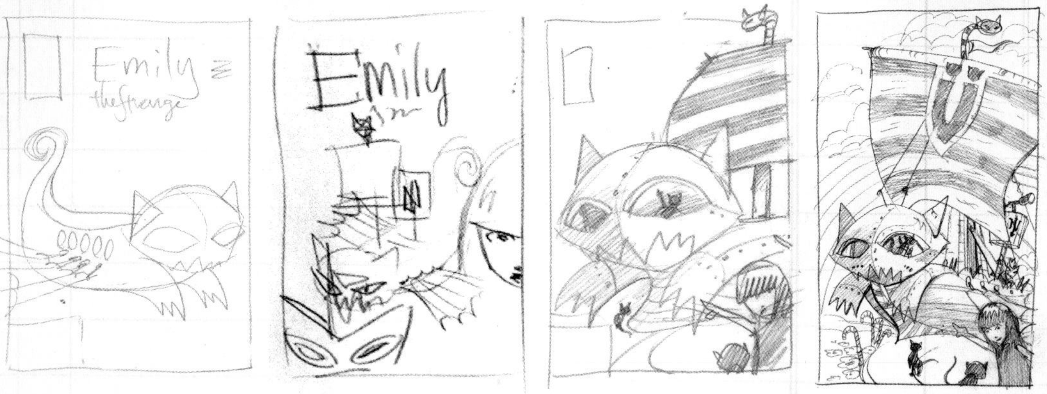
Emily the Strange
Emily

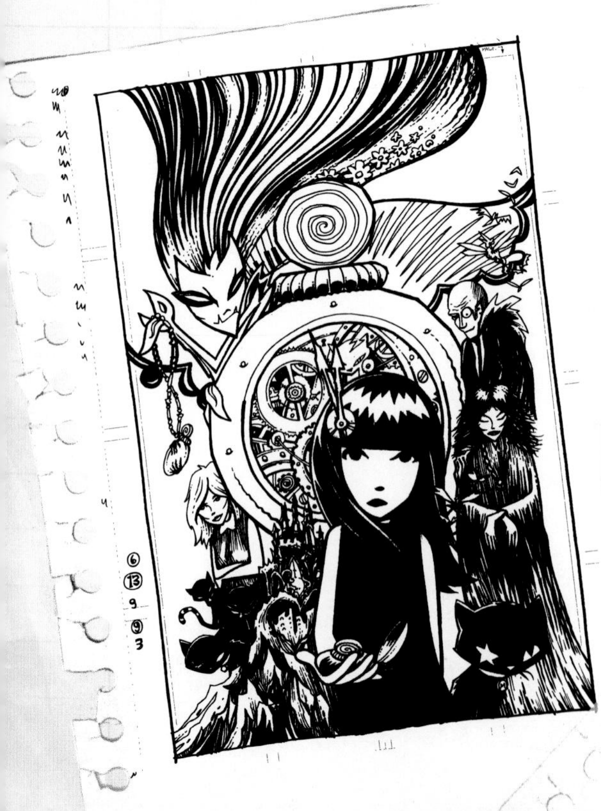

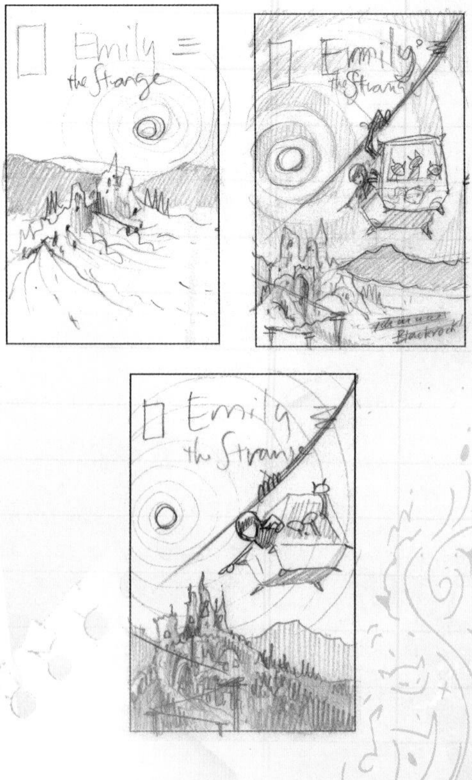
Emily the Strange
Emily the Strange
Emily the Strange

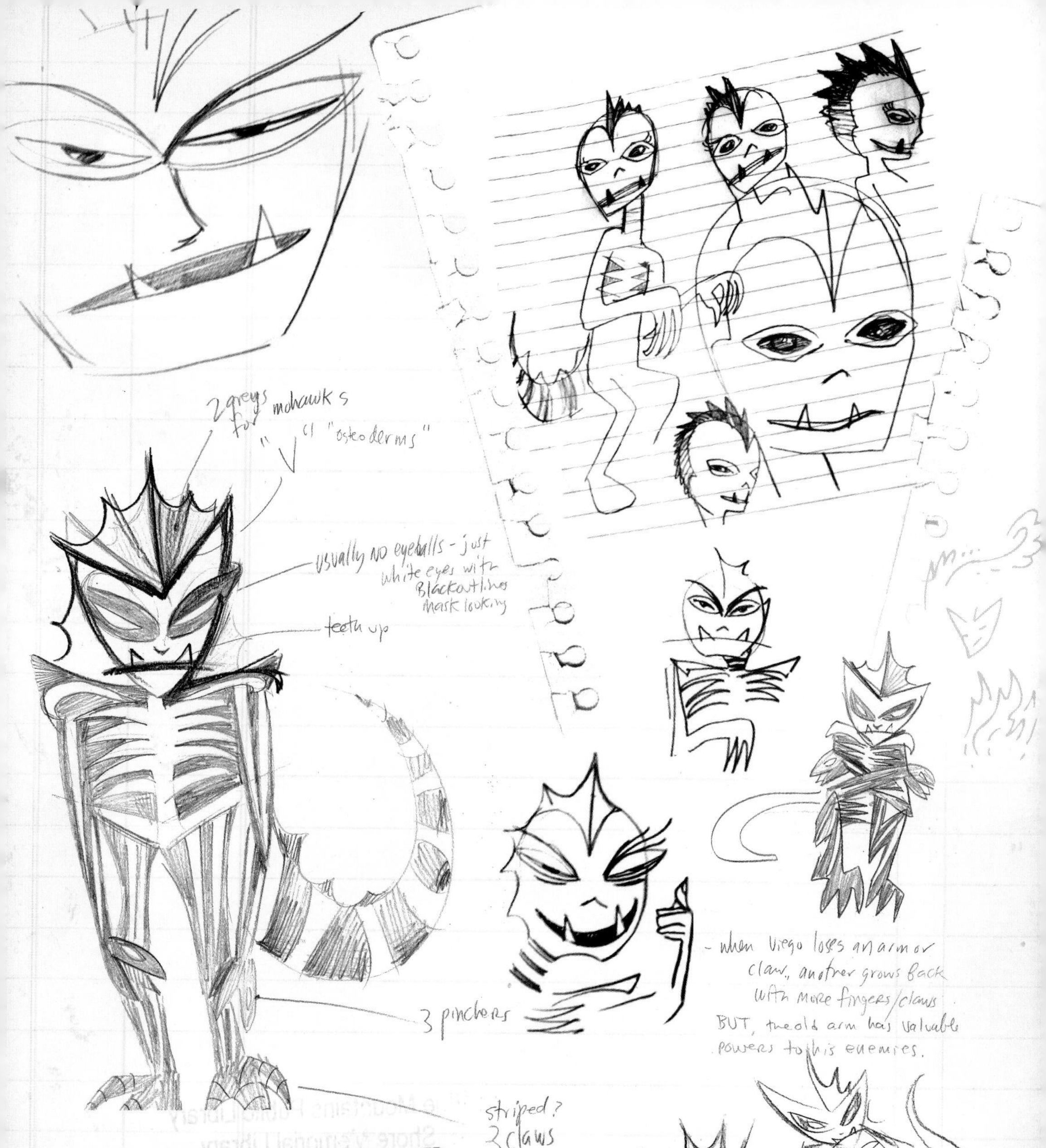
2 greys for mohawks
" " "osteoderms"
usually no eyeballs - just white eyes with Blackoutlines mask looking
teeth up
- when Viego loses an armor claw, another grows back with more fingers/claws BUT, the old arm has valuable powers to his enemies.
3 pinchers
striped? 3 claws

El Viego was a challenge to design because his character is both human and monster, which readers finally learned in issue 4 of this series. The name "El Viego" was derived from mixing up the letters in his human name—"Oglevie."

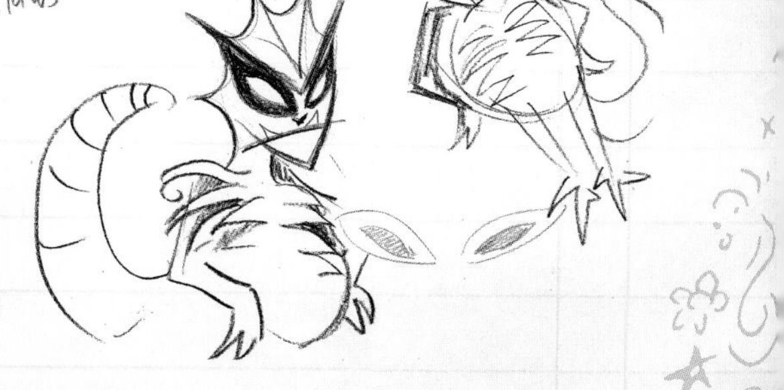

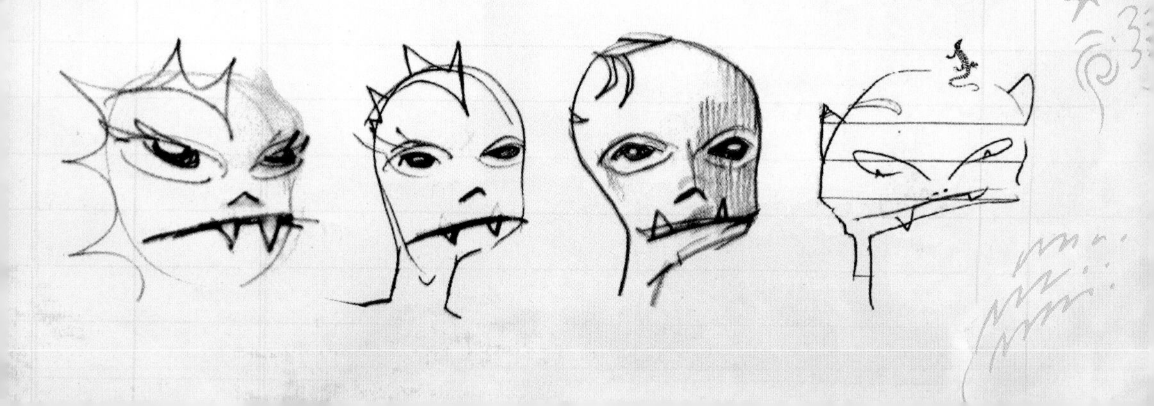

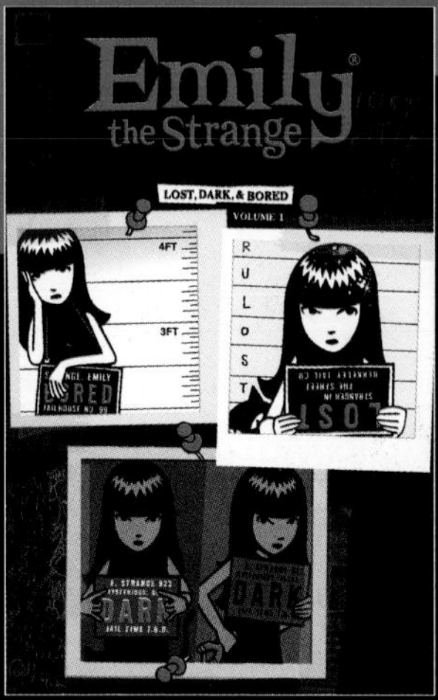
Emily the Strange
LOST, DARK, & BORED
VOLUME 1

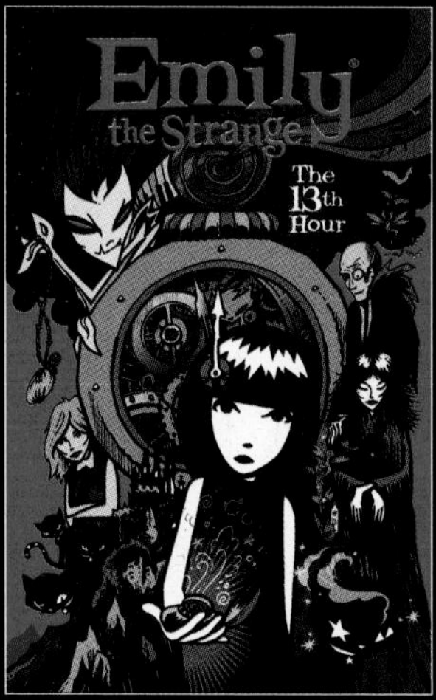
Emily the Strange
The 13th Hour

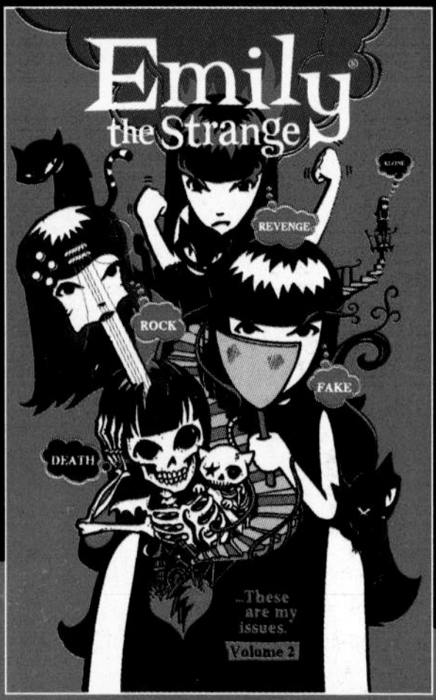
Emily the Strange
REVENGE
ROCK
FAKE
DEATH
These are my issues.
Volume 2

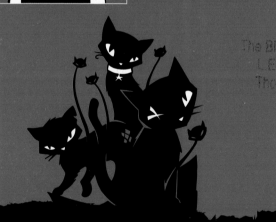

Emily® the Strange

Emily the Strange presents strange books for strange readers!

VOLUME 1: LOST, DARK, & BORED
ISBN 978-1-59307-573-6
$19.99

VOLUME 2: ROCK, DEATH, FAKE, REVENGE, & ALONE
ISBN 978-1-59582-221-5
$19.99

VOLUME 3: THE 13TH HOUR
ISBN 978-1-59582-700-5
$14.99

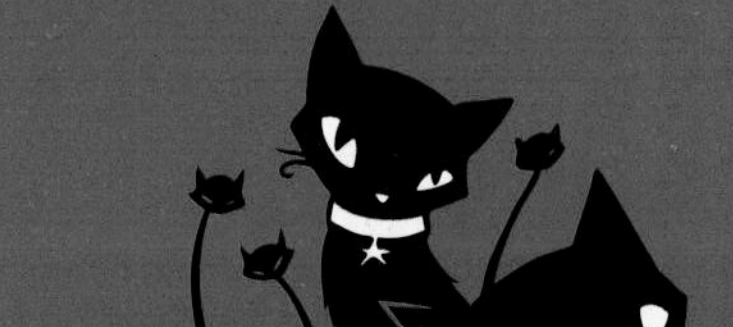

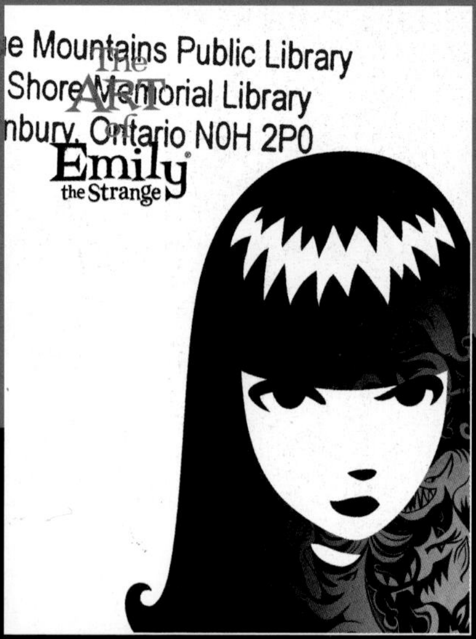
The ART of Emily the Strange

THE ART OF EMILY THE STRANGE
ISBN 978-1-59582-371-7
$22.99

DARK HORSE BOOKS
COSMIC DEBRIS

AVAILABLE AT YOUR LOCAL COMICS SHOP OR BOOKSTORE! To find a comics shop in your area, call 1-888-266-4226
For more information or to order direct visit darkhorse.com or call 1-800-862-0052 Mon.–Fri. 9 A.M. to 5 P.M. Pacific Time *Price and availability subject to change without notice.*